Praise for *A Stranger in the Family*

'With every breath in my body, I'm BEGGING you to read
Jane Casey's books! The plot! The characterisation! The
sexual chemistry! Delivers on every level! I LOVED it!'
No. 1 bestselling author Marian Keyes

'The ultimate just-one-more-chapter read'
Abigail Dean, author of *Girl A*

'Jane Casey is simply one of the best writers of
detective fiction today'
Liz Nugent, author of *Strange Sally Diamond*

'A twisting, seductive, sensational thriller'
Chris Whitaker, author of *All the Colours of the Dark*

'As tense as piano wire, intricately plotted'
Neil Lancaster, author of *The Devil You Know*

'The undisputed queen of simmering tension.
Explosively good'
Sarah Hilary, author of the DI Marnie Rome series

'One of the very best authors writing today'
Andrea Mara, author of *No One Saw a Thing*

'Smart, gripping and stylish'
Catherine Ryan Howard, author of *56 Days*

'Funny, sexy, and a character and a case
that will break your heart'
Jo Callaghan, author of *In the Blink of an Eye*

'   urprising as it was satisfying'
                                    ath Under a Little Sky

A
STRANGER
IN THE
FAMILY

Jane Casey has written fourteen crime novels for adults and three for teenagers. A former editor, she is married to a criminal barrister who ensures her writing is realistic and as accurate as possible.

This authenticity has made her novels international bestsellers and critical successes. The Maeve Kerrigan series has been nominated for many awards: in 2015 Jane won the Mary Higgins Clark Award for *The Stranger You Know* and Irish Crime Novel of the Year for *After the Fire*. In 2019, *Cruel Acts* was chosen as Irish Crime Novel of the Year at the Irish Book Awards. It was a *Sunday Times* bestseller. Jane's standalone thriller *The Killing Kind* has been adapted for television.

Born in Dublin, Jane now lives in southwest London with her husband and two children.

𝕏 @JaneCaseyAuthor
⊡ @janecaseyauthor

Also by Jane Casey

A
STRANGER
IN THE
FAMILY

JANE CASEY

HEMLOCK
PRESS

Hemlock Press
an imprint of HarperCollins*Publishers* Ltd
1 London Bridge Street
London SE1 9GF

www.harpercollins.co.uk

HarperCollins*Publishers*
Macken House,
39/40 Mayor Street Upper,
Dublin 1
D01 C9W8
Ireland

This paperback edition 2025
1

First published by HarperCollins*Publishers* 2024

A catalogue record for this book is available from the British Library.

ISBN: 978-0-00-840506-9

Typeset in Sabon LT Std by HarperCollins*Publishers* India

Printed and bound in the UK using 100%
Renewable Electricity at CPI Group (UK) Ltd

This book contains FSC™ certified paper and other controlled
sources to ensure responsible forest management.

For more information visit: www.harpercollins.co.uk/green

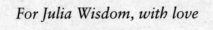

For Julia Wisdom, with love

'I have an habitual feeling of my real life having past, and that I am leading a posthumous existence.'

John Keats' last letter
30 November 1820

1

Did you notice anything out of the ordinary?

Afterwards, when the whole horror of it had been laid out, and their innocence – or rather, the degree to which they should feel guilty – had been debated by people who knew them, and many more who didn't, it was the small, uneasy details that lingered in the mind.

What went missing with her, and what did not.

What happened during the holiday a month earlier.

The argument two days before.

The car with a broken number plate, and how many times it was seen near the house.

The tiny, bare bedroom with blood on the floor.

The visitors to the house that week.

The letters before.

The phone call after.

The open door.

The river.

The bruises and scrapes.

The way her brothers reacted, or did not; the things they said, or did not.

The way her father cried.

Her mother. Her mother. Her mother.

But most of all, how long it was before anyone realised she was gone.

2

For some time now, Helena Marshall had been waking up every morning in a panic. It was instant, a punch of fear that struck before she was even aware that the day had begun. Today was no different.

She peeled off her eye mask and blinked at the ceiling, at the lightshade that probably needed dusting, and a smudge that had once been a mosquito in the corner, and the crack that wandered across the plaster, and a cobweb. The house was full of spiders because August was when they started preparing for cold weather, and it was an old house, with sash windows that were loose in their frames and gaps in the floorboards and fireplaces in bedrooms, and the chimneys needed sweeping now that she came to think about it but the sweep had been so *rude* the last time he came.

There was a notebook by her bed, with a pen, and she could start a list of jobs to do – *dust shade, remove cobweb, find new sweep* – but it was so *boring*. And no one else noticed these things, or did anything about them. It was always her job to sort out the house, and the children, and remember to buy school shoes (school shoes! that needed to go on the list that she wasn't making) and actually, she had better ways to spend her time. Work that needed to be done.

Beside her, her husband gave a long, quavering snore. If she was a man, no one would expect her to bother about the chimneys being swept and the gutters cleared (which they would need to be; there were thriving miniature rain forests in three or four places and August had been so wet and the brickwork would take any excuse to soak up damp and present it to her in bouquets of dull grey blooms on the wallpaper).

It was (she checked, peering in the half-light) ten minutes past six. The sun had risen, in theory, but it was a dull day and the forecast was for rain again and *that* didn't help her mood.

Her age, Dr Fuller said. Her age seemed to be the answer to every question she asked the doctor these days. The aches in her joints. The skittish unreliability of her memory. The way her skin looked in the morning, and the evening, and after a glass of wine. The sense of impending doom. There was no other reason for it. Her life was busy and fulfilling. She didn't like seeing the changes that time was making to her famously lovely face but that was what happened.

Count your blessings.

Lying there, Helena tried. She was *getting things done* when it came to her work, and that was good, even if it meant unpleasantness from ignorant people.

Her husband was rich, reasonably nice, supportive of her and *present*, unlike several of her friends' husbands who had slid away to new lives where they could pretend to be young again. Bruce was thirteen years older than her, which made him fifty-nine (and she would have to plan a party for his sixtieth; that was another job that would take up time she didn't have). They had met later than their contemporaries, married within six months, and he had already been fading into comfortable middle age. She had been a minor star, famous enough to have her picture in the paper, often, coming out of nightclubs or at the races. A sort of celebrity, on the guest list for parties and launches even if no one quite knew why. She had thought he was wonderful and he had thought she was beautiful and that had seemed like enough.

Then marriage, and motherhood, which was another life.

Helena was not the sort of person to run away from things, but she sometimes dreamed of packing a bag and going away for a week or a month, meeting a stranger, having a wild affair, and only coming back to the cobwebs and the draughts and the homework and muddy sports kit and maddening questions when she was good and ready. And *that* was why she hadn't overreacted on holidays.

That was why Bruce still snored beside her.

Helena wriggled her shoulder blades flat against the mattress to try to relieve the ache at the base of her neck. The boys should have come first on her list of blessings, probably. Ivo was fourteen and, overnight, had gone from sweet-natured compliance to frowning silence. He only seemed happy when he was playing some sort of sport (which, at least, he was good at). Magnus was twelve and (a squirm of genuine anxiety at this) insufficiently focused on his schoolwork. He was lazy, and not bright enough to get away with it. His school report had made it impossible to ignore the issue, along with the phone call from his headteacher suggesting that if things didn't improve he might be happier at a different school. So they were paying, at vast expense, for a tutor to come all summer.

And Rosalie, of course. They had Rosalie, who was nine. Rosalie's room was the smallest and it needed a new carpet thanks to her experiments with making perfume out of pilfered cosmetics and household cleaning products. Helena had been thin-lipped about it and Bruce had laughed. Rosalie was a wilful child, demanding in a way that the boys had never been. Girls were different, she'd been warned.

Helena kept her preferences strictly to herself but if she had to choose – in a fire, say – she would rescue her boys first (and of them, Magnus had her heart, but that was something she thought no one else knew. Ivo was a good boy but Magnus had charm). And then she would go back for Rosalie – assuming she hadn't *started* the fire in the first place. What Helena often asked herself was whether Rosalie was *disturbed* or just too bright for her own good. She was intelligent. Interested in everything. A sponge for facts. Prone to awkward questions, and doggedly focused about them. She had never been playful. Helena had thought it would come in time, and had been wrong.

She took several deep, slow breaths, focusing on the positives: they were as happy as most people could expect to be.

Enough wallowing.

She levered herself out of bed, braved the bathroom (chilly) and the bathroom mirror (unflattering), and pulled on a dressing gown. Now that she was upright, her anxiety had translated itself into energy. It was Friday but they were at the tail end of the summer holidays; it would be hours before anyone else woke.

On a whim, Helena went upstairs instead of down. The ceilings were lower up here but there were two large bedrooms and a bathroom that made their Bulgarian cleaning lady shake her head. The important thing was that the boys occasionally showered in it. She missed the soapy-clean smell that they'd had throughout their childhoods. Now a waft of sweat and muskiness and socks greeted her when she opened Ivo's door, like the men's locker room in a gym.

He was face down, his head turned to one side, his arms and legs trailing off the bed. A spasm of tenderness made Helena tweak the duvet into place to cover his (enormous! calloused!) feet so he didn't get cold. His room was neat – Ivo was an organised child and always had been.

Magnus's room next. It was wildly untidy. No chance of reaching the bed here, Helena registered, eyeing the floor. It was covered in clothes and miscellaneous crap that she wasn't allowed to throw out. Her favourite child was rolled up in the duvet like a sleeping gerbil. A tuft of his silky fair hair was just visible.

Was he breathing? Could he have died in the night? Was that the reason for the feeling of doom that had been shadowing her since she woke up?

Helena stared at the ball of duvet, which didn't move. She was a new mother again, terrified of cot death. Surely it should rise and fall; surely—

Magnus shifted and a low fart vibrated through the mattress. The porcelain-delicate newborn was long gone. She retreated, closing his door. It was a long time since she had checked on the boys while they slept and she wondered if it would ever happen again, which was depressing. What was it they said? *Long days, short years.*

She shivered as she hobbled down the stairs, trying to be quiet, thinking about the opinion piece she was writing for the *Telegraph* and whether it was too angry and might put people off. Tone was so important.

Not for a moment did she hesitate on the first floor. Not for a second did she consider going to check on Rosalie. Afterwards, she would struggle to explain that, but the last thing Helena wanted was company while she was writing, and specifically Rosalie, who would want to know what she was doing and why. No matter what Helena said, she would linger in the room like a black-eyed ghost.

Helena wandered into her study and turned her computer on, shuffling through her notes, already half absorbed. Back out of the study, into the sitting room, her nose wrinkling at the mess of squashed cushions on the sofa and a stale smell. She tidied the room briskly, shuffling papers, plumping cushions, mouthing good lines to herself as she went.

The supreme act of love, as a mother, is to give up a child to someone who can offer them more. Love isn't about blood, but care, kindness and guidance . . .

Too early for post, which was something of a relief given the sort of messages she'd been getting since the last time she was on *Woman's Hour*. But she couldn't allow herself to be intimidated into silence. She went down the steps to the kitchen at the back of the house and filled the kettle. All of this mattered, that was the problem. Life and death, literally. Wishing things were different wouldn't help, and in the meantime children were suffering. The best place for a child to be, Helena thought, was with a loving family. Producing a child didn't make you a mother, and—

A thin line of pale light ran down the edge of the back door. It wasn't properly closed. Helena had gone to bed before the boys and her husband, so one of them must have left it open, she thought, and strode across the kitchen, her slippers scuffing the floor in a way that would have the forensics officers shaking their heads a few hours later. The handle felt sticky as she shut the door. She sighed and went to the sink for bleach cleaner and a cloth. There was dirt on the paintwork – something dark – so she wiped it vigorously until it was spotless. The key wasn't in the lock, or hanging on the hook where it lived, and Helena sighed again, and went to make her tea.

And she never, for one minute, thought that there was anything to worry about, because she had been in practically every room of the house and nothing was missing.

3

The Toyota Land Cruiser bumped up the track, the four-wheel drive barely coping with the heavy rutted mud and large stones on the only access road to Windholt House. Heavy gates topped with barbed wire blocked the track every mile or so, with signs warning that this was private property. The fields on either side of the road were muddy and straggled with unkempt grass, since the sheep no longer cropped it. Their absence had left the land without a purpose, without life.

The rain had been constant for days. The third gate sat in a giant puddle that made the driver swear as he splashed through it, dragged the gate open, drove through, stopped, got out again and swung the gate closed. Easier with a passenger, he thought, and winced at that thought too. This wasn't a journey he made often.

Today was different.

Today was an emergency.

Tearing anxiety tightened his hands on the wheel and turned his stomach into a sea of acid. The letter was where he had flung it on the passenger seat. It had been waiting in the PO box he visited once a week, an innocent-looking white envelope with his name in familiar handwriting.

I don't know when you will read this but you will be too late.

He stopped at the last gate. The rain seemed to gather force as he got out of the car, drumming on his head and shoulders. Now that he was nearly at the house he was afraid of what he would find, and more afraid of what he might not find.

At first glance, everything at the house looked as it should: the Land Rover was parked near the front door. A light in the hall made the windows glow softly. He hurried around the side of the house, the wind catching the breath from his body as he faced into it.

In the yard the kennel was empty, but that meant nothing. The dog, a sheepdog, had died before Christmas. He hurried forward, stepping on something that gave under his foot with unpleasant softness. It was saturated with mud, but he held it up and shook it out. A jumper, hand-knitted, the colour impossible to guess. Pearl-pink buttons at the neck.

He gave a low moan and looked ahead, to the back door.

It was standing open.

He hurried through to the hall, leaving a trail of prints from his boots, careless now as he flung open doors. Empty rooms. He ran up the stairs, praying under his breath.

How could he have left her here?

How could he have done anything else?

The brass doorknob chilled his palm as he turned it, and he swung the door open on a nightmare.

4

'Are you sure you don't mind?' Ivo Marshall's voice was barely audible. The other man had to strain to hear him over the sound of the television from the room next to them. Racing commentary echoed through the flat, rapid and toneless.

'Of course I don't. It's not a burden for me to spend time with them. Not after so long.'

'I'd have thought it would be worse, seeing them like this.'

'Time takes its toll on us all.' He held up his stick. 'I'm not what I was either.'

Ivo smiled. 'You haven't changed, Mr Hood.'

'Dennis, please. And I've slowed down a lot since Lydia died.' He reached out and patted the younger man's sleeve. 'Take a weekend off, Ivo. Spend some time with your wife. I can help out with your parents, if that frighteningly effective young woman needs any assistance.'

'Sabiha?' Ivo looked around as if the carer was going to materialise behind him even though she wasn't due to arrive for an hour. 'She's brilliant, isn't she?'

'I'm tempted to steal her when I go. It can't be long now until I need someone to look after me.'

'Please don't lure her to Bristol. We couldn't manage without her.'

Hood blinked. 'I was only joking, Ivo. I can see it's been difficult. Your mother . . .'

'It must be a shock for you to see her how she is now.'

'Helena was so beautiful, you know. So vibrant.'

'I remember,' Ivo said flatly. 'But she hasn't been like that for a long time.'

'No. Of course not.' Hood tried to smile. 'My poor Lydia would be so sad to see her like this. Was it – was it a stroke? Is there any hope of improvement?'

'She has permanent brain damage because she tried to kill herself and that didn't work out. So no. There's no chance of her getting any better.' A hint of impatience had crept into Ivo's voice and he regretted it instantly as the older man drew back, alarmed. 'But she doesn't seem to be unhappy, exactly. It's worse for Dad.'

'At least they're still together.'

'In sickness and in health. Dad meant it.'

'I was the same with Lydia. I'd have done anything for her. But I had no idea about your mother.' Hood folded his hands on the top of his stick, a slight tremor running through him. 'We left Richmond before all of this happened.'

'I remember. You were our favourite neighbours.' Ivo's eyes were unfocused for a second. 'I remember waving goodbye when you drove off. All five of us together. Before Rosalie disappeared.'

'Awful.' Hood said it with true sympathy. 'Unimaginable. None of us could have known.'

'No. Of course not.'

'And Lydia and I didn't realise, you know. We thought – ah, well. With hindsight, we should have kept in touch.' He rallied. 'But I promise you, it's a pleasure to me to see your parents and to give you a bit of a break.'

'I need it.' Ivo ran a hand over his head and blinked, looking exhausted. 'I'll be away for the night on Saturday, but I won't be far from London if you need me.'

'Magnus doesn't help out?' Hood asked the question diffidently, almost as if he feared the question was in bad taste.

'No.' A quick, tight smile from Ivo. 'This isn't Magnus's kind of thing.'

'And you don't find it too much of a burden?'

'It's not as if I have a choice.'

'Oh.' Hood moved back, alarmed by the look on Ivo's face. 'It was a stupid thing to say.'

'No. No. Sorry. I shouldn't have snapped.'

'Dennis?' The television had gone silent without either of them noticing. Bruce Marshall's voice was still strong. 'Are you there?'

'Yes, I'm just coming.'

Ivo winced. 'Are you sure, Dennis? I can come back tomorrow. I'm used to it.'

'Don't be silly.' Hood moved to the door of the flat's sitting room, deft in spite of his limp. 'You go and relax. Don't worry about anything. I'll do whatever needs to be done. You can count on me.'

Ivo followed him into the sitting room where his parents sat in armchairs on either side of a fireplace that didn't work, staring at a big old-fashioned television. Horses galloped towards the camera in a foreshortened blur. The colour contrast was turned up so the grass of the racecourse was luminous green. 'Dad, I'm going now. Dennis is going to be here over the weekend, so if you need anything, he can sort it out for you.'

'You aren't coming?'

Ivo stopped, caught Dennis Hood's eye, and said, more firmly than usual, 'No. Not unless you need me.'

'Hm.' Bruce laced his hands over his stomach, staring unhappily across at the slumped figure of his wife. Her eyes were vacant and her mouth hung open. Grey hair straggled over her shoulders. Dennis Hood looked away from her, uncomfortable. Ivo bent and kissed his father's cheek.

'But if you do need me, I'll be here, I promise.'

'Let him go, Bruce.' Dennis sat down in the chair beside his friend and patted his arm. 'We have plenty of catching up to do.'

'Sabiha will make dinner and put Mum to bed,' Ivo reminded his father, pulling his jacket on. 'And Dennis said he'd be back tomorrow.'

'All day,' Hood confirmed. 'And Sunday. There's golf to watch.'

'Ah, good.' Bruce nodded and raised a hand in blessing. 'You go, Ivo. I'll see you in a couple of days. It will be nice to catch up with Dennis.'

Ivo bent over his mother, dropping a kiss near her forehead without actually making contact with her skin. As he left the room, Dennis Hood leaned over conspiratorially. 'Do you remember Sammy Moguel?'

Bruce clapped his hands and crowed, 'Do I? How could I forget her?'

Neither of them heard the front door close, and if Helena was aware of it, she made no sign.

5

I knew exactly where I was going as soon as I heard the address: a flat in a mansion block in Battersea, overlooking the park. I took down the details automatically, scrawling them in my notebook, distracted. I'd lived in Battersea, once, and I'd been happy.

In ordinary circumstances I would have been focused on the case, not where it was. Today's job seemed straightforward, though – tragic, but not complicated. As I drove I found myself on familiar streets, passing places I hadn't been for a long time, and I thought about the past instead of what was coming my way.

The address was on Prince of Wales Drive. I found a space and got out of the car, but instead of heading straight for the scene I stood still. The air was clear and earthy, and in the distance waterfowl honked in a minor key. Bare branches stretched over the railings, reaching towards the road and the red-brick mansion blocks that ran down the other side, symmetrical and magnificent, layered with white painted brickwork so they looked like elaborate cakes. They hummed of privilege and wealth and the finest Victorian building, and they would probably last twice as long again as the glass and metal high-rise flats that were springing up around the sturdy white chimneys of the old power station.

I had parked near one of the park gates. On a whim I slipped through it and fell back through time. Nothing had changed. There was the lake where ducks were squabbling over food thrown by two earnest small children in hand-knitted jumpers, their mother bending over them, and there was a dog walker managing a brace of mismatched hounds, and there, as ever, pairs of earnest ladies of a certain age, deep in conversation. I kept up a brisk pace – and it was barely a detour – but I was lost in my memories for a self-indulgent minute or two.

Until one of the less happy memories from that time resurfaced – a man who had watched me when I was in that very park, with every intention of causing me harm. A prickle of unease made me stop to scan the path behind me. I saw nothing except trees, a few joggers and a couple walking hand in hand. The sense of danger lingered, though, and I was happy to leave at the next gate, focusing my attention on the job instead of myself. I had run laps of this park hundreds of times, and I had read the papers on lazy winter afternoons in nearby pubs, and I had kissed my boyfriend by the river, and I had wondered about the people who lived in the mansion blocks.

Now it was time to think about how they died.

I walked through the gate and a hand closed around my elbow.

'*Christ*.' I yanked myself free before I thought about it, and my free-floating anxiety found a focus in the man who was smirking at me.

'No. Only me.'

Panic receded, replaced by irritation, but also wariness. DI Josh Derwent had a troublemaking glint in his eye.

'What are you doing? Were you *watching* me?'

'I was *waiting* for you to finish your nature walk and get on with some work, if it's not too much trouble.'

'All I did was walk through the park instead of outside it,' I began, hearing the note of apology in my voice and hating it. It was always the same: me on the defensive, Derwent self-assured and assertive.

'I know.' Derwent tilted his head to consider me and I took the opportunity to look at him too: something about him was different, but I couldn't pin it down. As usual, his suit was immaculate, his hair neat, his expression coolly amused by some joke he wasn't sharing. He looked thinner, and I wondered if he was training for a marathon or if there was some other reason for it.

What he made of me, I couldn't guess.

'You didn't look as if you were enjoying yourself,' he said at last.

'I felt as if someone was staring at me, so that ruined it,' I said accusingly.

'Like before.'

His thoughts had been running along the same lines as mine, then. 'I didn't think you'd remember that. It was a long time ago.'

'I remember. You know, given that you have so much experience of being in danger, you could do with looking around you occasionally. Paying attention to that little voice in your head.'

'I looked back.'

'I know.'

I folded my arms. 'Well, maybe if you hadn't been lurking here I wouldn't have felt as if I was under surveillance. Most people would just say hello.'

'I'm not most people.' He leaned closer, his voice low. 'You know what I am.'

The words spun through my mind: *friend, landlord, colleague, bad boy, worst nightmare, almost-lover* – and stopped on the right one.

'My boss.'

'Exactly.' He grinned. 'So do you want to visit the scene or just skip it and go for a stroll?'

'If anyone's holding things up, it's you.' I slid past him. 'Let's go.'

He was smiling to himself as we walked towards Leinster Mansions. It was halfway along the road, a fine six-storey edifice with a gathering of police vehicles and uniformed officers and forensic service vans in front of it. Outside the police tape stood a small cluster of gawkers who seemed typical of the local community: genteel elderly people with small dogs, ultra-fit runners, and a couple of men who might possibly have been drug dealers and would definitely have known where to score if

16

you needed to. I ducked under the tape, showed my credentials to the officer who was on scene guard and ran up the stairs to the second floor, aware of Derwent on my heels. The front door to the flat was open, revealing a narrow, dark hallway with a wheelchair folded against one wall. I stuck my head in and looked to the left, where there was the promise of daylight. A couple of paper-suited SOCOs were deep in conversation halfway along the hall. I recognised Kev Cox immediately. He was a bald middle-aged man, good-natured and hardworking, a brilliant Crime Scene Manager.

'Can we come in?'

Kev looked around and beamed. 'Maeve. I heard you were on your way. Just watch where you step. We're waiting for Dr Early.'

'What's the story?' Derwent asked from over my shoulder.

'The main area of interest is at the end, in the master bedroom,' Kev said. 'Working back from there off this hallway you have another bedroom, then a bathroom, then the kitchen, and last but not least the living room. It's quite a big place.'

'Swanky location.'

He pulled a face. 'A bit stuffy for me. We've already been told off for making too much noise on the balcony outside the living room.'

'What were you doing?' I asked. '"Don't Cry for Me Argentina"?'

He was one of the only people I'd ever met whose eyes actually twinkled when he laughed. 'You know I'm famous for my Evita impression.'

'And you look so like her,' Derwent said.

'Hilarious.' Kev nodded towards the living room. 'Your colleague is in there.'

I walked on the footplates that were laid down like stepping stones, and made it to the first open door where, with a flash of pleasure, I found Detective Constable Liv Bowen. She had been back from maternity leave for three months and every day I thanked my stars that she'd returned. She was standing by a large window that overlooked the park, her attention focused on her phone. I took a moment to consider the old-fashioned décor: the walls peach and the carpet dark green, the furniture overstuffed and the curtains fussy. A narrow balcony ran along outside the windows.

I was really looking for clues to the character of the people who lived there, but found very little – no books, a large and dated television, a couple of bland paintings on the walls. Through an archway there was a formal dining room with a long mahogany table that was polished but empty and slightly too big for the space it occupied. A painting leaned against the wall, face in. A medicine container marked with days of the week lay on the table, and a stick hung on the back of one chair. There was a single framed photograph on a low table, a family picture from a holiday somewhere hot. They were sitting around a table under a tree, caught in a sun-dappled moment. Two boys, one hunched and awkward, one sprawling in teenage lankiness, a little girl with dark hair who was staring at the camera, wide-eyed, the father with his mouth open as if he was talking, and the mother turning her head to one side, inscrutable behind huge dark glasses, her hair sleek and fair.

'What have we got?' Derwent asked.

'Oh – sorry.' Liv shoved her phone in her pocket.

'Is everything OK?' I moved towards her, concerned.

'Sonny's childminder thinks he might be coming down with something because he didn't eat much breakfast. I can't bear it if he gets sick again, Maeve. He's been snotty ever since he started going to her.'

'That's normal, isn't it? Being around other kids, sharing germs. It's good for him.'

'It's not good for me. I need sleep.' She had shadows under her eyes. 'That's the first thing to go when he's sick, and I'm always the one who gets up to deal with him. Joanne seems to be able to sleep through anything.'

'Annoying,' I said sympathetically, while wondering how soon I could ask her about the case without being uncaring.

'Joanne says I'm trying to do too much.'

'Does she?' And what exactly was Joanne doing if Liv was running herself ragged with childcare and work?

Derwent cleared his throat. 'This is fascinating, but what I wanted was to hear about the murder, if at all possible.'

'Two bodies. A husband and wife. He killed her and then himself,' Liv said. 'Their carer found them this morning in their bedroom.'

I shivered. 'I hate these cases. So bleak. There's always a sad story behind it.'

'And not really a crime.' Liv amended her statement before Derwent could jump on it. 'Nothing to investigate, I mean.'

'You seem very confident that you know what happened.' Derwent folded his arms. 'Have you even seen the bodies?'

'It looks very straightforward, honestly.' A faint flush of colour warmed Liv's cheeks.

'Kev said there were two bedrooms. Did they live on their own?' I asked quickly.

'They had a carer who came every morning and evening to cook and clean. She helped them get up and go to bed, but otherwise it was just the two of them. The second bedroom isn't really usable as a bedroom.'

'Why not?'

'It's full of archive boxes. Piled up to the ceiling, practically. The only space left is for a desk.'

'They'll be worth a look,' Derwent said. 'That's the sort of thing you can do, Liv.'

She looked startled. 'There's hundreds of them, though.'

'Then you'd better get on with it as soon as Kev gives you permission.'

'Why?' I asked. 'What makes you think it's important?'

'I don't know if it'll give us a reason for why they died, but at the very least it should be interesting.' Derwent looked past me to Liv. 'Didn't anything else occur to either of you about them? What about their names?'

I flipped my notebook open and read them again.

19

'Bruce and Helena Marshall.' As I said it, the names sounded familiar. 'Not the couple whose daughter disappeared twenty years ago?'

'The very same,' Derwent said with some satisfaction. 'The name rang a bell and I recognise the family in the photograph over there. It was actually sixteen years ago this summer. I'm betting the boxes in the spare room are to do with the investigation.'

'It's coming back to me.' Liv clicked her fingers. 'People thought they did something to her.'

'And Helena was the one they blamed, but I don't recall why,' I said slowly.

'Worth finding out, wouldn't you say?' Derwent was at his silkiest. 'In case someone decided blaming them wasn't enough.'

6

'What are we waiting for?'

We had been in the flat for ten minutes at the most but Derwent was pacing up and down like a caged wolf, snapping with impatience. Delays brought out the worst in him, and his best wasn't all that great.

'Dr Early,' I said. 'As Kev told you.'

'Dr Sorry-I'm-Late.' He turned to Liv. 'If the bedroom is out of bounds, why are we OK to stay in here and touch things?'

'The bedroom is the only place that wasn't forensically compromised. I was the first one here after the response officers, so I saw it before Kev got here. And you're allowed in here because he cleared this room already.' Liv looked around. 'There wasn't much to check, he said, thanks to the carer. Sabiha Qureshi. She was in here first thing.'

'Where is she? Can we talk to her?'

'She had to go to her next clients. The agency couldn't provide cover for her. But we can talk to her later,' Liv said quickly as Derwent's face darkened. 'And I did run through the timeline with her.'

'So what time did Sabiha leave last night?' I asked.

'Seven. She came back at a quarter to eight this morning and let herself in, which was normal – she had a key. She was a bit surprised Bruce wasn't up already. He was usually having his breakfast when she got in. She just assumed he was resting and left them to sleep for a few minutes while she did some household jobs.'

'Including cleaning? It smells of furniture polish in here.'

'Yep.' Liv pulled a face. 'I've never seen Kev so upset. Sabiha cleaned the kitchen and bathroom as well as in here.'

'For God's sake,' Derwent said. 'Why couldn't she have been lazy? No fingerprints, no DNA. Same as when the daughter disappeared, if I remember correctly.'

I had been taking notes. 'Did Sabiha usually put them to bed by seven? That seems early. How old were they?'

'Bruce was seventy-five and Helena was sixty-two but she was the one who needed support. The carer put her to bed every evening and last night was no exception. Bruce didn't always go to bed at the same time as Helena, but he didn't like watching television in here without her. He would go into the second bedroom and do some reading or writing if he didn't want to go to bed. He always got up by himself, quite early. Helena stayed in bed until Sabiha came in the mornings.'

'What did she say about today?'

'The short version? The flat was tidy but she gave it a once-over before knocking on the bedroom door. She didn't know anything was wrong until she went in.'

'No sign of a break-in?' Derwent checked and Liv shook her head.

'Was there a note?' I asked.

'No.'

'You'd think Bruce would have left something on the door.' Derwent was looking thoughtful. 'Dear Sabiha, don't come in, call the police, love Bruce. It would have taken him ten seconds.'

'Maybe he didn't think of it because he was distracted by planning to kill his wife,' I suggested, and got a glare for my trouble.

'Sabiha knocked on the bedroom door at five past eight. The door was closed but not locked. She opened it and found the curtains were closed and one of the bedside lights was on. They were both in bed and both very dead.' Liv closed her notebook. 'And that was all she had to say. She called a family friend because he'd been there over the weekend instead of the usual son – she wasn't sure it was the right thing to do but the son was away, apparently, so she followed his instructions and called the friend.'

'Don't they have two sons?' I looked over at the holiday photo, checking.

'I did ask. The second one is more or less no-contact with the family, apparently. The friend is Dennis Hood. He came round, had a quick look to make sure she wasn't mistaken, although I don't know how you could be wrong about something like that, and he called us straight away.'

'And where is he now?' Derwent demanded.

'The flat next door. He's waiting to be interviewed. He was in a bit of a state so the neighbours took him in. Poor man – it's not what you expect on a Monday morning.'

'I don't really want to talk to him until we've seen the bodies.' Derwent checked his watch and sighed. 'What about the sons? Have we tracked them down?'

'Not yet.'

'Why not?' Derwent asked the question with deadly politeness, but Liv knew him well enough to quail.

'I was here. Waiting for you.'

'They need to be informed, don't you think? As the next of kin?'

'I'll get on it straight away.' Liv hurried out of the room, her face red, and I shook my head.

'Not necessary and not kind.'

'She needs to raise her game.' He was standing with his back to me, looking out over the park. 'Concentrate on the job, not her kid.'

'She's doing her best.'

'No, she's not.' He glanced at me. 'If she's working with you, she needs to be alert. I don't want any harm to come to you while she's on the phone to her childminder.'

'I can look after myself.'

A genuine smile narrowed his eyes. 'It's sweet that you believe that. But someone usually has to keep you out of trouble.'

'Oh, is that what you've been doing? I don't feel you've done a very good job.'

'Imagine how much worse it could have been without me.'

'Or better,' I said. 'It might have been better.'

23

'Maeve . . .' A note of reproach this time.

I abandoned the teasing and wandered around the living room and dining room, taking a closer look at the few personal effects I'd noticed. Everything reinforced my first impression that this wasn't much of a home.

I picked up the painting that had been leaning against the dining-room wall and straightened to discover that Derwent was inches away from me.

'What have you got there?'

I held it out so we could look at it together. 'You might know – was that their house?'

'Looks like it. The house was in Richmond, wasn't it? By the river.'

'The river was at the end of their garden. I remember that much.' The painting was amateurish, the grain of the canvas visible through the thin layer of paint, but it was still recognisably a Georgian house with a fanlight and dormer windows at the attic level. Trees crowded around it and a wide lawn filled the foreground. I tilted the frame, trying to read the artist's signature, but it was a squiggle. 'One of the theories was that the girl drowned.'

'They never found a body.'

'You know bodies don't always come to the surface. It's possible she did.'

'Lots of things were possible. It was one of those cases. Many theories and not enough facts. Kidnapping, accident, murder or your best guess, but the girl never came to light again, dead or alive.' Derwent brooded on it. 'I knew the first SIO. I should let him know about the parents, as a courtesy.'

'I think it's strange that it all died down so quickly,' I said. 'We're both struggling to remember the details. You'd think the media would have covered the case over and over again, given that she was a pretty little girl from a wealthy family, but the story just faded out of the spotlight.'

'The mother was famous, wasn't she? A media type. They look after their own.'

I had a vague memory of a blonde with self-consciously tasteful clothes and a heavy hand with eyeliner. She had been famous for being famous before she turned into some sort of campaigner. 'I'm not sure she was a media type, but she was good at generating outrage, from what I remember.'

Derwent was standing behind me, so close that I could feel the warmth of his body against mine in the slightly chilly dining room. The flat's heating was switched off, to preserve the crime scene in the best possible condition, and I had been regretting the lack of my big coat. He had been keeping his distance lately, literally and emotionally, and I had wondered if I'd done something wrong. There was every chance it was nothing to do with me. A late devotion to professionalism, perhaps.

Or maybe it was the best way to deal with the attraction that had been smouldering between us since the previous summer – the attraction that I was never, ever going to admit again, let alone act upon.

And since Derwent was fully committed to his girlfriend, her son and the suburbs, I didn't need to worry about it.

But I still longed to lean back against him, just for a moment.

'Sixteen years ago,' he said. 'Do you think it prompted whatever happened here? Grief can be difficult like that. It hides for years and then it overwhelms you.'

He was all business, not lover-like. I gave myself a mental shake. 'Do you know what else can be difficult to live with? Guilt.'

'About the daughter?'

'I'm just saying, there were rumours about what happened. Both of the parents were arrested at different times, weren't they? The investigating team had a good look at them, anyway. Maybe some new information came to light.'

'Another reason to talk to my mate. Find out what the team really thought about the little girl.'

'Sorry to interrupt.' Kev leaned in through the open door. 'Dr Early has arrived at last.'

7

For someone so robust, Derwent had his squeamish side. He hustled me down the hall to the bedroom where the Marshalls lay dead.

'Let's get in and out before the doc does her stuff with the thermometer.'

I didn't argue; it wasn't my favourite part either.

Kev was standing by the door. 'Gloves. Stay on the footplates. Try not to move around too much or touch anything.'

'Seriously?' Derwent raised his eyebrows. 'Still?'

He grimaced. 'You never know, do you? You only need one bad day in court to play it safe forever.'

I stepped carefully into the room to find the doctor, thin and eager, surveying the bodies. She looked up.

'Sorry I'm late.'

Behind me, Derwent turned a chuckle into a cough.

'Have you seen them already?' I shook my head and she gestured to the bodies. 'Have a look.'

Kev had lit the scene in merciless detail with bright white halogen lights on stands. They bleached out the warmer glow from the bedside lamp on Bruce Marshall's side of the bed. A cordless telephone sat on the table too, along with a couple of books. On Helena's side of the bed there was nothing but a full water glass, a paper napkin covering it. The room was tidy. Nothing seemed out of place on the chest of drawers that faced the bed: brushes, a mirror, a man's watch. Cream carpet, cream walls, curtains striped in blue and green, the same old-fashioned style as the rest of the flat. It made me feel suffocated. The curtains stirred gently, moving in a draught. I drew the nearest curtain back with a gloved hand. The sash was raised a couple of inches but there were stops on either side so the window couldn't be opened any further. I rattled it to check it was secure, confirming that no one had come in or gone out that way.

And then I focused on the double outrage at the centre of the scene.

Helena Marshall was lying on her back, her face slack and hollow in the way of the dead. I remembered her as a tall, glamorous woman, but the figure in the bed was frail. Her eyebrows and eyelashes were sparse and her hair spread out across the pillow in lank strands. Her mouth gaped open, a dark void. I shone my torch over her face, feeling that I was intruding. Her skin was waxy yellow, flecked with red petechiae. There was a pillow lying crumpled against her side of the bed as if someone had let it fall there.

'Presumably that's what killed her,' Derwent said into the silence and I winced, as if we might disturb them by speaking too loudly.

'It's been photographed,' Kev said. 'I'll be bagging it.'

'I'd expect to find saliva on it if it was used to smother her,' Dr Early said, and Kev nodded.

'Worth checking for trace fibres too.'

'No blood?' I asked.

'Not that I can see at present.' Kev, cagey as ever.

'Then she probably died before that happened.'

That was lying in the bed beside her, and all up the wall behind the headboard, and sprayed across the lampshade and the phone: red, predominantly. The top of Bruce Marshall's head was a soft mass of blood and brain and pulverised bone and his face was horribly distorted from the explosive force that had blown his skull apart.

'I didn't know he'd shot himself.'

'Liv left that detail out.' Derwent was grim. He made his way around to Bruce's side of the bed for a closer look at the weapon. 'A Webley. We don't see that very often. Usually a shotgun for a gun suicide.'

'They're easier to come by. Do you think that was an old weapon?'

'Well, I don't think he went to Tottenham and borrowed it from his mandem.' Derwent was crouching by the bed, peering at it. 'I bet you a thousand pounds that was a service revolver. Could have been his dad's from the Second World War. It hasn't been cleaned in donkey's years.'

'He should have handed it in when they had the amnesty after Dunblane.'

'There must be thousands of firearms that were stuck in the back of a drawer decades ago, or in an attic, and no one even remembers they're there. This could have been one of them.'

'But he had ammunition for it.'

Derwent shrugged. 'Why would he dispose of the ammunition if he'd forgotten to get rid of the gun?'

'Have you seen enough?' Dr Early asked.

He nodded and stood up, but he was still looking at the two bodies as he moved towards the door, and he was frowning. I felt like frowning myself.

'Kev, were the bedcovers like this when you arrived?' I asked.

'Haven't touched them.'

I stood for a moment longer, taking it in. Even though I would be able to look at videos of the scene and crime-scene photographs, nothing was as good as being able to stand in the room with the bodies. This was the last place Helena and Bruce Marshall had breathed. This was where their souls had departed.

An act of love, some might think, or a final revenge, or something else entirely.

I caught up with Derwent in the second bedroom. He was looming over Liv.

'How's it going?' I looked from him to her, noting the suspicious sheen in her eyes. 'Is everything OK?'

'I've made a start on the boxes.' Her voice wavered and she cleared her throat. 'Reams of files about the daughter's disappearance. Interviews, maps, photographs.'

'Police files?'

'No, they hired private investigators. They must have spent a fortune. I recognised a couple of the names as retired cops, though.'

'That doesn't mean they did a good job,' Derwent said.

'No, but it tells you the Marshalls sought out professionals to be involved in the investigation. They really wanted to find out what happened to her.'

'I wonder if any of the private detectives worked on the original case,' I said. 'Maybe the Marshalls wanted people who had nothing to do with the investigation because they weren't happy that the police focused on them.'

'It must have been frustrating when the Marshalls knew they didn't do it,' Liv said.

'They were the most likely suspects,' Derwent said. 'Statistically.'

'Yes, *statistically*.' I caught a raised eyebrow from him and doubled down. 'There are exceptions to the statistics. We've caught a few of them ourselves.'

'There are also good reasons for looking at close family when someone dies. *Statistically* women are most likely to be killed by their partners, and here we are, another dead woman beside her loving husband.'

'Yes, but . . . ' I trailed off. Was I ready to start sharing half-formed theories with Derwent?

'But what?' His eyes narrowed with suspicion. 'What did you say to Kev when you were leaving the bedroom?'

'I asked him if the covers had been moved since the bodies were discovered.'

'The bedclothes looked fine to me. Nothing much was out of place, apart from the pillow.'

'Well, that's what I was wondering about.'

He considered it, frowning in concentration. I knew that he wouldn't ask me what I thought, that he'd prefer to work it out by himself.

'Wasn't there anything that bothered *you* about the scene?'

He hesitated. Then, 'I didn't want there to be anything wrong with it, if I'm honest. I wanted this to be straightforward.'

'But.'

'There was one thing. I don't know.' He stopped as a voice in the hallway made us turn; the doctor on her way out, calling goodbyes.

'Dr Early?' I hurried to the door. 'Could you come in here?'

She came, but she was checking her watch at the same time. 'I've got to go. I'm late. I'm sure you want to know time of death, but it would only be a guess at this stage.'

'No, I wanted to check something else before the bodies are moved. What was Helena Marshall's cause of death?'

'Probably suffocation with something soft such as a pillow. She had bruising to her upper lip and nose that's consistent with the application of considerable pressure – I suspect her nose was fractured. I'll know more when I've excised the damaged tissue and examined it under a microscope.' She pulled on her coat, preparing to leave. 'I should be able to fit in the PMs this afternoon.'

I tried not to think about the doctor removing chunks of the dead woman's face. Dr Early's assistants were magicians when it came to making bodies look presentable so their loved ones could recognise them afterwards, but I would know the truth.

'I noticed she was flat on her back with her arms by her sides, and the bedclothes weren't rumpled. Is it possible that she cooperated with being suffocated?'

'It's more likely she was unaware of what was happening.' She frowned. 'You'd have thought . . . it's involuntary, the kicking, and the arms coming up, when someone is deprived of oxygen. It's a reflex. She couldn't have remained still by force of will.'

'But if she was already unconscious?'

'If she was deeply unconscious her movements might have been slighter.'

'Or he straightened the bedclothes before he killed himself,' Derwent said. 'Left everything neat and tidy.'

'Yes, but there's a problem with that, isn't there? You noticed the position of the bodies too.'

He folded his arms, mulish. 'I don't know what you mean.'

'Liar,' I said, without heat, and saw a gleam of amusement in his eyes.

'Want to act it out?'

'No.'

'That's a good idea, actually.' Dr Early's scientific mind was always delighted by experiments. Liv shrugged at me, unable to intervene.

'Come on.' Derwent led us into the living room, taking off his jacket and rolling up his sleeves. 'More floor space in here.'

He lay down and patted the carpet beside him. 'You be Helena, Maeve. I'll be Bruce.'

No point in arguing. I sat on the floor and shuffled into position before lying back, my shoulder lined up with his.

'Closer,' Dr Early said helpfully. 'The bed was narrow.'

We edged towards one another until our arms were pressed together.

'Helena had her hands by her sides,' Liv pointed out.

My knuckles brushed against Derwent's thigh as I moved into the right position and I cringed, rigid with embarrassment. Why had I started this?

'The bedclothes weren't tucked in,' Dr Early said. 'So if she'd tried to fight him off—'

'They would have slid down. Let's assume Bruce was her murderer.' Derwent turned his head and stared into my eyes. 'I'm in bed beside you and I decide the time is right to kill you.' He sat up and twisted around, reaching across me. 'I press my pillow over your face.'

'No. He'd need more force than that.' Dr Early demonstrated. 'Two hands, pushing straight down. It's harder than you'd think to suffocate someone. People assume it's a gentle death but a few years ago at a music festival some Dutch scientists got a random selection of people of different ages and sizes to smother a dummy to see what the natural methodology is –

where they put their hands and weight, and how long they can sustain a lethal amount of pressure. It takes some doing. Big strong men are better at it than small, frail women, and a lot depends on the angle of attack.'

'I'll take your word for it.' Derwent frowned. 'Bruce wasn't a robust man, was he?'

'I think he'd have had to get out of bed, come round to Helena's side and smother her while standing over her,' I said. 'Or he did it before he got into bed.'

'That, or he would have had to straddle her. He could have held her arms down with his knees.'

'Go on.' Dr Early was intent on the experiment. My eyes went to Liv. She was chewing her bottom lip, half-amused, half-wary.

Beside me, Derwent shifted his weight onto his left hand and knee and eased his right thigh across my hips. His right hand came down beside my ear and he paused for a moment, his arms braced, his body over mine.

I tried to breathe normally, and failed.

Then, kneeling astride me, but as if I wasn't even there, he straightened up to address Dr Early. 'I'm not going to put my weight on her arms.'

'No, it would bruise. I'll take a close look at Helena's elbows at the PM.'

'But even if I didn't . . .' He brought his knees in tight against me so my arms were trapped. He leaned forward again, his hands flat on the carpet on either side of my head. He was watching me intently. I hoped I looked unmoved but he grinned down at me, not fooled for a second. 'I'm holding the covers down too, you realise. And in this position, I can exert maximum force. Neat and effective.'

'It wouldn't have taken long.' Dr Early took a picture on her phone, looking at me in surprise when I protested. 'Just for my records.'

'OK.' Of course the doctor hadn't taken a picture of us in that position for fun. I regrouped. 'But whatever approach he took, he would have had to move from his side of the bed. And even if he was holding her arms down, her legs would have been free to move as she died. He *might* have remade the bed afterwards, straightened things up, adjusted the covers so they were pulled up to mid-chest for both of them, and then – what?'

'Got the gun out,' Derwent said, levering himself off me and returning to his original position. 'Loaded the gun, possibly. He could have stashed it in his bedside table, ready to use.' He turned away from me, reached towards an imaginary table and loaded an imaginary gun, lay back and mimed pointing the gun into his mouth. 'He shoots himself in the head. Blood everywhere.'

'The recoil could have made his hand fall back on his chest,' Dr Early said.

'Yes, but look at how we're positioned,' I said. 'I'm dead so I'm not moving. He's been busy sorting out the bed and getting ready to blow the top of his head off. Where does Bruce end up?'

Derwent looked down at his shoulder, which was in front of mine. 'Yeah. That's not how it was.'

'His left arm was under hers.'

'So he was the one who died first.' Liv frowned. 'But the blood covered both of them – she had flecks of it all over her face. If he died first, the blood on her face should have been smeared by the pillow pressing down on it. His blood should have been all over the pillow too. And obviously he couldn't kill her if he was dead.'

I didn't want to say it. 'I think they might both have been unconscious when they died. Unable to fight back.'

'It was staged,' Derwent said softly, and I nodded.

'Not a murder-suicide after all. Just a straightforward double murder.'

8

The stairwell was quiet and I paused to notice the silence. The flats were solidly built and the soundproofing seemed excellent, which was good for the residents but bad for us. So far, no one seemed to have heard anything.

Derwent swung out of the flat behind me as if someone was chasing him. 'Where are you going?'

'To see Dennis Hood. He's been waiting for ages next door.'

'On your own?'

'Yeah, I think I can manage it by myself.'

He looked surprised and, for an unguarded moment, hurt. Then the mask snapped back into place. 'Maybe you can and maybe you can't. Let's not assume anything.'

I made a small helpless gesture. 'All right, come with me if you like.'

'I just—' He stopped. 'I haven't been working with you for a while. And I enjoy it. So I thought I'd come along.'

Straightforward honesty from Derwent; it was more unsettling to me than any sarcasm or insinuation. I wondered if it was a trick or if he really meant it, and it was only when Dennis Hood was sitting in front of us, blank-eyed with shock, that I stopped thinking about it and came back to full attention. We had all refused the offer of tea and the Marshalls' neighbour had retired, hurt, to her kitchen.

'I can't drink any more of it.' Hood looked down at his hands, which were shaking. 'She's given me cup after cup of it.'

'People don't know what to do or say in these situations. Tea is a way of providing comfort,' I said.

'I just don't like it much.' He was a slim man with cropped silver hair and a beard, and I wondered if the shock had aged him or if he was always so frail. He looked lost in the large, velvet-covered armchair.

'First of all, I'm so sorry. Were you friends with the Marshalls?'

'For a long time. Decades. With Bruce, really. We're the same age.' He gave a dry little laugh. 'We *were*. I should be used to this by now. Friends die off in handfuls when you reach this stage in life.'

'So you were close.'

'At one time. But I hadn't seen them in years. I had moved away, you see, with my wife, before Rosalie disappeared. When I lived near them I was friends with Bruce and I saw him regularly, but sometimes we would go a few months without seeing each other. We always picked up where we left off. I thought that nothing would change after we moved. Then Rosalie disappeared, and they were never the same again. I tried to keep in touch, but it was difficult.'

'It can be very hard to move on from something like that. Especially with the uncertainty. I sometimes think it's easier to know the truth, even if it's bad news.'

Mr Hood looked at me approvingly. 'You're a nice woman.'

'It's just that I've seen a lot of sadness.' I could feel Derwent studying the side of my face and I flipped the page of my notebook. 'Where do you live now, Mr Hood?'

'I have a house in Bristol. Not as grand as the one in Richmond, when I lived near Bruce and Helena, but I'm on my own now.' He sighed. 'They had a wonderful life with the family. Just the kind of thing you might dream of. Then Rosalie—' He broke off, shook his head. 'We were all devastated, of course. The investigation took up so much of their time and energy from that point on. I did try to be supportive.'

'That can be difficult,' Derwent said quietly.

'Well, Helena made it difficult.' He ran a hand down his thigh, suddenly awkward. 'I'm speaking frankly.'

'Please do.'

'She was the kind of person who took offence easily. She would wait for someone to say the wrong thing and then attack.

35

I suspected it was her way of relieving her pent-up feelings of grief and guilt, because she was bad at admitting that she had any emotions at all, but it was rather like juggling live grenades. It wasn't a case of whether there would be an explosion, but when.'

'So you lost touch?'

'I couldn't be around them. It was too painful.' He sighed. 'I feared that something like this would happen. They became completely dependent on one another in a very unhealthy way. They shut everyone else out. I didn't even know that they'd left the house in Richmond until the other day.'

'Why did they leave the house?'

'A combination of things, from what Bruce said. Money, for one. It was a beautiful house but always in need of some kind of repair. I remember Helena complaining that everything leaked. And then it was big for the two of them on their own once the boys left.'

'What about their health? How would you say they were?'

'I was shocked when I saw Bruce. He'd lost a lot of weight. He used to be fitter than me. Mind you, I'm on a stick too.' He managed a weak smile. 'I've had a new knee and a new hip and I think I was better off with the old ones.'

'What about Helena?' I asked. 'Do you know what was wrong with her?'

'She took an overdose, a while after Rosalie . . . you know. She was never the same. She barely spoke when I was with them over the weekend. I think Bruce was glad to have some company.'

'I can imagine.'

He hesitated. 'I wondered if Bruce was developing dementia. He was very vague at times. He seemed to lose the thread of what he was saying and once or twice he spoke to me about things I hadn't said, like that I was going to Egypt. I told him he had me confused with someone else and he became quite distressed. If you're talking to the boys you might ask them if they had noticed any cognitive decline.'

36

'Their GP would know, presumably,' Derwent said.

'They never saw the same one twice, according to Bruce. It's not like the old days where you knew your doctor and your doctor knew you. And moving wouldn't have helped, obviously. They hadn't had time to get to know people – neighbours, and so forth. Not like it was in Richmond with Dr Fuller.' His face softened at the memory, his eyes wet.

'Why did you come to see them now, after so long, Mr Hood?' I asked.

'I'd put it off and put it off. There was always some excuse for me to avoid coming to London. And then I thought I wasn't getting any younger and neither were my friends, and I should make the effort to travel while I could. The letter I sent them bounced back, but I got hold of Ivo.'

'Tell me about yesterday.'

'I was with them all day from about eleven until six. Their carer was there when I left. Bruce was fairly cheerful, if anything. I was planning to call in this morning to say goodbye and he said he'd see me then.' Mr Hood shook his head. 'Hard to imagine he was already planning to do what he did. When the carer called me, I was floored, absolutely floored.'

'Why did she call you?' I asked.

'I'd left Bruce my number in the kitchen in case he ran into any difficulties. Their son Ivo usually comes to the rescue, but Ivo had asked for the weekend off and I was glad to be able to help. I wasn't thinking of anything like this, obviously.' He raised a hand to his forehead, his fingers trembling. 'For this to happen when Ivo was away . . . but perhaps that was why Bruce decided to do it now. The carer rang me, I got dressed and went to the flat, which was five minutes from my hotel. I had a quick look at . . . the situation, called the police and removed myself so I wasn't in the way. I didn't want to stay.' He blinked, his eyes watering. 'Bruce was a good friend. To lose him like that – and to see what he'd done to Helena – it was upsetting. He must have thought it was the best way out.'

I leaned back, my elbow brushing against Derwent's arm. Both of us jumped. I recovered to say, 'Would it surprise you to hear that we're treating it as a double murder, rather than a murder-suicide?'

'What? Really?' He looked stunned. 'Someone *killed* them? Heavens. Their poor boys. Who could possibly— but then I was so upset to think of Bruce being in such terrible distress when I hadn't noticed.' He was talking to himself more than to us. 'I mean yes. Murder. My God, that changes everything.'

9

Dennis Hood was right. A double murder did change everything. An hour after Derwent had called our boss, Detective Superintendent Una Burt, there were eight of us standing in the faded, chintzy living room.

'Dr Early said it might take a while to get the lab results back so we can see if they were drugged,' I explained.

'Why would you need to drug them?' Pete Belcott looked around at our blank faces. 'They wouldn't have been difficult to overpower.'

'Shut up, Pete,' Derwent said. 'Just stop talking.'

Pete blinked, wounded. He was stocky, with heavily greased hair, and I had hated working with him since day one. Time and proximity had only made me sure I was right to dislike him. 'I was only saying—'

'We heard what you were saying.'

'If it was someone who knew them well, like a family member, they might have wanted to avoid a confrontation,' I said. 'Or maybe the killer didn't want to leave anything to chance.'

Una frowned. 'Is it possible Mr Marshall gave his wife an overdose and then killed himself? I don't want to commit major resources here unnecessarily.'

'There's the position of the bodies too,' I said quickly as Derwent's expression darkened. He didn't like being questioned, and particularly not by Una.

'The bodies could have been moved by whoever discovered them. This carer. And who else – their friend?'

'I spoke to the carer,' Liv said, 'and she was adamant that neither of them had touched the bodies, except that Dennis

Hood checked for a pulse in Helena's neck. He didn't bother with Bruce.'

'Given that half his head was missing.'

'Yes, thank you, Josh. Have we spoken to Mr Hood yet?'

'Just now,' I said. 'I sent him back to his hotel.'

'Are you suggesting that we got this wrong, boss?' Derwent asked.

'Hoping. The last thing I need is another complex investigation.'

'So what's the plan?'

Her mouth thinned. He was passing it back to her to make the final decision on what we did, as was right and proper, given that she was his boss, but we all knew there was really no choice about it. 'Treat it as a double homicide for now. Do you think the family background is significant?'

'The missing daughter? It's worth assuming there's a connection. Most families never experience one major crime, let alone two.'

'Little Rosalie Marshall,' Una said, almost to herself.

'I don't remember that case,' Georgia said, and Vidya shook her head too.

'It dropped out of the headlines quickly,' Derwent explained. 'The family didn't seek out publicity.'

'That's unusual, isn't it?' Colin blinked behind his heavy glasses. He was the sort of man who always looked as if his anorak was close at hand even if he wasn't actually wearing it. Today, he was wearing it. 'The families are usually desperate for publicity.'

'The Marshalls got the wrong sort of publicity,' Una Burt said. 'The reports started out sympathetic and then the tone changed. There were circumstances that made the investigation focus on the parents rather than widening the net. You can understand why they shunned the limelight after that.'

'I'd like to find out what the investigating team made of them,' Derwent said. 'I was planning to get in touch with the SIO.'

'Yes, good. Do that.' She looked at me expectantly.

'I'm going to speak to the carer again.'

'Who let her leave?'

'Sorry,' Liv's face was flaming.

'Liv didn't know there was any reason to keep her here,' I said, defensive.

'But you did, Maeve.' Una Burt was always one to put the boot in where she could. I knew the remark was intended to make Liv feel she had fucked up.

'People depend on her. I'm not sure I'd have insisted.'

Burt registered the dissent with a twitch of one eyebrow and moved on. 'Colin, can you review whatever security there was here? CCTV, obviously. I noticed a couple of cameras in the hall downstairs.'

'I've already been making a list.'

'Of course you have.' Her face softened. Una Burt lived for efficiency and people who kept their emotions neatly under wraps at work, and Colin was ideal in both respects. 'We need to speak to all the neighbours. Vidya and Georgia, start on the top floor and work down. Pete, you start on the ground floor. You can meet in the middle.'

Pete would do far less than the two women, and complain about it much more.

'Oh – you can go with him, Liv,' Una said casually.

Along with his many undesirable attributes, Pete regularly questioned Liv about her partner Joanne and what they might do with one another, so I knew she liked to avoid him. She looked down at the floor and blinked furiously. I turned to Burt, ready to argue the point, but Derwent got there first.

'If Pete isn't capable of routine enquiries on his own at this point in his career, he's in the wrong job.'

'Hey,' Pete said in protest. Derwent ignored him.

'Liv can keep working through the spare bedroom. There's stacks of information, literally.' He threw Liv his car keys. 'It's too much for you to take in one journey, so let's share it out between vehicles. Start with the first stack next to the door – it probably has the most recent material in it. I'll take that lot back to the nick.'

She nodded and I felt a glow of gratitude to Derwent for finding her a way out. I kept my face absolutely impassive, however. Una didn't like being bested and she didn't like people taking Derwent's side over hers and she didn't like me all that much. Recently she had received her longed-for promotion – and permanent control of our team – so she was two full ranks above Derwent, and therefore entitled to demand respect. The trouble was that Derwent didn't do respect. Moreover, rank had no influence on his opinion of people, which was one reason why he was still an inspector. The miracle was that he had ever managed to get promoted in the first place.

With seniority came wisdom about which battles were worth fighting, and Una wisely decided this wasn't one of them. 'Right, good. Is everyone happy?'

'Who's speaking to the family?' Georgia asked.

'It's just the two sons. Response officers are informing them,' Derwent said.

'You didn't think it was important to get their reaction? I would have wanted to go myself instead of handing the job off to uniforms.' Una Burt's neck was blotched with pink, a sure sign that she had lost her temper.

'I don't actually think it'll make the difference between a conviction and them going free if I'm not standing right in front of them when they hear the news. And the officers have body-worn cameras. We'll have a record of how they react if they don't know already.'

'Then that's all right.'

'Exactly what I thought.' He held her gaze for a moment longer, then looked away. There was no warmth between the superintendent and her inspector.

'Right, everyone. Get going. Josh, you'd better show me the bedroom.'

With very bad grace, Derwent set off and she followed, taking two strides to every one of his, bobbing along on stumpy legs without grace in her movements or her manner. And yet there was a part of me that respected her for her confidence. I wished I knew how she did it.

The room emptied after Burt left, Georgia and Vidya with their heads together, Pete yawning as he went. Colin had slipped away first, on the hunt for his CCTV. Liv sat down in the chair on one side of the fireplace and buried her face in her hands.

'Are you all right?'

'Sort of. Not really.'

I sat in the chair opposite her.

'What's up? Was it what Burt said to you?'

'A bit.' Liv ran her fingers under her eyes, smearing the tears away. 'She wasn't wrong. I didn't do a very good job when I got here. I missed loads of stuff, but I'm so tired. And I've got a headache.'

'I have painkillers.'

'I took some. An hour ago.' She sniffed. 'I'm falling apart, Maeve.'

'You're not. You're just exhausted. It's hard, coming back to work.'

'I thought I'd be happy.' Two more tears streaked down her cheeks. 'I was so glad to be back.'

'Was Josh giving you a hard time about it too?'

'No. Not at all.'

'I thought he made you cry earlier, after we viewed the bodies.'

'He was being nice.' She rubbed at her cheeks. 'He told me to make Joanne do her share and blame him if she complains. He said I was important to the team.'

Relief made me smile. 'It'll get easier. I still don't think you did anything wrong.' I lowered my voice even more. 'If I didn't know better, I'd think Una has it in for you.'

'She wanted me to leave the team, so you're probably right.'

'Because you can't work and be a mother?' I had one eye on the doorway in case Burt appeared unexpectedly.

'Apparently.' Liv shrugged. 'That's the choice she made, I suppose. But I can tell you she disapproves like hell of mine.'

'We all make choices. There's no such thing as the perfect life. Everyone has to sacrifice something, somewhere along the way.' I sat back, shifting my weight in the chair.

'Thanks, Maeve. You know, I was thinking—' She broke off. 'Are you even listening to me?'

I was pulling on a glove, preparing to delve down the side of the armchair between the cushion and the frame. 'I think I heard something – it rustled when I moved – hang on . . .'

It was a piece of paper, lined, torn roughly from a notepad. On it, someone had scrawled a few words in pencil.

BDK? How?
Check dates

The last line was underlined twice, so hard that the pencil had dug through the paper.

'What's that?'

'It was down the side of the chair. A note.'

'Is it important?' Liv was too good a police officer not to be interested instantly. 'Do you think it was hidden deliberately?'

'I'd say it was pushed down so no one could see it.' I snapped a picture of it with my phone. The writing looked urgent, as if it had been scribbled under great pressure.

Liv came over to look at it as I went hunting for an evidence bag. 'Does it mean anything to you?'

I slipped it into the bag. 'No. Not yet. But I'll work it out.'

10

'Is that all?' Derwent tilted the scrap of paper inside the evidence bag, as if it might reveal some hidden message.

'I just thought it might be relevant.'

'It's not exactly going to secure a conviction.' He handed it back to me and I pressed my lips together to stop myself from arguing with him.

'I have to go. I'm meeting the carer.' I was glad to escape the flat, which was beginning to look like it was in the middle of a thorough burglary. Every drawer hung open, every cupboard door was ajar, and every surface was piled high with things that we had ferreted out to inspect.

'I'll come too.' He hustled me towards the door, murmuring, 'If we stay she'll find something shitty for me to do.'

She was Una Burt, who had spent a lot of time making it very clear that she wasn't going to interfere with how Derwent ran the investigation, and then proceeded to do exactly that.

'Superintendent Burt to you,' I said, once we were out of range. 'She's not exactly wearing the promotion lightly. You are being careful with her, aren't you?'

He looked at me for a second with that unnerving focus. 'She can't get rid of me. I get results and that makes her look good. She doesn't have to like me to know she needs me.'

'Maybe. But play it safe.'

'Worried about me?'

'Frequently.'

He stretched, effortlessly arrogant. 'You'd miss me if I was gone.'

'Is that a statement or a question?'

'A statement. But I want to hear you say it.'

'Well, you can want. I'm not here to pander to your ego.'

That got a genuine grin from him and he fell into step beside me easily as we walked down the road. The weak spring sunshine made the bare trees in the park gleam. 'Where are we meeting Sabiha?'

'She has another client on Prince of Wales Drive. She should be free in a few minutes. I said I'd drive her to the next one so she can spare us fifteen minutes. The poor woman doesn't seem to have much time to herself – all her clients are within walking distance of here, but only just, and she's on the move constantly.'

'Crappy job,' Derwent said.

'A necessary one.'

'Well, obviously. They're like us. They clean up people's shit and don't get thanked for it.'

'I think our pay and conditions are better.'

'Only just, probably.' Derwent checked his watch. 'Do we have time to get coffee before we interview her?'

'No. And why are *we* interviewing her anyway? I'm starting to think you're checking up on me again. I thought I'd proved myself today.'

'Hood wasn't what I'd call a difficult interview.' He relented. 'You got him to trust you. You made him like you. Classic Maeve.'

'So shadowing me when I interview Sabiha isn't because you think I'll do a bad job.'

He looked surprised. 'No. Of course not. I was only teasing when I said that about Hood.'

'Then . . . why?'

'What do you mean?'

Tread carefully, I thought. 'It's just that over the last couple of months, if anything, I'd have said you were avoiding me. As you said, we haven't worked together much.'

'That's ridiculous.' He seemed relaxed to the point of torpor. It was only the tightness around his eyes that was a giveaway.

'Is it? I've barely seen you since Christmas. You've been working with Vidya a lot.'

'Jealous, are we?'

'Certainly not. I noticed it, that's all. And so did Georgia, who feels left out.'

'Vidya's got the potential to be a decent copper, unlike Georgia.' A sidelong glance. 'She appreciates my expertise.'

'I'm sure she does, but so do I. You've left me to work with Liv—'

'Liv needs a sympathetic colleague while she settles back into the job.'

'Yes, and Chris Pettifer needs what exactly?'

'We don't have time to make a list of everything Chris needs.'

'Well, he doesn't need me,' I said. 'And as for Liv, she would be furious if she knew you were encouraging me to hold her hand. The best way to get her confidence back is to let her face the difficult situations head on instead of protecting her from them. It's not that I don't want to help her, but she's got to feel she can cope on her own.'

'That's not always easy, Maeve.' He said it gently, but there was something in his tone that brought me up short. There was more going on here than I could understand. If I wanted him to be honest with me, I needed to risk being honest with him.

'Look, I know I sound whiny. It's just that I miss you when we aren't working together.'

His mouth tensed, but he said nothing.

'And I think you miss me too, which is why you're acting like my shadow now that we have the excuse to be together.' I stood still and he carried on for a couple of paces, then slowly, reluctantly, came back to face me. 'But I don't understand why we need an excuse, Josh.'

'It was after last summer.'

'Last summer,' I repeated. 'When we were undercover.' We had been posing as a couple to catch a killer.

'You know what happened.'

'Nothing.' I said it quickly and he raised his eyebrows.

'Not quite accurate, is it?'

I knew that I was blushing. 'Nothing that need trouble anyone.'

'It troubled Melissa.'

'Oh. But that's not new, is it? She's always been . . . protective of you.' Melissa had transformed Derwent into a family man instead of the restless womaniser he had been when I first knew him. I assumed it had taken constant vigilance, at least in the early days of their relationship. Delicately pretty and gentle, she had been sweet to me, but with a touch of reserve that I recognised as a warning. *Back off. He's mine.* And until recently, I hadn't minded.

Derwent gave me a rueful grin, knowing exactly what I meant. 'This was different, I suppose. The amount of time we spent together, and the circumstances. And . . . how I was when I came back.'

I knew how he had been: unhappy and unable to hide it.

'What happened? Did she make you promise not to work with me?'

'She tried. I said no. I told her she couldn't control my job, and how I do it. I let her call the shots in almost every other aspect of my life. I decide how often I see Luke, and I decide what happens at work, and other than that, she's in charge.'

Luke was Derwent's son, a self-possessed twenty-something who was the result of a teenage one-night stand. Melissa had not been pleased when he resurfaced, threatened by the new relationship Derwent was forming with him, which was ridiculous, I had wanted to tell her. Derwent had been devoted to her since he met her and her son, Thomas. He had committed himself to making them happy, whatever sacrifices that required him to make. She needed to learn to trust him, whatever she felt about me. I didn't care if she didn't like me much – it was nothing to do with me – but something Derwent had said stuck like a burr.

'If you're the one who decides what happens at work, it was your choice not to work with me.'

'No.' He looked around, then took a step closer, lowering his voice even though no one was near enough to hear us. 'Melissa got in touch with Una. She convinced her that you and I were on the verge of having an affair, if not actually over the side yet. She wanted you to be kicked off the team.'

I went hot and cold. 'She couldn't have.'

'She did. And she didn't hold back.' His face was grim. I had known Melissa was possessive of him but not the extent of it. That was the difference I'd noticed in his face earlier: tension, skilfully hidden. 'Una decided I shouldn't work with you unless there was no alternative. God, I sacrificed enough of my dignity to wring that concession out of her. The only thing that swung it in the end was that she knows you well enough to be sure you wouldn't have done anything with me yet and you never would. Una told Melissa that she would keep an eye on me – on us – and you know what she's like.'

'A steam roller in drip-dry non-iron polyester,' I murmured. I was still thinking about what he had just said. *You never would*. He hadn't left a pause for me to comment either way, probably deliberately. It was what I thought myself, so why did I jib at hearing him say it? 'And you didn't tell me any of this because . . .'

'Because I didn't want you to know. It was bad enough letting Una into my private life. I have to give her credit, she hasn't held it against me.'

'She's not that kind of person. She plays fair. But she expects the same in return.'

'Exactly. And that's what I've been doing. I've worked with everyone but you.'

'I thought it was something I'd done.'

'No, definitely not.' He made a move as if he was going to touch my arm, but seemed to change his mind. 'I still see you in the office, and on cases like this – Una's kicking herself, by the way, because if she'd realised the investigation into the Marshalls was likely to be complicated, she'd have made someone else the SIO. But I'm hanging on to it, and to you. I told her it would be more awkward to take you off the case than to let it run. I promised I'd be on my best behaviour.'

'God, that must have been hard.' I expected him to make a joke in response, but there was a shiver of hurt in Derwent's voice when he replied.

'You have no idea.'

I would think about what he had said later, I decided. I checked my watch.

'We'd better get going. Sabiha will be waiting.'

11

Sabiha was a tiny, sweet-faced woman in her twenties who wore a beige veil over her hair. She had suggested meeting at her client's home, but when I phoned her to tell her we had arrived at Cornwall Mansions, she asked me to wait outside. She emerged from the building a few minutes later, out of breath. Her eyes were red.

'I'm sorry. I thought we could meet inside but my client wasn't happy.' She squeezed her hands together, agonised. 'I think she was worried the neighbours would assume she was the one who was in trouble with the police.'

'And now I'm wondering if she has something to hide.' I smiled to show that I was joking. 'Please don't worry, Miss Qureshi.'

'Sabiha, please.'

'Is there a café anywhere near your next client where we could go?'

She shook her head. 'But we can talk here, on the street.'

The wind had picked up and there was a keen edge to it.

'You're shivering,' Derwent observed. 'So let's not do that. We'll sit in the car if you don't mind.'

'Oh – thank you.' She blinked up at him doubtfully, as if she wasn't used to being on the receiving end of much thoughtfulness. 'I'm not cold, really, but I can't stop shaking.'

'That's shock.' I unlocked the car and held open the door so she could climb into the back seat. 'Have you had anything to eat?'

'I didn't feel like it. I had a glass of water.'

'Leave it with me.' Casually, Derwent leaned on the door with his full weight so it slid out of my hand and closed on her

51

with a soft thunk. He muttered, 'I'll get her something while you talk. She looks scared of her own shadow.'

'I would guess most things scare her after what she saw this morning. It wasn't pretty.' Bruce in particular was going to recur in my nightmares, and I'd seen plenty of violent deaths in my time.

'I'll try to be quick.'

I watched him lope across the road and disappear into the park, a tall and broad-shouldered figure with enough natural authority to make the traffic stop for him with an imperious raised hand, on a mission to make an insignificant young woman feel slightly better on the worst day of her life. Then I gave myself a mental shake, looped around the car and got into the back seat beside Sabiha.

'It might be easier to talk if I sit beside you – is that all right?'

She nodded, biting her lip.

'I'm just asking you questions because you're a witness to what took place in the Marshalls' home, not because you're in trouble. I'm sorry to make you talk about all of this again. It must have been a difficult morning.'

'A difficult day.' She raised a hand to her head, her fingers trembling. 'Nothing has gone right for me. I can't seem to think properly.'

'I'm sure it was traumatic to find them like that.'

'It's not the first time that I've tried to wake a client and discovered they had passed – some of our clients are very old and very sick. I have seen them die, even, but never from any violence before this. And the blood . . . the way he looked . . .' Her eyes filled with tears again. 'He was always so kind, so pleasant. Not like some of the clients. That he would do that to Mrs Marshall, and then himself . . . it's hard to believe.' She leaned back against the seat and closed her eyes for a moment, looking exhausted.

'When did you start working for the Marshalls?'

'About . . . five months ago. They liked to have the same person as much as possible so they didn't have to explain every time what they wanted their carer to do, and it was good for me to have regular clients in the same area. The managers never schedule enough time for us to travel from one person to the next one, and if you are delayed by something – someone takes a little longer to eat a meal or to get ready for bed – the next client is upset. So you learn you need clients that live in a small area.'

'And it was seven days a week?'

'Twice a day, but only every other weekend.'

'What were your duties?'

'Mainly cleaning and housekeeping but also to help Mrs Marshall dress and undress and wash.'

'Was she very unwell?'

'She never spoke – a word here or there. She couldn't move very much or hold small items or cutlery. She couldn't manage for herself. Mr Marshall spoke for her if I asked her a question. She ate because he told her to.'

'He was in charge.'

'He was keeping her alive.' Sabiha smiled, remembering. 'He said, one day she would bloom again.'

'And would she have recovered?'

'It was permanent, her condition. Her brain was affected when she took an overdose. She had almost died, Ivo said.' She said his name with a slightly different emphasis, lingering over the two syllables with tenderness that aroused my interest.

'What about Bruce?'

'He was older than her. He needed a stick. He went for a walk every day in the park though.'

'What about his mind? Was he forgetful?'

Her brow furrowed. 'He was very careful not to forget things. He wrote everything down.'

'Where?'

'In a notebook. He kept it in his pocket.'

'What did it look like?'

'Small, red, lined paper, a – a wire holding it together.'

I took a moment to translate that. 'Spiral bound?'

She traced circles in the air with her finger. 'Like this down the side. Not expensive. Just easy to carry around, I think.'

We hadn't found anything like that in the flat, as far as I knew. I took out my phone and opened the picture of the note I'd discovered down the side of the chair, zooming in so only a few letters were visible.

'Does this look like Mr Marshall's writing? And does it look as if the paper came from the notebook?'

'Yes, his writing. It could be the same paper, but I can't be sure.'

I put my phone away. 'Now, I want you to think about this morning. Try to remember what it was like when you went into the flat first. Did you notice anything different? Anything unusual?'

'No. Nothing. That's why I cleaned the other rooms.' The trembling was back, I noted. 'The police who came were angry that I'd done it but I would never have touched anything if I'd known.' Her small hands were clenched into fists in her lap. 'There was a note in the kitchen with Mr Hood's phone number. Ivo always came at weekends. I was glad he had a weekend off. And then, when I found them, I couldn't think. I just remembered that I was supposed to call Mr Hood and I did. And he came. I was sitting on the kitchen floor when he arrived and I don't remember how I got there.'

'I know what that's like,' I said, with sympathy. 'How did Mr Hood get in?'

'There's a key-safe beside the door. He had the code.'

I looked up to see Derwent coming back to the car. He got into the front seat and handed a cardboard cup to Sabiha, and another to me. She had tea; mine was coffee and I felt myself reviving as I sipped it.

'Careful, it's hot,' Derwent warned.

Sabiha was gulping her tea down. 'It's sweet.'

'I put two sugars in. You need it when you've had a shock.' He passed a paper bag back to her. 'That's just a pastry but it should make you feel better.'

I waited until she had finished it before I asked my next question, aware that I was pushing into difficult territory.

'What about in the Marshalls' bedroom? Did you notice anything unusual or out of place aside from the Marshalls themselves?'

'I didn't really see the bodies. I was trying not to look at them. I opened the door and it smelled wrong and it was too quiet so I knew something bad had happened. And the light by the bed was on, which wasn't usual, so I looked for a moment and then – then I looked away.'

'What else? Try to remember the rest of the room.'

'There was a pillow on the floor next to Mrs Marshall's side of the bed.' She dropped her chin to her chest. 'You'll be angry.'

'We're never angry when someone tells us the truth.' Derwent sounded as if he was more or less incapable of losing his temper, as unflappable as an air traffic controller.

'I picked up the pillow. Only for a second. Then I realised I shouldn't touch anything and I put it down again.'

'How did you hold it?' I asked.

'By one corner.'

'That shouldn't be a problem.' I was thinking of what Dr Early had said about the force needed to smother someone. Sabiha could hardly have obliterated any traces of the killer by holding on to it in one place. 'We'll need a sample of your DNA so we can be sure to eliminate you from our enquiries, but we would have wanted that anyway.'

'Oh thank goodness.' Tears welled up over her lower lashes. 'I was so scared, all day. I've cried so much my head has been aching. I don't know why I did it.'

'You said it was unusual for the lamp to be switched on in the morning. Was there anything else that was unusual? Was it normal for them to sleep with the windows open in their bedroom?'

'No, unless it was very warm, and even then they preferred to keep them shut because Helena didn't like any noise from outside. Were they open? I didn't see that. The curtains were closed.' A tiny gasp. 'Did someone break in?'

'There were locks on the windows so you couldn't climb in or out.'

'That's what I thought.'

While I made a note about the windows, Derwent asked, 'Did they have many visitors?'

'No. Very few. Only their son. Maybe old friends like Mr Hood, but not often.'

'Did anyone else come to see them recently?' She shook her head. 'Was Bruce worried about anything?'

'He was always worried about his wife. Nothing else.'

'Is there anything you want to tell us before we let you go?' Derwent said at last. 'Anything strange that happened lately?'

She frowned. 'There was a man who tried to talk to me two weeks ago, outside the building. He seemed to know I was working for the Marshalls. He asked me about them.'

'By name? What did he want to know?'

'If they lived there and which flat they lived in. I ran inside and shut the building door so he couldn't follow. Then Mr Marshall called Ivo and he came, and when I left there was no sign of the man.'

'Could you describe him?'

'Maybe forty? Thin. He kept saying he was sorry to ask, sorry to bother me, sorry if I was upset, sorry to be a nuisance. He seemed . . . shy. Not angry. He seemed . . . worried. He said he needed to find them.'

'And would you recognise him if you saw him again?'

'I think so,' she said. 'I might.'

I left Derwent to go back to the crime scene while I drove Sabiha to her next client, and I chatted to her about where she lived and how long she had been in London and what she wanted to do with her life, but all the time I was thinking about the apologetic stranger who had wanted to know where he could find the Marshalls.

He didn't sound like the typical murderer, if such a thing existed, but then this wasn't a typical murder.

12

I came back to the crime scene after dropping Sabiha off and made it as far as the door of the building, where Una Burt was lying in wait.

'Maeve, can you follow up with the sons? No one from the team has seen them in person yet, and I'm not happy about it.'

'Absolutely.' I hesitated, finding it hard to look her in the eye, given what I knew about her opinion of me. 'Has Josh okayed it or—'

Her face was stony. 'He's gone back to the office with some of the files from the flat.'

'Right. Of course.' I took the sons' details from her and went back to the car. I rang Ivo's number first and confirmed his address (Clapham, a ten-minute drive from the flat in Battersea) and that he would be there all afternoon. He sounded calm and controlled, not at all like someone recently and violently orphaned, and I felt a prickle of curiosity. I rang Magnus's number and listened to his voicemail greeting, which was brief, left an equally short message with my number, and made tracks for Clapham.

At first glance, Ivo Marshall's home was a grand, red-brick Victorian villa with a huge stained-glass door, and I braced myself for ostentatious wealth. When he opened the door I realised the house had been divided into two properties and he had the lower one. In contrast to the Victorian exterior the flat looked modern, with pearl-grey carpet, pale walls and discreet recessed lighting all the way down the hall. Ivo Marshall himself was tall and well-built, with light-brown hair. He had a square jaw and a straight nose: deeply conventional good looks that could be more or less attractive depending on the personality that went with them.

'Sergeant Kerrigan? Thank you for coming. You must be so busy, it's very good of you to take the time.'

Instant warmth, instantly likeable. I felt myself relaxing. Whatever our conversation involved, Ivo was the kind of person who would strive to make it easy for both of us, and I didn't encounter them too often in murder investigations. I could see why Sabiha might have had a crush on him.

'I'm sorry we couldn't get to see you earlier.' I noticed he was barefoot and slid off my shoes.

'Oh – you don't mind? The carpet is new. We haven't accepted it will ever look dirty.' He led the way down to the back of the flat. I caught glimpses of a sitting room with red-painted bookshelves, a study with yellow walls, and a pair of bedrooms, one in tones of pale green, one pale blue. At the back of the hall a short flight of stairs went down to the basement, which contained an enormous and very modern kitchen where none of the appliances were visible and everything was either black wood or gleaming brass. A mid-century dining table stood in front of a vast abstract oil painting, and a low fleecy sofa that looked like a cloud faced the television. Somehow they had contrived to make the space light and airy despite being below street level, facing steps that rose to the lawn. It was like walking into a cover shoot for *House & Garden*.

'This is fantastic. Did you do it yourselves?'

'Yes, just finished it a couple of months ago. This flat was a wreck before and the basement didn't exist. My wife is an architect. She designed the whole thing and project-managed it. It's a way of showing clients what she can do.'

'And you get to live in it.' I didn't try to hide my envy.

'But I also got to live through two years of building work.'

Ivo's excellent manners extended to offering me a cup of tea, or glass of water, or a drink of any kind, all of which I declined despite being curious about where the fridge might be hiding in the inscrutable kitchen. I realised he was using politeness as a delaying tactic, warding off the moment when he would have to talk about his parents.

'I just have a few questions, Mr Marshall. Where would you prefer to sit?'

'Oh. Yes. Sorry.' He chose a chair that was clearly a Danish design classic, leaving the sofa to me. I perched on the edge, trying to maintain my dignity instead of sinking into it.

'What do you know about what happened?'

'Um . . . the police – your colleagues – told me they were found dead this morning by their carer.' He shrugged, uneasy. 'I understood there were suspicious circumstances, given that both of them were dead at the same time. They said there was a murder investigation but they couldn't tell me anything more. Or wouldn't, I suppose.'

'Do you know how your parents died?'

'N-no. They didn't say.' He had folded his arms tightly, so he was hugging himself. 'They said that the bodies had been identified already.'

'We'll be able to confirm it with DNA, but Sabiha was able to identify them, and Mr Hood confirmed it.'

'Hood – he was there, was he?'

'Sabiha called him.'

Ivo nodded and smiled, although a muscle spasm in his cheek ruined the effect. 'The one weekend I have off in years and this happens.'

'Do you think it's significant that you weren't in charge this weekend?'

'You mean, do I think Dad took the opportunity to kill my mother? I'm assuming that's what happened.' The muscle spasm was worse now.

'There were aspects of the crime scene that made us question whether that was what happened.'

He frowned. 'She couldn't have done anything to him, if that's what you're thinking. She was almost completely helpless.'

If he was pretending that he didn't know how they had died, I couldn't spot it. 'I gather her poor health wasn't a recent development.'

'No. She'd been in that state for years. So you can't possibly suspect her, can you?'

I left that one unanswered. 'At the moment we're keeping an open mind about what happened.'

'But it's suspicious.'

'No doubt about that, I'm afraid. They both died violently.'

'Violently?'

'It looks as if your mother was suffocated and your father was shot.'

'*Shot?*' Ivo's voice cracked.

'Did he have a gun?'

'A shotgun? He used to go shooting with friends but I don't remember him having a gun.'

'No, a handgun.'

'What, a *pistol*? No. They're illegal, aren't they?'

'Was your father the sort of person who would have obeyed the law and handed in a gun . . . even if it had some sentimental significance?'

'It's an old gun, then? It's possible he decided to hold on to it, I suppose. He was a private sort of person. I'd never have gone through his belongings without his permission.' He paused, gathering his thoughts. 'He was *shot*? Where?'

'In their bedroom. He was in bed.'

'I meant . . .' He raised a hand and gestured at his body.

'It was a head shot.'

Pure shock in his face. 'Poor Sabiha, walking in on that. I'm glad Hood was around to help her. He's a capable sort of person. The Hoods were good friends but they hadn't been in touch with my parents for a long time – so long that he wrote to the old house to try to find them.'

'How long is it since your parents moved into the flat?'

'Must be . . . three years.'

I blinked. 'I assumed it was more recent. They didn't seem to have moved much in.'

'They didn't have much left. They sold the Richmond house

and most of the contents, but they'd borrowed so much against it that they only had a small amount to live on.'

'It must have been possible to find somewhere cheaper to buy.'

'They didn't buy it. The flat is a loan from a friend of my mother's. It belonged to her godmother, and she didn't need it when she inherited it. My parents paid rent but it was a really tiny amount.'

'Where did their money go?'

'I think there was less of it than they pretended even when things were going well, but they spent a fortune on medical bills and other expenses in the last few years.'

'Because of your mother?'

'Not just that.' He swallowed, looking down. 'My sister disappeared.'

'Rosalie.'

'Oh, of course you know.'

'I know what happened but I don't know the details,' I said, and he sighed.

'There isn't much to tell you. She disappeared from our house one night sixteen years ago and no one ever saw her again. No one knows where she went or what happened to her. She was only nine. And it broke my mother's heart.'

'I understand Helena took an overdose.'

'A little while later, yeah. She lived but only just. She was brain-damaged. She wound up in hospital for months and months.' Ivo shook his head as if he was trying to get rid of the memory of that time. 'Just disappeared, like Rosalie. And even though Mum came back, she wasn't the same. We lost both of them.'

'She needed help with basic tasks, is that right?'

'She couldn't do anything, and she never got better.' Ivo ran a hand over his face, wincing. 'We got angry with her, my brother and I. We were used to her sorting our lives out. We didn't like her being ill. Suddenly she needed looking after and no one had any time for us.'

'Anger is completely understandable. You were kids too.'

'Teenagers – at least I was. Magnus was twelve. I was fourteen. She'd always been a bit of a tiger mother. I was relieved when she backed off after Rosalie disappeared. Then that was another thing to feel guilty about.'

I felt deeply sorry for him. 'Did you ever talk to anyone about it? A professional?'

He grinned suddenly. 'It's a pretty dark scenario to have to explain to a counsellor. They're used to bad divorces and absent fathers, not catatonic mothers and a family mystery with no solution. We had a couple of family sessions when Mum was in the rehab place trying to learn how to speak again, and it was too traumatic for Dad. He gave us a list of people we could talk to. People he could trust not to sell a story about us. Other than that, we didn't speak to anyone about Rosalie. The whole thing was hushed up.'

'Most people want media interest when a family member disappears.'

'Not us. Dad spent a fortune on PR advice and legal fees, so journalists would be too scared to write about us in case they got sued for defamation. He wanted me and Magnus to have our privacy, growing up.' He shook his head. 'The only thing media coverage ever got them was trouble. Mum had been a bit of a star before Rosalie disappeared – she wrote articles and gave speeches, and she was on *Thought for the Day* or *Woman's Hour* or some other radio show every couple of weeks. She loved being controversial. She was the sort of woman everyone loves to hate. And of course, the circumstances made it even more ironic.'

'What circumstances?'

'I think Mum always wanted to be famous. She came up with the idea of campaigning for adoption instead of letting children go into care or leaving them in dangerous situations with their own parents. She wanted the process made quicker and safer for the kids, with the added advantage that nice middle-class parents like her could get their hands on babies rather than traumatised and difficult older children. I'm paraphrasing, obviously. She made common ground with the pro-life brigade, even though that wasn't her main interest – but they were pushing adoption as an alternative to abortion. That annoyed a lot of people.'

'Which meant they were pleased because she hadn't managed to keep her own daughter safe? That seems harsh.'

'It was. But she'd been pretty unbearable, I think. And Rosalie was the poster child for her scheme.'

'So Rosalie . . .'

He was nodding. 'Rosalie was adopted.'

13

'Nothing like a bit of tragic irony to get the media interested.'

'It explains why they were publicity-shy,' I said. My phone was propped on one of the boxes in the second bedroom of the Battersea flat while I tried to organise the reams of paper that remained after Liv and Derwent had taken a carload apiece. I was on my own, so I'd taken the risk of putting Derwent on speakerphone. 'You can imagine after the second or third think-piece about it, they started to feel attacked.'

'That and the fact that they were suspects.'

'Adopting a kid is difficult. Maybe they struggled with her. Ivo said he thought the reality of having Rosalie was a shock to his mother. She sold an idealised vision of herself as a parent through her media work but it was hard, at times, from what he remembered.'

'You think they were responsible for her disappearance?'

'I don't know enough about it.' I levered the lid off a box and sighed at the sight of a stack of newspaper clippings. 'They used a cuttings service. That costs a fair bit. Medical bills, lawyers, a PR company, private detectives. I'm beginning to see why they had no money left.' I had already explained to Derwent how they had come to live in the flat.

'Or they were being blackmailed.'

I paused. 'Is that just a guess?'

'Wild speculation. That's pretty much all we have at the moment.'

'Have you found anything interesting in the boxes you took away?'

'As if I'm going to bother reading any of it,' Derwent said cheerfully. 'I have you for that.'

'And Liv.'

'If she has time. I'll try to get her to do some more interesting tasks so she gets the love back for the job and feels appreciated. I don't want to tie her up with boring old background reading. I'll leave that for you.'

'Oh, thanks very much.'

'You don't want anyone to think I'm playing favourites, Maeve, do you?' Derwent's voice was soft, too sweet to be sincere.

I rolled my eyes as I lifted another box off the pile in front of me. 'You wouldn't.'

'What did Ivo say about his parents' marriage?'

'Before Rosalie disappeared they were a pretty impressive partnership – he made the money and facilitated her work, and she kept the house running smoothly. They had nannies but at the time Rosalie disappeared there was just a tutor for his brother, part-time, and various other members of staff who came and went – a cleaner, a gardener. The brothers helped with Rosalie if Helena wasn't available.'

'Did they mind having to look after their little sister?'

'Ivo said not. He seems like the type who just does what needs to be done and doesn't complain. After Helena's overdose Bruce gave up work to look after her. It was a total change of lifestyle, but Bruce was devoted to her. Ivo thought the way he behaved towards Helena was him taking his vows seriously – you know, in sickness and in health.'

'Or Bruce felt guilty about murdering Rosalie, which was the reason Helena OD'd, and he wanted to stop Helena from telling anyone what he'd done so he made her totally dependent on him.'

I stopped leafing through a file for a second. 'That's dark, even for you.'

'But a possibility, nevertheless.'

'Well, Ivo didn't think of it. He made sure he was available to help whenever they needed it.'

'That must have been a huge commitment.'

'Yes, but he didn't seem to question that either. I think the family was in a state of crisis from the moment that Rosalie disappeared. They were fighting fires all the time. They didn't have time or space for introspection.'

'What about this man who accosted Sabiha two weeks ago? Did Ivo tell you anything about him?'

'Yes and no. He didn't get to talk to him – the guy ran away as soon as he caught sight of Ivo. He disappeared through the park. Ivo couldn't give me a proper description of him either. It was drizzling by the time he arrived, and the man had his hood up, but here's an interesting thing that I don't think Ivo clocked: *he* definitely recognised Ivo, because he took to his heels. Ivo could have been anyone walking down the street, but our mystery man knew exactly who he was and didn't want to hang around to chat.'

'That fits with him asking Sabiha about the Marshalls by name.'

'Maybe he wanted to talk to the parents but he didn't fancy an argument with their grown-up son.'

'If he recognised Ivo, presumably Ivo would have recognised him.'

'Very possibly.'

'And he didn't want to be recognised.'

'I also thought that.'

'Because he was up to no good.'

'I think we can assume that was the case.'

'So we need to find this man.'

'Any ideas?'

'Not so far.' He yawned. 'I'm trying to get hold of my mate who investigated Rosalie's disappearance. What about Magnus?'

'I've left him some voicemails but he hasn't replied.'

'I never listen to your voicemails either. Did Ivo tell you anything useful about him?'

'Magnus didn't help with the parents at all. He seemed to be no-contact with the whole family. Ivo said Magnus went his own way.'

'What does that mean?'

'I think we'll have to ask Magnus that.'

'Ask Magnus what?'

I almost dislocated something as I whipped around to face the man who was standing in the doorway. He was in his twenties, and fair, with the kind of thin skin that flushed easily. He looked enough like his brother that it didn't take much guesswork to identify him, but unlike his brother he gave every impression of someone who didn't mind being rude at all.

'How did you get in here?'

'Maeve, what's going on?' Derwent sounded sharp and much too loud. I picked up my phone without taking my eyes off the younger Marshall son.

'It's fine. I'll talk to you later.' I thumbed the phone off without waiting for a reply, which I knew would earn me an earful of abuse at some point in the future, but I wanted to stop Magnus from heading for the door. 'Magnus? I'm Sergeant Maeve Kerrigan. I've been leaving you messages all day.'

'Yeah. Sorry about that. I didn't really listen to the messages, to be honest with you, once I got the gist. I thought I should come and see for myself what was going on.'

'And the scene guard let you in?'

'He was talking to the neighbours.' Magnus tossed his hair off his forehead with a jerk of his head that was pure arrogance. 'I didn't wait for him to notice me.'

'Well, you're here now. You might as well talk to me here as anywhere else.'

'Talk to you? About what?'

Um, your murdered parents? I settled for a polite smile. 'If you'd like to go into the sitting room we can talk more easily in there.'

'Where's that?' He was looking around vaguely, as if he'd never seen the room or its contents before.

'Is this your first time here? I thought your parents had been living at this address for three years.'

He shrugged, his eyes as blank as a mannequin's. 'I never visited them, to be honest with you. I knew they'd moved out of the family home because Ivo emailed me on my work address to see if I wanted anything from it as a souvenir.'

'And did you?'

'Mate, I didn't even reply.'

I'm not your mate. I moved towards the door. 'The sitting room is on your right, past the kitchen.'

'The kitchen,' he repeated. 'Any chance of a cup of tea? I'm parched.'

'Sorry,' I said, not managing to sound sincere. 'But I won't keep you for too long.'

He prowled around the sitting room, peering out of the windows at the shadowy trees. 'Nice place.'

I couldn't tell if he was being sarcastic or not. 'Why did you avoid seeing your parents?'

'Not just my parents. The whole family. I wanted a break from them. They were . . . what's the buzzword that therapists use? Toxic.'

'In what way?'

He was crouching, turning the picture frame around to inspect the painting I'd found that morning. 'Jesus, look at that. I haven't seen this in years. I wonder why they kept it and nothing else?'

'Who painted it?'

'My nanny, believe it or not.' He glanced at me with a wry expression that made me like him a fraction more. 'Sadie, her name was. Like the song.'

'You mean the Beatles song? "Sexy Sadie"?' I raised my eyebrows. 'And was she?'

He pretended to be horrified. 'I was a *child*. She was just the face I looked for in the crowd when I came out of school. But I remember my mother saying it was appropriate.'

I was forming dark suspicions about why Sadie might have left.

'It's a pretty picture.'

He gave a bark of laughter. 'It's shit, beautiful.'

'You can call me Sergeant Kerrigan,' I said, unmoved; I had worked with Derwent for too long to be flustered by someone calling me 'beautiful'. 'Maybe they were sentimentally attached to the picture.'

'Dad? Sentimentality is not his thing. Or it wasn't, I should say. Mum wouldn't have cared.' He looked around, wrinkling his nose. 'There were decent paintings they might have kept. They had a Duncan Grant that was all right, and a very underwhelming Augustus John but it would have been worth a bit.'

'You sound as if you know your art.'

'I studied it. Now I work for an auction house.'

'That must be interesting – getting your hands on amazing paintings and treasures.'

He laughed. 'It's not Sotheby's. It's a small specialist outfit. You won't have heard of it. Rafe and Gunther.'

He was right; I hadn't heard of it. 'Ivo said your parents ran out of money. Presumably the paintings were sold.'

'Not on the open market. I'd have known. But a discreet private sale, sure. As long as the dealer is respectable and the sale is recorded it doesn't have to be turned into a song and dance.'

'Why did you say your family was toxic?'

He sat down and slung one leg across the other. 'Back to that, are we? Well, it wasn't the ideal situation. Mum was a zombie. Dad was a benign dictator. Ivo was his loyal servant. Rosalie was the ghost that everyone pretended to ignore. I realised there was nothing in it for me. I just wanted to live my own life. Make my own mistakes.'

'What about Ivo?'

'He still wanted Dad's approval.' Magnus snorted. 'The best way to get it was to walk away. Dad respected that. He didn't respect Ivo or his wife, Lisa. She's another doormat.'

'She didn't mind Ivo being so attentive to them?'

He shrugged. 'She never said it to me. But she doesn't like me.'

'And you don't like her?'

'I don't think about her enough to have an opinion.'

'When you heard that your parents were dead, what did you think?'

'That he'd killed her, and then himself. Was I wrong?'

'I think you were.'

'Not an accident.' He read the answer in my face. 'Then . . . someone did this to them?'

'That's how it looks.'

'How did they die?'

'They suffocated your mother and shot your father while they were in bed.'

He got to his feet, his shock propulsive and unfeigned. '*Shot* him? Where's the bedroom?'

'You can't go in there. It's sealed in case there needs to be further forensic work. Anyway, it's not very pleasant. Did he own a handgun?'

'Did he bollocks,' Magnus sneered, and then, as something occurred to him, his face dropped. 'At least – I don't know. An old Webley?'

'Yes.'

'Then, yes. I saw it once. It was in a box on top of a glass-fronted bookcase in Dad's study and I thought it was a Christmas present. I climbed up and knocked the box down, which cracked the glass in the bookcase. No way to hide it.'

'You must have been in trouble.'

'I got the spanking of my life. I must have been ten, eleven? Something like that.'

'Was there ammunition with it?'

He closed his eyes, frowning. 'Um, yes. I remember having to hunt around on the carpet for the bullets. I think there were six or seven.'

'Where did he get it?'

'He didn't tell me. It could have belonged to his father, though, I suppose.'

'And who else would have known he had a gun?'

'No idea. Didn't Ivo come across it when he was helping them to move in here?'

'He said not.'

Frank incredulity on Magnus's face. 'And you believed him?'

'He seemed to be telling the truth.' I was aware that I sounded uncertain.

'Well, that's Ivo's trick. People take him at face value and assume he's a good guy.' Magnus shook his head slowly. 'But I'd have thought someone like you would know better.'

14

Unhelpful to the last, Magnus declined the opportunity to help me carry some boxes of papers out to the car. He did confirm with a quick look around the flat that most of the furniture hadn't been in his family home.

'This stuff is grim. They had better taste than that.'

'So everything was sold?'

'I suppose so. Dad would have minded that a lot. I doubt Mum would have noticed or cared, but before she became ill she was proud of the house.'

'Did you know they had run out of money?'

'They couldn't hide it. Dad gave up work to look after Mum and they spent a fortune on doctors and the like. No holidays, no new cars, no presents at Christmas. Their standard of living plummeted.'

'Was that why you decided there was no point in staying in touch with them?' It was a rude question but I was under no illusion that Magnus and I were ever going to be friends.

'No. It wasn't. I never wanted a penny from them and I wouldn't have taken it if they'd offered it.' He picked up his coat. 'I left the family because it was broken, and it was breaking me. They were selfish people and they got worse once they had an excuse to look for sympathy. Ivo seems to have felt some obligation to let them use him, but I didn't. They were adults and they made their own choices.'

'They didn't choose to lose Rosalie.'

He looked at me for a moment, his eyes cold. 'Didn't they?'

'Do you think they were involved?'

'I don't know. I've never known.' He pulled the coat on. 'And now I suppose I'll never find out.'

The flat seemed to vibrate with his anger and distress long after he'd gone. He was an awkward and unhappy young man, I thought, and I could understand it if he truly suspected his parents had been involved in the disappearance of his little sister. I didn't quite believe Magnus when he said Ivo was a fraud, but I didn't dismiss it either. I'd met Ivo for an hour – less – in the aftermath of his parents' death, so I wasn't sure I'd seen him as he really was. Magnus, for all his younger-brother truculence, had grown up with him. And I was used to people lying to me. Maybe Ivo's wide-eyed cooperation wasn't everything it had seemed to be.

I stacked boxes in the hall, checking the contents so I had some idea of what I was taking back to the office: a whole archive of obsession. I'd calculated I could take seven boxes in my car, but that meant seven trips down the stairs and along the street to where I was parked. There weren't any spaces closer to the flat. I did three trips before I needed a break, not so much because I was tired but because the special constable on scene-guard duty annoyed me. He was young, soft and red-faced, and seemed to feel he was entitled to comment on what I was doing every time I passed him.

'Got your hands full there, love.'

'Put your back into it. Get it done in no time.'

'What you need to do is put one under each arm. Half as many trips.'

'You know, you could help,' I snapped in the end.

'I've got a job to do here.'

'Is that the job you were doing when you let the victims' son walk into the crime scene unannounced?'

'I don't know what you're talking about.'

'You were chatting to the neighbours.'

He looked wounded. 'I was reassuring them that they were safe.'

'You don't know that they're safe. And *I* wasn't safe, since you weren't doing the very basic job of watching who was entering the premises. It could have been anyone who walked past you. It could have been the killer.' Magnus had caught me unawares and I didn't like it.

'Sorry.' He swallowed, his eyes wide. I thought he was about twenty-two, and now he was terrified. I went back into the flat for a glass of water and some much-needed time out.

On the fourth trip, the special constable was silent as I stalked past him. It was a shame that I'd broken him, because although I didn't know it, I was about to need him. As I levered the main door open and stepped out into the night, I saw a man leaning into a car down the street, then straightening up to examine something he had retrieved from it. I took a moment to realise it was my car he had been searching, which meant that he had broken into it.

My initial reaction was outrage; my second was interest. It wasn't my car, after all, but a job car, and he was peering at a file he had liberated from one of the boxes. He hadn't noticed me yet and I took the opportunity to note every detail of his appearance. He had fine dark hair that was sparse on top and straggled over his collar, a weak jaw, thin limbs and sloping shoulders. Inoffensive was the word that occurred to me first, along with the suspicion that it was an image he cultivated. I guessed he was a journalist getting a different angle on the double-murder story that would merit a couple of paragraphs in the newspapers the following day. Una Burt believed in press releases that were low on detail and big on jargon, so even the most gothic crimes sounded tedious. If he had worked out who the Marshalls were, and their connection with Rosalie, this guy had already done better than most of his colleagues. Finding the family files on Rosalie's disappearance would be a major scoop.

I put down the box I was holding and ducked back into the building, calling up the stairs to the constable. In as few words as possible, I explained to him about the man outside and that I needed him to secure the building at the front door.

'But I thought I was supposed to guard this crime scene. That's what you told me to do.'

'And now I'm telling you to take charge of the building's security.'

'What about you? Why can't you do it?' Panic edged his words.

'I'm going to tackle the man who broke into my car.'

'But he could be armed.'

'If you're worried, call for back-up,' I hissed, thoroughly irritated. 'But I've dealt with worse. What if he's there as a distraction and someone's real intention is to gain access to the crime scene while we're both engaged with him?'

This possibility had obviously not occurred to him. He goggled at me, silent.

'So would you mind coming down to the hall and keeping an eye on the box of papers, and the building, and on me?'

'I'm not sure.' He was fingering his radio nervously.

'I am. Get down here and do your job.'

My tone made him move at last. I slipped out of the front door of the building and across the road, thanks to a helpful gap in the traffic. I walked briskly along the park railings, apparently lost in thought, actually focused on the man who was rifling through the car as if he was a terrier hunting for rats.

At the next lull in the traffic I crossed back and came up behind the man.

'Excuse me, sir, what are you doing?'

He gave a start and everything he was holding cascaded to the ground: files, a torch, a metal rod and a screwdriver. The screwdriver rolled towards me and I kicked it deftly under the car.

'Hey, that's mine.'

'Is it? Is that the tool you used to break into my car? Are you admitting it's yours?'

'I – no, I—'

He fumbled his phone out of his pocket and keyed in the code to unlock it at the second attempt, his hands shaking.

'Are you planning to record this conversation?'

'I am, yes.' He had managed to open the camera and had switched it to record video, but he was struggling with the record button.

'Not working? That's a shame. Let me see.' I picked it out of his hand and dropped it, sending it after the screwdriver with a swift sideways shove.

'That's – that's mine too. My personal property. You can't do that.'

'It was an accident,' I said, my eyes wide with innocence. 'I'll get it back for you before we go to the nick.'

'To the – you mean, you're going to arrest me?'

'You broke into my car.'

'I didn't. It was open.'

'It certainly was not.' I wobbled the window of the passenger door. 'And this wasn't loose when I left it. And you just admitted the tool I found was yours. Where did you learn to break into cars?'

'Reddit,' the man said sulkily. 'And I was just doing research.'

'Are you a journalist?'

'In a way. I'm working on a podcast.'

'Oh.' I eyed him. 'About the Marshalls, by any chance?'

'How did you know?'

'You tracked them down. You approached their carer a couple of weeks ago.'

His jaw sagged. 'How did you know *that*?'

'Intuition.' I relented. 'And you fitted the description she gave me. What's your name?'

'Tor Grant.' His voice acquired a new resonance and confidence, as if I should be impressed. I remained underwhelmed.

'And you make podcasts?'

'Yes. Well, this one. This is my first. It's going to make my reputation. People love this kind of unsolved mystery.' He looked back over his shoulder at the building behind us. 'And now this has happened. I mean, what an opener. Bang.'

'Bang?' I repeated.

'Bang. Straight into the story.'

76

So he hadn't been making a reference to Bruce Marshall's death – or he had and he was covering up with his twit-of-the-year routine.

'The thing is, podcasts about missing kids are ten a penny – that's what a producer told me. You need something extra, they all said. Some hook. I thought this case had it all, but everyone said it wasn't enough. Some of them said it was too long ago and some of them said it was too recent. But now, this is current. It's exciting. It opens the whole story up.'

'And they can't sue you for defamation now.'

'No, well exactly. That occurred to me.'

'They haven't even been dead for twenty-four hours.' I couldn't keep the revulsion out of my voice.

'Oh, and I should wait, is that it? How long is respectful? A day? Two? A week?'

'How did you even know about it?'

'I was doing some recording – children playing in the playground, birds singing, that kind of thing. Colour for the podcast. I saw the police cordon.'

'And when you heard the Marshalls were dead you decided you needed to kick your investigation up a notch.'

'Other podcasters will be all over this. People with funding and sponsorship and big organisations behind them.'

'Well, you're not going to get anything done tonight.' I hooked my cuffs out of my jacket and snapped one on his right wrist without any warning. 'I'm arresting you—'

'No!' He flailed so I couldn't get hold of his left hand. 'You can't do this!'

'Stop fighting me.' I dodged to avoid getting an accidental elbow in the face. He wasn't athletic or coordinated but he was lanky and I couldn't pin him down easily if he was determined to be uncooperative. 'I'm not letting go.'

He threw his head back and yelled: 'Help! Police brutality! Help!'

There were areas of London where that would have drawn a crowd, all with phones out to record video that would travel the globe faster than a lie. In Battersea, on Prince of Wales Drive, the windows remained genteelly shut. I wrestled with him for a bit longer, increasingly irritated. I managed to get hold of his left arm but I'd lost my grip on the hand I had already cuffed and he was waving it around, turning the cuffs with their solid central bar into a decent weapon.

'Stop it, you little *fucker*,' I hissed, peripherally aware of a car screeching to a halt in the middle of the road, hazards on, blue lights flashing: the back-up summoned by the constable, I assumed, right up until I recognised the figure coming around the car with a face like thunder. Without any preliminaries or noticeable effort, Derwent cuffed Tor Grant on the side of the head, spun him around, slammed him against the car hard enough to knock the breath out of his body and hauled his wrists together so he could put the handcuffs on properly. While Grant was protesting about that, Derwent twisted to check on me.

'Are you OK?'

'I could have got the handcuffs on him myself,' I said, furious.

His eyes narrowed. 'Not how it looked to me.'

'I'm *bleeding*,' Grant said faintly.

'Good,' Derwent said, and manhandled him to his car, where he formally arrested the podcaster. I waited until he had gone through the caution and slammed the door on Grant.

'I am a police officer, I have plenty of experience of arresting people, and I didn't need your help.'

Derwent leaned against the car, ignoring the knocking and muffled shouting that was coming from the back seat. 'Yes, yes, and no. You didn't have a hope.'

'Well, we'll never know.'

He jerked a thumb at the back seat of his car. 'Is this the person who interrupted you when you were talking to me?'

'That was Magnus, the second son. I got rid of him. This is Tor Grant, the man who approached Sabiha. He says he's making a podcast about the Marshalls. I was arresting him because he broke into my car. His phone is under my car along with a bit of kit he used to get the door open.'

Derwent went over and dropped to the ground. He reached under the car to retrieve them, sliding them over to me before he stood up, dusting his hands off.

'Stick him on for assault as well as breaking into the car. It should only take you a couple of hours to process him. Then the paperwork. You'll be finished by midnight, probably.'

'But I was moving the files,' I protested.

'You're not going anywhere in that car. It needs to be recovered and repaired, so you might as well deal with this twat. Call a van to take the pair of you to the nearest nick and I'll take the boxes back myself.'

'No – wait . . .'

'Got somewhere better to be?'

His tone was irritating enough to bring me out in hives but I tried very hard not to let it show. 'What if we need to interview him about the Marshalls? He's been hanging around, he bothered Sabiha, and now he's here trying to look through the evidence I was collecting. What if he's our killer? I don't want there to be any issue about me questioning him if he's separately charged with assaulting me.'

Derwent snorted. 'You think *that* is capable of killing?'

'I think I don't want to assume he isn't,' I said evenly.

'Look, hand him over to the local CID once you get him booked in. I'll call their skipper and let them know. They can interview him about the car and the assault. At the moment I just want him out of the way. They can drop the assault charge in the morning. You're not really hurt, are you?'

Parts of me were aching and I knew I'd feel worse in the morning but I shook my head.

'And the car's a job one so that doesn't matter much either.'

'No, like me it doesn't matter at all.'

He gave me a reproving look. 'Come on, Maeve. Self-pity isn't your style.'

It was when I actually did feel sorry for myself, but I didn't argue with him. I went in the van with Tor Grant to the nearest police station, where the custody skipper was reluctant to accommodate an unexpected detainee and the detectives were obviously irritated to have to interview him.

None of this was my idea, I wanted to say, and didn't, and Tor Grant slipped through the system with all the ease of a brick on a sandpaper slide.

15

I came out of the police station and headed with purpose for the nearest taxi rank, focused on getting home.

My phone buzzed against my hip. I hooked it out of my pocket, knowing who was calling before I looked.

'Josh.'

'Maeve.'

He had used exactly the same measured tone of voice as me, and I grinned to myself.

'How was the nick?'

'I've just left, actually.'

'I know.'

I stopped walking. 'Are you *here*?'

A car horn tooted softly across the road and I scanned the cars until I spotted a familiar one.

'*Why* are you here?'

'Not the warm and welcoming reaction I was looking for.'

'It's just – don't you want to go home? It's three in the morning.' I yawned widely enough to crack my jaw.

'Christ, I've seen sharks with a less intimidating bite. I needn't have worried about you being mugged.'

'Is that why?' His car window was closed and the streetlight was reflecting off it so I couldn't see him. 'You were worried about me?'

'Just checking up on you. You did get a bit of a going-over from Grant.'

'Oh.' I was surprised, and warmed by his thoughtfulness.

'I took the boxes from your car back to the office. Then I thought I'd come back to see how you were getting on. I didn't think you'd be out for a while.'

'Only the six hours this time. I was lucky. I'm going to get a taxi home.'

'I'll drive you.'

'It's completely the wrong direction for you.'

'I know where it is.' He sounded amused; it was his flat, after all, and I was only renting it from him.

'Are you sure?'

'Maeve. Get into the car.' He ended the call. I ran across the road, caught between embarrassment and a sudden, unexpected happiness that I didn't choose to analyse too closely.

'Well?'

'Well what?' The first couple of minutes of the journey had passed in silence and I was relaxed, almost sleepy, my body slack against the seat. Derwent's question made me literally sit up.

'Did Tor Grant say anything interesting? What was he looking for in the boxes?'

'He didn't say specifically. He said it was too good an opportunity to pass up.' I yawned. 'He said a lot of other things. I don't think the detectives could have shut him up if they'd tried.'

'Did he talk about the Marshalls?'

'He talked about the podcast a lot.' I did some sums and came up with not enough sleep, but all the same . . . 'Should I go and interview him about the Marshalls in the morning after they let him go?'

'There are other things that are more important at this stage. I'll tell CID to make sure we know where we can find him. But if you're wondering if he killed them, I'd say no. Why would he?'

'To generate interest in his podcast?'

Derwent shook his head. 'He's the sort of true-crime fanatic who loves to talk about it but he would shit his pants if he met an actual killer. I mean, you scared the living daylights out of him and you're hardly intimidating.'

'Excuse me, I'm terrifying when I want to be.'

He grinned, concentrating on the road. 'If you say so. You had hours hanging around there doing nothing. You'll have spent some of that time thinking about the case, if I know you. Did you have any other thoughts?'

I had spent a fair amount of time thinking about Melissa and what she had said to Una Burt about us, but it would have taken serious torture for me to admit that to anyone, let alone Derwent.

'The scrap of paper I found down the side of Bruce's chair bothers me.'

'Go on.'

'It must have been something he wanted to remember, and presumably the shorthand made sense to him. "BDK" has to mean something, and it relates to an important date – maybe when Rosalie went missing.'

'So?'

'So what if he was aware that he was developing dementia? What if it was a reminder to him to look up the date his daughter disappeared, and the shock of forgetting such an important event pushed him into taking action?'

'By killing his wife.'

'Yeah, that's what I meant.'

He was frowning. 'We ruled it out because of the way the bodies were lying.'

'I know. But I was wondering if we saw what we wanted to see.' I said it in a small voice and got a swift glance from Derwent.

'You think it suits me to make this into a bigger case than it seemed at first? Why?'

'Um.' I squirmed. 'You don't like being told what to do. And this is one way of getting around Una Burt's rule about us not working together. You said as much yourself.'

'You came up with the idea of it being a third-party murder rather than a murder-suicide, and at the time you didn't know what Una had decided, or why.'

83

'I know.'

He was driving smoothly, untroubled. 'It worked out for me, don't get me wrong. But I think there were enough issues with this case to trigger a proper investigation, not least the daughter's disappearance. I don't think we're overreacting.'

It worked out for me. What did that mean? Nothing romantic. He had literally stepped away from that when he'd had the opportunity the previous summer, and I closed my eyes for a moment to allow a wave of scalding shame to pass over me at the memory of how I had waited, expectant, for him to kiss me. What had I been *thinking*?

'What are you thinking?'

I jumped, but managed to come up with, 'Was it very convenient that Ivo invited Mr Hood to visit so he would be technically out of the way?'

'Suspicious of you.'

'Well, Magnus has been filling my head with doubts about his brother. Apparently I wasn't anything like wary enough when I interviewed him.'

'What's he like?'

'He's charming. Very handsome.'

Derwent made a noise that was somewhere between a huff and a snort.

'I'm joking. He was a spoilt brat.'

His shoulders lowered a fraction. 'That's a surprise.'

'He wasn't in touch with his parents and didn't seem bothered that they were dead. He said the painting of the old house was done by the nanny, Sadie, and it was almost the only thing they kept from the old days.'

'Presumably Bruce decided to keep it. Helena had checked out, remember?'

'Helena used to say "Sexy Sadie" was an appropriate nickname for the nanny.'

'Did she?' Derwent looked thoughtful. 'Maybe we should try to find this Sadie.'

'Yes, that should definitely be a key objective at this stage of the investigation.'

'It's all part of the picture of what happened before Rosalie disappeared. Sadie would be what – forty now? I'm betting still fit.'

'What else do we need to do?'

'Get the results of the post-mortems from Dr Early. You and I can collect the last boxes from the flat. And I need to talk to Billy Howlett who ran the initial investigation into Rosalie's disappearance. He's retired now.'

'What was he like?'

'Painstaking. The sort of person who wouldn't like giving up on the investigation when he had to hand it over to someone else. Quiet, but you wouldn't want to get on the wrong side of him.'

'Is he still alive?'

'I'd have heard if he died, I think. Someone would have let me know.' Derwent shook his head. 'Those messages about all the old bosses dying off. I never get used to them.'

'And one day it'll be you.'

Derwent squinted out through the windscreen. 'Long walk home from here.'

'I didn't say it would be soon,' I protested.

'Better not.'

We bickered gently all the way through central London and out the other side to the flat where I lived, a first-floor one-bedroom place where Derwent had spent some wild years, I suspected. It was on the corner of a pretty Victorian street of similar maisonettes, mostly owned by house-proud yuppies, and it was within walking distance of nice shops and the underground station. He had renovated it beautifully, and even though I'd almost died in it, I liked it a lot. After years of moving in with boyfriends and out again when the relationship ended, and a succession of grim rental properties, I thought of it as home. In fact, the only problem with it was the lack of on-street parking. When we turned into the street Derwent stopped in the middle of the road with the hazards on. I pointed.

'There's actually a space on the left, look. I never get that lucky.'

He hesitated. 'I was just going to drop you off.'

'And what? Drive back to Sutton?' He was living a long way south of the river, not far from where I'd grown up and my parents still lived – so close, in fact, that they looked after Melissa's son Thomas from time to time. 'It's hardly worth it. If we're going to Battersea together in a few hours we might as well start from here.'

'I'm heading back to the office. I can sleep there. I've got a toothbrush and a change of clothes.'

'I can lend you a toothbrush. You can have the sofa.' I nudged him. 'I'll even let you use the washing machine if you ask nicely. The quick cycle has saved me from a laundry crisis more than once.'

'Better not.' He said it with the kind of decision that I recognised: he'd made up his mind. And I shouldn't have pushed further, but I found myself saying what came into my head.

'Because you'd get in trouble with Melissa for staying with me?'

A glower. 'Because it's not a good idea.'

And that was all I was getting. I put a hand on the door handle. 'Are you picking me up in the morning?'

'No, I'll see you at the flat in Battersea at nine.' He revved the engine. 'Go on. See what some beauty sleep can do for you.'

'Nothing much, I imagine.' I was hurt, and embarrassed, but trying not to show it. If I'd got a taxi home I would have had to make my own way to Battersea, too, but somehow this was different. I got out, thanked him and closed the car door. He waited while I took out my keys and let myself into the flat (which was exactly the kind of thing he would do, in case I was murdered on my doorstep and he missed it). Then he drove off with a brief wave.

What else had I expected?

I trudged up the stairs, feeling lonely for the first time in a long time.

All very well for him to blame Una Burt, but I had a suspicion that wasn't the whole story. Derwent had been avoiding me for his own reasons. I just didn't know what they were.

16

Derwent had told me to be at the flat in Battersea at nine, which meant he would be there by 8.45 at the latest. I arrived ten minutes before that with two coffees and two bacon sandwiches. I leaned against the railings, enjoying the morning air and the birdsong from the park and the feeling of superiority that came from being on time. I'd put some colour in my cheeks with the help of the blusher my mother had given me for Christmas (along with a meaningful look). I was feeling surprisingly well, which was adrenalin, and also anticipation.

The thought tripped me up. Anticipation of what? Spending the day with Derwent, came the truthful answer, which was pathetic.

Oh yes, and what if he rings you to tell you he's not coming and you can handle clearing out the flat on your own, needled a mean little voice in my head. *What if he's thought better of spending time with you, like he did last night?*

I wouldn't mind, I thought, knowing it was a lie. I took out my phone to check that I hadn't missed the soft hum of a message delivering bad news, so I was staring at the screen – *like a teenager with a crush*, the mean voice observed – when he strolled up, his hands in his pockets.

'What's this?'

'Breakfast.' I handed him his coffee and sandwich.

'Lifesaver.'

'I thought we'd need it.' I watched him wolfing the food down. He had shaved with care and his suit was immaculate, but nothing could hide that he was hollow-eyed with fatigue.

'How are you feeling?' He said it around a mouthful of sandwich. Perfunctory, that was the word.

87

'Fine. How did you sleep?'

A grimace. 'I managed a couple of hours on the sofa in the break room.'

'Well, you did have an alternative.' *Keep it normal, keep it light.* I wanted to see how he would react, so I could work out how he really felt about what had happened, and by extension how he felt about me. He ate the last of the sandwich and looked at me.

'Are you nearly finished?'

'Not yet.'

'Well, do you mind getting on with it?'

'I just don't eat like a starving Labrador.'

'Oh sure. You're too much of a lady for that. Unless you're really hungry in which case all bets are off.' He sounded as if he was thinking about something completely different.

'Any news on Tor Grant?'

'They've let him go. They got an address for us.'

'It'll be a shame if he turns out to be our killer after all.'

I said it as a joke, but Derwent looked gloomy. 'That could still happen.'

'Is it the lack of sleep, Josh, or is something else making you grumpy?'

Instead of answering, he walked away towards the building. I scrambled to gather up the empty cups and the remains of my breakfast, then dropped the lot in the bin on my way.

He was holding the door open for me, which was something. I waited in the hallway, letting him take the lead. All the little tricks were coming back to me, the techniques I had learned to deal with him in the years when he was relentlessly rude and confrontational. Nothing to do with me, or something I'd done? My thoughts were interrupted by a door opening as we started up the stairs.

'You there. Are you the police?'

A big man, stooping over a stick. He had a white beard and white hair which gave him an immediate touch of the old St

Nicks, but the red in his face was high blood pressure rather than jolliness.

Derwent came back down two steps. 'Yes, sir. What can we do for you?'

'I wanted to complain about the *noise*.'

'We're conducting a murder investigation, sir. Unfortunately it does involve a certain amount of coming and going.'

The man was oblivious to the tone of reproach that Derwent reserved for members of the public who had transgressed. 'It's been intolerable. You're right over our heads, you know. People dropping things, dragging things, tramping around on the balcony. Totally inconsiderate.'

'Sorry about that,' Derwent said, not sounding it. 'We'll be finishing up shortly.'

'I hope so. Can't concentrate on the wireless.'

'You must have very good hearing,' I said, and he threw back his head like an old elephant.

'Got these new hearing aids. Didn't want them but they talked me into it. Now I can hear everything. Marvellous.' He turned to face away from us and I thought he was going back into his flat, but he barked, 'Say something, quietly, and I'll tell you what it was. Not even looking. Go on.'

I didn't dare catch Derwent's eye. 'Twinkle, twinkle, little star.'

'How I wonder what you are,' he finished, triumphant, working his way back around. 'You see? I leave them in because they're fiddly little things so sometimes I get woken up during the night.'

'Did that happen the night before last?' I asked.

'Early yesterday morning.' He shook his head, irritable. 'That was it. I was wide awake.'

'What time?'

'Five, it must have been.'

'Do you know what woke you? Could it have been a gunshot?'

He considered the question. 'No. Thumping and banging. From eight or so there was a lot of coming and going, which was you lot.'

To Derwent, I said quietly, 'Kev mentioned that he got in trouble for making too much noise on the balcony.'

'That's the worst place for it,' the man said. 'Sounds like a herd of bullocks trampling around.'

'Could I ask your name, sir?' I asked.

'Hartley Goring. I'm in flat 3.'

'Mr Goring, did you ever hear anything that was unusual or suspicious from upstairs? Arguments? Odd sounds?'

'They were good neighbours, until recently. Their son – he dropped in once. I had a leak. Thought it was coming from their flat. He came and found out what was wrong. Nothing to do with them, as it happened.'

'Was that Ivo?'

'Nice young lad.' Mr Miller was leaning more heavily on his stick, as if standing was an effort. 'Well, that's all I had to say. About the noise.'

'We'll keep it in mind,' Derwent said smoothly. 'And I do apologise. Is it possible to adjust your hearing aids?'

'Yes, I suppose it is.'

'Maybe turn them down a little for the next hour. We'll be moving boxes around.'

'But this should be the last of it,' I added.

Mr Goring looked unimpressed, but he tapped away down the hall.

Derwent was grinning when I turned back to him. 'Twinkle, twinkle?'

'It was the first thing that came into my head.'

'I wonder why.'

'Don't over-think it,' I said, following him up the stairs. 'What would you have said?'

'Not that.'

I dropped my voice so it was a mumble, barely audible. 'Mr Goring didn't hear a shot.'

'Maybe the killer used something to muffle the sound,' Derwent murmured back.

I frowned. 'We didn't find anything.'

'No, he could have taken it with him.' Derwent leaned closer. 'Or the hearing aids might not be as good as all that.'

'You're still whispering,' I pointed out.

'Better safe than sorry.'

He let us into the empty flat. The living room felt cold and abandoned. We spent a few minutes in the main bedroom, which was marginally better without the bodies and bloodied bed linen, but found nothing that could have muffled the shot.

'It would have been covered in blood. Maybe Kev took it,' Derwent said at last.

'The killer would have had to hold it over Bruce's face, wouldn't he? Risky. Unless he was sure neither of them was going to wake up because they were unconscious.'

'If they were unconscious, it needn't have been a man.'

I sighed. 'We're making the wrong kind of progress.'

'Adding suspects instead of eliminating them?' Derwent grimaced. 'I keep waiting for it all to fall into place but it doesn't. Who would want to kill them? Why now? What if it has nothing to do with Rosalie and we're barking up the wrong tree?'

'That's the job, isn't it? Trying all the trees until you find the right one?'

'That's life.' He leaned against the wall, his head tilted back, a troublemaking stance if ever I saw one. 'Speaking of which, are you seeing anyone at the moment?'

I blinked at the change of topic. 'Like?'

'Like your ex?'

My ex, Rob, who had resurfaced briefly after years of silence. 'He's long gone.'

'How do you feel about that?'

'Fine. I feel fine. And you shouldn't ask me about him, or this. It's not appropriate.'

'Keep your hair on. I'm just saying.'

'Well, don't.'

He peeled himself away from the wall and went into the second bedroom, whistling, which meant he was pleased with himself. I wondered why I'd been looking forward to spending the day with him and took a second to retrieve my self-possession. I spent it looking at the windows which had been open, but that Sabiha had sworn were usually closed. No one could have come in or gone out that way, but I kept worrying at it. Whether it was relevant or not, it was *different*, and that made me suspicious.

I found Derwent shifting boxes, moving them into the hall. 'I'm organising them by weight. The ones nearest the door are the lightest. You can carry them down to the car. Leave the ones on the right to me.'

'I can manage.'

'OK.' He dumped the box he was carrying into my arms and, unprepared, I almost dropped it. I eased it down.

'Fine. You've made your point.'

'Of course I still see you as my equal, blah blah blah.' He grinned at me and went back into the bedroom. A long scuffing sound as he dragged a box from one side of the room to the other made me wince: Mr Goring wouldn't like that at all.

I was just lifting one of the lighter boxes when he spoke.

'Maeve? Could you come here?'

'What've you got?' I looked through the doorway and found him hovering over the last row of boxes by the window, balancing on one foot.

'I think we fucked up.'

'What? What do you mean?' I went to stand next to him and he put his arm out to stop me from touching the boxes.

'Who's been in here? You, me, Liv . . .'

'Kev and his crew. Magnus, the son. I don't know who else. Why?'

'Someone was here.' He had taken a torch out and was playing it over the space behind the boxes. I braced myself on his shoulder and looked. A rust-coloured piece of fabric stuck out from behind the last boxes, and there was a smear of the same colour along the wall.

Derwent swore, quietly. 'That'll be whatever was used to muffle the shot, in case you were in any doubt that this was connected with the murders.'

I looked at the window for the first time, noticing that it looked out on the balcony. 'Is the window unlocked?'

'Looks like it. Come on.' Derwent hurried around to the living room, where he opened the door and peered out along the balcony. 'Shit.'

'What is it?'

'An easy drop down to street level. You'd have to be fit, but not exceptionally so. You could do it.'

'Oh well, in that case.' I looked, though, and was inclined to agree with him. 'So our killer came and went through the window. Colin can stop wasting time looking at CCTV from inside the building. Those noises Mr Goring heard on the balcony – that would be our guy leaving. At least we know how he got out, and we have some idea of when he left.'

'But we don't know when he arrived, or how he got in. And we've obliterated any worthwhile forensic evidence in the second bedroom and the balcony.' Derwent clasped his hands behind his head and walked around in a small, frustrated circle. 'Apart from that, we're doing a great job.'

17

One small thing went our way: William Howlett hadn't moved far from London when he retired. His house was in rural Sussex; a small 1960s bungalow on a tree-lined country lane, with a view of rolling hills dressed in sharp spring green. He was outside when we arrived, raking the grass, a slight grey-haired man who had wiry strength in abundance and who wanted, passionately, for us to leave him alone.

'It's good to see you,' Derwent said with feeling, and the two men shook hands, holding on marginally longer than I would have expected. Mutual respect, I gathered, or a test of strength. Impossible to tell who had won.

'You too, Josh. Inspector now?' Howlett shook his head. 'How on earth did you manage that?'

'Wrong place, wrong time. This is my colleague, Sergeant Kerrigan.'

'Ah.' He nodded to me.

An understated man, Derwent had told me in the car on the way there. 'Old school but he's not old. He would have been the type who joined young and did his thirty and retired to enjoy the pension while he was in his fifties. Don't make the mistake of thinking he was a card-index kind of detective. He retired in 2016.'

'He's barely middle-aged and you're still young. Got it,' I said. 'So I shouldn't expect him to be a sexist dinosaur.'

'I don't know. That attitude runs deep, doesn't it? I seem to remember his team was mostly blokes, apart from the civilian staff. He wasn't married, except to the job.' He looked across at me. 'Basically, I'll do the talking.'

Now I stood a pace behind Derwent, letting him take the lead.

'As I said on the phone, it's regarding Rosalie Marshall.'

'I always expected that one would come back to haunt me. I have to say, I didn't anticipate it would be because her parents were murdered.' He had a quiet voice, just above a mumble, and a distracted manner, which I thought had probably misled more than a few criminals in his time. 'There's no doubt about that, I suppose? They were both murdered?'

'No doubt at all.' Not now that we had found the cushion used to muffle the gun.

'That's a shame. A very great shame.' He dusted off his hands. 'Come into the house. I'll make tea.'

The kitchen was small but very clean and looked modern, with a polka-dotted blind at the window and shiny red cupboards that didn't seem to fit with what I knew of Howlett. It was a happy space, light-hearted.

'Do you live here on your own?' I asked.

'No, with my wife. I'm sorry she's not here but she's out volunteering at the local school this morning.'

'When did you get married?' Derwent was looking startled.

'A couple of years ago. I thought I'd never marry. Then I met Sheila.' He smiled and I saw the warmth that had been missing from his manner before. 'Never too late to be happy.'

'Good for you.' Derwent clapped him on the shoulder.

'And are you married, Josh?'

'Not yet.' There was an odd undertone to his voice.

Marry Melissa? I hadn't even thought of that, I'd been so sure that Derwent wasn't happy with her. *Just like every Other Woman since the dawn of time*, the mean voice in my head informed me, *not that you've made it to Other Woman status*. Maybe I only saw what I wanted to see. I tuned out of the do-you-remember conversation that Derwent and Howlett were having, following in silence as the retired superintendent put mugs on a tray and carried them into a sunny living room. A wedding photograph stood on a side table: Howlett in a suit with a rose pinned to his lapel, smiling widely as he held hands with a beaming dark-haired woman in pale pink. The picture was a million miles away from misery and missing children and I understood why Bill Howlett had picked a time when his wife would be out, and why he had chosen to put off talking about the Marshalls until he couldn't avoid it any longer.

Howlett sat in an armchair that looked comfortably worn, crossing his legs and holding his hands up in front of his mouth, the fingers interlaced. 'Why don't you begin.'

In a few brief sentences, Derwent outlined what had happened: the bodies, the causes of death, the room full of boxes and the balcony.

'Our current assumption is that it was something to do with Rosalie's disappearance. There doesn't seem to be any other reason why two frail and elderly people would be murdered in their beds.'

'You've ruled out burglary.' He murmured it, as if it was hardly worth floating the idea.

'The pathologist thinks they were drugged with chloroform before they were killed, which is unusual for a burglary. And they didn't have many possessions any more,' I said. 'There was nothing to steal.'

'Interesting. Chloroform?'

'They're doing more tests but it looks like it. The pathologist said it's easy enough to make it, if you know how.'

'Hm. They were well off, you know, when I knew them. At least, that was how it looked to an outsider like me. Big house, staff, the kids went to private schools, and no one had a real job. What did the sons say about that?'

'The same – the parents had run out of money.'

'Nothing to inherit,' Derwent said.

'Nothing to fight over.'

I smiled. 'Magnus could start a fight in an empty room.'

'That's also interesting,' Howlett said. 'He was a nice boy. A little wild, perhaps. He was devastated when his little sister disappeared.'

'And Ivo?'

'He was older, of course. A teenager. He was more closed off. But certainly upset.'

Derwent leaned forward, his elbows on his knees. 'You got the first impression of the case before the waters got too muddy to be able to see anything. You must have had your own theories about what happened.'

Howlett considered it for a moment. 'Well, you know how she disappeared. A cool August night. No windows left open downstairs, no doors unlocked according to the Marshalls. No sign of a break-in. Helena Marshall was first to get up that morning and went downstairs without checking on Rosalie, though she did visit the bedrooms of her other two children. They were asleep.'

'Why did she leave Rosalie out?' Derwent asked.

'She didn't want to wake her up.' He shrugged. 'Nothing to say that was a lie. Rosalie was usually the first one down in the morning, everyone agreed, and sometimes she would make herself breakfast. But on this particular morning, there was no sign that anyone had been up already, except for marks on the back door that Helena claimed to have seen. The door itself was open.'

'You said the doors were all locked.'

'Exactly.' Howlett smiled at me. 'That's what Helena and Bruce told me. When she came down, Helena assumed someone had opened the door again after she had gone to bed, and had forgotten to lock it. She shut it, then cleaned the door, then couldn't find the key. There was no damage to the door. Bruce said he had locked and bolted the door at the top and bottom before he went to bed. Someone unbolted it at some stage, and we never found the key.'

'Someone who was inside the house. Could Rosalie have done it?' Derwent asked.

'She couldn't have reached the bolt at the top of the door, even if she'd been standing on a chair.'

'So do you think that's how she left the house?'

'Possibly. Or one of the boys opened the door and wouldn't admit it in case they got in trouble. One theory was that she climbed out of her bedroom window, or someone climbed in. The window was loose and it was possible to rattle it in its frame and dislodge the lock. I did it myself to test it.'

'Was her bedroom disturbed?'

'She spent some time in her bed, from the way the bedclothes were left. Nothing was particularly out of place, but then there wasn't much to be out of place. It was bare, I remember that. Very little that a child would love. Some books, a couple of toys.' He stared into space and I knew he was back in that room. 'Then of course there was the blood on the floor.'

'Blood?' Derwent and I said at the same time.

'Yes. Not much – a few drops – but it came back as Rosalie's when we tested it. Now, it wasn't fresh. It had been there a while. Helena claimed that she had scraped herself on something and it wasn't unusual for her to have cuts and bruises. She said she was a clumsy child.'

'If a parent said that to me in an investigation I'd think it was a red flag,' I said.

'Indeed.' Howlett's voice was quiet but the way he spoke – slowly, halfway to a drawl – made me sit up and mind my manners. I noticed Derwent was smirking to himself. 'I didn't take it for granted that she was telling the truth. But I spoke to a lot of people who knew Rosalie – teachers, her nanny, her siblings – and they all agreed that Rosalie was careless and dreamy. She was one of those kids who wants to climb trees but falls out of them. No sense and no idea of what her limits might be.'

'She sounds brilliant,' Derwent said and Howlett smiled.

'By the end of my time on the investigation, I felt as if I knew her. She was bright and imaginative and fun. Her classmates were devastated when they heard she was missing. Her teacher cried.'

'What about her nanny?' I asked.

Howlett paused. 'That was a different situation. The nanny's name was Sadie Pilchrist. She was twenty-four and she was absolutely furious with the Marshalls, who had sacked her a couple of weeks earlier. I had to take that resentment into account when I considered what she told me, especially where it didn't match up with what other witnesses alleged.'

Derwent looked at me, triumphant. 'I told you the nanny was important.'

I unclenched my jaw to ask, 'Did you discount her evidence because she was a young woman?'

'I didn't discount it at all, but I'm afraid I didn't weigh it as heavily as the evidence from the family doctor, for example – Dr Fuller. Sadie Pilchrist alleged that Helena occasionally administered physical punishments to Rosalie when she was angry with her – a slap, a spanking, that kind of thing – but I couldn't find anyone to corroborate it. Dr Fuller had never noticed anything out of the ordinary with Rosalie. She'd had concussion – that happened at school – and a broken wrist that she got playing football, but also the usual childhood ailments, chicken pox and chest infections and so forth. Dr Fuller was horrified when I asked about violence in the home but couldn't recall any evidence to support the allegation. And the boys flat-out denied it.'

'They might not have said anything if they were scared of Helena too,' I protested.

'Sadie was almost certainly sleeping with Bruce Marshall, and she was sacked after the family holiday that year in France,' Howlett said with the air of someone playing a winning hand. 'She wouldn't admit it to me, and Bruce denied it, but the boys both told me, halfway through the holiday there was a huge argument between the adults and Sadie cried a lot and then she went home. After that Helena was doing all the childcare.'

'Were Bruce and Helena getting on, then, at the time Rosalie disappeared?'

He grimaced at Derwent. 'They had patched things up but no, I'd say there was little love and no trust between them. They supported each other during the investigation, and then Helena overdosed and after that she was totally dependent on him.'

'Was Sadie ever a suspect in Rosalie's disappearance?' Derwent asked.

'She had an alibi for the night in question. If she had wanted revenge on Helena, I think she would have gone to the papers and revealed what she was like behind closed doors. Helena was just famous enough for them to have done a story about it. She didn't need Rosalie to be missing.'

'Why didn't she do a tell-all after Rosalie disappeared?' I asked. It seemed like an obvious earner for her, in the circumstances.

'She did. They got it spiked. The Marshalls spent a fortune on lawyers. Every newspaper editor in London had a solicitor's letter at one point or another.'

'If you ruled out the nanny, who did you rule in?' Derwent sat back. 'Strictly off the record.'

'One of the problems we had was the sheer volume of people who were suspects. Helena was a divisive figure. She had death threats before and after Rosalie's disappearance. Bruce had business interests that annoyed animal rights campaigners. Investigating that took up a huge amount of time and money and it got us nowhere. They had anonymous letters – I mean, you always will in a case like this, but it was on a scale that I hadn't experienced before. And phone calls. It drove Helena over the edge.'

'That's what caused her to try to end her life?'

'I assumed so.' Howlett looked at me, his eyes shrewd behind the thick lenses. 'I never knew for certain.'

'Who else was a suspect?'

'Easier to tell you who wasn't. The house was full of people in the weeks before she disappeared – strangers, neighbours, friends of the family. Someone saw a strange car outside a number of times, but we never got a proper description or number plate. Any one of them could have taken the key to the back door, and then let themselves in at their leisure. The door was bolted but the kidnapper could have been in the house already that evening, hiding.'

'Or they could have been in the house already because they lived there,' Derwent said, and Howlett nodded.

'It's possible.'

'What about Rosalie's birth family?' I asked.

'Her parents were both dead – George Canning, his name was, and the wife was . . . Sarah. George was a painter – artist, not houses. They were very young – seventeen when she got pregnant with Rosalie, twenty-one when George killed Sarah.'

'Jesus.' Derwent flinched.

'He was mentally ill. Schizophrenic, they thought, but he hanged himself on remand and so he never had a formal diagnosis. There was no warning. They lived in a tiny little cottage somewhere in Cornwall, in absolute poverty, and Sarah didn't tell anyone that he was unstable. I don't think they had a phone, even. She did little bits of work here and there – cleaning, I think, and looking after children.' He sighed. 'We did wonder if it was a family member who'd taken Rosalie when she disappeared, but they were totally uninterested in her. She was in a foster family for a couple of years before Helena made contact with them. Rosie Canning became Rosalie Marshall when she was five years old, and she disappeared when she was nine, and her birth family didn't see her from the day she went into care until she disappeared. Six years, no contact. Their choice.'

'How did the Marshalls get to adopt her?'

'Helena was involved with a charity – some sort of religious organisation. She wanted a little girl – not a baby, because a baby was too much work – and she jumped the queue to adopt Rosalie. She was quite candid about it with me. She had a list of criteria and Rosalie met all of them – no living parents, intelligent, a girl of school-going age but young enough to be malleable.'

'Was that the word she used?'

Howlett nodded, the distaste on his face mirrored on Derwent's. 'She didn't waste a lot of time finding out about the birth parents. I think she didn't want to know much about them. Helena was never very interested in anyone but Helena.'

'Mr Howlett, what do you think happened to Rosalie?' I asked.

'I think someone took her and put her in the river. We never found a trace of her. Not a footprint, not a hair. It was just at the bottom of the garden. I saw the river, that first morning, and I knew she was already dead.' He took off his glasses and polished them on his shirt, absent-mindedly. His eyes looked vulnerable without them, defenceless. 'I looked for that child every day for a year. In some ways I've never stopped.'

On the doorstep, he said, 'I don't talk to my wife about the cases. She doesn't need to know everything that keeps me awake at night.'

Derwent nodded. 'They never leave you alone, do they? The ones that didn't work out, especially.'

'Part of the job,' Howlett said soberly. 'You'll take them with you when you go. And it's not always the ones you'd expect that cause the most pain.'

18

Bruce

'Daddy . . . Daddy . . .'

Bruce folded his arms more tightly across his chest. He was leaning back in his padded desk chair, congratulating himself (not for the first time) on establishing that he needed an office at home, and that the furnishing of the office must be left to him. He had spent a lot of time and a considerable amount of money on the ox-blood leather chair that had made Helena shudder.

'It's vile.'

'It's comfortable. For my back,' Bruce had added quickly, thinking, *for my naps*. And it had proved to be a loyal companion when he was in his study, 'reading papers' and 'making calls'. Bruce did of course make calls but they were largely to friends to arrange golf outings, which counted as work because that was how he made the right impression on the right people, who then invited him to be on the right boards and chair the right committees. He had a carefully cultivated reputation for being reasonable and not asking the difficult questions that could derail ambitious business plans. He didn't like to look the gift horses in the mouth too closely – not with two sons in private school and every prospect that little Rosalie would be the same, even though he had tried hinting to Helena that it wasn't quite as important for her. It wasn't that she was adopted and therefore didn't deserve the expenditure, he had explained, but more that the boys needed to meet the right people, and through them Rosalie would meet the right people. Helena had been furious – *it's a hostage to fortune and every journalist will ask me about it, quite rightly. Do you want me to look like a fool* – so he'd backed off, but he hadn't given up. Bruce was a practical man and he didn't feel that girls repaid their education in the way that a son might. They had other things to offer. He cherished a vision of himself walking Rosalie down the aisle, her face obscured with a cloud of white lace which was convenient because, try as he might, he couldn't imagine her looking like anything other than a black-eyed urchin—

'Daddy . . . . *Daddy* . . .'

She was sitting outside the closed door to the study, and she would sit there until the door opened or Helena found her and shooed her away. She was quiet enough – just that insistent repetition of *Daddy* every few seconds which was enough to drive a less patient man insane. Every so often a piece of paper would slide slowly under the door with a scuffing sound that always seemed sinister. 'My story' Rosalie would tell him, or 'a letter to you, Daddy', or 'a drawing I just wanted to do and I think it's quite like what I imagined?'

He rarely looked at them properly, truth be told. Little grubby scraps of paper went on the fire, when it was lit, and in a drawer when it was the summer. He appreciated it in a way. No matter what he gave Ivo and Magnus it was the wrong thing – the wrong brand of cricket bat, the wrong type of trainers, the wrong game for their infernal computers. But throw a box of crayons in Rosalie's direction and her peaky little face lit up as if he'd given her diamonds and rubies.

A shout came from outside, somewhere in the garden. He swivelled in the chair to look out of the window. There: Ivo running backwards in defiance of gravity and wisdom, all his focus on the cricket ball that was arcing towards him. There was a lovely inevitability in the way the ball curved into Ivo's outstretched palms, a pure moment of grace as he took it from the air, but he'd had to hustle to get it.

'Oh well done,' Bruce murmured, imagining himself at Lords on a sunny day. 'I say.'

'Good. That's it. Back to me.'

Ivo lobbed the ball back to the trainer who remained invisible behind the shrubbery. Trainer was a grand word for the boy, Nathaniel, only a few years older than Ivo, but prodigiously talented. He had come up through the cricket club's outreach scheme and he needed the money, the coach had told Bruce. Nathaniel was lined up to go on a cricket tour to South Africa in the winter so he was spending his summer training Ivo and boys like him, giving them one-to-one attention, for a very reasonable hourly rate. And Ivo was improving, Bruce thought. Decent fielding, excellent batting. Not an all-rounder, unlike Nathaniel, but you hardly ever got that. He'd put in the hours down at the nets, dogged and determined, and that was Ivo for you; he'd break his heart striving to be excellent before he'd admit defeat. Whereas Magnus—

'Daddy . . . *please*, Daddy . . . I want to show you my *story*.'

'Rosalie, Daddy's working,' Bruce barked, sounding more annoyed than he really was. She wouldn't dare to open the door and he was managing to ignore her quite well and there was Ivo again, racing to an imaginary boundary. He was good, Bruce thought, and he could be even better, and Lords wasn't an impossible dream – it had to happen for some parents. Why not him? (*Why not me* was the philosophy that had taken him this far through life. It was a useful means of eliminating self-doubt if you were weighing up whether to go for a job or not, and it was a very good way to avoid the nagging concern that you'd gone a long way on privilege alone. Would he have achieved as much if his parents hadn't been wealthy? Perhaps not. But since he couldn't do anything to change that, why not enjoy the benefits? The guilt wasn't his when it was sheer luck that he'd been born in the right circumstances. Everyone was entitled to ride their luck.)

'Daddy, when will you be finished work? Daddy? *Daddy?*'

She sounded as if she was close to tears and Bruce clenched his fists in irritation.

'Not for some time, darling. Go and play.'

'I did play. And I did writing. Now I want to show you. It's about Medusa. With the snakes. From my book.'

She was obsessed with a book he had given her on Greek and Roman myths, something he'd seen in a bookshop window and picked up on a whim. Magnus had given up on it after flicking through the pictures, and Helena had told him it was too old for Rosalie, but she had fallen in love with it. She had read it for weeks now, lying on the landing on her front, breathing heavily as she worked her way through the stories, lost in other worlds. It had led to awkward questions about Leda and Zeus and what exactly he had done when he was pretending to be a swan. Bruce tried to remember the story of Medusa – pretty much sex-free, he thought. Like his marriage? Better not think about that.

'Go and show Mummy.' Bruce pulled a face at his own audacity. This was the dance that two working parents did, even when they were both working at home. Working. That was what Helena called it but it was largely writing long screeds for her blog (horrible word) and going on the radio and allowing herself to be interviewed and writing important articles for the broadsheets about parenting adopted children. Well, she could try parenting the one she had; that would be a start, Bruce thought, swelling with self-pity. Where was Helena? This had all been a lot easier when Sadie was around.

Sadie.

He shut his eyes.

He had been stupid, of course, about how he handled it, but Helena had overreacted, and he had let her, because it was easier than arguing, or trying to explain.

It had ruined the holiday for him. For all of them, actually. Rosalie crying all night, her little voice hoarse from it. The child was hollow with grief. Ivo and Magnus unable to look him in the eye. Helena, rigid with disapproval and rage.

And no Sadie. He was surprised by how much he missed her, there and at home: her smile, her gleaming tanned limbs as she arced into the swimming pool, her laugh. Her very round, very full breasts, generously displayed in skimpy sundresses.

He wasn't stupid enough to ask Helena if she had got around to replacing Sadie yet. That didn't mean he couldn't encourage her to get on with it.

Bruce got up and went to the door. When he opened it, Rosalie fell backwards, landing on her elbows. She looked up at him reproachfully.

'I was leaning on the door.'

'I know.' He held out his hand. 'Give me the story.'

Her eyes widened and then she scrabbled for it, so eager he almost laughed. He skimmed through it, murmuring *oh very good* and *that's a nice phrase* at intervals, taking in very little of it (but it did seem to be nicely expressed, spelling and handwriting aside).

'Really, Rosalie, this is excellent.'

'Is it?' She hadn't looked away from his face since he started reading, focused on every nuance of his expression.

'You've excelled yourself.' He handed it back to her. 'Now go and show Mummy.'

'She said she's busy.'

Bruce smiled. 'Don't take no for an answer. She'll be so pleased when she finally reads it.'

'Like you?'

'Absolutely like me.' He pretended to steal her nose, which he wasn't good at, and she laughed dutifully and a little too loudly, as she always did, and Bruce closed the study door on her with the comfortable feeling that he had killed two birds with one rather clever stone.

He would reward himself, he decided, with a little nap.

Helena

If she was honest (and Helena always tried to be honest), she had been nervous about the interview. The publication wasn't one of her usual sources of commissions and that was something she was determined to change, even though *politically* she doubted that she would see eye-to-eye with the editor, but of course that didn't matter. What mattered was the message about adoption. Helena was confident, as ever, that she could win this journalist over, but she didn't expect it to be effortless.

'I hope you'll be fair,' Helena said.

'I'm always fair.' An easy reply, instant, questionably sincere. He was lean and whippy with dark hair that flopped over his forehead and small round glasses and he wore a white shirt with the sleeves rolled up to reveal a few inches of tanned forearm: muscular intellectual was so strongly Helena's type that she felt slightly weak.

'I read your profile of that racehorse trainer.'

He raised his eyebrows, amused. 'Reading up on me?'

'Of course. Forewarned is forearmed.' She refused to be embarrassed about it, even if he was suggesting she should be. He had presumably done his homework on her too. 'You gave him a hard time.'

'Not as hard as he gives his horses.'

'He has a job to do.'

'And he does it a certain way.' The journalist shrugged. 'All I did was describe it. I can't help it if it doesn't read well to most ordinary people.'

'I don't want to look like a bitch,' Helena said, holding his gaze.

He laughed, holding his hands up. 'I promise not to put words in your mouth.'

And then she thought he was genuinely impressed by the set-up in the sitting room, with a tray of biscuits and coffee and two chairs facing one another and a table in the middle for his recording device because Helena knew a good recording was vital if he was going to be able to write an understanding profile of her. He had looked at the paintings on the walls and admired the secretaire desk that was a wedding present from her mother. She thought they were getting on very well, in fact. So well that she found herself saying more than she usually would about how the current approach to adoption involved social workers sacrificing children's chances because their awful birth families wanted to keep them, so they grew up in squalid, unsuitable conditions and were neglected until they were just as hopeless and drug-addled as their parents.

'Family is something you should earn, not something that's given to you as a right just because you're too stupid or careless to avoid getting pregnant.'

The journalist looked up at that and smiled. He had a crooked mouth, an angular face, nicotine staining on his fingers. Not handsome, Helena had thought, but *interesting*.

'I've read your blog. Do you really think that unemployed people should be required to use contraception to qualify for benefits?'

'I think if they had any sense they would choose to anyway,' Helena said carefully, thinking *yes, obviously*. 'Not having any proper income or stability should rule out having children.'

'But having a child could be a great motivator for someone to find work and change their circumstances.'

'They should do it beforehand, not afterwards. Nothing is easier once you have a child to take into consideration.' Helena leaned forward. 'I'm not suggesting a baby is a reward for good behaviour. No one should have a family out of indolence or self-interest, that's all. Parenthood is the purest kind of self-sacrifice, an investment with no return except the satisfaction of seeing a human reach their full potential.'

'And what about drug users? Alcoholics? Should they have to use contraception to qualify for medical care?'

Helena shuddered. 'The pill seems to be the one drug it's impossible to persuade them to take. And then the babies are so damaged when they're born. Even if they're adopted into a loving home they can experience great difficulties.'

'So do you think long-term drug-abusers and alcoholics should be sterilised?'

'No, and I didn't say that.' She shook her head at him, mock-severe. 'People should be encouraged to make good decisions but as we all know some of them can't, or won't. I think it would be better if they didn't have children, but if they *do*, we can't expect them to take on that responsibility. These are people who can't even take responsibility for themselves. What matters then is the child. Their safety, their happiness, their health. I don't see what's controversial about wanting them to be brought up in a loving, caring environment where their emotional and spiritual needs will be met.'

'And you don't think that would happen if either or both parents had a history of drug abuse?'

'In very rare cases, maybe. *Very* rare. As I say so often, everyone is concerned about the rights of the parents to have children and keep them. *Someone* has to advocate for the children who have no voice.'

'And that's you.' Another, warmer smile.

He was definitely attractive, Helena decided. She bowed her head. 'I would rather not. I don't seek the limelight, believe me. But I feel a responsibility to speak up.'

'You've started making quite an income from it too, haven't you? Fees for speaking at conventions in the US, payment for articles, TV and radio appearances – they add up.'

Helena's face was burning. The glow of mild sexual interest had turned to a different kind of heat. 'What does that imply? And how do you know about it anyway?'

'Your accounts are filed with Companies House. I did a little digging.' He handed her a couple of pages, printouts from the internet. 'I was curious to know what kind of gatherings you were invited to attend.'

She glanced at them, saw a familiar logo and had to resist the urge to shut her eyes in horror. 'Look, I don't see how that's relevant to this interview. I am very professional about spreading this message. Various kinds of people are interested in what I have to say. I don't limit who can buy my book or read my newspaper articles or my blog so why should I pick and choose who gets to hear me speak?'

'Can you go into more detail about what kinds of people you're talking about?'

'Not really.' Helena was defiant now, the disaster unstoppable. 'That organisation that booked you to attend their annual convention, that first one I showed you – they present themselves as Christians with a particular commitment to the family. That fits in with your ethos, doesn't it?'

Helena found herself touching the cross that hung around her neck and took her hand away, irritated that he was getting under her skin. 'I mean, in part. But just because I speak somewhere that doesn't mean I agree wholly with the aims and beliefs of the organisers.'

'They're a far-right neo-Nazi interest group with links to the Ku Klux Klan. Did you know that before you went to Florida last year to speak to them about adoption and limiting procreation for what you called "undesirable parents"?'

'I don't want to talk about this.'

'I can understand that, but I'd love to know how it came about that you went there.'

'I had an email from the organiser.' Helena's face felt stiff. 'I get lots of emails. Lots of requests to speak. I turn down many of them.'

'But not this one.'

'No. It was a generous offer.' She tried to smile. 'Too generous, in retrospect. They were paying my expenses plus a fee. I – I should have looked into it more closely. But I'm not a politician, I don't have staff. I don't have an organisation behind me. It's just me, and I try to share information that I consider to be important and potentially lifesaving and if the audience wasn't my usual one, they were polite to me and didn't expect me to espouse their – er – odder beliefs.'

'So when did you realise about their – er – odder beliefs.'

She sat up straighter, irritated by the mimicry. 'When I arrived.'

'But you didn't think about pulling out of the convention.'

'I – no. I was a key speaker.' She swallowed. 'They had my picture on the advertising. I didn't feel I could let them down. And I knew what I had to say wasn't hateful. It was an opportunity to reach out to people. I'll talk to anyone. Maybe I helped to moderate their opinions, you never know.'

'They had your picture on the fliers. They also took your picture on stage.' The journalist handed her another printout, this time an image from a website. The reproduction was fuzzy but unfortunately all too recognisable: Helena in full cry with some dubious (at best) imagery behind her: a stylised tree that was the logo of the organisation, a banner that read RAHOWA and another with a sentence written down it, red on white, illegible thanks to the way the ink had bled into the paper. Deniable, Helena thought, although with her fair-haired beauty she had an Aryan-mother look to her that was at best unlucky in the context of the setting.

'Do you know what RAHOWA means?'

Helena prised open her lips, which had tightened. 'I do now, yes. I didn't at the time.'

'What is it?' He smiled again. 'I'll say it, shall I? Racial Holy War. That's a very well-known white supremacist concept. And what was on the banner on the left?'

'I – I didn't read it.'

'Hard to miss it, surely. It's a sentence known as the fourteen words.'

'I don't know anything about that.'

'It says, "We must secure the existence of our people and a future for white children". That didn't make you uncomfortable when you saw it was your backdrop?'

'I was just there to deliver my speech.'

'You're an intelligent woman. You must have known these people were racists and fascists. They were hardly hiding it.'

'As I said, I felt obliged to speak.' Helena squirmed. 'They had arranged my transport. I was depending on them. This place was in the middle of nowhere. A swamp, literally. I had no choice.'

'They forced you?'

'Not exactly. I didn't— I just thought it was best to get it over with as I'd agreed to do it, and then go. And that's what I did.'

'And took the fee.'

Helena opened her mouth to reply and then closed it. There was nothing – literally nothing – she could say to explain why she had kept the money that didn't sound selfish. But she had earned it, talking to those awful people in ridiculous humidity when she was tired from the flight and the long car journey with a vile, low-grade woman who had not stopped talking for even a minute, and it was a *lot* of money and the roof had been leaking in three places so they had needed it . . .

'What would you have done?' she said instead.

The reply was instant. 'Donated it to a suitable charity.'

'How do you know I didn't?'

'Did you?'

It was like tennis, back and forth, back and forth. Helena hesitated. To lie or not to lie. She couldn't prove she *had* but he couldn't prove she *hadn't*. Or maybe he could. She could be vague about which charity so he couldn't track it down but he was clearly thorough; he was capable of putting in the hours to prove her wrong.

The silence was heavy. Helena met the journalist's eyes, which were warm, inviting her to laugh, inviting her to admit that she'd been wrong but she would never do it again, she promised . . . Or maybe he liked her. Maybe he was getting a frisson out of this, a Cary Grant and Katharine Hepburn moment where arguing led to mutual admiration. Helena couldn't read him at all and for once she didn't know what to do. Flirt? Argue? Deny everything? Cry? All of the options sounded equally awful. For a mad moment she imagined herself leaning across, putting her hand on his knee.

Let's forget about the interview . . . let's settle this argument another way . . .

A clatter at the door made her jump and she exclaimed, irritated.

'Mummy . . .' The hoarse little voice, the aftermath of tonsillitis that had afflicted Rosalie since they came back from their holidays. It made her sound like a forty-a-day smoker.

'Not now, darling.' It came out high, a sing-song, tinny with insincerity.

The journalist tilted his head towards the door. 'Your daughter?'

'Mummy, Daddy told me to show you my story.' The handle of the door started to turn.

'Not *now*.' What was Bruce thinking? Helena jumped up and yanked the door open. Rosalie was holding a piece of paper with both hands, her expression wary, her body poised for flight. She looked terrified, which annoyed Helena even more. 'For God's sake, Rosalie, I told you not to bother me.'

'I just wanted to show you—'

'Yes, I know! And it can wait! It's hardly urgent. I'm busy.' Helena was shaking. It was a reaction to the stress of the interview more than anger. A bitter whiff made her clamp her arms against her sides; she had sweated through the top she was wearing. So unfair to be interrupted when she was trying to think, so impossible to come up with an explanation for what she had done . . .

Rosalie's eyes filled with tears. 'I'm sorry, Mummy. But you're always busy.'

Helena glanced back to see that the journalist had got to his feet, his face concerned. This was intolerable and it was all Bruce's fault for sending her to find him, and for what he had done with Sadie so they couldn't have a nanny any more, which was humiliating and enraging too. All of the bitterness and anger seemed to slosh around inside Helena's chest, splashing acid into her throat.

Ultimately, and because she was standing in front of Helena, it was Rosalie's fault for not taking no for an answer. Just for a moment, Helena's self-control slipped.

'Go to your room,' she hissed at her daughter, leaning forward. 'Go on. Get out of my sight. I can't speak to you now.'

'When – when can I come out?'

'When I say so and not before.' Helena swung the door closed, managing not to slam it but only just. She stood for a second with her back to the journalist before she turned to him, a smile pinned to her face. Perhaps he hadn't heard. 'Where were we?'

The journalist was looking shaken. 'That was your daughter?'

'Rosalie,' Helena confirmed. 'She's quite the little attention-seeker, I'm afraid. Sometimes she drives me *mad*. I've completely forgotten what we were talking about.'

'Your . . . adopted daughter?'

Helena's lip curled. 'What does that have to do with anything?'

Silence.

Time to take control, Helena decided. 'I'd love to pursue this discussion but we probably need to wind this conversation up, I'm afraid. As you can see, I'm very busy. I have three children to think about.'

'It just seems ironic, doesn't it. With her being adopted, and you not having any time for her.' He was pale with anger, she realised with a rush of fear.

'Please don't take her word for it. She has a very shaky grasp on reality.'

'Is that so?'

She made one last attempt to find common ground. 'Look, do you have kids?'

'I don't think that's relevant. We're talking about you.'

'Not any more.' Helena took a step closer to him. *Rat-faced little creep, opinionated pipsqueak*. He was *so* unappealing now that he was looking at her as if she was something he'd stepped in, with his pseudo-intellectual styling. 'The interview is over.'

'Can we arrange another meeting? I had a few more questions.'

'I'm sure you did.' She held the door open for him. 'You can email me, if anything comes up.'

He fumbled his recorder as he picked it up, swinging his leather satchel onto his shoulder, grabbing for the tweed jacket he'd hung on the back of his chair, flustered and furious. 'I don't know if I can do a good job, you see. If you don't address the issues, I mean. You might not be very happy with what I write.'

'That's a risk I'll have to take.' It didn't matter, Helena thought. The readers of that rag wouldn't be on her side anyway. Do-gooders never actually did good. They didn't *do* anything. They just patted themselves on the back for being wonderful.

'Could I go to the toilet before I leave?'

Pathetic. 'The *lavatory* is at the top of the stairs, on the right.'

'*Mum*. MUM. Ivo hit me.' Magnus, shouting for her from the garden. As if this horrible situation could get any worse.

'Er, thanks. Sorry. I won't be long.' The journalist scuttled past her.

'Fine.' She wanted to shove him up the stairs; Magnus was capable of saying literally anything about her, as long as it was an insult. 'Just . . . hurry up.'

Rosalie

The carpet in Rosalie's room had been thin and worn before she ever came to live with the Marshalls, and now it was patched with stains from various incidents that Rosalie classed as unimportant. Still, she preferred to lie on the floor instead of sitting upright on the bed. The floor was better: you could arrange your toys around you and they didn't fall over, and you could write in your notebook as if it was on a table whereas on the bed it was too soft or you had to write on your knee and either way, it was annoying. And she wasn't allowed to lie on the bed – her mother disapproved of it because it rumpled the covers.

And she wasn't supposed to be in her room most of the time anyway, which was all right because it wasn't a very nice room. It was small, with faded curtains that smelled musty, and there was only room for the bed and a chest of drawers that had a book shoved under one side to keep it from tipping sideways and a drawer that stuck an inch out and could never be closed properly. The walls were covered in white paper garlanded with green wreaths, and the curtains were pink, and the carpet had been a strange shade of grey before she had spilled things on it, so none of it had ever really gone together. The wallpaper was old and blotchy with brown stains like a fawn's coat but she liked tracing the garlands of leaves with a finger when she was waiting to feel tired enough to go to sleep. Her bedtime was earlier than she would have liked, but her mother was strict about it, *young girls need their sleep*, and it was useless to protest that she wasn't sleeping but lying in the half-light listening to life going on without her.

She wasn't allowed to put posters up, like the boys, and there wasn't room for a bookcase, but there was a shelf where she kept her dolls and she had five books on it: *Ballet Shoes* (which made her wish she had two sisters instead of brothers, and made her wish she liked ballet lessons but she did not), *Charlotte's Web* (which made her love spiders), *Harry Potter and the Philosopher's Stone* (which was hallowed twice over because Sadie had given it to her and she had read it and reread it until she knew it more or less off by heart), a book of Bible stories (either terrifying or boring or incomprehensible, with hideous illustrations that reminded her of rainy-day trudging around the National Gallery), and her book of Greek and Roman Mythology which was the second-best thing she had ever read after Harry Potter.

Rosalie flattened out her notebook. She was writing a new story, about the Minotaur, or really what had happened *after* the Minotaur when Theseus had forgotten to change his sails from black to white because he was so excited to go home and his father had thrown himself off a cliff, maddened by grief, assuming his son was dead. Rosalie tried to imagine her own father throwing himself off a cliff because he was maddened by grief, and could not. But she did know all about one small mistake made with the best of intentions, followed by disaster.

Rosalie put her head down on her arms, squeezing her eyes shut. That was what had happened on holidays, with Sadie. But she hadn't known when she took the picture of the swimming pool. She hadn't seen them. It was Magnus who had pointed it out.

And then everything had gone wrong.

'Rosalie?'

At the sound of the stranger's voice, Rosalie sat up, rubbing her eyes. He was leaning around the door of her room: the dark-haired man who had been talking to her mother.

'Are you all right?' He stepped inside the room and crouched in front of her, setting down his leather bag on the floor. 'What are you up to, Rosalie?'

'How do you know my name?' she asked, instead of answering him.

'Your mum told me.'

'Are you friends with her?'

He smiled. 'Is this your room? It's very nice.'

Rosalie decided instantly that he was another adult who told lies when it suited them because there was no world in which her bedroom could be described as 'very nice'.

'You like reading, do you? Do you like Harry Potter? He's great, isn't he.'

She nodded, although it wasn't really Harry Potter himself who was great as far as she could see. He was so slow to realise what he could do with his powers, which was frustrating when you knew exactly what you would do if someone came unexpectedly and told you you were *actually a wizard*.

'What are you doing? Writing?'

She put one hand across the page in front of her so he couldn't read it. 'It's not finished.'

'But you finished another one, didn't you, because you wanted to show it to your mum. I'd love to read it.' He had a soft voice and kind eyes behind his little round glasses but he smelled funny: a bitter kind of smoky smell that made Rosalie's nose sting.

118

'I'm actually a writer myself. It's my job. So I'd be really interested to see it, if you didn't mind showing it to me.'

She had been sitting on her story, flattening the page under her, and it was warm when she handed it to him. He sat on the edge of her bed and smiled at her before he started reading.

It was the first time anyone had read anything of Rosalie's the way she read books, concentrating on every word, line by line. He didn't say anything while he was reading, unlike her dad, and he didn't hand it back to her with a comment about her handwriting after a quick glance, unlike her mother, and Sadie had always sighed and said she didn't know anything about writing and she was too busy to stop and read something when she had so much to do and couldn't Rosalie see it was a bad time? But this man was really interested. He read it through, and then read it again, nodding this time.

'You did a really good job on this, Rosalie. A really good job. I like the way you described the snakes on her head hissing. And this line about Perseus being braver than handsome – I liked that a lot. You're a very good writer.'

Rosalie felt shy, and happy, and absolutely unable to say anything in response.

'I bet English is your favourite subject in school. It was always my favourite too. Which school do you go to?'

'What are you doing?' Her mother, in the doorway, staring at them. 'Rosalie, what have you said?'

'Nothing. She hasn't said anything. It was me.' He was standing now, the story crushed in one hand, forgotten. 'It's not her fault.'

'You shouldn't be in here. You shouldn't be talking to her. This is so inappropriate I can't even begin to— you know you shouldn't have done this. Get out of her room.' Rosalie's mother was shaking with anger, her eyes bright and hot.

The man picked up his bag and slid out of the room without speaking to Rosalie – not even goodbye. He had shoved her story into his jacket pocket but she was afraid to ask for it back.

It wasn't her fault – he had found her, he had sat on her bed, he had asked her questions and wanted to read her story.

And she had known it was wrong.

She had just wanted him to tell her she was special, that she was as different as she felt, that she had power no one knew about.

Her mother had shut the door but they were standing right outside and Rosalie could hear everything she was saying. The man was completely silent which was the right course of action, Rosalie had found, when her mother's voice was low and sharp and terrifying and her words came out so quickly they all ran together *well-you've-made-quite-the-mistake-here-haven't-you*.

'You obviously came here with an agenda. You want to write a profile of me that implies I'm not a good mother and I'm a white supremacist, and you're prepared to go and interrogate a *child* to get evidence against me. She's pathetically trusting – she wouldn't have the first idea why you were talking to her or that she should be wary of you. You took advantage of her and you know it was wrong.'

'I was just checking she was OK. She seemed upset.'

'As if it's your place to do that. As if it was appropriate for you to lie so you could make your way up here and find her where there was no adult supervision. I suppose I should be relieved that you were both fully clothed.'

'It wasn't like that!' His voice was louder now, angry. No one shouted back at Rosalie's mother. No one except Magnus, and he always regretted it in the end.

'Here's what's going to happen. If you write anything about me – anything at all, even the most basic and bland profile – I will publicise the fact that you approached a vulnerable child in her bedroom, alone, and lied to do so, and that you were interrupted before you could do anything else but that I have grave concerns about how safe you are around young children. You will lose your job and you won't find it easy to get another one. You might be able to damage my reputation but believe me, you'll regret it when you lose yours entirely.'

Silence. Rosalie held her breath.

'Now, when you leave, I'm going to call your editor and explain to them that you were rude and intrusive and behaved inappropriately. I think you'll find this interview simply won't have happened.'

'Helena—'

'Get out.'

Footsteps retreated from the door, moving down the hall, and then down the stairs, and the front door banged, and a car engine started just below Rosalie's window, and the car drove away. She went to the window to see it: small, red, gone.

When Rosalie turned back the door was open again, and her mother was standing there, watching her. Although she couldn't have put it into words, she had a child's instinctive and immediate understanding of what was happening: that her mother was angrier than she had ever been before, that she had not vented enough of that anger on the man to relieve her feelings, and that Rosalie had been bad enough to make whatever happened next justifiable.

Jay

'Magnus, come on. It's easy.'

Magnus, hanging upside down over the back of his chair, didn't answer.

'Magnus . . . your parents would be really cross with me if I let you skip this. They're paying me to teach you.'

'That's their choice.' Magnus straightened up, turned and plumped down on the seat. His face was glowing red and his hair was wild. 'And it's my choice not to bother trying to understand any of this.'

'You have to understand it. You're failing maths, your mum said.'

'Your mum said you were a fucking dork.'

'Shut up.' Jay said it too fast, giving away his real feelings. Better to have ignored it, obviously, but he'd reacted. Magnus

121

gave him a slow smile and he was able to translate what it meant: *I know what annoys you now*. 'Look, it's just a simple equation. It's like a puzzle. On one side, you've got the answer, here – thirty-nine. And therefore we know everything on *this* side adds up to thirty-nine even if some of the numbers are represented with an x.'

'We do know that but we don't give a fuck.'

'You will when you're back at school and your teacher finds out you didn't learn anything over the summer.'

Magnus opened his eyes very wide. 'It's not my fault. I had a shit tutor.'

'I'm not shit.' Jay kept his voice level this time. 'And I'm trying to teach you but you said yourself you're choosing not to understand any of it.'

The twelve-year-old's face contorted with rage. *'I don't care.'*

What Jay wanted to do was scream back *I don't care either*, throw the maths paper in the little turd's face and walk out, but he held on to his temper. He needed this job. In a month he would be packing his little car with everything he needed for university and driving up to Oxford, on his own for the first time in his life. It was strictly forbidden to work during term time, because the terms were only eight weeks long, and he understood that and respected it – he didn't want the distraction from his studying which he knew would be demanding but ultimately rewarding. Equally it was vital for him to have some money because his *fucking stepdad* had made it clear to him that he was on his own now that he was eighteen. Going to Oxford was his chance to reinvent himself, which had started already with the way that he'd told everyone he was to be known as Jay and had grown his hair out so it hung over his eyes and curled on his neck and the new trainers he'd bought at staggering expense with the first money he'd got from tutoring. He wasn't the old version of himself anymore, the wimp who got bullied in school, who was afraid to open his mouth most of the time. Oxford would be different, but he'd need money to enjoy it or he'd end up staying in his room on his own the whole time.

Like you do now.

No. Intolerable. He had to make this work.

Jay leaned back and crossed his ankle over his knee, folding his arms across his chest. It was a smug pose but he'd earned the right to it. *I am going to Oxford and you, Magnus, are going to get expelled.* 'You think you're never going to understand this so you're getting angry with me to distract me. It must make you feel really thick that you can't get the hang of it because it's easy, let me tell you.'

'I'm not thick.'

'I didn't say you were.'

'I'm telling my mum you called me thick.'

'You can if you want, but I didn't. I said you feel thick because you haven't understood this yet. But you can. Come on. Look at it with me. Thirty-nine. And then on the other side, we have a three outside the bracket and inside the bracket—'

'This is too hard.' Magnus was fidgeting, his face still brick red. He was on the verge of tears.

'It's so simple.' Jay stared at the paper in front of him, trying to find a way to explain it. $3(2x + 5) = 39$. He could read it like a sentence. As so often he found himself trying to communicate it to Magnus telepathically *(x equals 4 . . . x equals 4 . . .).* It would possibly be easier for them to learn telepathy than algebra.

'What are you doing?' Rosalie had wandered into Magnus's room, unobserved. She was standing beside them, staring at the page. 'What's that?'

'Maths,' he and Magnus said in unison, and Magnus added, 'It's too hard for you. You won't understand it.'

'Explain it.' She put a finger on the page, pointing. 'Why are there letters if it's maths?'

'Because it's evil.' Magnus sounded sulky, and tired.

'Time for a break.' Before the words had fully left Jay's mouth, Magnus had shot to his feet.

'Can I get a snack?'

'If your mum says it's OK. But you have to come back here in ten minutes.'

'Yep. I will.' He slammed out of the room and Jay listened to him rattling down the stairs, and the silence as he jumped the last few steps on each flight.

Ten minutes. That would be half an hour, if he was lucky. Magnus didn't wear a watch and also Jay wasn't totally sure the kid could tell the time. Meanwhile, here was Rosalie, puzzling over a sum that was far too advanced for her. She was wearing a pink cotton skirt and a white T-shirt that was a fraction too short. An inch of skin appeared when she leaned on the desk, one foot propped on the other.

'Explain it to me.'

'No. I'm bored with this one. Your brother doesn't understand it but I have to make him understand it.' Jay leaned on the desk, looking at Rosalie. She had long eyelashes and a pretty mouth, like an anime character. 'Why don't I tell you about the question I was asked in my interview for Oxford?'

She turned to look at him, interested. 'What's Oxford?'

'A university. I'm going to study there.' He took a clean sheet of paper and started drawing on it. 'Look, I was asked all about rectangles. Do you know what a rectangle is?'

'Yes. I'm nine.'

'Of course, sorry. I just – I didn't know . . .' It was happening again, as usual: why couldn't he ever manage to talk to people? What he meant and what he said seemed to be two completely different things.

'What about rectangles?' Rosalie asked and he recovered. She was actually *interested*.

'Well, the question was how many rectangles you can fit in a square so that you fill it. And the rectangles have to be a certain shape – the long side has to be twice as long as the short one. But they can be any size as long as they fill the square completely, with no overlapping.'

She considered it. 'What if you had a really big square and really tiny rectangles?'

124

'You'd fit lots in. The point is to work out if there are any numbers of rectangles that you *can't* fit in. Look . . .' He started drawing, the ruler making a silky sound as he swept it over the page. Outside someone was mowing a lawn, and downstairs there was banging on pipes, and in the garden Ivo was yelling, but it all receded. There was only him and the page and the girl leaning over his elbow, watching, her breathing tickling his skin. 'So one rectangle obviously won't fill the shape of a square. That means we can cross off one on our list of numbers.' He wrote it to one side of the page with a line through it.

'But two would?'

'Yes, definitely. Side by side. Or one under the other.' He drew a line and showed her how to measure the rectangles, one centimetre by two, in his neat little box. 'Now the rectangles can be any size as long as they're in the right shape, or what's called *proportion*.'

The hard crack of a bat hitting a cricket ball. A magpie scuffling in the gutter by his head. The whisper of his pen on the page, busily drawing, unfolding the explanation – the *beauty* of it – and he felt all over again the thrill of rightness when he had come up with the solution in his interview, after minutes of silence and panicked staring and trying to concentrate, to think, to remember . . .

'Because if you divide the rectangles in two, you get squares. And we know you can divide each of those squares into rectangles again, and our number is going up in threes because every time we divide one rectangle into four rectangles we go up three numbers because four minus one is three and we've already counted the one. So any number of rectangles we have can go up in threes.' He was talking faster, the words spilling out of his mouth, explaining it badly but striving to get to the point anyway. 'And then we know multiples of the numbers that work will also work, don't we? And we start seeing that we could go on forever.'

'I know. Like a pattern. It just goes on and on.' She pointed at the list of numbers he had been scrawling beside the shapes,

125

so he could tick them off or cross them out. 'Eight, nine, ten. All of them work – you checked them. And it goes up in threes. So there won't be any gaps after that and you only need to work it out for the little numbers.'

'No gaps,' he repeated. 'Rosalie, you are seriously clever, sweetheart. Did you know that?'

'I'm bored,' Rosalie said, and slid off the chair, pushing her hair off her face with the back of a hand that was none too clean.

'No, don't go. Stay here for a while.' He got to the door before her, just in time to slam it shut and hold it there. She was very small when he was standing up. Tiny. 'Stay here, little one. There's – there's something else I want to show you.'

Magnus

He was hungry and he did want a snack but after he'd eaten it he had no intention whatsoever of going back up to his bedroom under the eaves, where it was hot and airless, especially because that arsehole JV was there. 'Jay'. As if he was ever going to be anything other than JV. As if Jay was a cooler name than JV. What a twat. He had a rash of acne on his cheekbones and neck, the skin red and inflamed, and he smelled weird, a musty odour from his body overlaid with detergent and deodorant and whatever he put on his hair that made it look as if it would be hard to the touch – wax? Gel? Magnus wasn't clear on it and he certainly wasn't going to ask J fucking V.

(He kept an eye on the bathroom for the arrival of new products he could try but so far Ivo hadn't bothered with anything like that. Ivo kept his hair short. He wasn't interested in changing his image. He didn't need to. Sports Boy was a good enough look. Whereas Magnus was nothing. Xbox Master, maybe. Which in itself was typical, because he had asked for and wanted a PS2.)

Coming down the last flight of stairs to the ground floor, Magnus became aware of how much noise he was making. He took exaggerated care to avoid the creaking step three from the bottom, holding his breath as he lay down and slid over the final stairs, sprawling on the tiled floor by the telephone table. His mother was talking to someone in the sitting room and his father's study door was closed, but if the phone rang now, he was fucked. He commando-crawled through the hall to the kitchen, toeing the door shut behind him before he addressed himself to the fridge, and found nothing.

He grabbed a banana from the bowl on the table and sidled out through the back door. In the fresh air it was possible to shake off everything that had happened that day. Magnus ate the banana and dropped the skin behind a shrub, then set off at a run towards the river. The garden sloped downwards and he had a route that involved jumping off a small outcrop in the rockery and vaulting over a low wall. Ivo said you couldn't call it parkour but he was working up to doing a front flip off the rockery instead of just a jump. The trouble was that his front flip wasn't 100 per cent reliable and there had been a couple of times where he'd under-rotated and face-planted, or missed his landing and tipped backwards. That was OK when he was in the gym at school or on grass – painful, winding, but not *dangerous*. If he front-flipped off the rockery, though, he'd be landing on concrete with chunks of granite behind him. The potential for serious physical harm was too high even for Magnus. He gave a war cry and settled for jumping higher than ever before as he levered himself off the rocks and flew through the air—

'Magnus, you *dick*.'

He landed awkwardly, his ankle buckling under him and pain spearing up through his calf and knee. He crouched, clutching his leg, twisting to see Ivo marching towards him looking furious. 'What's your problem?'

'We're practising here, shithead. You almost got hit by a ball.'

'Why did you have to shout at me like that? My fucking ankle, Ivo.'

'You deserved it.' Ivo, ice cold, hands on his hips, looking down his nose at Magnus as usual. Magnus felt the rage begin to bubble up from the pit of his stomach.

'Fuck you. You don't own this garden.'

'One day I will. Mummy told me she's leaving the house to me.'

'She can't do that.'

'She doesn't want us to sell it. She wants it to stay in the family. That means it has to go to one of us and she picked me because I'm the oldest.'

'That's – that's not fair.' There was nothing Magnus could do about being born second, after all.

'I think it's sensible.' Ivo looked past him, his eyes sweeping over the back of the house with proprietorial pride, so he wasn't aware of Magnus shifting his position, preparing to attack. Under his palm a rock moved and his fingers closed around it without him even consciously deciding to pick it up.

'Magnus, no!' Nathaniel was already running towards them, full tilt, and Ivo made the mistake of looking at him instead of Magnus. He was completely unprepared when his brother reared up and bowled the rock at his head.

None of the three of them would ever forget the sound it made as it collided with Ivo's skull. He crumpled to the ground, his mouth open in a scream that was, at first, silent. For a moment Magnus stared down at him, petrified by horror. Then he ran, half stumbling, sobbing with dry eyes, until he reached the house where his father was standing at the back door, looking down the garden in bafflement. In broken sentences, Magnus managed to convey that an ambulance was needed, urgently, that it was Ivo who was injured, that Nathaniel was with him, but not that he, Magnus, was the one who was ultimately responsible.

'All right. Good lad.' As his father swung into action, Magnus felt himself sagging, physically, shock weighing on him like atmospheres of pressure when he'd been learning to scuba dive. He knew he should go back to Ivo but he slid into the house

128

instead, past his father in the hall on the phone, and started up the stairs.

The house was dark and cool after the glare of the garden. Magnus had his head down, so he didn't see Rosalie crossing the landing until he registered the movement of her bedroom door closing out of the corner of his eye.

'Sally?' It was the nickname he had for her. 'Are you OK?'

There was a pause before she answered. 'Yes.'

'Don't come downstairs, OK? Someone's hurt and it's not nice.'

'Who?'

'Ivo.'

Another pause. 'OK.'

Magnus was self-absorbed and spoilt and over-privileged to the point of being almost completely unbearable but he genuinely liked his little sister and even in the depths of his own misery he noticed two things: Rosalie had never, in the four years she'd lived with them, *not* wanted to be at the heart of whatever was going on in the house, and she sounded as if she was upset. He went over to the door and listened. 'Sally? Are you crying?'

''m OK.'

'You sure?'

'Yep.'

The door remained closed, the white paint uninformative. He touched the handle with a fingertip, but didn't try to turn it. 'Should I leave you alone?'

'Yes, please.'

With a shrug Magnus turned away; he had his own problems, after all.

Why had Rosalie been upset?

What was going to happen to him if Ivo was really hurt?

Could he go to prison?

He was so absorbed in his thoughts that he had genuinely forgotten JV would be in his bedroom, where he'd left him.

He was halfway across the room before he saw the older boy hunched over at the desk, his arm moving in an unmistakable rhythm.

'What the fuck – what are you doing?'

'It's not – it's not—' JV had half-risen and was trying to button his jeans. 'Look, please—'

'Fuck off.'

'Look, please, I was just bored. I was just—'

'Don't ever come back. I don't like you and I don't want you in my room ever again.' Magnus's voice had risen to a yell. He watched JV spilling pens, shoving papers into his bag and finally scuttling out of the room with his head down.

Magnus climbed onto his bed and pulled the duvet over his head. In the warm, cotton-clean dark, something broke inside him, and, quite suddenly, he burst into tears.

19

I stood in the doorway of the meeting room, staring at the piles of paper and lists and stacked boxes that had been my work for the last ten days.

'Coming or going?' Liv asked from behind me.

'Neither. I'm stuck here for good.'

She edged past me, carrying a mug. 'We're making progress.'

'If you say so.' Since the trip to see Bill Howlett, I had barely seen daylight. With Liv, I had worked through every single box methodically, cataloguing their contents and creating a single timeline of the events before and after Rosalie's disappearance. It was painstaking work, and frustrating, and I had fallen into doing it through a trap Una Burt had set in a briefing the day after Derwent and I had spoken to the retired superintendent.

'I'm just wondering,' she had said, 'about the value of one or two officers essentially reinvestigating Rosalie's disappearance, when we have an active murder investigation running alongside it that is complex enough to absorb your entire team.'

Derwent had looked at her quickly and I knew he heard it as a criticism of how he was handling the case, setting the narrative up for some future reckoning when it had gone wrong. I found myself leaping in.

'I think we'd be incredibly remiss not to start with Rosalie, especially when we have access to all of this material. Yes, it's a time-consuming task, but I don't know if anyone has ever gone through everything in one concentrated effort so it may be that we find details that turn out to be more significant than anyone thought up to now. I can't see how we can lose by putting one or two people on Rosalie. If it turns out we need to borrow more bodies for the main case, we can always put reading the material on hold.'

'Good point,' Burt said, with an air of satisfaction. 'It does seem like a critical aspect of the investigation if you put it in those terms. And I think because you have such a good understanding of its relevance to the overall investigation, Maeve, you should take charge of it.'

Derwent made a small movement that might have been a protest, but when Una turned to look at him his face was completely impassive. I matched it as best I could, and so all the joy that Una got out of us was a nod of agreement each. But it had condemned me to endless days spent leafing through the notes and records that Bruce Marshall had so carefully preserved. I was aware of the real action of the investigation taking place elsewhere as the forensic reports came in (the bloodied material in the second bedroom had once been a pale pink cushion and would have made an excellent silencer; there hadn't been any usable DNA recovered from the second bedroom; the post-mortems had confirmed the causes of death and that the two victims had been drugged with a chemical mixture that bore some relation to chloroform, and that, apart from some test results that were still to come, was that). Derwent was even more absent than before: a figure in the distance, and at briefings, and a voice on the phone checking, irritably, to see if I had finished with the boxes yet. When I arrived at work, he was already there, and when I left his jacket still hung on the back of his chair, but I rarely spoke to him. So much for working together. From what I saw of him, he looked neither well nor happy, and I had too much time to think about it as I ploughed through witness statements and diaries and photographs and newsprint. Now and then, when I noticed Una Burt pausing to watch me and Liv working together, it was hard not to read smugness into her expression.

I dropped a file back into its box and carried it across the room to the wall of boxes we had looked at already. I pushed the box into place at the top of one stack and wiped my hands on the seat of my trousers, regretting it instantly. 'Did that leave a mark?'

'No one will notice.'

'Someone always notices.'

From the door, Derwent drawled, 'Are we dusting your arse for prints, Maeve?'

'The boxes just breathe dirt, as you'd know if you'd spent any time in here over the last week and a half.' I twisted to see the damage and swiped at the fabric, irritated. 'What do you want?'

'I want to see if you've finished this wild goose chase yet. I know you think you're going to find her even though better police than you tried and failed, but can we just accept the trail has gone cold? The chances of solving this mystery are nil and it's a massive distraction from the actual case.'

I looked at him, surprised at his tone. It was flat, entirely lacking in his usual mischief. 'You agreed this was important.'

'I didn't disagree.'

'That's a fine distinction.'

He was staring at the whiteboard. It contained a list of anyone, no matter how obscure, who had contact with the family that summer, and a timeline we had rewritten a hundred times as new nuggets of information appeared. The list of names was long: workmen, students, a cleaner, colleagues of Bruce's, friends of the family – everyone who had been caught up in the hurricane of the original investigation.

Derwent folded his arms with a wince, as if his shoulder or back was hurting. He had cut himself shaving, I noticed, which was unlike him: a straight graze just above his collar that had bled into the pristine whiteness of what looked like a new shirt. The folds and creases down the cotton were unmistakable: straight out of the packet.

'Maybe I should go.' Liv was edging towards the door.

'Stay,' we said in unison, and she stopped, but she was still poised for flight. Derwent had brought an atmosphere of jangling tension with him when he walked in, and Liv wasn't a fan of confrontations.

'What if this has nothing to do with the Marshalls being killed? It's been sixteen years since Rosalie disappeared. Why kill them now if it has to do with their missing daughter?'

'Why bother at all if it's not?' I countered. 'They were no threat to anyone.'

'That we know of.' Derwent closed his eyes briefly, as if he was exhausted. 'But people kill for lots of reasons. What if it was the carer?'

'*Sabiha?* I can't really imagine—'

'Or one of the kids. Magnus. He seems like a dickhead.'

'Doesn't make him a murderer.' I hesitated. 'Look, do you want to sit down? You look shattered.'

'I'd feel OK if we were making any progress. This investigation is dead in the water.'

I nodded. 'Being frustrated makes everything worse.'

'Tell him about the new lead.'

He looked around at Liv, surprised. 'Don't tell me you've actually found something.'

I tapped the board. 'This guy. Paul Lavender. He's a journalist who did an interview with Helena shortly before Rosalie disappeared. He was never interviewed by the police in any of the investigations. We only know about him because Bruce mentioned him to a writer when she took him out to lunch – I think she charmed his socks off and he gave her lots of details that don't appear anywhere else in the files. But he still scared her publisher into dropping the book she proposed to write about Rosalie. He paid her a kill fee as compensation and in return she typed up her notes with her impressions of him, which were on the flattering side, and gave it to him. She wrote, "In case this is helpful" across the top of it, and signed it with a kiss.'

'Very friendly,' Liv observed drily.

'Well, we know Bruce was a flirt. I imagine she played on that. It's what I would have done.'

'No surprises there,' Derwent said, not looking at me. 'So what's the significance of this Paul Lavender?'

'He was interviewing Helena for a magazine feature, and it didn't go well. Bruce said the interview never appeared in the end.'

'Maybe they didn't want to run it after Rosalie disappeared.'

'You'd think it would be more newsworthy, though. There were loads of profiles of her in the press but nothing by Paul Lavender.' The profiles had been a large part of the initial coverage of Rosalie's disappearance. Helena, even as a desperate mother, did not come across well.

'Why didn't Helena mention this to the police?'

'That's what I'm wondering too. It feels significant. I'm just about to look for him.'

'Maybe they forgot about him.'

'That list on the board is mainly from Helena and Bruce. It's incredibly comprehensive. They even included the men who delivered a new sofa to the house and probably spent less than ten minutes inside it. I don't believe that Helena would have forgotten an entire one-on-one interview – which never appeared in print, by the way. She was hiding something.'

'I'll come with you,' Derwent said as if he was conferring an enormous honour on me, and Liv sighed.

'I'm never going to get out of this room.'

20

Paul Lavender was living in Brighton, in a terraced house overlooking a square. The house had seen better days. It had been painted white, but not recently, and the white was stained with brown where the balconies had corroded. The stucco looked as if it had the structural integrity of a sugar mouse and might dissolve at any moment in the sea air. The house had four floors, all divided into flats, and Paul Lavender, inevitably, lived in the attic.

'Why,' I said plaintively, 'is it always the top?'

'Because we need the exercise after the drive.' Derwent took the stairs two at a time and I followed more slowly.

Lavender had agreed to speak to us when I tracked him down through LinkedIn, sounding, if anything, pleased. I identified him as the kind of man who likes talking about himself, regardless of the circumstances. I had seen the headshot he used for his journalism, a moody black-and-white picture of him frowning into the middle distance, his hair artfully dishevelled and his jaw squared. It was not the choice of someone who had a low opinion of himself.

The years had not been kind to Paul Lavender. He had softened and faded: his features were blurred by the weight that had crept on. The sparse beard that was designed to hide a second chin drew attention to it instead, while the hair that had tumbled over his forehead was now scraped back into a ponytail. I thought very few men could carry off a ponytail with any conviction, and Paul Lavender was not one of them.

'Come in, come in. Oh, you're both so tall. Mind your heads, won't you? The ceilings . . .'

136

The flat was in the eaves, so the ceiling sloped dramatically from right to left across his living room. It meant that much of the living room was more or less unusable, unless you were prepared to crouch. There were books everywhere, particularly around the desk that was jammed against a dormer window with a view over the square. An old computer squatted on the desk, which was covered in papers. The wall was stained around the windows, as if they leaked, and the kitchen was none too clean, with dirty plates piled in the sink. The air in the flat had a chemical, fruity smell which I traced to the vape that lay beside his computer. He noticed me looking at it.

'You've spotted my vice immediately. It's the best I can do, as I tell my doctor. I was a smoker for twenty years so it's a big improvement on the old days. Sit, sit.'

We watched from the sofa as Paul made his way to the chair in front of the desk. He spun it round and sat in it, moving with the kind of over-emphatic posturing that gives away the person is consumed with thinking about how they look: *see how I turn the chair with a flourish, watch as I sit down with casual grace and throw one leg over the other because I am relaxed, above all, and a little bit amused at this interruption to my day, but prepared to be very helpful . . .*

'Thank you for taking the time to speak to us. We'll try not to keep you too long.' Derwent was sounding hesitant, which was unlike him, but Paul Lavender beamed.

'Not at all, not at all. This isn't one of my teaching days so I have plenty of time for you.' He waved a hand, expansive. 'Ask me whatever you like.'

'You aren't a journalist any more? You're a teacher?'

'English as a foreign language.' He shrugged at me. 'It's a good gig – plenty of students around here. I turn work away.'

Yes, you look as if you're flush with cash. I kept the thought off my face and smiled.

'Don't you miss writing?'

'Journalism is a dying profession. No one wants to pay for words any more. If you don't want to write for free someone

137

else will.' He stretched, propping his hands behind his head. 'Now, this was about Rosalie Marshall, you said?'

Derwent made a big show of checking his notebook. 'You haven't been interviewed about her before, have you? They missed you in the original investigation.'

'I assume so. Not that there was any reason to interview me about her at the time. Or now, really. It's a pure coincidence that I was there at all.'

'Why were you there?'

'I was interviewing Helena Marshall. I couldn't believe it when I saw she was dead. Terrible.'

'What date was the interview?'

'Now, I looked this up.' He spun on the chair and pawed through the papers on his desk. 'It was the ninth of August. A Monday. And it was in the afternoon, as I recall.'

Eight days before Rosalie disappeared.

'Tell us what happened.'

He laughed. 'Nothing happened. I interviewed her and drove home in my little car. I don't have a car these days – I sold it. I don't really need one in Brighton. Everything is walking distance.'

'What was your impression of Helena Marshall?' I asked.

'Not my type.' He grinned at me. 'Sorry, sweets, but it's natural. That's the first thing I always think when I meet a woman. Yes or no.'

'So you didn't want to sleep with her,' Derwent said evenly, heading off the question of which category I might fall into. 'What else?'

'Helena was a bit of a ballbreaker despite the pretty face. She had one idea, which was to hammer home this notion that adoption was the answer to all of society's ills, as long as it involved taking babies away from unfit mothers and giving them to nice decent middle-class families who would bring the baby up in a Christian environment, with the right values and opportunities. I don't know which came first, adopting a kid or this idea, but it was the way she'd raised her profile from dolly bird to talking head. Being cynical, I suspect she wanted attention and Rosalie was the best way to get it. I flirted with her a bit, which she liked, and then when I'd softened her up I gave her a hard time, which she didn't. We'd found out that she was a headline speaker at a white supremacist rally in Florida the previous year. She was really angry that I'd found out about the rally, but she couldn't deny it.'

'Was she a white supremacist?' I asked.

'Probably not. She was OK with taking their money, though.' He sighed. 'I miss doing that job, you know. I miss that moment where you get someone in a corner and they can't slide away, and all they can do is get angry with you but you've got them by the throat so they have to tell the truth. You must know what I mean.'

I smiled blandly. 'Did she get angry with you?'

He grinned. 'That meant I was doing my job properly, so I didn't mind.'

'It sounds as if you had her on the ropes,' Derwent said. 'But the interview never appeared, did it?'

'Well, no. But that was the timing. The girl disappeared – what – a week later? It wasn't really appropriate at that stage for me to go after Helena Marshall for her activism. She wasn't a popular person but we'd have been lynched if we published a hit piece. That changed once people started talking about whether the Marshalls had been involved in their daughter's disappearance, but by then the moment had passed.' He spread his hands with a flourish. 'Story of my life.'

'And you couldn't sell it anywhere else?'

'I wasn't allowed to. Not the done thing, you know. The commission had come to me through a magazine and they were the ones who'd hunted out the information about the rally in Florida. I wanted to keep in with my editor there because it was a good source of work. That was worth more to me than getting paid a few quid for an article somewhere else. It was just a wasted day, you know? I filed the notes away and got on with my life.'

'Do you still have the notes?'

'Somewhere.' He waved a hand at the box files and books that filled the living room. 'I never throw anything out.'

'Could you find it for us?'

He pursed his lips. 'I'll have a go. See what I can do. It'll take a while, though. I can send you anything I find, how's that.'

'I'd prefer you to look now.' Derwent sounded much more forceful, all of a sudden, and I saw the other man blink at the change of tone.

'Well. I'll try. Is that everything?'

'Not quite. I can see why Helena would have wanted the interview to go away,' I said. 'But you were a top journalist. An investigative reporter with a good reputation. You could easily have sold a colour piece about the Marshalls in the aftermath of Rosalie's disappearance, and even if you didn't mention the rally specifically you could have hinted at it. There would have been a way around it.'

'I didn't want to, all right? Maybe I felt sorry for them. Maybe I wanted to leave them alone.' He gave me his crooked smile. 'People think journalists are all immoral but we're people. We can be kind.'

'Of course,' Derwent said politely. 'So can we.'

He laughed. 'Yes, you'd know. You get a bad rap too. But so far, one interviewer to another, I'm impressed. This isn't too painful at all.'

'And we're nearly done.' Derwent was looking at his notes. 'Just thinking about that day in August, did you happen to see any other members of the family when you were in the house?'

He was shaking his head. 'Not that I recall.'

'You didn't see Rosalie?'

'I was focused on Helena.' He held up his hands a few inches apart, palms facing one another, and moved them away from his face. 'Tunnel vision. Eyes on the prize. I assumed that the reason the police didn't want to talk to me at the time was that I hadn't seen anyone else when I was in the house. Just Helena, for coffee and a bit of an argy-bargy. Then I made my excuses and left.'

'And that was it?'

'That was it,' he confirmed. 'Now, if there's nothing else . . .'

'Nothing much,' I said. 'But what you were saying earlier, about enjoying getting someone in a corner and making them tell the truth . . .' I smiled again. 'I like that too.'

'Oh yes?' He swivelled the chair so he was facing me, striking an attitude with an index finger propped against his temple, amused. His eyes were warm, inviting a moment of understanding. I could see how he had appealed to Helena Marshall, once upon a time.

'We spoke to your editor. The one who spiked the article.'

Instantly, he flushed an ugly red. 'What – how did you know who I was writing it for?'

'Good police work. Not mine. A colleague tracked her down.' Liv had followed the trail like a terrier until she had run the editor to earth. 'She told us about the incident with Rosalie.'

'With . . . God, you can't think that I—' He caught himself, stopped. 'You've got no evidence of any wrongdoing on my part.'

'Just her account.'

'Which is hearsay.' He looked from me to Derwent. 'And Helena Marshall is dead.'

'That's right.' Derwent sounded grim, all the diffidence gone from his manner, leaving cold disapproval. 'All we can say for sure is that you lied to us about not meeting Rosalie when you were in the house. In fact, you were alone with her for an unknown period of time, in her bedroom, eight days before she disappeared, and no one knows what you did while you were there.'

21

By mutual consent we sat in silence for a minute before setting off to London, allowing the echoes of Paul Lavender's hysterical pleading to fade. He had begged, and wept, and bellowed at the top of his voice about entrapment. Then, with great reluctance, he went back over the events of that day and this time described the way Helena had spoken to Rosalie.

'She was taking out her frustration on the child. I felt – I felt terrible.' He sucked on his vape desperately. A sweetish cloud billowed out of it. Derwent leaned over to open a window.

'The little girl was so small, I remember. Tiny and – and fragile. I just remember Helena looming over her like a – like a breaking wave that was going to smash her to bits. It got to me, you know? And if she was like that in front of me – a stranger, and a journalist at that – what was she like the rest of the time?'

'Did you have the impression it was how she always behaved towards Rosalie?'

'I don't know.' His hands were shaking. 'I mean, yes. Because she was scared of Helena. She looked terrified before Helena said anything to her, and she didn't look surprised when it all went wrong. I'm not just saying that, you know, because it's any benefit to me. I'm trying to help you. I always thought that Helena was the most likely suspect for what happened to Rosalie. If she lost her temper and lashed out and hurt her or killed her by accident, well, the river was right there.'

'But you didn't feel you should come forward when the original investigation was going on?' Derwent's words were clipped.

'I was afraid to get drawn in. A young man, not married. And I had been in Rosalie's room. I knew if I pointed the finger at Helena, she would point straight back at me, and I thought I'd come off worse.' He laughed, bitterly. 'And I was right.'

'There might have been evidence that could have helped you at the time,' Derwent said. 'If you'd come forward. Forensics to corroborate your story.'

'Oh yes. I'm sure it would have worked out very well for me.' He clutched his head, half in tears again. 'All because I wanted to check the little girl was all right. It was a moment of madness, you know? A compulsion. She looked hopeless. Bleak. As if there was no one she could rely on. I thought it would be wrong to turn my back on her. I thought I could make a difference to her. I asked to use the toilet and when I was upstairs, on my own, I went for a bit of a wander to see if I could find her.'

'What happened next?' I asked. 'In your version of events.'

'Oh, so you have a version already? From Helena?' He sucked on the vape again. 'It's hard to contradict a dead woman, isn't it?'

'Try.' Derwent sounded as if his well of patience had run dry some time before.

'I just talked to her.' He rubbed his eyes with the heels of his hands. 'I found her bedroom – which was tiny, by the way, and bleak as fuck. She was on the floor, writing. I asked her about the story she'd been trying to show her mother, and I read it, and it was decent, of its type. I wasn't expecting much but it was genuinely good. I was just chatting to her, you know? Grown-up to kid. What's your favourite subject, that kind of thing. And then Helena flung open the door and started acting as if I'd been trying to *seduce* her. I don't know which of us was more scared, me or the little one. It was nothing. Absolutely nothing. Helena saw an opportunity to shut me up and she took it and that's the truth of it.'

He had given us his notes (which he'd found immediately; so much for not being sure where they were) and spent another twenty minutes pleading with us to understand his position and why he hadn't come forward before. When it became clear that he was just going to keep repeating himself until we left, Derwent stood up.

'Don't go anywhere, Mr Lavender. If you disappear, I'll have no hesitation in using every means at my disposal to hunt you down, and I will take it as an admission of your guilt. You know how you'd look to a jury, don't you? You've got a job that brings you in regular contact with young people. You live alone. You've never married. It all adds up, doesn't it?'

'It's not fair. It's not fair.' Lavender was grizzling like a giant baby.

'We'll be in touch.' It sounded like a threat, and Derwent knew it.

Now, with the quiet of the car ringing in our ears, he sighed. 'Do you think Paul Lavender would refer to that little scene as "a bit of an argy-bargy"?'

I started to laugh. 'Absolutely.'

'I feel traumatised.' Derwent slid down in his seat. 'We didn't even go in all that hard.'

'No, but it was useful.' I adjusted the rear-view mirror, pleased to be getting to drive for a change. 'We need to speak to the nanny. She was the other person who said Helena was abusive.'

'I told you the nanny was key. I said that from the start.'

'And no one's got hold of her yet? Well, let's see if Liv can track her down.'

'She will. And when she does, she needs to find out if Sadie's still fit.'

'I'll make sure that's the first question she asks.'

He yawned. 'Did you believe Lavender's version of events?'

'Not sure.'

'No. Me neither.' A pause. 'I might have a nap.'

'Go for it.'

He folded his arms, closed his eyes and was asleep in seconds, his breathing regular and slow. Exhausted, I thought, glancing at him from time to time as I drove out of Brighton and onto the motorway. There were blue shadows under his eyes and the cut on his neck looked sore. It wasn't like him to check out like that, not when we'd just been interviewing a suspect. He should have been full of plans for the next stage of the investigation.

It wasn't until we were well into London and stopped at a traffic light that he stirred, sitting up and looking around him to get his bearings.

'Oh. Sorry. I slept for longer than I thought I would.'

'Don't worry. It's fine. You were tired.'

'Yeah.' He yawned. 'Thanks.'

Now or never.

'Is everything all right, Josh?' I was aware of a sudden stillness on the other side of the car, sleepy relaxation tightening into something altogether more wary.

'Why wouldn't it be?'

'Answering a question with a question. I think I taught you that technique.' I was keeping my tone light.

Silence.

I braced myself. 'So when were you going to admit that she kicked you out?'

'What are you talking about?'

'You haven't been home, Josh. You're in the office every morning when I get there and you disappear in the evenings when I'm leaving but you don't go home. You're wearing the same two ties in rotation and they don't look great on it. That's a new shirt, straight out of the packet, and you got blood on the collar this morning when you put it on after shaving, but you're still wearing it. The Josh Derwent I know would have washed and ironed it before he ever wore it, and he certainly wouldn't have spent the whole day with a dirty mark on his shirt.'

'Maybe I didn't notice.'

'As if.' I glanced across at him. 'The only way you'd be looking like this is if you had no choice.'

He slumped in his seat. 'Fuck. Does everyone know?'

'Nope. But you shouldn't have tried to pretend everything was all right with me. You should have known I'd spot it.'

'I thought you might not.'

'I'd have noticed sooner if I hadn't been shut in the office with Liv.' A beat as the full meaning of that sank in. 'You didn't want me around in case I realised what was going on.'

'You were doing useful work.'

'You couldn't have known that.' I kept my eyes fixed on the road. 'All to avoid what? My support?'

'Don't.'

'I just want to help,' I said, and I did, but I also desperately wanted to know what was going on. 'When did it happen?'

'A week ago.'

'You've been staying in the office for a *week*? Why didn't you stay in a hotel?'

'Because I thought I'd convince her to change her mind.' He propped his elbow on the door and squeezed the bridge of his nose as if he had a headache. 'Sounds pathetic, doesn't it?'

'There's nothing pathetic about wanting to be at home. And Thomas—'

'Yeah, and Thomas.' Derwent swallowed. 'It's not fun.'

'I can imagine.' I let the silence play out so the only sound was the car's engine and the swish of tyres on the road. 'So what happened?'

'She gave me an ultimatum about something—' he broke off to glower a warning— 'and I'm not telling you what it was. If I said no, she wouldn't let me see her and Thomas, let alone live with them. I said no. She left a bag on the doorstep with some clothes in it and locked me out.'

'I can't imagine you taking that on the chin. Did you try to get in?'

'No. I tried to talk to her. She called 999.' I risked a fleeting look in his direction and caught the bleak expression on his face as he remembered it. 'They turned up just as I was leaving.'

My hands were cold on the steering wheel. 'Did you get arrested?'

'No. They could see I was about to go when they got there, so that helped, and I cooperated fully. I hadn't even got angry with her. I just wanted her to listen to me.' He let his head fall back against the headrest. 'I didn't make the mistake of pulling out the warrant card either. The trouble is, the officers interviewed her after I left and she said I threatened her so it was recorded as a domestic. I've had Burt asking me about it already.'

'Did you threaten her?' I had to know.

'Of course not.'

'Did Melissa think you were going to hurt her?'

'I can't tell you what she thought.' I could feel that his eyes were fixed on my face. 'I would never hurt her. She knows that. And so should you.'

'She ran away from her ex-husband because he was violent, so I suppose she's likely to be scared easily.'

'You still have scars from your last boyfriend,' Derwent said slowly, 'and you know me pretty well. Would you be scared?'

'No.' No hesitation, no doubts. I trusted him completely.

'Well, that's something.' He said it under his breath. I was thinking through the situation.

'So until you give her what she wants, you aren't going to have anywhere to live.'

'It doesn't seem so. And I'm still not telling you what she wants. It's not an option. Leave it at that.'

There was no point in speculating. I focused on the practicalities instead.

'You can't live in the office. Come and stay in the flat.'

'With you? Absolutely not.'

'Come on, Josh. We've lived together before, and it was fine. You'd have to sleep on the sofa, but you have a big investigation to run – the last thing you need is more stress because you don't have anywhere to wash your pants.'

He laughed at that, a little, and then sighed. 'This isn't what I wanted, Maeve.'

'I know,' I said, without really knowing what he meant. 'But it'll do, for now.'

22

I had expected that Derwent and I would fall into the easy companionship we had enjoyed the previous summer when we had pretended to be a couple. But that had been his idea – I was the one who had needed to be convinced. The current situation was the opposite.

Derwent said almost nothing the whole way back to the office and avoided me for the remainder of the working day. I waited until the office was more or less empty before I tried to speak to him; I didn't want an interested audience. He wasn't at his desk. I scouted around meeting rooms and corridors until I ran him to earth in the kitchen, where he was staring blankly at the rota for cleaning out the fridge.

'It's late. Ready to go?'

He looked at his watch, distracted. 'Go without me. I've got stuff to do here.'

'Like what? You're just standing in the kitchen. It's hardly productive.'

He leaned against the worktop and folded his arms, the picture of unflappable calm. 'I'm making tea.'

'With what? The power of your mind? No mug, no tea bag.' I picked up the kettle and shook it. 'Empty. You need a better cover story.'

'Evidently.' He pulled a face, which was apparently meant to convey *you-got-me* and *sorry* and *I'm-still-not-budging*.

'Anyone would think you were hiding in here,' I said coolly.

He raised his eyebrows. 'From you?'

'Are you?'

'Obviously not.'

I sighed. 'Come on, Josh. You must have spent enough time in the office over the past few days to last you a lifetime. You can always bring your laptop back with you. I promise I won't get in the way.'

'You are literally getting in the way now. You're standing between me and my desk.'

'Yes, and I'm not moving until you agree to get out of here.'

'For God's sake . . .' But he gathered his things and followed me to the car park without further protest.

He was a tense, brooding presence beside me on the journey back, clearly miserable. It felt strangely intimate to walk to the flat side by side, like a couple, his bag knocking against my leg once so he swapped it to the other hand with a muttered apology. All of this could have been avoided if I had let him make his own way back from work, I reminded myself. He had known it was going to be awkward, even if I hadn't had the wit to realise it.

There was also the question of how I'd left the flat that morning. I was certain there were bras and knickers drying in the bathroom, and unwashed dishes in the sink. He might not comment on the underwear but he would certainly notice it, and he would never forgive the washing-up.

'I was thinking . . .' he took a step back, just as I slid the key into the door. 'I should go and get some food, for dinner. I bet you don't have anything worth eating.'

I hesitated, trying to remember the contents of the fridge. 'We could get a takeaway.'

'Kerrigan cuisine.'

'I cook. Sometimes.' *And sometimes I eat toast for dinner.*

'You like salmon, don't you?' He put his bag down beside me. 'Look, I'll be ten minutes. Shove that bag in the hall. Don't bother carrying it upstairs. I'll do it when I get back.'

'I can manage.'

'But I said to leave it.' He turned and walked away, and he was already pulling his phone out of his pocket as he disappeared from view. A last-ditch attempt to persuade Melissa to give in, I guessed.

I miss you. Please let me come home.

I squared my shoulders. So I was second-best, and a very distant second-best at that. What on earth had I expected?

Nothing, came the small, dull reply. I tidied up, and laid out a duvet and pillows on the sofa, and reminded myself more than once that I was helping out a friend and colleague, no more, no less.

When the friend and colleague returned with a full shopping bag, he cooked dinner and we ate it and then he stretched.

'I'm shattered.'

'Me too. I was going to go to bed early.' I would have to, if he wanted to go to sleep. The flat was much smaller than the house we had shared. If he was sleeping in the living room, I was limited to the very tiny kitchen and bathroom and my bedroom.

'Sounds like a good idea.' He was gathering plates and I put out a hand to stop him.

'I'll tidy up.'

'No, I'll see to it. You have first crack at the bathroom.'

I spent a scant ten minutes in the bathroom, including getting changed into my night clothes, then tapped on the closed living room door. 'I'm finished.'

'Thanks. Goodnight.' No sound of him coming to say it to my cleansed and moisturised face. I went slowly down the hall to my room and shut my door, knowing I would lie in bed listening to every noise he made until he finally went to sleep.

In the morning I felt a lot better, as you tend to after several extra hours of rest, even if you didn't want them. The living room door was still closed when I came out of my room. I went into the kitchen, which was flooded with sunlight, and got out two mugs, humming to myself as I put the radio on. I listened to the second half of a grim news report on asylum seekers who were risking their lives and their children to get to the UK. The journalist was sympathetic, the politician she interviewed less so. Not our responsibility, was his message. We had enough problems without inviting more to join us. It made me think of my parents, and how they had kept a low profile when they arrived in England first, when an Irish accent could trigger anger and fear. Anyone could be arrested on the off-chance they were connected with the IRA. They had walked a careful line, keeping to themselves, safe within the Irish community. It hadn't been easy.

The sound of Derwent's voice in the sitting room interrupted my train of thought. I listened for a couple of minutes while I finished making the tea: he was telling Bill Howlett about our interview with Paul Lavender. I went in when he was finished and found him standing by the window, fully dressed. The duvet and pillow were neatly stacked on the sofa. He turned and gave me a swift, assessing look, taking in every detail of the oversized T-shirt I had thrown on as nightwear without thinking about how it might look in the morning.

Focus, Maeve.

I handed Derwent his tea. 'What did Bill Howlett say about Paul Lavender?'

'He'd never heard of him. Helena never mentioned him. Bill was livid. I can't say I blame him. He's spent sixteen years trying to solve this while missing a piece of the puzzle.'

'This is why it's worth going back to what happened when Rosalie disappeared,' I said. 'Things change. People decide to talk about things they didn't want to talk about before.'

'I've never disagreed about that. It still doesn't mean it's relevant to the Marshalls' murders.' Derwent flipped his phone over a couple of times, thinking. 'Howlett's sure we're going to find out what happened to Rosalie.'

'Isn't that what he wants?'

Derwent's mouth twitched. 'I think there's a part of him that doesn't want someone else to succeed where he failed. Having said that, he was keen to help. He suggested finding out what car Lavender drove. There was that vehicle outside the house on numerous occasions in the week before Rosalie's disappearance

– no one got the plates, unfortunately. He suggested that could have been Lavender. It might help us to put pressure on him if we can put him in the area when there was no reason for him to be there.'

'I'll get Colin Vale onto it. Did Howlett suggest anything else?'

'Talking to the neighbours at the time. They were a close-knit bunch.'

'We can cross Dennis Hood off the list, anyway. We're ahead of the game there.'

Derwent's phone purred and he glanced at the screen, then answered it quickly. He stood straighter, obviously pleased. Melissa, I assumed.

'Hey. How are you?' As happy as he ever sounded. This was not going to be tolerable, I registered, and began to retreat. He looked at me, mouthing 'wait'.

'Did you? And how was that?' A smile warmed his voice. 'Nothing would surprise me, Luke.'

Luke. Derwent's long-lost son. It shouldn't have made any difference to me but it did. He was silent, listening. I tried to read his expression.

'Take it slowly. Either you want her or you don't, and if you do it's worth the wait. Nothing worth having comes easy.' A laugh. 'So I should hope. Yes, definitely still on for Saturday. See you then.' He ended the call.

'What's on Saturday?'

'Football. Five a side.' He looked at me sheepishly. 'I'd forgotten how much I enjoy playing football until last summer. Luke plays every week. I don't always.'

'Sounds like a good way to get to spend time together.'

'That's what *I* think.' And Melissa didn't. He didn't have to say it; I knew.

'Were you giving him relationship advice?'

He looked down, suddenly disconcerted. 'I'm the expert, as far as him and his friends are concerned.'

'Well, you've certainly put in the time over the years.'

'Maeve . . .'

'Plenty of experience, good and bad. And ugly, from what I've heard.'

'I can make you stop talking, you know,' he said calmly. 'I've done it before.'

He had and I remembered how. He was one step away from me; it would be the work of seconds for him to take hold of me and put his mouth on mine. I blushed and I knew he'd noticed it, because he turned away.

'I'm glad you have him,' I said quickly, more or less at random. 'Luke really loves you.'

'Why wouldn't he?' Derwent said, with a hint of the old swagger. I was almost glad to see it.

23

I spent the morning tracking down the Marshalls' old neighbours and reading up about the mysterious car. After a few hours I went to find Derwent, who was sitting at his desk for once, deep in concentration. I perched on the edge of it.

'I want to go and see the house. The Marshalls' place.'

'Why?'

'I want to have a look around. Get a feel for what it would have been like. See how close the neighbours' houses are, and what the river's like there.'

'I'm guessing the house has changed a lot in the last sixteen years. And the new owner might not want us sniffing around either.'

'No harm in asking,' I said, and he sighed.

'No peace until I let you, I suppose. All right. Get in touch with them. It might be interesting to hear what they made of the Marshalls too.'

I went off and did just that, and came back to him, grinning. 'Do you want the good news or the bad news?'

'Good, obviously.'

'I spoke to Louisa Stern, the new owner. She says we can have a look around the house tomorrow.'

'What's the bad news?'

'She wants advice on home security.'

Derwent groaned. 'Why is there always a price to pay?'

'From what she said, living in a notorious house has involved paying a fairly high price too. They get drive-by tourists and people coming to the door.'

'Yeah, but presumably they got it for less because of the history.'

154

'I didn't point that out. I don't want to piss her off until we've had a look at it.'

'I'll save that question for the end of the tour.'

'If you could.'

I wasn't sure if everyone in the office knew already that Derwent was staying with me, but there were few secrets in a room full of detectives. Nonetheless I was circumspect about how we left work that day, meeting him in the car park. He drove us back and stopped at the gate again.

'Your turn to get us something to eat.'

'What do you want?'

'Surprise me.'

I wondered if I'd done something wrong, because he was sounding grim. He saw the expression on my face and shook his head with a quick smile.

'I'm just hungry.'

Maybe he was and maybe he wasn't. I walked to the corner shop and spent a long time prowling up and down the aisles before I settled on sausages and mash – everyone liked sausages and Derwent would enjoy mocking me about the potatoes which was fine; I could take it. I bought some strawberries because they looked luscious, and beer because I knew he liked it. Decisions came slowly, uncertainly. I should know him better than this, I thought. Just at the moment, I didn't feel as if I knew him at all.

When I got back to the flat, laden with bags, I understood immediately why he had wanted to get rid of me. From the bottom of the stairs I could hear a voice: Melissa's. The sound had the muddy quality of a video call, the treble pitchy so she sounded shrill.

'—don't know why I'm surprised that you're being so selfish. You've never put us first. Not once. And don't say that it's not true because I remember many occasions when you've left us sitting around waiting for you. You always have somewhere more important to be, don't you? The little hero, running off to rescue everyone.'

I stood in the hallway, wondering what to do. Derwent would hate it if he knew I could hear her.

'I should have known better. I don't know what I was thinking, getting involved with a police officer. You all have a God complex. Always on a power trip, aren't you, Josh? Always the centre of attention. What am I, as far as you're concerned? Someone to fuck occasionally?' She laughed. 'Not even that lately.'

Oh hell. I stood stock still, trying to avoid making any noise. The potatoes were heavy and my once-broken collarbone was starting to complain.

'At least Mark knew I existed. At least he *wanted* me.'

Mark Pell was the husband she had fled, hiding in a high-rise tower block to get away from his abuse, with their son Thomas who was the light of Derwent's life. I felt myself go hot with anger. How could she suggest Mark was a better choice than Josh?

Up until now he had been completely silent. When he spoke, I barely recognised his voice. It was quiet and emotionless. 'I've explained why I can't do what you want.'

So he wasn't even going to address the fact that Melissa was comparing him unfavourably to the man who had brutalised her?

The realisation was like a punch in my chest: this wasn't the first time she'd said that to him, or screamed at him, her voice edged with rage.

'Oh yes, you've explained. Look how fucking reasonable you are.'

'Mel—'

'I know exactly what you're doing. You're with that *whore*. You couldn't wait to get at her. You must think I'm some sort of moron—'

He cut into the diatribe, louder than her, still striving to sound calm and reasonable. 'Tell Thomas I'll see him soon.'

'You won't. Not unless you—'

Silence. He had cut her off.

I bit my lip. If I'd moved when Melissa was shouting, I might have made it to the doorstep, but I was at the foot of the stairs. I measured the distance by eye. If I crept back I could bang the door and pretend I'd just arrived—

'Are you coming up?' He was leaning over the banisters, his expression interested. He didn't look flustered, which was an achievement because my face was red and I hadn't even been involved in the conversation.

'Sorry. I wasn't listening. At least, I was, but I didn't mean to.'

'I know.' He came down the stairs and took the shopping bags from me. 'These are heavy.'

'Tell me about it. I was standing there for a while.'

'I heard you come in.' He went back up, leaving me at a loss in the hall. Was that it? He wasn't even going to mention what I'd overheard?

I found him in the kitchen, unpacking the shopping.

'Are you all right?'

'Yeah, why?'

'Josh . . .'

'Leave it,' he said briskly. 'Don't get involved. It's nothing to do with you.'

'It didn't sound like that?' I made it a question, because I wasn't sure of myself. Generally when he told me to butt out of his business, I did just that, but this felt different. 'Is that how she is with you all the time?'

He turned and leaned against the counter. 'I'm not an easy person to live with, Maeve. She gets frustrated. I'm used to it.'

'You shouldn't have to. The things she was saying—'

'I've heard worse.'

'You can't stay with her. You can't live like that.' It wasn't premeditated, but it was the truth. He went still for an instant, and then the wall went up.

'Don't worry about me. Worry about yourself. You've got bigger problems than I do.'

'I heard what she said to you and it was hurtful and unfair and *wrong*.'

'You heard one conversation and you're an expert.' He folded his arms, his eyes hard. 'Tell me, how's your love life, Kerrigan?'

'Better than yours, by the sounds of it, because I still have some self-respect.'

For a moment, neither of us blinked. Then he stepped towards me and I backed into the hall, unsure of what he wanted. When he spoke, it was in a conversational tone.

'You know, I'm not that hungry after all. I'm going to go for a run.'

'What, now?'

'Yeah.' He moved me to one side gently, so he could get past me, and disappeared into the sitting room. Again I was treated to the closed door. When he came out he was wearing a black T-shirt and matching shorts, and headphones that he was adjusting so he could shut out any attempt at talking to him. 'Cook for yourself. I'll get something later.'

'Josh, you can't run away from this situation.'

He smiled at me, jogged down the stairs, and did exactly that.

24

I had been looking forward to seeing the Marshalls' former home, and I was still curious about it, but when we parked in front of the house I didn't even look at it.

'Are you going to sulk all day?'

I didn't answer. Derwent sighed and got out of the car, slamming the door with enough force to make my ears ring. I followed suit, ignoring him. The sun was bright and warm, spring getting underway all around us, and I shaded my eyes to scan the front garden. Mature trees lined the high wall, screening it from a road that was narrow and quiet. In the distance, there was traffic, but here, for a moment, it felt peaceful.

I, on the other hand, was simmering with rage, and I had been for roughly fourteen hours, since Derwent had sauntered in after a very long run, spent an age in the shower, and emerged to tell me, casually and without looking at me, that he had bumped into the neighbours from the flat downstairs.

'They're going to Australia for a month. They were worried about leaving the place unoccupied for that long. Jonny asked me to keep an eye on it since I'm here, but I thought I could go one better. I'm going to stay in their flat while they're gone.'

'Stay in their flat?' I repeated stupidly.

'Instead of here.'

'Is this because of what Melissa said?'

'No. Nothing to do with her.' He had been frowning at his phone, only half-engaged with the conversation. 'You and I could do with a bit of distance from one another, given that we have to be together at work. You don't want me camping on the sofa for the next few weeks.'

I let that go. 'When are you moving in?'

His answer was to hold up a set of keys. 'I'm just going to pack.'

'Without even discussing it with me?'

'Why on earth would you mind?'

And when I hadn't come up with an immediate answer to that question, he had got his things together and left.

Because it was my job, and only because of that, I went to stand next to Derwent, who had just rung the doorbell. The front door was painted pale pink with bright, polished brasses, and someone had coaxed a climbing plant up trellis that was attached to the house.

Derwent glanced at me. 'Good of you to join me at last.'

'Are you really doing this?' I found myself asking.

'Conducting this interview? Yes, that was the plan.'

I unclenched my jaw to say, 'You know that's not what I meant.'

The door opened before he could reply, which was probably for the best. I tried to look pleasant for the sake of the woman who was smiling in welcome. Louisa Stern was in her early sixties and had a demure look, like a housewife in a fifties sitcom. She wore a cotton dress with a wide skirt, a cardigan, flat shoes and large pink earrings that matched the colour of the front door. Her hair was greying and elegantly bobbed.

'Ah, the police.'

I'd been greeted in many ways over the years, but rarely with a beatific smile.

'I'm glad you contacted me. I was wondering if I should get in touch with you.'

'Was something worrying you?' Derwent asked politely.

'Well, yes. But you never know if it's useful or not, do you? I don't want to waste your time.' She laughed. 'I'm wasting it now, my husband would say. Come in. You wanted to look around, so please do.'

'I'd rather deal with your concerns and then look at the house. That seems more important.'

And it meant he could avoid being alone with me for another

160

few minutes. Louisa Stern took his gallantry at face value and was pleased. 'I was sitting outside in the sunshine. Would that suit?'

'Perfect.'

She led us around the side of the house to the back garden where we perched on garden furniture. It was slightly too cold to be outside, I thought, but I admired the pots filled with spring flowers that brightened the paved area around us, and the long sweep of lawn down to the river.

'That's what sold the place to us. My husband has always wanted a boat. He had his eye on the house for a very long time but we never thought the Marshalls would sell. In the end we contacted them and they agreed to a private sale. Quite a good deal, as it happened, but then I suppose not everyone would want to live here.'

'It's a lovely house,' I said. 'Most houses of this age have some sad stories attached to them.'

'And ghosts, sometimes. But not this one. Not that I've seen, anyway.' She folded her arms, hugging herself. 'That's what one of them asked me. If I'd ever seen Rosalie's ghost. But I hadn't.'

'One of them?'

'Oh, the people.' She waved a slim hand. 'The ones who came. We had such a rush of them. When we bought the house we knew there was public interest in it even for people who didn't know about the little girl, because it is impressive. A landmark building, I've heard it called. The houses on either side are much smaller.'

We agreed that it was definitely the nicest property on the riverbank.

'So people try to gain access because they're curious,' Derwent prompted.

'Often. Driving past, going slowly, or even walking up the drive. We do have a sign to say this is private property, but people ignore it. That's why I thought you might have some suggestions for our security.'

'A big dog,' Derwent said. 'Best deterrent there is.'

'Mm, but think of picking up the turds.'

'You could throw them at the rubberneckers.'

She gave a squeal of delighted laughter. 'So we could.'

'Is this an ongoing issue,' I asked, 'or has something changed?'

'Well, it was every couple of months, one or two people, fairly casual. Just in the last month or two, though, there were more. One of them came by boat, rowing up to our jetty, which was very annoying, I thought, but he said he knew it well and he seemed very knowledgeable about the area and the family.' She pulled her cardigan around her. 'He was making a programme about it. He wanted to record me talking about the house.'

That caught my attention. 'Was it for a podcast?'

'That's right. As soon as he said that, I lost interest. I don't listen to them much, and when I do I don't like the true-crime ones. I prefer something funny.'

'Me too,' Derwent said. 'Do you remember his name?'

'Tor something. Not short for Torquil, he said, which was what I thought originally. That's why I remembered that part. You never meet a Torquil, do you, except in books. He was very diffident. Very polite. I just didn't want to be involved.'

'Did he ask you where he could find the Marshalls?'

'Yes.' She looked nervously from me to Derwent. 'I told him their address. I wouldn't have, but he was a friend of the family.'

'Is that what he told you?'

'Was that untrue?' She went pale. 'I probably should have checked with Bruce, but Tor seemed very familiar with them. With the sons. He knew all about them. He said he used to be their neighbour.'

Derwent looked at me and I shook my head slightly. No one named Grant had lived on the road at the time of Rosalie's disappearance, but I thought Tor Grant would have put in the time and effort to research the family well enough to fake it.

'When was this?'

'About a month ago?'

It would have been around the time he turned up at the Marshalls' flat and frightened Sabiha. Tor Grant was a walking

162

red flag, with his soft, woolly manner that was so at odds with the persistence he demonstrated. He was prepared to break the law to get what he wanted, which was access to the Marshalls and their story, even to the extent of breaking into my car.

'That was one person who approached you recently,' I said. 'Who else?'

'No one important. A couple of new age traveller types, which I didn't like. They didn't seem like the Marshalls' sort of people either, so I assumed they were up to no good. And a couple of garden fanatics.' I thought she wasn't enjoying herself any more, that the attention and excitement of the interview had faded away into stark fear that she had done something unforgivable in sending Tor after the Marshalls. 'Are you nearly finished? I do have phone calls I need to make.'

'You're shivering, Mrs Stern,' Derwent said gently. 'Can I get you a blanket?'

'No, I'm all right.' She rubbed her arms.

'We'll try to get through the rest of the questions as quickly as possible.' I didn't want to lose this opportunity.

Derwent got up and took off his jacket, draping it around Louisa Stern's shoulders. She clung on to it gratefully.

'That's very kind. Very thoughtful. But won't you be cold?'

He shook his head, sitting down and concentrating on rolling up his shirt sleeves, which gave her the chance to recover her composure and for me to reflect that he knew what he was doing, most of the time, and when he got it wrong it was telling. He had got it epically wrong with me, but what it was telling me, I didn't know.

'Can we talk about the other people who bothered you, Mrs Stern?'

'Well, I wouldn't say they bothered me exactly. But it was just odd, after all this time, that we had people get in touch with us who wanted to find the Marshalls.' She looked pensive. 'When they left they didn't seem to tell all of their friends because we had Christmas cards and letters and things for them for months and months. You know, I don't think the Marshalls wanted to leave. When we arrived on the day of completion and wanted to move our stuff in, the house was full of furniture and belongings still. Junk, most of it.'

'Did you keep anything?' I had visions of an attic full of more boxes, more things to look through in search of the link to Rosalie, and didn't know whether to be relieved or sorry when she shook her head.

'I got a house clearance company to come and get rid of everything. I'm an interior designer. I needed a blank canvas.' Louisa Stern smiled. 'This house has got me quite a few clients over the years. It's no wonder they didn't want to go.'

25

When we eventually went into the house, Louisa shut herself away in a pretty sitting room at the front of the property. She was still wearing Derwent's jacket, despite being indoors, and I wasn't sure she was planning to give it back.

We started in the kitchen. I took out a handful of pictures.

'Compare and contrast. These are images of the house taken at or around the time Rosalie disappeared. Louisa said the house hadn't changed much but it looks different to me. I think she meant it hasn't been extended or rebuilt. I suppose her standards are different, being a professional.' We were standing in the kitchen, which wasn't large but overlooked the garden. It was painted a rich egg-yolk yellow which was warm and cheering and a whole lot nicer than the powder blue of the Marshalls' era. 'These windows are new. There was a door in the middle of that wall which was the one that was found open on the morning Rosalie disappeared.'

Derwent took the pictures and shuffled through rapidly, barely glancing at them. 'God, she can talk.'

'Louisa? I thought you were getting on with her.'

'Needs must.'

Yes, you'll say whatever you have to whenever it suits you. Thanks for the reminder.

I took back the photographs and separated out the ground-floor ones, giving them back to him. 'I'll start at the top. We can meet in the middle.'

'You don't want to walk through it together?'

'Sorry,' I said blandly. 'I thought you were the one who wanted to keep your distance.'

He sighed. 'Fine. Go. Whatever you want.'

Whatever *you* want, I thought and didn't say, and knew that he knew I was thinking it.

There were three rooms on the top floor: two bedrooms and a bathroom in the middle. I matched one to the picture labelled 'Ivo's Room' and the other to Magnus. Both were wallpapered in pretty florals and had a pristine guestroom quality that was very different from the teenage-boy bedrooms that were in my photographs. The windows were the same, little dormers that gave a limited view over the front and back gardens. Ivo had kept his room tidy, with an austere bookcase on one wall, a desk and chair, and clothes folded with geometric precision. A single poster of a fighter plane hung on one wall, where now there was a framed Victorian sampler. The bathroom had been remodelled and I shuddered at the photograph of what had been there: chipped tiles, limescale stains and flooring that was peeling away around the base of the toilet and the shower. Now it was immaculate in white with brass fittings. Magnus's room was heroically untidy in the pictures but then he had been twelve, I thought, caught halfway between childhood and being a teenager. Clutter, everywhere, and toys, and a general air of chaos had pervaded what was now a perfectly pleasant bedroom. I thought of what Bill Howlett had said about Rosalie's room being bare, and how it had looked in the crime-scene pictures. I wondered if Magnus had resisted passing on his more childish toys, or if Rosalie had simply wanted to be more like her older brother.

On the middle floor, I found a large master bedroom and bathroom which overlooked the river. At the front of the house, two other rooms flanked the tiny hall bedroom that Rosalie had slept in. I decided to save her room until last. Each of the other rooms had a large tree outside the window, currently coming into leaf. I looked at the photos, frowning.

'Wondering who needs this many bedrooms?' Derwent was standing in the doorway, his hands in his pockets. 'It's just the two of them, you know.'

I knew he wanted me to agree with him that it was a waste to have all of this space and no one living here, but the words stuck in my throat.

'They have grown-up children. Presumably they stay sometimes.'

'OK.' He said it on an exhale. 'So what's wrong? Why are you frowning?'

'The trees.'

He shrugged, looking baffled.

'Howlett told us there were sightings of a car with a broken number plate passing the house. He said the car was never traced.'

'So?'

'In the files, there are lots of references to a car, at various times and in various accounts of what happened. But they all come back to one person. Helena. She was the only one who ever saw a suspicious car lurking outside the house, or driving past slowly, or parked on the road. She repeated her concerns to everyone. She talked about seeing the car from the house – looking out and watching it drive past.'

'And?'

'You can't see the road. You can just about see it through the trees and hedge now, but you certainly wouldn't have been able to see it in the summer, when Rosalie disappeared. Not from the ground floor, not from these rooms, not from the attic. And you wouldn't have been able to see a broken number plate.'

Derwent came to the window. I waited, sure I was right. The gate to the road was over in the far left, tucked away from the house. The trees I had noticed on our arrival screened the road entirely. As he looked out a car drove past, invisible.

'You can't even see what colour it is, let alone make and model and a broken licence plate.'

'She could have seen it when she was driving in and out.'

'She could have, but that's not what the files say. It just isn't possible, especially in August. Look at the pictures. The trees are in full leaf. And I know it's a long time ago, but the trees are mature. They wouldn't have looked much different sixteen years ago.'

'So Helena lied.' He turned to lean against the windowsill, folding his arms. 'So what?'

'Why was she trying to sell the police on a lead that was impossible to follow? Classic misdirection. She wanted them looking outside the house, not at the people in it.'

'Her family.'

'At a guess.' I sat down on the edge of the bed. 'The timing of her overdose always bothered me, Josh. She coped, after Rosalie left, and then something happened that changed everything. She was under intolerable strain, and she snapped.'

'That can happen. Bearable becomes unbearable like that.' He clicked his fingers.

'There's generally something to trigger it. What if it was one of the boys who did something to Rosalie?'

'What if it was Bruce?'

'He stayed loyal to her,' I said slowly.

'Out of guilt?'

'Maybe. He might have been afraid she would tell the world what she knew if he didn't look after her. Or he was a devoted husband who was completely innocent.'

'No one ever connected him to Rosalie's disappearance. He was there when Helena woke up that morning.'

'She went to bed first. He was the last one awake in the house. And it's a big house. You wouldn't necessarily hear something happening on the ground floor if you were in the master bedroom.'

'It's suspicious,' Derwent agreed. 'I can't see why none of the neighbours reported seeing this car around the place, if Helena saw it repeatedly.'

I pulled a face.

'What? I was agreeing with you, you nit.'

'No, but if Bruce was the one who killed Rosalie, that doesn't get us much closer to finding out who killed him and Helena.'

'Maybe Helena persuaded someone to kill him and they got carried away and offed her too.'

I shook my head. 'You can't argue with the forensics. The blood on Helena's face wasn't smudged by the pillow when she was smothered. She died, then he died. And we still don't know why, let alone who. I want to know what happened to Rosalie – I need to know, now – but I'm beginning to think Una was right and this isn't going to get us any closer to solving this murder.' I got up and smoothed the coverlet where I'd rumpled it. 'Let's have a look at Rosalie's room.'

The photographs in the file had documented every inch of the small space – every smudge on the wallpaper, every curl of dust under the bed. Louisa had transformed it into a small office in a highly feminine style, with white furniture, patterned curtains and flowers on the desk. Gold details gleamed everywhere: the light fittings, the handles on the desk, the legs of the chair. For all that, I was instantly aware of how small the space was, and how cramped it felt – even the ceiling seemed low. If I had stood with my arms outstretched, I would have been able to touch both walls. I turned and found Derwent had followed me in, which made the space feel even smaller.

'Did you look out of the window?'

'Same story. No view of the road.'

He nodded, his attention on his surroundings rather than on me. It was not going to be possible to get past him, I noted, and waited for him to realise that.

'They had her sleeping in here? That tells you a lot, doesn't it?'

'Does it? It's close to the master bedroom. Maybe Helena wanted to keep an eye on her because she was younger than the boys.'

'The other bedroom we were in is closer,' Derwent pointed out. 'And bigger. And they would still have had a decent-sized guest room, plus this one for emergencies.'

'A small room can be cosy.'

169

'You saw the pictures. Howlett said it was bleak in here.'

'I remember that. It didn't look very nice.' I sighed. 'Poor Rosalie.'

'She wanted attention,' Derwent said. 'And love. Kids like that are so vulnerable. Abusers have radar for them. They grow up into adults who get into terrible relationships with manipulative people.'

'If they grow up at all,' I said softly.

'Helena loved her boys and tolerated Rosalie, until she didn't. Maybe Helena is the one we should be looking at. Maybe Helena was trying to divert suspicion from herself, not one of the others. The fear of getting found out made her try to take her own life.'

'Could be.' I shivered, my skin tingling as if something unwholesome was touching it. 'I know Louisa said she'd never seen a ghost, but I really don't like it in here.'

He grinned. 'I'll protect you.'

'Forget it.' I pushed him out of the way, far too close for one excruciating moment. Just as I slipped past him and stepped through the doorway his fingers closed around my wrist and he hauled me back.

'Maeve, wait.'

'Just leave it,' I said, and his grip tightened briefly.

'If you want me to apologise for moving out—'

'Not at all. Why would you?'

'Yeah, I was about to say I wasn't going to.' He frowned at me. 'I don't know why you mind so much about me moving into the flat downstairs. I thought you'd be relieved. I hadn't exactly settled in.'

'I noticed that. You didn't think it was a good idea from the start, and I'd like to know why.'

'Of course you would. You always want to know everything.' He let go of me with a little shake. 'I will tell you, some time. Not now.' His eyes were sad. 'But believe me, it's for the best.'

26

Rosalie

Rosalie was a very lucky little girl to be staying in the South of France, in a villa with a pool (a-villa-with-a-pool was one word as far as she was concerned, it had been talked about so many times in the months before the holiday). Such a long journey across to Calais and then down through France on the wrong side of the road until they got to the tiny village after dark. Her first impression was one of strangeness in the black night: strange hot dry air, strange insects clicking in the undergrowth, strange glaring lighting in the sparsely furnished rooms, strange humming fans in the ceilings that swept the air with their paddles. There were four bedrooms: Mummy and Daddy, Ivo and Magnus, Sadie, and Rosalie. Rosalie didn't like being on her own and Ivo didn't like being with Magnus but Magnus flatly refused to share with Rosalie, so all three of them were cross from the very start of the holiday, and that made Mummy cross, and then Magnus and Rosalie cried. And there was a mosquito in her room darting at her and retreating on a miserable whine, and she got bitten all over the legs and she had a nightmare and Sadie got in trouble for sleeping through the screaming, and that was just on the first night.

Then she had heard the conversation between her parents.

'Honestly, it would be easier to stay at home.'

'No, we should leave the children at home and go away by ourselves.'

Her mother sighed wistfully. 'The dream.'

'Do you ever think, if we hadn't taken on Ro— Well, Magnus won't want to come on holidays with us in a couple of years.'

'Rosalie will. We have years of this ahead of us.' Another sigh, this one less dreamy, more despairing.

'It was your idea to adopt her.' Her father sounded irritated. 'You can't treat the girl like a prop and just take her out to show her off when you need to, for the sake of your career. It's a lifetime commitment, like I told you.'

'Oh, stop it, darling, you were pleased to take her on. Anyway, I didn't know what it would be like. Girls are so different. Such hard work. I had *no* idea.'

Rosalie went and sat in her little bedroom on her own for ages after that, until Ivo called her for lunch, and it was hot, and the food got stuck in her throat but no one noticed that she was sad.

And the swimming pool was out of bounds, her father said, because she wasn't a good enough swimmer and she could only go in with an adult, but he wanted to read his book and Mummy didn't swim and Sadie had to walk into the village to buy something for tea and she didn't want Rosalie to come with her. The boys didn't want to play with her. They didn't want to do anything. They were bored, they said, and told her to go away. She spent the afternoon pretending a clump of trees was actually a gateway to a fairy kingdom, and that was all right, but when Sadie told her to come to dinner she got in trouble for having a rip in her dress and dirty legs.

Two days into the holiday they went to the coast and she paddled for hours in the sea, only up to her knees unless Daddy was prepared to come into the water with her. The salt stung the grazes on her skin and the sun made her shoulders red and she loved it, she loved every second of it.

Three days into the holiday, her dad came up with the idea of giving her his digital camera so she could take pictures of the house and the garden and the hills in the distance and the vineyards that stretched around the village and the insect she found crawling by the pool and the flowers on the bush on the other side of the fence and the funny mirror in the bathroom, so he didn't have to get up and look every time she called him. He sat by the pool in the shade of a parasol with a glass at his elbow, ice dissolving in it, and reviewed the pictures every so often while she hovered, wanting to talk about what she had found (the bird's skull, the mouse running flat out over open ground, moving so fast it seemed to be floating, the silver-leaved scrub and the olives on the trees and the fat purple bolsters of lavender waving as she walked through them and the quick flash of brown lizards in the low stone walls . . .).

Four days into the holiday they went to Tourtour, the prettiest place Rosalie had ever been, and drank Orangina that came in glass bottles, sitting outside a café in a cobbled square, and Sadie sketched a house with flowers outside it and talked about coming back with her watercolours and they had chips for lunch which were called *pommes frites* and a *croque monsieur* which was a toasted sandwich that was too hot. And that night she had a nightmare which was because of the cheese, her father told her, when he tucked her back in under the thin, stiff sheet.

Five days into the holiday, she took a picture of Ivo diving into the swimming pool with the villa in the background, his hands carving a line through the air, his body a bow, and showed it to Magnus, who never looked at her pictures but looked at that one, and then took the camera and showed his mother that there, in the black shadow of the doorway, her father was standing so close to Sadie that you couldn't see any gap between them. If you zoomed in – and her mother did – you could see that his face was right up against hers and his hands were on her arms, holding her tightly. And Sadie had been wearing little white shorts which you could see, and a bikini top that you couldn't make out unless you knew what to look for. Her skin was brown and smooth and Bruce's hair was thinning on top and her mother had laughed, and cried, and said *There's no fool like an old fool* and *I should have known* and *She has to go* and her father said things like *You're overreacting* (which made it worse) and *Calm down* (she hadn't) and *This is ridiculous* (which made her mother throw a bottle of wine at him that stained the white wall of the living room and left tiny jewels of glinting glass everywhere). Sadie packed her things, and got a lift to the nearest town (with the man who ran the *boulangerie* and liked her and always gave Rosalie an extra *goûter* which was another of the French words she had learned so far) so Sadie could catch a train to Paris, and they would never see her again and her mother was very angry when Rosalie asked if never meant really never because she loved Sadie.

They stayed in France for another nine days but after Sadie left, the holiday was over.

And everyone – from Magnus and Ivo to Sadie and her father, and even the man from the *boulangerie* – looked at Rosalie as if it was all her fault.

27

'Sadie Pilchrist, you are not an easy woman to find.'

She laughed and flicked her hair off her shoulder. 'Well, for starters, you shouldn't have been looking for Sadie Pilchrist. I'm Sadie Cartwright now, for my sins.'

'And before that you were Sadie Manners.'

She rolled her eyes. 'Please. We don't talk about that. He was a big mistake.'

'We all make mistakes.'

'Yeah, but we don't all marry them.' She had a husky laugh and Derwent was prompting it a little too often for my liking. I suspected he knew that I wasn't enjoying it as much as he was, which would make it all the more entertaining for him.

It had taken Liv the best part of a week to track down Sadie after we visited the old house, a week of painstaking phone calls and electoral register searches and dead ends. She had finally located Sadie on the outskirts of a small Surrey village where she lived in a substantial house with stables. I had known Derwent was keen to interview the ex-nanny himself, but I'd thought Liv would want to go with him and was surprised when she shook her head.

'You go. I've had enough of her.'

'Don't you want to get out of the office?'

'Not with him.' She mouthed it, eyeing Derwent, who was standing in the doorway of Una Burt's office, complaining about something. His mood hadn't improved noticeably despite having his own space to live in. I saw him in the mornings and evenings but we spent no time together outside work. He went running every evening, I presumed on the old routes that he had followed when he lived in my flat. It was obsessive behaviour and I was worried about him.

None of my business.

'And you think I want to go?'

'Yeah, I do.' Liv narrowed her eyes at me. 'Every time I look up from my work, you're staring at him like you're making a nature documentary about him and you're hoping to observe some rare behaviour, which in Derwent's case is probably smiling.'

'He smiles.'

'Not at me.'

And not at me either, lately. When he came out of Una Burt's office Liv shared the good news about Sadie's location and I volunteered to go with him the next day, which got me a grim nod but no actual encouragement.

He had been very slightly more cheerful in the car on the way to the interview, as I teased him.

'What if she's not fit?'

'I've seen the pictures in the files. She'll be ageing like fine wine. Anyway, forty's not old.'

'No, but it can hit you hard.'

'I have faith in Sadie. She'll have looked after herself.'

She was grooming a horse when we walked into the yard, briskly drawing a brush over its gleaming hindquarters. Her skin-tight jodhpurs clung to long legs and a firm, round bottom. Thick fair hair hung straight around her shoulders and when she turned, her face was tanned. She had laughter lines around her eyes, but she was undeniably attractive. On our way into the house Derwent spared a second for a smug look in my direction, then proceeded to flirt up a storm, much to Sadie's delight. When I was too bored to put up with it any longer, I cleared my throat.

'Did you know that Bruce and Helena Marshall were dead?'

'Not until your colleague called.' She blinked, her long sweeping lashes too perfect to be real. 'I don't pay any attention to the news. Why get upset about whatever is happening in the world if it doesn't affect me?'

I could think of a few reasons, but I smiled politely. 'We're trying to work out who might have had a reason to harm them, and of course we're interested in what happened to Rosalie.'

'Yah, well, that would have been after I left, so.' She ran her hand into her hair and flipped the weight of it from one side of her face to the other in a practised move.

'How long did you work for the Marshalls?' Derwent asked.

'Three years.'

'And you were a full-time, live-in nanny.'

'I officially didn't work at weekends but the rest of the time I was expected to be on duty unless the kids were at school, and if I was around I'd help out, even on weekends. I got paid, I had a roof over my head, a car . . . It was the perfect job as far as I was concerned, at that stage of my life. Now, I wonder how I could bear being there all the time, but it was such a different world from how I grew up that I loved it. So grand, so posh. Everything seemed incredibly glamorous.'

'How old were you when you worked for the Marshalls?'

'I started when I was twenty-two, then left when I was twenty-four – nearly twenty-five.' She looked at Derwent. 'Don't do the maths, please.'

'I've never been any good at maths.'

For God's sake. I said, 'So what did you do before that? University?'

'I left school when I was sixteen. Never did A-levels or any further qualifications. I'd done various jobs – barmaid, stable hand, carer – and then I worked for a bit in a nursery that my mum's friend owned. I started babysitting for the kids, and then one of the families asked me to be their nanny, which I did for a couple of years.'

'And then you started working for the Marshalls.'

'The Marshalls were looking for someone to help with Rosalie because Helena was getting busy with her campaigning and Rosalie was a bit . . . challenging. She was six when I started working for them. It wasn't difficult but she wanted attention all the time. Basically she was a lonely little kid and they preferred to pay a stranger to look after her than to actually talk to her. I could see that Rosalie was going to be a lot easier than a baby, a toddler and a four-year-old.' Sadie shrugged. 'It was a no-brainer.'

'The Marshalls didn't mind about your lack of qualifications? I'd have thought Helena was keen on that kind of thing.'

'They realised that I was really good at the job and Rosalie was happy. But towards the end, Bruce was helping me to apply for courses, actually.' She sighed. 'All of that went to the wall when I left. I never got around to going back to college.'

'You seem to have done very well.' The house was large and comfortably furnished, and the stables behind it were full of horses. She ran a riding school but it was at the top end of luxurious.

'That's what happens when you get a good divorce settlement and then use it to meet and marry a rich man.' She looked at my hands. 'No rings. You need to get a move on, don't you, darling?'

I smiled sweetly while hot murderous thoughts crowded into my mind.

Derwent cleared his throat loudly, and when he spoke, his voice was slightly strained: suppressing laughter, if I knew him. 'Going back to Helena. What was she like?'

'A bitch.' Sadie shrugged exaggeratedly. 'I know she's dead, but sorry, she wasn't a nice person.'

'In what way?'

'She was condescending. Mean. Treated me very much like a servant and her social inferior, which I suppose I was. And she was a cow when she was angry. I don't know what Helena's problem was with Rosalie, but that girl couldn't do anything right. She was always in trouble. I used to try to intervene where I could but I couldn't always stop her from being punished.'

'How did Helena punish her?'

'All kinds of things. No pudding, sent to her room, made to stand facing a blank wall, made to do lines or extra homework.'

'Was that all?' I asked.

Sadie wriggled. 'You've read the files, so you know what I said.'

Yes, but I want to know if it was the truth. 'Tell me again.'

'She hit her, sometimes. At least, I heard her screaming at Rosalie and then Rosalie cried, but she never did it in front of me and Rosalie would always come up with a reason for any of the injuries she had, and she *was* clumsy so there were always bruises and grazes. Looking back, I should have said something, but I was young. I didn't know what to do.'

'You talked to the police about it,' I said.

'When it was too late.' Suddenly Sadie's eyes brimmed with tears and she ran a knuckle under each of them, struggling for composure. 'I wasn't brave enough to do anything when it might have made a difference. I only spoke up about it after I left, so I wasn't employed by the Marshalls any more and I had nothing to lose. And no one believed me.'

'What makes you say that?' Derwent asked gently.

'The cops thought I was bitter about getting the sack, because that's what Helena and Bruce told them. They ignored my evidence. I think they were misogynist bastards, if you really want to know. They wrote me off because I was young and pretty and whatever I said couldn't possibly matter.'

'I can assure you, they did take it seriously,' Derwent said. 'But there were other accounts of how things were at home that contradicted yours.'

'Oh yeah? Like whose? Helena's? Bruce's?' She threw out a hand, frustrated. 'It's not as if *they* had any reason to lie, is there?'

'Why do you think they would have lied?' I asked.

'Isn't it obvious?' Sadie blinked at us, her eyes lingering on Derwent for a fraction longer. 'They were the ones who offed her.'

'What makes you say that?'

'Oh come *on*. Everyone knew it at the time but no one had the nerve to say it. They got rid of me so there wasn't anyone to stop them and then after it happened they sued the arse off anyone who suggested they had anything to do with it. They killed her, either by accident or because they were worried about her talking to someone about—'

She cut herself off, breathing hard, her chest rising and falling rapidly. I presumed Derwent was busy enjoying the view but I was more interested in what she wasn't saying.

'They're dead, Sadie. You can't be sued now, whatever you say about them. And you could never have been sued if it was true.'

'I couldn't take the risk.' Her voice had dropped to a whisper and she was gulping back tears again. 'Not then. I couldn't have coped if they'd sued me. But they set me up so they had a reason to get rid of me because I knew too much, and the way they did it meant that no one listened when I tried to talk about them. I tested the waters with what I said about Helena – and I know other people knew, the cleaner knew and people who came to the house, friends of the boys, the fucking *tutor* knew – but no one would corroborate what I said. What was the point in getting myself in deeper when Rosalie was gone and there was no evidence?'

She had left me behind and obviously Derwent felt the same way. 'Hold on, evidence of what?'

Sadie sniffed. 'When we were on holidays in the villa in France, Rosalie was in a room by herself. And I was down the hall, in another room. I got in trouble for not hearing her crying on the first night we were there – I mean, I was shattered. I was sleeping like the dead. But after that I was really on edge in case she cried and I didn't hear her, so when there was a noise from her room in the middle of the night, on the fourth night of the holiday, I went to see if she was all right. And Bruce was in there with her.'

'Doing what?'

'He heard me coming. I called out to her as I left my room.' She closed her eyes tightly and rubbed her forehead, frustrated. 'He wasn't *doing* anything when I came in, but he had no reason to be there.'

'What did he tell you?'

'He was my boss. I couldn't just interrogate him. He said something about wanting to check on her because she'd got hold of one of Helena's sleeping pills – and she was really out for the count, so much so that I believed she was drugged, but I thought he'd given it to her, and then you have to wonder *why*. He said it was because she didn't want to wake up in the night again, given that Helena had been so angry about it, but you know, she was a little kid. Would she even have thought of that? And once she was drugged, anything could have happened to her.' Sadie sighed. 'But I had no proof. None at all.'

'Was it just that one incident? Did you talk to him or Helena about it?'

'The next day, I was confronting him, and Rosalie took a picture of her brother in the pool. We were in the background. It looked dodgy as fuck – he was holding my arm and pressing me against the wall and you couldn't tell he was angry instead of horny. He let Helena think he'd been fucking me and she sent me away. I was so upset, it didn't even occur to me to tell her what I'd seen the night before. She was furious. Devastated. I've never seen anyone tear themselves apart that way. I suppose it made her feel as if she'd been betrayed, but actually there was a far bigger betrayal going on with Rosalie.'

'If he was abusing her,' I said quietly.

'Yeah. If.' She blotted her eyes with a tissue. 'I always thought it was likely he decided to kill Rosalie because she knew what he'd been doing to her, but I also wondered if Helena had decided to get rid of the competition. She couldn't bear the idea of him being interested in someone else. She threw me out so fast my feet didn't touch the ground. And she resented Rosalie anyway. How easy would it have been to kill her, really, with no one there to stop Helena? She could have done anything in that big house and no one would have known.'

'Did you ever tell her about what you saw?' Derwent asked.

'Not until later. A long time later. Months after Rosalie disappeared. I called, one day. Disguised my voice. I said she should ask Bruce about what he'd done to Rosalie. I said I knew he'd been interfering with her.'

'And?'

'And nothing. I was still in touch with one of the neighbours – Mrs Moguel, who lived next door. It was her kid JV who tutored Magnus in maths, and he was a little weirdo, incidentally. But I liked Mrs Moguel and she had this really hot new husband who worked in Dubai and always flirted with me when he was around. I mean, she was on her third marriage, which at the time I thought was scandalous but now I can see how it happened, you know?' She gave a loud laugh that faded into awkward silence.

'What did Mrs Moguel tell you?' I prompted.

'Oh – that Helena had overdosed and almost died.' Sadie bit her lip. 'I always wondered, did I do that? But really it was Bruce's fault, if it was connected. I didn't do anything wrong.'

'No.' Derwent leaned back and folded his arms. 'You know, Sadie, I imagine you never do.'

28

We were both quiet on the way back from interviewing Sadie. I didn't even have the heart to tease Derwent about the hungry look she'd had when she'd stared at him. He shook his head when I asked what he'd made of her.

'Not a lot. She didn't care about anyone but herself, and she still doesn't really care about what happened to Rosalie.'

'Do you think it would have made any difference if she'd reported Bruce to the cops when she got back to the UK?'

'Maybe not. There was fuck-all evidence of him doing anything to the girl, and it happened in France.'

'But no one was looking for evidence of anything like that. No one asked Rosalie about it.'

'If she was drugged she might not have known . . .' He trailed off, then, and a muscle tightened in his jaw.

'Are you OK?'

'I don't like hearing about it. Not when there's nothing we can do.'

'I meant in general.'

He glowered at me briefly. 'I'm all right.'

'You don't seem to be.' And when I wasn't all right he intervened, always, whether I wanted him to or not.

'It's just this case.'

I thought about pushing him on it, wondering what he would do if he was in my place. Something dramatic and borderline unforgivable. I didn't have the nerve. 'It's worth asking Howlett about it.'

'It is, and I will when we get back.' He yawned widely, which made me yawn too. 'Actually, do you mind if we don't go back to the office? I'm shattered and it's hardly worth it this late in the day.'

When we got home Derwent said a brief goodbye and disappeared into the downstairs flat with an air of finality. I had been planning to suggest we had dinner together to discuss the case, so that I could be sure he ate something. I let myself into my flat and went up the stairs slowly. The last time we had been at close quarters the job had involved being all over one another, performatively in love, and this time there was no job: there was just a miserable real-life relationship that seemed to my outsider's eyes to be doomed, and me on my own, wondering why I couldn't seem to stop thinking about it. Irritated with myself, and sticky thanks to the beautiful spring weather, I stripped as I walked through the flat and went straight to the shower, standing under tepid water for long enough to pucker my fingertips and chill my skin.

My mobile was ringing when I got out of the shower and I ran to answer it: Colin Vale.

'What's up?'

'Good news.' He did sound pleased with himself. 'We managed to trace Paul Lavender's car at the time Rosalie disappeared. Still on the road, believe it or not. It's changed hands a few times but it's still going. We've taken it for forensic analysis, because Kev said there was a chance we'd be able to recover something from the upholstery, even after all this time. Body fluids, that kind of thing.'

'Grim.'

'Useful,' Colin corrected me happily. 'It matches the description of the car that was seen repeatedly near the house before Rosalie disappeared. Down to the last details, Maeve.'

And what did that mean? Did it matter? I thanked him and dried off quickly, then changed while I thought about the car and whether I was wrong about the trees, and Helena, and Paul Lavender, who triggered so many alarm bells it was deafening. I curled up on the bed and called Derwent, who answered immediately.

'Hey, I thought I'd get you before you went for your run.'

'How did you know I was going for a run?'

'It's what you always do.'

He sounded amused. 'I'm not going until later. There are too many slow-moving pedestrians around now.'

'It'll be dark later.'

'I'm not scared of the dark.'

'That's your male privilege showing. It's all right for you, but if I went out running at night you'd flip.'

'Yeah, I probably would. What's up?'

I filled him in on what Colin had told me about the car.

'It's worth putting it through the forensic process, isn't it?' Derwent said.

'Expensive and time-consuming.'

'And essential if we want to rule Lavender out. Helena didn't tell Howlett or anyone else about him, but she described his car. Maybe she didn't realise it was his.'

'Or she was trying to divert attention towards him and away from the family, because she didn't like him and she wanted to get him into trouble.'

Derwent didn't sound convinced. 'She could have done a lot more to push the investigation in that direction if she'd wanted to.'

'Maybe it suited her to muddy the waters. Paul had a story to tell too, didn't he? She might not have wanted him to be found. But if we had found Rosalie's body and there was evidence of abuse, she would have wanted there to be an external suspect. She was pushing that outsider story all the time, until Sadie called her and broke the news that she had suspicions about Bruce. Then Helena snapped when she realised the situation was out of her control.'

'Or she was horrified at Sadie's allegations, which were bullshit, and he really *was* lurking around the house and Helena was telling the truth.'

I could hear footsteps: he was pacing around the flat downstairs as we talked.

'You couldn't see the road from the house, Josh. Helena lied.'

'You can't discount everything she said just because Sadie didn't like her.' There was a very slight reverberation from his words: he was in the room below me.

'You don't trust Sadie any more than Howlett did.'

'Yeah, and it's not misogyny or whatever crap she suggested. She was worried enough about Bruce to talk to Helena, who she hated, but not worried enough to call the incident room. I think Sadie wasn't completely honest about what she told us, and I think I know why.'

'You think she was trying to blackmail the Marshalls?'

'Makes sense, doesn't it?'

'And . . . do you think they paid her?'

'It's possible. We can go back and look at bank records but all we can do is confirm that they paid her money and she's the only person who can say what it was for. The Marshalls can't give evidence against her now. Sadie likes living well and she seems ruthless about it. That's not something that came to her later in life. She liked their lifestyle and she wanted it for herself. They ended up losing everything. The money had to go somewhere.'

'Which suggests they had something to hide.' I thought about it and came to the only conclusion I could. 'Poor Rosalie.'

'Very much so.'

There was a pause. This was the best conversation we had managed for a few days and I didn't want it to end. Apparently, Derwent felt the same way – or he was just lost in thought, I told myself, embarrassed at how quickly I assumed it was a personal and emotional connection rather than work. *Get a grip, Maeve.*

Then he said, as if he didn't want to ask the question but he had to, 'Are you in bed?'

Four words. The tone of his voice was subtly different: warmer, deeper. I stayed very still while my mind raced, and eventually I asked, 'How did you know?'

'I didn't. I do now.'

I sat back against the pillows. *Make a joke of it.* 'Just for a second I thought you were going to ask me what I'm wearing.'

'Don't need to. I can guess.'

I looked down at myself. 'I bet you can't.'

'What do you want to bet?'

'Tenner.'

He was silent for a beat, but it was as if he was considering the implications of playing this game rather than because he needed to think about it, because when he began to speak it was without hesitation.

'I heard you have a shower when you came in. You would have come round to talk to me about the case if you'd got dressed afterwards, but you didn't. You rang me. But you wouldn't talk to me if you were naked, or just in a towel, even on the phone, because that would feel far too intimate' – his voice dropped on that word, *intimate*, and I felt it in the pit of my stomach – 'and you want to keep things professional. You put some clothes on before you picked up the phone to call me. We're both tired and you weren't planning to go out again and it seemed natural to you to get into bed before you called, so night clothes.' He paused for a second and I thought I heard a mattress spring protesting. He was lying down, in the bedroom right below me, and when he spoke again his voice was lower, slower. 'You wear shorts in bed, at least in warm weather, and you generally don't wear anything underneath them. You'll be wearing an old T-shirt with the shorts, a worn-out one that isn't good enough for daytime any more. Right so far?'

'Uncanny.' I was glad I sounded cool and a little amused rather than exceedingly flustered, which was my actual state of mind. 'Which T-shirt though?'

'I think your favourite – the grey one with the lion on the front.'

I swallowed. 'What makes you say it's my favourite?'

187

'It's worn around the neckline. The material is falling apart. You didn't wear it when we were doing surveillance because the V neck is too low and you were self-conscious about how revealing it is, but any of the times I've come round unexpectedly and got you out of bed, you've been wearing it.' He paused. 'I like it.'

I said the first thing that came into my head. 'It's a tiger, not a lion.'

'Then the stripes have faded since you bought it.'

I looked down. They had, too. The tiger coat was a flat pale orange and the shaggy ruff of fur around its face looked like a lion's mane. 'I never noticed.'

'I did.'

And what else did you notice, I thought and couldn't say. The material was so softened by wear that it draped over my body, thin and clinging, and I realised that every curve was visible; I might as well have been naked. *How revealing it is.* He had looked at the neckline enough to see it was fraying; he must have looked at what it was framing too . . .

'You've considered this in detail.'

Instead of answering, he sighed, and that was enough to make it absolutely clear he was thinking along the same lines as me. I closed my eyes as I slid my hand down to my stomach, pressing it flat against my bare skin, which was cool from the shower. The tip of my little finger slid under the waistband of my shorts, and then the ring finger. A shiver of pleasure ran through me. It would have been easy to slip my hand down, between my legs – easier than not doing it, at that moment. I pressed my body into the mattress, and made a tiny noise of pure frustration.

What if he kept talking.

What if he let himself in with his key to this flat, and came up the stairs.

What if he came into this room. What if he slowly peeled off every single thing I was wearing.

What if.

Silence on the other end of the line, but I knew he was there, listening, and I knew as clearly as if he'd said it out loud that he could picture exactly what I was thinking about, and what I wanted. Then, as if in confirmation, he spoke again, and this time his voice was heavy with regret.

'You see why we can't be in the same flat, Maeve.'

And then, 'You owe me a tenner.'

MAN FOUND DEAD AT ISOLATED HOUSE

A man's body has been found at a house in Cumbria, in an isolated location five miles from Keswick. A council worker discovered the body on Tuesday when he visited the property to secure power lines damaged by high winds. Cumbria Constabulary have opened a murder investigation.

Local sources say the man was the owner of the house. He has been positively identified but his name has not been released as next of kin have yet to be located. He was 39. The sources described the house as 'remote' and said the man 'kept himself to himself' and had few visitors.

Police have refused to confirm reports that the man was shot dead. 'The investigation is at an early stage,' Chief Superintendent Eli Parker said at a press conference yesterday. 'We are keen to speak with anyone who might have visited the property in the last year. We don't yet know when or how this man died.'

They also want to locate a red Ford Transit registered at the property, registration AD15 XCM. Anyone with relevant information should call 101 and ask to be put in touch with the incident room at Keswick police station.

29

Because of the car, and because he was still a suspect in the disappearance of Rosalie Marshall, and therefore a person of interest to our enquiry, I went to Brighton the next day to search Paul Lavender's flat. In the passenger seat: Georgia, who was wildly over-excited to be getting a trip out of the office. It was just the two of us, because Una Burt was playing a constant numbers game to try to cover our workload. I had hoped for Liv but she turned me down, preferring to stay in central London in case Sonny needed her.

'Isn't this the perfect opportunity to show you still love the job?' I whispered. 'Didn't you want to prove yourself?'

Her eyes narrowed and she stood very straight, as if that would add enough inches to let her look me in the eye. 'I prove myself every day.'

'I know that. I miss you, that's all. I was looking forward to spending the day with you.' I pulled her in for a quick hug which made Pete Belcott whistle appreciatively from the other side of the office.

'At last. Do you know how long I've waited to see you two getting physical with one another—'

He broke off as Chris Pettifer put a meaty hand over his face and held it there, muffling his words so all that came out was inarticulate honking.

Chris nodded to us. 'You're welcome, ladies.'

And so I had Georgia. She was buzzing with happiness, having received permission from the CPS two days earlier to charge someone in the stabbing she had been investigating, and she wouldn't shut up about it.

'I mean, I thought the evidence was all there as far as it went but he didn't confess and you know there are no guarantees with the CPS. Even if you have loads of forensic evidence and eyewitnesses you can't be sure you're going to be able to convince a jury, but I know he did it and I was absolutely bricking it in case the lawyer said no. I think I sounded too surprised when he said yes because he laughed.'

'Was that the first time you called the CPS yourself?' I couldn't believe she had been a detective for so long without doing a fairly ordinary part of the job. On second thoughts I could absolutely believe that someone else would have intervened to do it every other time. I'd done it myself.

'Josh said it was my case and my responsibility so I should make the call.'

My hands tightened involuntarily on the wheel. I hadn't spoken to him since the night before, only seeing him in meetings, looking focused and professional. I put a ten-pound note on his desk before I left for Brighton. It seemed like the best thing to do. *Of course I didn't take it seriously when we were talking on the phone. Of course I was just playing along. Of course I wasn't shaky with desire when I hung up, and of course I didn't spend the whole evening and most of the night thinking about you.* The flat downstairs had bare floorboards in most of the rooms; I had heard him walking up and down for hours, pacing like an animal looking for a way out of a cage.

In a way it was a blessing to have Georgia there as a distraction. She chattered all the way. I managed to make it seem I was interested in what she was saying while my thoughts spun in circles: Derwent, Rosalie, the Marshalls, Paul Lavender, Derwent . . .

The reason Derwent had stayed in London, as far as anyone else was concerned (and perhaps it was the truth), was that he needed to supervise the interview that Chris Pettifer and Colin Vale were currently conducting with Paul Lavender. Paul was spittingly angry about us going through his things, which made me feel that it was worth the effort. Derwent, I had heard from

Pettifer, thought men would be more effective when questioning Lavender, given his propensity to flirt with women. I wondered if that was true or if I'd been dispatched to Brighton deliberately. Out of sight, out of mind. It wasn't working that way for me, whatever about Derwent.

My phone rang just as we came into the city centre and I glanced at it to see, inevitably, Derwent's name on the screen. Georgia reached across and grabbed the phone before I could stop her.

'Hello-o?'

A brief silence as she listened, biting her very perfect bottom lip, while I floated on a sea of rage. Why had she picked the phone up? Why had I let her? What was she saying? What was *he* saying?

'Yes . . . No, she's driving. You can tell me if you— oh, really? OK. I'll pass it on, then, shall I?' She looked at me and rolled her eyes. 'Yes, she's fine. We're almost there. Yes, when we're finished. OK. Bye.' She hung up.

'What did he want?' It came out as a croak.

'He just said we should look for anything that connected Lavender to Rosalie which, I mean, I know? He never trusts me, does he? Just points out the obvious in case I've missed it.'

I thought of a hundred things to say in response to that, and discarded them as being too mean.

'It's my phone. He was ringing me.'

'Oh yeah. I forgot.' She looked out of the window, humming under her breath, and I wrestled with myself. She would have mentioned if he'd sounded different or said anything unusual, wouldn't she? But I couldn't just leave it, I discovered.

'Did he know it was you who answered the phone?'

'Straight away.'

'You do have a very distinctive way of saying hello.'

'I do!' She grinned happily.

'What exactly did he say?'

'He asked where you were and I said driving and he said to look for items that relate to Rosalie, like press cuttings or pictures and I said yes, and he asked how you were and I said fine and he said you should call him and I said later, when we're finished and then he said goodbye. And that was it! No drama, just him being a moody git.'

'He sounded moody?'

'No more than usual.' Georgia slotted the phone back into its holder and brought up the satnav again. 'Maeve, we've gone completely the wrong way, look. We'll have to go around again.'

I had got lost, I realised, and dragged my mind back to focus on the route, concentrating like a learner driver as we threaded our way back to Paul Lavender's flat.

He had phoned me. He wanted me to call him.

Forget it. Concentrate.

Concentrate.

I had warned Georgia about what she could expect but the full horror of it didn't sink in until we arrived and I ushered her inside.

'Oh my God.'

'And you were pleased to be sent to do this.' I pulled a mask up over my mouth and nose. The sun was streaming in, which really brought out the stale food and body odour undertones of the atmosphere. 'I don't think housework has been a priority for Mr Lavender since he moved in.'

Georgia was looking around, dismayed. 'I don't even know where to start.'

'We need his computer and any external hard drives. That's a priority. And then go through the rest of the place.'

'Including all the books?'

'Yep.' I scanned the shelves. They were crowded with books and papers, folders and files. 'You know, when we were here before, Lavender was able to find exactly what he wanted as soon as he looked for it. There has to be a system.'

'But if there's something to find, it's going to be hidden, so it's not going to conform to the system anyway.' Georgia reached up and took down a handful of papers. 'So we might as well just go for it instead of wasting any time trying to work out how everything is shelved.'

She was right. I took the papers from her nonetheless; I still didn't totally trust her. 'Why don't you do the kitchen and bedroom and I'll do the bathroom and the shelves.'

'Have you seen the bathroom? Because I glanced in and God, I wouldn't volunteer to do it.'

'I have seen it . . . but I've also seen the kitchen.' I patted her arm. 'Let's see how quickly we can do this.'

For the next few hours, we searched. I opened the windows to make it bearable and the salt-laden air blowing off the seafront was a bonus. The shelves yielded various bits of paperwork relating to the period of Rosalie's disappearance and Lavender's journalism, but nothing that linked him to her. I had no doubt that he was a connoisseur of the darker corners of the internet, legal or not, but it was all hidden on his computer and it would be someone else's job to search that. Georgia also came up empty-handed in the kitchen, giving me a running commentary on the horrors she found in the fridge and larder ('this is four years out of date. Four years! If I don't throw it out could I be done for attempted murder?') and then the bedroom where all I heard was the occasional cry of disgust.

Having dealt with the bathroom I went to join Georgia. She was lying face down on the floor, shining a torch under the bed, and she looked up at me with reproachful eyes.

'I wish I'd done the bathroom.'

'No, you don't.' I indicated the wardrobe. 'Have you gone through his clothes?'

'Not in there. I went through the chest of drawers.' She got up. 'Help me lift the mattress?'

Together we wrestled with it, finding only the bed's stained base and a condom wrapper.

Georgia let the mattress fall back. 'Ugh. Imagine coming into this flat and deciding "yes, that's a man I'd like to have sex with".'

'I'd rather not.' I was thinking Lavender's soft white flesh would have been enough to put me off long before I'd climbed the endless flights of stairs to his lair. 'He teaches English as a foreign language. Do you think he ever invites students here for extra coaching?'

'Definitely.'

'We should mention it to Josh. They can hint at it in interview and see if it gets a reaction.'

I turned my attention to the wardrobe, a poky space built in between two support beams. The base of the cupboard was about a foot lower than the floor of the room by some quirk of architecture, and I hoped I wouldn't have to climb into it. Because it was narrow and deep, a bar ran from the front of the cupboard to the back rather than from left to right, which meant that I would have to lean right in to reach all the clothes that hung on it. Every fibre of my being wanted to refuse. I started at the front, taking every hanger out and going through the pockets of trousers, shirts and jackets at speed.

'You're so fast at that.' Georgia had stopped to watch me.

'Practice.' I whipped through the six or seven hangers that were loaded with multiple items of none-too-clean clothing, wrinkling my nose at the smell of body odour that was making its way through the mask, and found nothing but rubbish and a couple of crumpled bank notes. When I'd taken out the last of the hanging clothes and folded them at my feet, I shone my torch into the space, catching glints from wire hangers that had fallen to the floor at some point, and a few coins that had slid out of pockets, and a button shank that proved to be attached to a leather button, which was sewn onto tweed. It was, inevitably, right at the back.

'Hang on.' I stepped into the cupboard, cursing quietly. It was a jacket, crumpled and dusty, and as I shook it the empty casings from moth larvae floated down to the floor. 'Gross.'

I backed out carefully and examined my prize. The label and the lapels suggested it was from the 1970s and at one time it had been an expensive piece of clothing, with a silk lining. The lining was now fraying and stained, and the moths had feasted on the creased tweed so that it was only fit for the bin.

'That's disgusting,' Georgia said, and I agreed. I made myself check the pockets, discovering a dry, dead roll-up cigarette, and a folded piece of paper that had slipped into the lining through a hole in one pocket.

'What is it?'

A child's handwriting, straggling on a diagonal across the page . . . 'It's a story.'

'What kind of story?'

'Medusa.' I looked up at Georgia. 'I wonder if we have any samples of Rosalie's handwriting.'

30

When we had finished searching the flat, I took out my phone to call Derwent, steeling myself to sound normal, casual and focused on the case: all the things I was not.

'What are you doing?' Georgia's voice was edged with unease.

'Calling Josh. I want to tell him about the story and that idea we had about Lavender taking advantage of his students.'

'No need. I texted him already.'

I blinked. 'You did what?'

'Texted him. I sent him a photo of the story. I thought it was better to let him know as we went along, so he could feed the information to Chris and Colin during the interviews if they decided it was relevant.'

'You . . . thought that.'

'It made sense.'

I felt as if my skull had been filled with wet cement that was now sloshing around unhelpfully. 'Well. I thought I was going to tell him.'

'Usually we wouldn't wait until the end of a search to share any useful discoveries.'

'No, but—' I broke off.

That Georgia had acted on her own initiative was good, really, and it was just that I hadn't thought of it.

I should have thought of it.

I was not going to blame Georgia for my own shortcomings, I decided, and tried very hard not to feel blazingly angry with her for doing what I should have done.

'Well, thank you. But Josh wanted me to call him back anyway.'

'Maeve.' She put her hand over my phone. 'Don't.'

'What do you mean?'

A flicker of something that might have been pity. 'Look, you know a lot more than I do about investigating murders. You're a much better detective than I am. I'd never tell you what to do if this was work. But I know men, and I know you shouldn't call him.'

I welcomed the surge of rage that swept through me, lighting up synapses in my brain. 'Why the hell not?'

'You'll just get hurt,' she said softly. 'He's a married man, Maeve.'

'They're not married, actually.' I corrected her without thinking about how that sounded, and her face fell: definitely pity now.

'He lives with her. She's his partner.'

'None of this is news to me.'

'Yes, I know. But I think you haven't thought about what that means. He's not going to leave Melissa for you. The only thing that will happen if you get tangled up in a relationship with him is that you'll lose your self-respect.'

'I think you should mind your own business.'

She folded her arms, uneasy. 'I'd like to, believe me. I'd prefer that. But I feel like you need someone to stop you from making bad choices and it seems to be up to me to do it.'

'You are very much mistaken about that.'

Ordinarily my tone would have made her shrink and scuttle away but she stood her ground. 'Who else is going to intervene? Liv? For what it's worth, she thinks it would be disastrous too, and if she was here she'd be saying the same thing as me.'

'Oh, you've discussed it?'

'Of course.' Georgia blinked, earnest. 'We worry about you. And you were the one who dragged us into the situation.'

'I absolutely did not.'

'You did. Last summer. You invited me to stay with you when Josh left unexpectedly—'

'That wasn't my choice. It was the boss who sent you.'

A wave of her hand; it wasn't important. '—which was after something happened between you, which I know because you called Liv looking for a shoulder to cry on. She tried to warn you that he wasn't being fair to you.' A shrug. 'I totally get that you didn't want to listen, by the way. The two of you there on your own – it must have been impossible to resist him.'

'There was nothing to resist.' I swallowed, my throat suddenly tight. 'You said that yourself. No romance. All professional. You told the others that.'

'Yeah, because I was looking out for you. I said the same thing to everyone who asked, but you and I know it's not true.'

'What makes you say that?' I managed.

'Maeve, I have *eyes*.'

I should have known, I thought bitterly, that Georgia, who was oblivious 99 per cent of the time, would have picked up on the slightest hint of sexual tension between me and Derwent. And it had been more than a hint; even I had to admit that. But, 'Don't get too excited. If you and Liv have talked it over in detail, she'll have told you it was nothing. Not even a proper kiss.'

'Yes, but I think that's worse. It makes it more exciting, not less, that nothing really happened. If you'd had sex it would be an embarrassing memory by now, but you didn't.' She tilted her head, all sympathy. 'It feels like love at the moment because he's unattainable. And because he's Josh Derwent, obviously.'

'I don't – I wouldn't say *love*.' I stopped, tripped up by a wave of unexpected emotion. What would I say, if I was trying to explain it? How did I feel? I couldn't even name it to myself.

'I'm really sorry, Maeve.' She sounded it, too. 'But this only ends one way – with you on your own, hating yourself. There's no happy ever after.'

My knees felt weak. I sat down on the edge of Paul Lavender's bed and put my head in my hands. 'Well, obviously I don't want that.'

The mattress dipped as Georgia sat beside me. She put her arm around my shoulders. 'What do you want? If you could have anything you wanted in the whole world, right now, what would it be?'

The answer came surprisingly easily. 'I'd want to find out what happened to Rosalie.'

'You would.' She was smiling when I looked at her. 'But it's not a bad idea. Throw yourself into the case so you don't have to think about your love life.'

'You never know,' I said. 'It might even do some good.'

By the time I got back to London I had endured almost two hours of intensive emotional support, including a hands-free chat with Liv, who backed Georgia up. They had clearly bonded over the Josh situation, as Georgia insisted on calling it, and I was mordantly aware that the next thing they'd suggest would be a karaoke evening *á trois* with tequila shots and a hangover worthy of commemoration in an epic poem. I nodded and said all the things that they expected me to say before I dropped Georgia off at the office, ended the phone call with Liv and drove back to the flat. I hadn't gone into the office, even to find out how Paul Lavender's interview was going. Better not to see Josh, Georgia and Liv had urged me. Better to leave it for today.

'You need some space. Some time,' Liv had counselled.

Georgia had agreed. 'And another man to take your mind off him.'

My mind wasn't on him, I assured myself, glancing at the windows of the downstairs flat as I parked on my street. The lights were off. No one home.

Not that it mattered to me.

In the silence after the engine stopped, there was nothing to distract me any more. I had been stupid, I thought. Liv and Georgia had spotted it, and I hadn't. Derwent had known too, carefully avoiding me, blaming Una Burt and Melissa for the distance he felt he should keep from me. And I had been oblivious, stubborn, trying to persuade him to come closer instead of realising he was making every effort to stay away, and why. I could say lots of things about Josh Derwent and the way he behaved but one of the truly consistent aspects of his nature was that he always wanted to do what was best for me.

And the previous night, on the phone – all he had asked me was whether I was in bed, which could have been for a hundred reasons. I was the one who had turned the conversation into something different, something that still made my body hum with unfulfilled longing. So he had gone along with it – that meant nothing, really. That was Josh as I'd known him first, when he was relentless in his pursuit of women. That side of him was hidden, not gone. I'd drawn it out of him, which was nothing to boast about.

I put my head down on the steering wheel and sighed. I needed to make it right and I wasn't sure how to start.

31

The following morning we had two hours left of Paul Lavender's company before we had to charge him with something or let him go, and the interviewers had made no progress. I steeled myself and went to find Derwent, who was watching the live feed from the interview room. He was sitting on his own, scowling at the screen, his arms folded. I stopped in the doorway.

'Hi.'

'What do you want?'

'Time to let me have a go.'

A minimal shake of his head. 'He'll run the clock down bullshitting you.'

'As opposed to what he's doing now?' I watched the interview for a few seconds, assessing the body language. Lavender was relaxed, his head tilted to one side, his expression supercilious. Pettifer's shoulders were up around his ears and Colin Vale seemed to have shrunk into himself. 'They're not getting anywhere.'

'I don't think it's worth changing our tactics at this point. He'll know we're desperate.'

'If he can tell the time he should know that anyway.'

Derwent rubbed his eyes with the heels of his hands. 'You're right.'

'I know. Look, it can't do any harm to let me try. There's something he's not telling us. Even if I can't get him to talk, I might be able to work out what it is.'

When I walked into the room, I got my first proper look at Paul Lavender since he'd been in custody. He was slumped in his chair, his eyes swollen and red from lack of sleep, even though we had been punctilious about giving him breaks, but he didn't seem cowed. 'Sending in reinforcements? Did I break the other two?'

I waited to answer until the digital recording was running and I had explained who I was, careful to follow the rules. 'I asked if I could have a turn.'

'Really? Couldn't stay away?' He gestured at the room. 'I've had better locations for first dates, but we might be able to make it work.'

'I asked if I could interview you because I wanted to ask you about this.' I slid the story across the table, sealed in its evidence bag.

'The others already asked me about it.' His voice was rough and he took a moment to sip some water. 'I told them, I don't remember anything about it. I didn't know it was in the flat.'

'I was the one who found it.'

He stopped with the plastic cup a few inches from his mouth. 'Oh? Does that mean you've been through my things?'

'Yes.'

'You didn't find a set of keys with a hippo keyring, did you? Only I lost them a while ago and I've been hoping they'd turn up.'

'Sorry.' I tapped the story. 'Tell me about this. Tell me about the tweed jacket.'

'The tweed— oh Lord, is that where it was?' He did a convincing job of looking surprised and a little embarrassed. 'I hadn't cleared out the pockets, obviously.'

'It was a good jacket.'

'My father's.' He leaned back in the chair, clasping his hands behind his head and narrowing his eyes at me. 'Lovely thing to wear, when it fitted me. They don't make them like that any more.'

'Were you wearing it when you went to interview Helena Marshall?'

'Probably.' He sniffed. 'I must have been, I suppose. It was the only decent jacket I had at that point in my life – I tried not to turn up in an anorak when I was interviewing people. I was young. They underestimated me anyway, which was useful, but the jacket made me feel respectable. Was the story really just shoved in the pocket?'

'It had slipped into the lining.'

'Ah.'

'Was it Rosalie's story?' I asked, knowing that he had said he didn't know when Pettifer asked. I had emailed a photograph of the story to Ivo and Magnus, asking if they recognised Rosalie's handwriting. There had been no reply from Magnus, which didn't surprise me, but a cautious 'possibly' from Ivo. It was the kind of thing Rosalie had written, he confirmed, and it might have been hers, but he couldn't say for certain.

Lavender drew it towards him and read the first page. 'Yes. She wrote it. I remember it. *Persues was very hangsom but he was braver than hangsom and cleverer than brave.* God, you can't deny she was a bright little thing. If you fixed the spelling I'd be happy to write that sentence now, let alone at the age of nine.'

'Why did you tell my colleagues you didn't know if it was hers?'

'It doesn't mean anything, does it? I said I didn't know because I didn't like them and I had forgotten about it. Then I remembered shoving it in my pocket. I didn't dwell on it. I wasn't *obsessed* with her. I was just . . . interested. She was unusual and she seemed to be having a pretty miserable life for herself and it all made me curious.' He leaned forward. 'You strike me as the kind of person who understands being curious.'

'I do. It's part of my job. And at the moment I'm curious about you.' I closed my notebook as if the interview was about to be over, subtly indicating that Lavender could relax. 'I know you haven't told us everything. I know you're hiding something that you don't want us to know because you don't think we'll find it out ourselves.'

He blinked. 'Like what?'

'We went to the house to get the lie of the land. I wanted to imagine what it was like when the Marshalls lived there. I spent some time looking out of the windows. During the investigation into Rosalie's disappearance, Helena described seeing a car at the house, repeatedly, in the previous weeks. That car matched the car you were driving down to the last details – but it wouldn't have been possible for her to see the car, not as she described it, glancing out of an upstairs window. Helena lied about it.'

'So what?' Lavender shrugged. 'Helena lied about a lot of things, darling. If you haven't worked that out yet, I don't hold out much hope for this investigation.'

'Lots of people lie to us, Mr Lavender,' I said, unruffled. 'You've lied in this interview. What's interesting to us is why people lie, and what they lie about. There was no need for Helena to mention your car at all, was there? She didn't tell the investigating officers about your visit to the house – the one that went so badly. She didn't name you. If she didn't want them to find you, her best approach would have been to suppress any mention of you.'

'I don't know why she talked about it. You're asking me to speculate about someone else's thought processes. I can't see the point.'

'You're right, this is just speculation.' I smiled. 'Indulge me, just for a couple of minutes. I think Helena was worried about you. I think she was concerned that you were involved in her daughter's disappearance, and I'd like to know what prompted that. She saw your car, we know that. She noted certain details of it, like the broken numberplate. She remembered it. Something about it worried her.' I leaned across the table. 'What did you do that worried her, Paul?'

'I was there. I saw how she treated Rosalie. I suppose I was a loose end.'

'Were you there more than once?'

He pressed his lips together and shook his head; not *no, I wasn't there* but *no, I'm not telling you.*

206

'Cards on the table, Paul. We haven't found anything that ties you to Rosalie except for this story and the description of your car, so I think you're probably going to drop down our list of suspects. My personal opinion is that you're more important as a witness. You saw Rosalie. You spoke to her. You aren't a member of the family and you weren't influenced by any fondness for the Marshalls. So stop thinking about when you can leave, and start helping us. What haven't you told me?' I put my notebook and pen on the table and folded my arms. *This is just a chat, a walk down memory lane . . .* 'What happened when you went back?'

Silence for a moment, and I thought I wasn't going to get anywhere with him after all.

'What I've always wondered,' Paul Lavender said quietly, 'is whether I made a bad situation worse. I did go back to the house. Just once. I didn't go in. The gates were closed and I pulled my car in, off the road. I was curious. Concerned. I wanted to know that Rosalie was all right, after what had happened. I thought Helena might have taken it out on her after she found me in Rosalie's room.'

'What happened?'

'Rosalie was in the front garden, playing on her own. There was no one else around. She was messing about and I called to her. I said hello.' He swallowed. 'I never went into the garden. I never touched her. I just asked her if she was all right. I told her to keep writing, I think – you know, encourage the young. That's why I like teaching. You can make a difference.'

'What happened then?'

'Helena came out of the house and saw us. I – I ran. A fully grown adult man, and I scurried away as if I'd done something wrong.' He shook his head. 'Twice, I ran and left Rosalie behind to deal with the consequences. And then she disappeared. I've always felt guilty about it. I could run away, but Rosalie couldn't, and I've always worried that I was the reason Helena lost her temper with her for the last time.'

'You think Helena killed her.'

'I think she was capable of it.' His chin was trembling and his eyes were wet. 'When Rosalie disappeared, I wasn't surprised. The only thing that surprised me was that Helena never got arrested for it. I tried to help that little girl, and I think – I think I was the reason she died.'

32

'It was a wonderful place to live. We were all so happy there, such a community.'

I was glad I was on the phone so Samantha Moguel couldn't see me. I had started to slump over onto my desk from sheer despair ten minutes into the call when she had repeated the line about being 'so happy there' for the third time. The miracles of modern technology: Mrs Moguel now lived in Florida but the line was clear and crackle-free. I could hear every single word she was saying without any difficulty. Unfortunately none of it so far was worth hearing.

'There were the Marshalls and the Hoods and the Spekes and Nestor Campbell, who was an impresario and always had interesting guests, and one or two other people who were in our gang. We socialised together and shared advice about cleaners and workmen and so forth, and Dr Fuller was wonderful with the children when they had health issues and Emory Speke was a solicitor so he was the go-to man for conveyancing and wills and divorces. Everything was *easy*. Also it was lovely to be by the river.'

'Lovely,' I repeated dully.

'I have such happy memories of being there,' Mrs Moguel droned on, 'as if the sun was always shining, which, I mean, I know it *wasn't* – how could it have been, in London.' A tinkly laugh, and a sigh. 'But in retrospect we were all so happy. So happy.'

Paul Lavender had walked out half an hour earlier, a free man, threatening us with legal action of an unspecified and unlikely nature.

209

'Go and chase up any loose ends you can think of,' Derwent had ordered, his jaw tight with anger as his case came apart around a suspect who simply wasn't suspicious enough. 'Anything you have on your action list – now is the time to get on with it. If we can't find any evidence against Lavender, he gets away with murder or he's not the one we're looking for. Either find me something to throw at him so I can arrest him again, or find me a new lead, because at the moment we've got nothing.'

'Mrs Moguel . . .' I tried.

'You can call me Sammy, dear. And you should know that I've divorced Jacques Moguel. I'm Sammy Hillard again for the first time since I was in my twenties. But never mind – you were asking about the Marshalls. They were wonderful neighbours. Such good friends, through all my ups and downs. I moved in as a newly-wed with my second husband, Christian Rothwell, but I already had my son, from my first marriage. I was so relieved that Helena had boys too, even though they were younger. I thought they would be company for one another, but of course there was always a huge gap between them, being five and seven years younger than my boy and it makes a big difference at that age. But then at that stage I thought I would be living happily ever after and that was wrong too – Christian was unfaithful from the very start. It absolutely broke my heart. Of course I behaved badly too, to retaliate. He was a gentleman though. I got the house when we divorced, which was wonderful because my son was settled in school and I was happy there, and then I met Jacques and he seemed like heaven on earth and he wasn't around much because he was working in Dubai so I suppose I was able to keep my illusions about him. But he was really a liar and a cheat. They all were. Tony, Christian and Jacques. One disaster after another. And here I am on my own again, although I will say that I date a lot.' Another giggle; she was sliding back and forth between sorrow and glee with dizzying speed.

'So who lived in your house at the time that Rosalie disappeared? I'm trying to get a full list of everyone in the neighbourhood,' I explained.

'Just me, most of the time. I'd divorced Christian when my son was ten. And then it was the two of us. Then Jacques was only around a few weeks of the year – Christmas and Ascot and so forth. I used to go to Dubai to stay with him whenever I could, which I loved because he had staff and such a lifestyle and the heat . . . well, it's no accident I've ended up living in Florida where it's warm all year round. I could never live in the UK again, never. The cold just seeps into your bones.'

I rubbed my forehead with the heel of my hand, trying to ease the headache that was gripping me around the temples.

'So it was just you and your son?'

'No, not then. I remember because it felt like such a shock – I had been bracing myself for the empty nest and crying over the fact that my boy was heading off to university, though of course I was so proud, but I had thought we'd have the summer together, but he was just . . . gone. He never came back, in a sense – I mean, I saw him occasionally but he never lived with me again. He grew up that summer. He'd started to pull away – changing his hair, wanting to be called Jay instead of JV, which was what I'd always called him, unless he was in trouble in which case it was his full name and he knew I meant it. That's what he does, you see, when he wants to change his image. The name goes along with everything else; I mean, honestly, it's hard to keep track sometimes. But then he had this moment of madness and packed up his things and that was that, he was gone. And as I said to Helena, she had a terrible shock when Rosalie disappeared but she also had two other children. I was on my own, without warning.'

The idea that it had been worse for her was breathtaking in its self-centredness, but I let it go.

'And JV was what age when he left? Eighteen?'

'Almost nineteen, actually. His birthday was in August but I'd held him back a year so he wasn't disadvantaged by that.'

'And – forgive me, I'm being stupid – he left before or after Rosalie disappeared?'

'Oh, before. He went off backpacking, or fruit-picking or something. He had been tutoring Magnus so he'd built up quite a little pot of money and I suppose that was all he felt he needed. He barely said goodbye. Rosalie disappeared about a week later.' A sniff. 'It felt as if I'd spent the whole summer crying. When Helena wound up in hospital, I almost envied her. I had to keep going, you see. I couldn't just give in to my feelings.'

Unlike selfish old Helena who had indulged herself with a suicide attempt that had left her brain-damaged. I was sitting up straight now, trying to concentrate on the thread of interest that ran through the acres of flannel that Sammy Hillard was wadding into my ear. 'So JV left unexpectedly?'

'Well, yes. That's what I've been telling you.' For the first time she sounded irritated. 'The plan was to spend the whole summer together, for the last time. The two of us were so close. Jacques was busy in Dubai and it was too hot to go out in the summer, I thought. I was going to go in September and stay for a couple of months rather than rattling around the house on my own. I have never liked being on my own much.' Another laugh. 'I suppose that's why I keep getting married.'

'Let me just see if I've asked you everything I wanted to know . . .' I stared at my notes. I was playing for time. It was essential that none of that urgency and excitement I was feeling crept into my voice. 'Mrs Mo— er, Ms Hillard, I mean – I've been through the files and I don't think JV was ever interviewed about Rosalie's disappearance.'

'No, he wasn't. He had already left then, as I said. What could he have possibly contributed to the investigation?'

'Absolutely, he wouldn't have been on anyone's list at that stage. It's just that, given that he was in the house so much that summer, tutoring Magnus, I think it would be helpful if I could speak to him. We're trying to get a full picture of who was there and what the family dynamic was like.'

'After so long?'

'Because of what's happened to Mr and Mrs Marshall. In case there's any connection with what happened to Rosalie.' I had explained this already, at the start of the phone call.

'Oh yes. Of course. So sad. Well, I'm sure JV will want to help if you think it's important.' There was a scuffling sound. 'I have his number here, on the fridge. He lives in London now so you're in luck.'

Not dead, not on the other side of the world. I was liking the sound of JV more and more.

'Here it is.' She read it out, repeating various parts as she lost track ('no, one-four-three-ONE') and I read it back to her a couple of times, making sure I had it right. The number looked familiar to me and I puzzled over it for a moment, confused. Where had I seen it before? Or was it just reading it out two or three times that had made me think I remembered it from somewhere else?

Someone was standing beside me, looking over my shoulder. Derwent, I knew, before I glanced up. He was focused on the number I'd written down, frowning at it with the taut concentration of a hunting dog. So it meant something to him too.

'Ms Hillard,' I said into the phone, 'what is JV's actual name? What's his surname? Is he Hillard, or Moguel, or—'

'He has my first husband's name. He's John Victor Grant. JV to me, Jay to his university friends. But these days he goes by—'

'Tor Grant,' I said, my eyes locked on Derwent's.

'Yes,' Sammy Hillard said happily. 'How did you know?'

33

After I got off the phone I looked up at Derwent. His expression was as bleak as I'd ever seen it.

'We couldn't have known Tor Grant would be a person of interest.'

'Except that I said he'd turn out to be our murderer.' He shook his head. 'I fucking said he was. I knew it.'

'No, you didn't. I said it first anyway. And we still don't know that he killed the Marshalls.'

'OK. That's fair. If he killed them, it's hard to see why he would come back and draw attention to himself by breaking into your car, unless he was looking for something that would otherwise incriminate him.'

'The note from down the side of the chair?' I had a copy of it taped to my computer monitor and now I looked at it again.

BDK? How?
Check dates

'The dates – maybe Bruce wanted to check when Tor left for university.'

'Maybe.' Derwent grimaced. 'He has to be top of the list now for Rosalie's abduction. He never came to the attention of the original investigation because he wasn't around when she disappeared, but he knew her. His behaviour changed that summer. He also changed his plans unexpectedly. He left before she did, as far as anyone else knew, but he could have come back to take her.'

'Why would he want to make a podcast about it if he was the one who took her?'

Derwent raised his eyebrows ironically. 'You think there was ever going to be an actual podcast?'

'Yes, I do. He's got a website for it. Social media accounts. If it was fake he went to a lot of trouble to publicise it.' I had been typing and now I showed Derwent my screen: a comprehensive list of results for 'WHO STOLE ROSALIE?', broadcast date to be confirmed.

Derwent shrugged, changing tack effortlessly. 'If I wanted to control a narrative – if I wanted to point the finger at anyone but me, and suppress any evidence that might get me in trouble – I might decide to make a podcast.'

'He was worried about someone else doing a podcast about Rosalie,' I said. 'Maybe he thought they'd focus on him.'

'If he claimed his was the definitive one, it would put off other podcasters, I suppose.' Derwent closed his eyes for a moment, looking exhausted. 'We wasted time on Paul Lavender.'

'Maybe,' I said, troubled. 'But what he told us feels like part of the picture. I just don't know how it fits in.'

'It doesn't, in any meaningful way. I have to go and explain all of this to Una Burt now, including the fact that we had Tor Grant in custody at one point.'

'You can try to convince her that it's good news. We've had contact with him already, and recently, so we should be able to pick him up relatively easily.'

'Or we had our chance and he slipped through our fingers.'

'That would be bad luck,' I allowed.

'When have we had any other kind? Try Grant's number and see if you can talk him into coming in, but get response to go round to the address he gave us too. See if we can pick him up quickly, before he has a chance to slip away.' He turned, scanning the room. 'Colin, Liv, dig into his background. I want to know everything about him – if he's been arrested before, if he's ever been charged with any crimes, what jobs he's done, where he's been living, everything. I want to know more about Tor Grant than his mother does by the time he's sitting in our interview room.'

'That might not be difficult,' I said. 'I don't think his mother has the least idea what he does or where he is. She just has that mobile number for him, and . . .'

Derwent groaned. 'Don't tell me.'

I held out the phone so he could hear the recorded announcement. *This number is out of use. Please dial again.*

In one way we were back to square one, but it helped that Tor Grant felt like a promising lead for the first time. Una Burt was brisk; she wasn't given to I-told-you-so unless you really deserved it.

'Well, it's a shame, but you couldn't have known.'

Oddly, I thought, Derwent would have preferred a proper bollocking instead of Una Burt's pragmatism. If she wasn't going to beat him up, he would have to do it to himself. Grim-faced, he shut himself away with Chris Pettifer to work on the questions they would put to Tor Grant, also known as Jay Grant, also known as JV Grant, also known as John Victor Grant.

'And who knows if he ever borrowed a surname from one of his stepfathers,' Liv said. 'That gives us another few options for pseudonyms.'

'Split the list with Colin,' I suggested, reaching out for my phone, which was ringing. 'Maeve Kerrigan speaking. Yes . . . Right. That's a shame. No, it's not a surprise. We thought he might be . . . Oh really? Thanks anyway.'

'Tell me that was good news,' Liv said as I hung up.

'That was the response PC. He moved out two days after he was arrested, according to the landlady. Took everything, didn't leave a forwarding address. She thought it wasn't the first time he'd done a runner like that.' I had one eye on the meeting-room door. I would need to interrupt Derwent to give him the bad news and I wanted to choose my moment. Preferably that moment would be when I was a long way away so I could avoid the worst of the explosion.

Liv leaned closer. 'How are things going with Josh? You seem stressed.'

'Why don't you discuss it with Georgia?'

She bit her lip. 'Ouch.'

'Yeah, well, imagine how I feel. I never thought you'd talk about me behind my back.'

'We were worried about you.' Liv's eyes were shiny with concern. 'It's just a toxic situation for you. Living with him again—'

'I'm not living with him. He's in the flat downstairs.'

'That's a technicality. What did you think was going to happen if he moved in with you?'

I couldn't look at her. 'He needed somewhere to stay.'

'He could have gone anywhere. He could have stayed with anyone. Why you?'

'Why not me?'

'Maybe a better question is what did you want to happen?' I was familiar with that silky tone of voice; I'd heard it in enough interviews when she landed the killer question.

'Seriously, Liv, it's not a big deal.'

'That's not what Georgia said you said.'

My phone rang again and I snatched it up, glowering at Liv the while. *Georgia? Seriously?* 'Maeve Kerrigan speaking.'

'You said I should call you if I thought of anything else that might be relevant.' Magnus's voice was loud and immediately distinctive, which was just as well, given that he hadn't bothered to say who he was. 'You sent that story to us.'

'You didn't reply.'

'I knew Ivo would. Did he say it was Rosalie's writing?'

'He said he thought so but he wasn't sure.'

Magnus snorted. 'Typical. He never paid any attention to me or Rosalie. We were insignificant as far as he was concerned. It was definitely her story. Her writing. Unmistakable.'

'OK. Thank you. Was that all?'

'You don't seem very excited.'

'Well, the investigation has moved on since I emailed you the picture of the story, and someone else had already confirmed it

217

for us. It's still helpful to know that you think it was her work, but it's not where our focus is.'

'Where is your focus, if you don't mind me asking?'

'Look, I can't talk to you about the investigation. We're making enquiries about an individual, and I can't say any more.'

'For fuck's sake.' A horn blared so loudly it must have been next to him, a double beep from an irate moped.

I twisted to look at the open window behind me. 'I heard that. The horn.'

'Yeah?' He sounded uninterested. 'It was loud.'

'I mean, I heard it through the window, not down the phone. Are you somewhere near my office?'

'I wanted to talk to you. I told you, I thought of something. I don't know if it's relevant or not but you wanted to know if I remembered anything. The address of your office is on your card and it's not far from my work so I thought I'd come round.'

'Your speciality is turning up uninvited, isn't it?' I grabbed my bag. 'I'll come down and meet you outside. We can get a coffee.'

'You're buying.'

'Of course.' I hung up and caught Liv's eye. 'What?'

'Making a getaway. Am I supposed to break the news to Josh about Tor Grant being in the wind?'

'You could.' I was edging away. 'If he comes out of the meeting room. If he asks.'

'Maeve.'

'I have an important witness to see.'

'Maeve!'

'You'll handle it better than I would.' I checked; the door was still closed, thank God. 'I'll be back soon. Good luck.'

'I won't forget this,' she called as I slid out of the office, barely daring to breathe until the door was safely shut behind me.

Magnus was leaning against a wall outside the building, smoking, all floppy hair and privilege in a blazer and chinos. He made to throw the butt away when he saw me, but stopped himself.

'You're not going to arrest me for, like, littering, are you?'

'In a heartbeat. I have nothing better to do.'

He grinned. 'Cute.'

'Find a bin.'

I took him down the street to a small and pretentious coffee shop, instinctively feeling that I'd get more out of him if I kept him in familiar territory. He gave the barista a detailed and complicated coffee order that I only half understood, and smirked when I ordered a flat white.

'The Fiat 500 of coffees. All the girlies love a flat white. I bet you don't even know how they make it.'

'I bet I don't care,' I said evenly, and paid, and followed him to a table at the back. The décor involved a lot of brass, mirrors and taxidermy which I could have done without. Our table was watched by an owl in a glass case, one withered set of talons wrapped around a mouse.

'This is nice,' he commented. 'Not what I was expecting from the Old Bill. I'd have thought a greasy spoon was more your cup of tea.'

'What did you want to tell me?'

'Straight down to business.' He took his time, sipping his coffee and making an appreciative noise. I resisted the urge to fidget, knowing that he would take longer if he knew I was impatient. 'OK. Well, I was thinking about the gun.'

'Go on.'

'When I knocked it down . . . I wasn't on my own. I'd forgotten. Rosalie was there.' His voice softened when he said her name.

'Rosalie? You're sure?'

'She helped me find the bullets. I was lying in bed the other night and I remembered there was one that had gone under a cupboard. I couldn't fit my arm underneath it but she was tiny. She was holding the bullet when Dad came in and found us.'

'Did she get in trouble?'

'Not with Dad. He was always nice to her. He told her it was very important and precious and dangerous, and she promised she'd never touch it. Then he must have let her go because I don't remember her being there when he leathered me to within an inch of my life.'

As I considered this new piece of information, I accidentally made eye contact with a screaming weasel, frozen on a branch in a glass case behind Magnus and looked back at him in a hurry. He was a more pleasant sight than a dead weasel, but only just. 'OK. And no one else saw it? Ivo?'

'Not that I recall.' He sat back. 'I thought you'd be more pleased.'

'I'm ecstatic. I'm just thinking, that's all.' I turned the spoon over in my saucer. 'What about anyone else who might have been in the house?'

'Like who?'

In for a penny . . . 'What about your tutor?'

'My tutor?' Magnus frowned. 'You mean – JV?'

'Yes.'

'Why are you asking—' He broke off and his eyes went wide. 'You think JV was involved?'

'It's a line of enquiry.' I leaned across the table. 'Please, Magnus, keep it to yourself. We're at an early stage and—'

'He was gone. He'd already left. When Rosalie. He was gone.' The flush had faded from his cheeks; he had turned a shade of green that I associated with extreme seasickness. The smooth drawl had become choppy, incoherent, panicked.

'Are you OK, Magnus?'

'No, but.' He ran a hand through his hair and I saw his fingers were trembling. Sweat glinted on his forehead and upper lip. 'If it was him. I thought. He was gone, so I didn't.'

'You didn't what?'

'Tell the police about him.' All the cockiness had gone, leaving raw honesty. 'I should have. I didn't. I was just a kid. But I should have. I—'

He hurled himself towards the door of the café, cannoning off chairs and tables, and when I followed him outside I found him bent over, throwing up into the gutter as if he might never stop.

34

'I feel as if I've been split open and emptied out. I mean, there are places where you'd have to pay for that.' Magnus was back on form, regrettably.

I led him through the lobby, heading for the main door of the building. I had waited for him to stop vomiting, which took longer than I expected, and then dragged him back to the office and a quiet interview room. I sat opposite him with a notepad in front of me, recording the entire conversation on my phone in case I missed a detail.

'Tell me everything you remember about JV. Absolutely everything.'

To give him credit he had done his best to do just that over the next two hours, digging deep into his memory. The shock of hearing JV's name in the context of his sister's disappearance and his parents' murder had been enough to jolt him out of his habitual drawl and belligerence, and I found myself warming to him as he talked. For the first time I could see the nice little boy that DI Howlett had met, the brother who had been devastated when Rosalie disappeared.

'I hope it wasn't too traumatic,' I said now. 'I know it's hard to revisit a painful time in your life, but the information you've given me might be really useful.'

'Are you going to arrest him?'

'Yes.' If we can find him, I didn't add.

'Good.' He blew out all the air in his body, relief softening his expression. 'You know, I do feel better. This is why people go to therapy, isn't it?'

'It's one reason.' I hesitated. 'Look, Magnus, I think it might be an idea for you to get some proper counselling. All of this stuff about Rosalie, and your parents – it's a lot to sort through by yourself.'

'We should have had counselling at the time. Me and Ivo. My folks didn't do anything to organise it.' He winced. 'I mean really, what chance did we have to be normal?'

'You don't get on with Ivo, do you?'

'I think in an ordinary family the gap between us would have narrowed as we got older, but that didn't happen for us. We were frozen as we were when Rosalie disappeared. He didn't have any interest in me and I resented the fuck out of him. And that's how it is now. Childish, but there we are.'

'Maybe it's time to get to know each other, now that it's just the two of you.'

'It's too late.'

'It's never too late.'

'Unless one of us dies.' Magnus gave me a twisted little smile and I remembered that he had just lost his parents, shockingly, and that no matter how old you were or how distant you might feel from your parents, losing them meant something.

'Yeah, that's pretty final. So don't let it happen. Sometimes you have to make the first move. Let go of the anger first. It's not doing you any good to hold on to it.'

He tilted his head back, looking down his nose at me, all arrogance. 'Why do you care?'

'I think you've missed out on enough, that's all. I have a brother,' I found myself saying, slightly to my surprise, 'and I don't see much of him, but I know he'd be there for me in a heartbeat if I needed him.'

A raised eyebrow as his chin came down. 'You're a bit of a sweetheart, aren't you, Sergeant?'

'Don't tell anyone.'

'I won't. And I promise I'll think about therapy, and my brother. He's all I have left, after all. So thanks.' He leaned over and kissed my cheek, his expensive aftershave covering any hint of vomit or sweat. That was Magnus all over, I thought, keeping the real version of himself hidden. It wasn't for me to convince him to change, but I hoped he would.

'You're welcome. And if you think of anything else—'

'I'll be in touch.' He waved and headed for the door. I watched him until he was out of sight.

'Who was that?' Derwent came to stand beside me, his expression dark.

I started, one hand to my chest to keep my heart from leaping out of it. 'You have got to stop creeping up on me.'

Derwent snorted. 'Maybe if you hadn't been staring into your new boyfriend's eyes—'

'Let me stop you there. That was Magnus Marshall.'

He had the grace to look embarrassed. 'Oh. Sorry. I didn't know.'

'Evidently not. He wanted to tell me that Rosalie also knew where the gun was in his father's study.'

'Huh. What's the significance of that?'

I shook my head. 'Not a clue. It might not matter at all. I suppose she might have told someone. But get this, I asked him about Tor Grant. Magnus went to pieces. He said he didn't talk to the cops about Grant when the original investigation was taking place, and he didn't think it mattered because he knew Grant had already left home when Rosalie disappeared, but somehow it had always bothered him that he didn't say anything.'

'About what?'

'He said Grant was a creep – his word. He asked Ivo and Magnus if they'd ever done anything with girls and tried to get them to look at a nudie magazine once when he was babysitting.'

'Grooming them.'

'Possibly. Magnus was adamant that nothing happened, but Ivo must have said something to his mother because when Rosalie arrived, there was no more babysitting work for JV. He wasn't around much after that, until Magnus started struggling in school and needed a tutor.'

'Did anything happen?'

'He's not sure. He remembers a day when he left Rosalie alone with Grant, in Magnus's bedroom right at the top of the house. Rosalie wasn't with Grant when he got back but she was upset, Magnus thought.'

'What upset her?'

'Magnus never found out, but when he went back to his bedroom, JV was there, sitting at the desk, masturbating.'

'That fucker,' Derwent said softly. 'What did he do to her?'

I shook my head, trying not to imagine the details. 'Magnus was relieved that JV never came back to the house after that day. He never told anyone that he'd caught JV, even after Rosalie disappeared, because he was embarrassed about it, and he felt guilty. He assumed that JV went away because he was mortified and couldn't bear to live next door to him any more.'

'Which might be true. There's nothing as sensitive or self-conscious as a teenage boy, especially when it comes to sex.'

'Or he did something to Rosalie and he was afraid she would tell her parents.'

'Or that. That might be more likely.'

I shivered. 'Whatever happened in that room, JV found it exciting.'

'I'm not making excuses for him, but you know boys that age spend pretty much every spare moment wanking.'

'They don't run away from home afterwards, though, as a rule.'

'You can still have him as a suspect.' Derwent grinned. 'I want to see you asking him about it in interview.'

'Nothing would give me greater pleasure,' I said with feeling. 'I take it there's no sign of him?'

His expression darkened again. 'Not at the moment. But we'll get him.'

'I know.'

'Coming up?' He started towards the lifts and I followed.

'You usually take the stairs.'

He pressed the button. 'I must be tired.'

The lift doors slid open obediently and he stood back so I could go in first. I let him press the button for our floor, and the doors closed, and we were alone.

He leaned against the other side of the lift, his hands in his pockets, his eyes fixed on the floor. It was late in the day and his shirt was limp, crumpled, the sleeves badly creased where he had pushed them halfway up his forearms. His tie was askew and I longed to reach out and straighten it, but I pressed against the wall behind me, the maximum distance between us, the air charged with things unsaid – or completely normal if your mind wasn't running along the same lines as mine. He would be thinking about Tor Grant, I thought. He would be concentrating on the case, on our next moves, on what remained to be done before we could leave for the day.

He looked up and our eyes met. I felt the shock of it run through me like a current.

'Are you OK?'

'Why wouldn't I be?' I said, and he made a tiny movement, instantly arrested, that I recognised as frustration. Well, if he wanted to ask awkward questions, I could do the same.

'Why do you always take the lift with me, Josh? Always the stairs on your own, always the lift with me.'

He moved to stand in front of me, his hands still trapped in his pockets, his feet wide apart, his face inscrutable.

And the lift stopped with a self-satisfied jounce: our floor. I stepped out ahead of him, outwardly composed, inwardly trembling; he was right on my heels, as close as a shadow, and his voice was a slow, honeyed murmur only I could hear as we walked along the hallway to the office, for the last few moments that we were on our own . . .

I might have fainted from sheer longing if I hadn't been listening to what he was saying.

'You get winded on the stairs and pretend you're not. I feel like I'm in a documentary about the Death Zone on Everest.' His breath against the side of my face, like a caress, as he leaned closer. 'I might as well be watching a middle-aged tourist

225

preparing to die in the most expensive way possible. If they ever install oxygen and hire some Sherpas, we'll start taking the stairs together, all right? Until then, the lift.' He got to the door ahead of me and held it open, smiling sweetly as I walked past him, my face flaming.

God, I was such an idiot.

Georgia looked up when we came in. She instantly spotted the colour in my cheeks, her expression changing to horror. I shook my head at her as discreetly as I could.

'Did you talk to Magnus?' Liv asked, and I filled her in on what he had told me about Tor Grant.

'Wow, it would have been helpful to know that for the original investigation.'

'He was just a kid,' I said. 'I can understand why he was too shy to speak up about what he'd seen.'

'Don't be rude about Magnus,' Derwent warned Liv. 'Maeve likes him.'

'What's that supposed to mean?' I asked, stung.

'Nothing. Just that, as usual, you're determined to see the best in someone who doesn't deserve it.'

Derwent's mobile rang and he answered it with his eyes on me, bright with mischief. He was enjoying teasing me far too much, I thought, trying to remember how I had coped with it before. I hadn't minded then, that was the problem. Now I minded all too much.

I turned to go back to my desk, and he reached out to take hold of my arm.

'Wait,' Derwent said to me, serious now, and into the phone, 'no, sorry, go on. You were saying.'

I stood beside him, watching his face change as he listened, trying to guess what had happened to make his eyes narrow and his mouth tighten.

'Yeah. Of course we will. As soon as we can. Thanks for letting me know. No, definitely of interest. I can't quite believe it.' A short huff of amusement, the release of tension. 'I bet you couldn't either. One where you check the results again.

226

Yeah, twice over. Absolutely. I'll let you know our ETA. This number good? OK. See you soon.' He ended the call and stood completely still, processing whatever he had just heard.

'What is it?' I asked. 'Bad news?'

He looked at me as if he'd just woken from a dream, coming back to himself slowly. 'Yes. Maybe. For someone.'

35

The car was silent as we drove through empty, still streets in the blue light before dawn. My eyes were sore from lack of sleep and the early start. I thought back to the night before, when Derwent had wanted to leave for the Lake District straight away, but Una Burt intervened.

'It's what – six hours on the road?'

'At least.'

'And it's getting on for eight in the evening now. You'll get there in the middle of the night. Nothing will be open and the locals won't want to stay up waiting for you and there's no point in visiting the scene in the dark. Go in the morning.'

'Is that an order?'

'Call it an order, if it makes you happy. You can leave early.'

'If we get on the road at half past four we'll be there mid-morning,' Derwent said to me. 'Probably not worth trying to do there and back in a day. We'll need to book a hotel. Nothing fancy.'

I phoned a budget Keswick hotel to make the reservation and hung up to discover Georgia was at my elbow.

'How many rooms did you book?'

'Two.'

'If you give me the number I'll call them to book an extra room.' She beamed. 'I'm coming too.'

'Whose idea is that?' My voice was sharper than I'd intended it to be, and she actually took a step back.

'The boss.'

'Josh?'

'Una.'

I felt myself relax a fraction, but not completely. 'Why is she sending you?'

'She didn't suggest it. I asked if I could go. It sounds interesting.'

'Interesting,' I repeated, and looked across the room to where Liv was watching us. She turned away, pretending to read the piece of paper in her hand, a little too self-conscious to be for real. 'You cooked this up with Liv, didn't you? Just in case being alone with him was too tempting for me and I did something I shouldn't.'

'No, that's not it at all.' She didn't sound convincing but I didn't have the heart to pursue it.

Anyway, I wasn't entirely sure she and Liv were wrong.

'Did you sleep?'

'What?' Derwent glanced at me, the angles of his face silvered by the white glare of the streetlights.

'Did you manage to get any sleep? You were up late.'

'A couple of hours. Sorry if I kept you awake.'

'No, you didn't,' I said quickly. 'I wasn't sleeping and I looked out of the bedroom window. I could see the lights were on downstairs.' Lozenges of golden light framing patches of grass, glassy with dew, unsettling in the blackness. I had stood and watched for a shadow, a hint of where he was or what he was doing, until I realised I was shivering with cold.

'You can have a nap now if you want.' He checked the rear-view mirror. 'Georgia's out of it.'

I turned to check, half suspecting she might be faking to see what we would talk about without her supervision, but her head was tilted back at an awkward angle. There was no way she would have allowed her mouth to hang open like that if she'd been conscious of it. So we were effectively alone.

What I chose to say, now that no one else was listening, was the supremely romantic, 'We should make good time. I'll take over from you in a while. You don't have to drive the whole way.'

'I don't mind. It helps me to think.' A pause. 'Especially if no one is talking to me.'

I folded my arms and stared out of the window, mock-outraged. 'I can take a hint.'

'Sandbach services is roughly halfway. I'll stop there. We'll need fuel and a pit stop. You might as well sleep between this and then.'

Instead of arguing that I couldn't, I wouldn't, that I would much rather talk to him about anything at all – not the case, necessarily, if that was off limits, but ordinary conversation about this and that and nothing in particular – I shifted position until the headrest was doing its job properly. It was an opportunity to think uninterrupted, as Derwent had said. I needed to try to make sense of the new information, which was what had kept me awake all night. I shut my eyes. Even if I didn't sleep, I—

'Maeve.'

'What?' I struggled upright, peering out at petrol pumps and trees starting to come into leaf and a clear blue sky. 'Where are we?'

'Services. Georgia's gone to get food. Do you want anything?' Derwent had the car door open. 'I'm going to fill up.'

'OK.' I rubbed my eyes, trying desperately to come to full consciousness. 'Fine.'

After a trip to the bathroom in the filling station I felt a lot more like myself: the wobbly legs and stiff neck had worn off a bit and I was glad I'd slept. I came out to find Georgia settling into the passenger seat in the front.

'What are you doing?'

'Getting ready to leave.' She pointed to the cupholders, tentative now. 'I got us all coffee.'

'Thanks,' I said automatically. 'But why change seats?'

'Josh suggested it.' She looked past me. 'Here he comes, you can ask him.'

I wouldn't, I thought, and he didn't volunteer an explanation, and before I had driven us a mile down the motorway he was asleep himself, sprawling on the back seat in total exhaustion.

Georgia maintained a constant flow of trivialities and observations all the way to Keswick ('which is near Derwentwater, isn't that funny?'). There she switched into map-reading mode with surprising efficiency, directing me away from the town on a narrow road that climbed sharply to higher ground. The mountains lifted around us and I felt comforted, in spite of our reason for being there; in spite of everything. The sky was wide, filled with plump white clouds scudding across the horizon, and the ground on either side of the road was bright with spring grass. White water veined the mountains in the distance. I longed to pull the car over and stare, instead of snatching an opportunity to look at the view now and then.

I turned onto a road so tight it made the previous one feel like an avenue. Grass snaked up the centre, breaking through the tarmac, and the view was of patchworked fields stitched together with drystone walls. After a couple of bone-shaking miles, Georgia pointed across me.

'There. On the right. That gate. They said there'd be a marker.'

A strip of police tape fluttered from the top bar, dancing in the wind. Derwent got out and opened the gate so I could drive through and I waited for him to jog back to the car, watching in the rear-view mirror as he closed the gate.

'There are six more gates between us and the house,' Georgia announced as he got back into the car. 'I can't see it yet, can you?'

I shook my head. Fields, yes, and the bare flanks of the mountains, and an endless sky where birds flirted and dipped in the crystal-pure air, but no house. There was no habitation of any kind.

'I wouldn't have a clue we were in the right place without the directions and the police tape, would you?'

'No.'

'They said it was isolated, but . . .' She trailed off. Even Georgia was capable of being silenced by the magnificence of the mountain scenery, I gathered. It seemed impossible that this existed in the same country as the grey streets we had travelled a few hours earlier, where the natural world was represented by a scruffy fox prospecting for an unsecure bin or a spiky stand of rosebay willowherb on a patch of waste ground.

A long way up the track, we came to the first police vehicle, a Toyota Hilux that was blocking the way. The driver got out and watched us approach, his face impassive. I pulled in where he indicated, on a small patch of grass to the side of the next gate, and we climbed out of the car to stretch.

'Morning. I need to ask you to transfer to this vehicle, please. That one will get stuck in the mud on the way to the house.'

'Is it much further?' Georgia asked, eyes wide, and he smiled at her, his stiff manner evaporating. Whatever he'd been expecting, it wasn't the Pollyanna of the Met.

'Not too far but it's like the Somme. You'll see. You'd get bogged down straight away. We've already had to tow the boss out.'

The boss was standing outside the house when it finally came into view, a dark figure in an overcoat that whipped around his knees as the sharp wind caught it. The house looked forbidding behind him: heavy grey granite, symmetrical windows, five across the top and two on either side of the front door.

'Windholt House,' the driver announced.

'Whoever built it really wanted to get away from it all,' Derwent commented.

'They liked their own company,' the police officer confirmed, driving through a massive puddle that sent wings of muddy water arcing out from both sides of the vehicle.

He stopped on gravel in front of the house and the boss walked across to greet us: a tanned, tall man with a worried expression and no more than a suggestion of hair left on his head.

'Superintendent Parker?' Derwent shook his hand. 'Josh Derwent.'

'Good to meet you.' He nodded to each of us in turn as Derwent introduced us. 'Found the place all right, then.'

'Thanks to your directions. It's not exactly easy to find, is it?'

'Deliberately so. No one comes up here from one end of the year to the next. Most of the gates were padlocked when we got here. The homeowner used to collect his post in Keswick. No deliveries, no tradespeople. When we spoke to the local press, we appealed for anyone who'd been in the property during the last twelve months to come forward, and no one did. It was the talk of the town so anyone in the area would have known we wanted to trace visitors to the house or even just to the farm. Windholt House was completely cut off.'

'What do you know about the homeowner?' Derwent asked. I knew he wanted to get into the house, to see the crime scene, but I also knew that he would follow Superintendent Parker's lead, and Parker seemed to need to talk first.

'Piers Wilmington, aged thirty-nine. He lived here all his life. This place was in his family for generations, I gather – and the estate consists of a few hundred acres of good farmland in addition to the house, by the way. He was an only child. Got the lot. The Wilmingtons always had money and they didn't like spending it.'

'What did he farm?' I asked, looking around at empty fields that stretched away from the house, ribbons of grass rippling in the wind.

'Sheep, largely, but he'd sold them all. He'd stopped everything over the last few years. He even sold some land, over on the edge of his property. Got a good price for it – enough to live off for a while, especially given that he was frugal. Not the brightest, according to the people who knew him, but decent.'

'And now he's dead,' I said.

'And now he's dead. Very.' Superintendent Parker moved towards the side of the house. 'Come on. I'll show you what we've got.'

36

'They used this door as the main way in and out of the house,' Superintendent Parker said over his shoulder as he walked through a filthy cobblestoned yard. He was making for the back door, which stood ajar. Specks of maroon paint flaked off it, and the glass window set into it was grey with dirt. 'Very common around here not to use the front door, so when the contractor from the council came round, he went straight to the back of the building and found the door open.'

'No one knew he was coming, I take it.' Derwent held out a hand to me as I slithered on a particularly slick bit of mud, and hauled me to firmer ground.

'No, it was emergency repair work. Some power lines had come down thanks to high winds. He'd gone to sort it out but the access road was blocked with a chained gate. He needed to get to the affected area so he came to the house to see if there was another way there or if the gate could be unlocked.'

We stepped into a stone-flagged corridor. It was icy and I shivered.

'No heating left on.'

'No heating at all. The boiler is an antique that could just about cope with making hot water but not much of it. There's a range in the kitchen and fireplaces in most of the rooms.' Parker walked ahead of us, gesturing at open doors. 'Parlour. Dining room. Kitchen's the other way.'

'It's like a museum,' Georgia said in awe, peering through open doors. In the dining room a linen cloth covered the table and a big brass-bound family Bible stood on a lectern. I imagined the Victorian residents spending their Sundays reading improving texts from it, and how boring that must have been, and how there had been no escape in any direction.

'You're right there. Nothing has changed here in a hundred years. More. All this furniture went in when the house was new. Imagine them hauling it up here by cart.' Parker started up the stairs. 'Watch your step. Some of the treads are rotten.'

'What's your best guess for when this happened?' Derwent asked from behind me.

'Good question. We know Piers was in Keswick in January, because the post in his PO box goes back to the fifteenth of that month. If he paid any other visits, he didn't pick up his post. A lot of people in remote parts of this area would only go to town once or twice a month. So maybe it happened in January. Maybe February. There was some food in the fridge that had been bought mid-January, but not much, so it could be that he'd eaten a lot of it over the following weeks.'

'What about the body?' I said. 'Doesn't that help?'

'The body wasn't in a good condition at all, even though it's like a fridge in here. There were . . . vermin.'

Georgia made a tiny noise of pure revulsion and I didn't blame her.

'They've done the PM – that happened the day we recovered the body,' Superintendent Parker continued, oblivious. 'The pathologist won't give us his best guess until all the tests come back.'

'They're annoying that way,' Derwent said, with feeling.

'One thing we haven't found is the van. There was a red Ford Transit registered to this address, but there's no sign of it. We included the details in our initial appeal for information but no one seems to have seen it.' The superintendent paused. 'You'd need a vehicle to get out of here. No public transport. You could walk but it's a hell of a long way.'

'He could have sold the van before he died. Or scrapped it,' Derwent said with his usual unhelpful logic, and Superintendent Parker sighed.

'We've thought of that too. At the moment, it feels like our only lead. The van can't have disappeared into thin air. It must be somewhere.'

'No one's seen it in what – two months?' Derwent pulled a face. 'Good luck.'

We had stopped in front of a door at the end of the hallway. On the way down the hall I glanced through open doors to see bare rooms, almost unfurnished, with neither curtains nor carpet. Cool pearly light slanted in, filtered through smudged windows. It felt like an abandoned building, down to the arctic chill that was seeping into my bones.

'Was he moving out? There's hardly any furniture up here.'

'That was how he lived,' Eli Parker said, opening the door with something of a flourish. 'And this is how he died.'

In contrast to the other bedrooms, this room was over-furnished with small armchairs and tables full of trinkets littered here and there. The room occupied the entire width of the house from the front to the rear, and it was big enough that I felt it was something of an achievement to make it feel cluttered. Heavy chests of drawers stood on either side of the fireplace and between the windows, and a massive wardrobe filled one wall. Faded velvet curtains hung at the windows and a four-poster bed squatted behind the door. There was a smell of old smoke from the fireplace which was still full of ash, and overlaying that, the unmistakable odour of human decay. I almost gagged at it but caught myself in time. Georgia reversed sharply, her boots loud on the wide floorboards, fleeing to the safety of the hall again.

Focus.

It was the damage I noticed next. A fine mist of blood sprayed up one wall, between the windows. A small round table lay on its side, as if someone or something had fallen against it. A large, wavering stain marked the rug in front of the bed, and the mirror above the fireplace was smashed, a spiderweb of damage radiating out from the point of impact on the right so that half of the mirror was unusable.

'What are we looking at?' Derwent asked.

'Two shots. One bullet was in our victim, Piers. The other hit the mirror. We recovered the bullets and sent them off for analysis, as you know.'

'And the ballistics expert matched them to the bullet that killed Bruce Marshall.'

The impossible, undeniable fact of it. I had seen the close-up images of the bullets lined up, carefully lit, the marks on the ammunition that were, even to my untrained eye, identical. One dead body in remote rural Cumbria, another, presumably killed weeks later, in central London in a luxury flat.

Parker nodded. 'That was our first clue that this wasn't going to be straightforward. Two murders, a few weeks apart, in different locations, with what seems to be the same weapon. We already knew we had to involve the Met, even before . . . the rest.'

'The rest'. A nice way of saying 'the unthinkable'.

He pointed to the floor. 'This is where Piers died. We don't know if it was instant or if it took a while. The bullet hit him in the chest and nicked an artery before it lodged in his spine, but he bled out slowly, into his chest cavity. A doctor could have saved his life, the pathologist said, but he would have been paralysed from the waist down whether he got treatment or not.'

'So he might have been conscious while he died? But he couldn't move?' Derwent checked, and the superintendent nodded.

'There were fibres from the rug under his nails. He died hard.'

I caught sight of myself in the fractured mirror: endless versions of me, all frowning. 'If the bullet didn't pass through him, where did that blood on the wall come from?'

'Another good question. Not him. This is where we got the second DNA sample we recovered.'

'And there's no doubt about the DNA?' Derwent turned to look at Parker, his face bleak.

'None at all. They've tested it three times and it always comes back the same.' I knew what he was going to say next, but it still sent a chill through me. 'Rosalie Marshall was here.'

Not dead. Not in the river by her parents' home. Rosalie was alive, and an adult, but still lost to us.

'How old is the blood on the wall?' I asked.

'The lab said it was recent. The sample hadn't deteriorated.'

'Fuck.' Derwent's voice was flat. 'If we find her, are we going to have to arrest her for murder? That's not how I wanted this to go.'

'Maybe she had her reasons,' I said softly. 'The blood . . . maybe he was cruel. Violent. Maybe he was keeping her here against her will. Maybe she was kidnapped and trafficked and he bought her. It would explain why he didn't want to have any visitors.'

'He certainly took steps to avoid anyone coming to the house,' Parker said. 'But that was only in the last few years, from what we've heard. He'd become reclusive. The nearest neighbours – and they aren't close – said it was six or seven years ago.'

'So we can guess she was here for the last few years, whether it was of her own free will or not.' I looked at Derwent. 'That's a fair assumption, isn't it?'

'It's a possibility. You can assume it if you like.' He was frowning. 'The gun. How the hell would she still have the gun if she took it when she left home? She was only a little girl. She couldn't have hidden it for sixteen years. That's impossible.' Derwent shook his head. 'None of this makes sense.'

'Unless whoever took her kept the gun. Unless they shot Piers,' I said. 'And killed her parents. You might not have to arrest her after all, Josh.'

'There's something else,' Parker said slowly, almost reluctantly. 'Something I didn't tell you yesterday on the phone because I didn't know about it. We were focused on this room and the rooms downstairs, as far as forensics went. The SOCOs only made it into the other rooms up here this morning. We weren't expecting to find anything of interest.'

He opened the door to reveal a shame-faced Georgia, who he sidestepped so he could go down the hall. 'In here.'

It was another bedroom, this one desolate. A double bed was almost the only furniture. The mattress was lumpy and stained, and there was only a single blanket for bedclothes. There was a small bookcase without books, and a second blanket at the window where a curtain should have hung. The walls, the window, the bookcase: every surface was dark with fingerprint powder that highlighted hundreds – thousands – of overlapping handprints.

'Oh God,' I said under my breath and Parker gave me a quick, sympathetic look.

'I know.'

'How many?' Derwent's voice was tight.

'Two complete sets. Not Rosalie. Not Piers Wilmington.'

'They're so small,' I whispered.

'Yes. Children.' Parker looked around and shook his head in sheer disbelief at what they'd discovered. 'There were children here too.'

The hotel might have been fairly low on frills, but it had a residents' lounge with a fireplace in it. The night manager had been happy for us to light the fire ourselves. Derwent proved to be deft with firelighters and kindling and Georgia helped, reminiscing happily about her time in the Guides, and none of that surprised me. We drew three overstuffed armchairs close to the hearth, the privilege of being more or less the only guests mid-week. The options for electric light consisted of a searingly bright overhead bulb and I switched it off once the fire was blazing. In the dim firelight the basic country-chic décor looked cosy, the warm glow illuminating displays of mounted antlers and old books and copper pans. Our conversation, on the other hand, was not cosy at all.

'He was violent towards her, she needed to get away, she shot him, she took the children and she drove away in his car, in a hurry, leaving nothing behind. No note. No explanation.'

I leaned my chin on my hand. 'That part could make sense. But it doesn't explain the gun.'

'So why didn't she go to the police for help, or to a hospital? Why did she go to London?' Derwent asked.

'Because she killed him,' Georgia said. 'She was scared she'd be arrested.'

'And she still had something to do.' Derwent stretched out his legs, crossing them at the ankle. 'Kill her parents.'

'No,' I said. 'I don't agree. She was scared of going to the police because she was brainwashed into not trusting us by whoever kidnapped her. Maybe she thought we'd take the children away.'

'Do we think they're hers?' Derwent's face was grave in the firelight.

'Of course they're hers,' I said, impatient with him. 'She took them away. Piers was abusing her and she had to kill him so she could leave. That house – those poor children. No wonder she felt she had to escape.'

Derwent shook his head. 'I can't help thinking there's a lot of empty space out there in the mountains. If it was January, they wouldn't have lasted long.'

'She couldn't have.'

'It happens.' His voice was harsh.

'I'll believe it when there's some evidence of it,' I said. 'And we don't know that she was the one who killed the Marshalls either.'

'We know she had the gun,' Georgia said.

'We know someone had the gun and used it in the house where she seems to have been living,' I corrected. 'We don't know it was Rosalie. And we don't know why she used the gun a second time, if it was her. She must have known that using the gun would draw attention to her, especially if Piers's body had been discovered.'

Derwent shrugged. 'She wanted to send a message. There was no reason to use it otherwise. She could have smothered both of them.'

'Then it wouldn't have looked like a murder-suicide,' I pointed out.

'It fooled us for about five minutes.'

'Because you're a pair of geniuses,' Georgia said. 'It would have convinced me.'

'That trick where someone pretends the top of their thumb has been cut off would convince you,' Derwent said, but kindly. I couldn't stop myself from grinning.

'I actually really hate that trick. It gives me a funny feeling in my tummy.' Georgia got up. 'I'm going to my room. I want to ring my boyfriend.'

'Sleep well,' I said.

She bounced out, her attention on her phone, leaving us on our own for the first time. An old clock on the mantelpiece ticked, the sound heavy and deliberate, like a heartbeat.

Derwent raised his eyebrows. 'Are you OK?'

'Tired.'

'It was a long drive. I'm going to bed in a minute.' He yawned widely. 'We'll go back to London tomorrow. Do you want another look at the house in the morning?'

'I think I saw plenty today. I keep thinking about how isolated it is. You can't see any other houses, or even a road – just mountains stretching into the distance, like walls. Imagine living there all the time.'

'It's beautiful.'

'Only if it's not a prison. We don't know if she could come and go. No one knew she was there, Josh. Piers never took her to town. She didn't have a doctor or a dentist that the local police have managed to trace. If those were her children, she had them on her own, without medical help.'

'You don't know that she wasn't happy,' Derwent said. 'Maybe Piers was what she wanted.'

I thought of the picture Parker had shown us. 'He was handsome, if you like fair hair.'

Derwent grinned. 'I didn't think posh boys were your type.'

'If I have a type, which I doubt, it's men I should avoid at all costs,' I said tartly.

He let it go with nothing more than a slight narrowing of his eyes. 'There's every chance our pal Piers fitted into that category.'

'Superintendent Parker said he was decent but decent people don't keep women hostage.'

Derwent stretched. 'I feel sorry for him. What a way to go – completely helpless, knowing he was cut off from civilisation, feeling himself getting weaker and weaker. It must have been slow torture. Whatever he did to Rosalie, or didn't do, I can't believe he deserved that.'

'What if she didn't kill him, Josh? What if someone else did, and then took her and the kids away? We don't even know that Piers was responsible for her blood being on the wall. Maybe she tried to fight back and was overpowered.'

'That's a possibility. I'll mention it to Parker in the morning.' He got up and put the fire guard in place. 'Either way, we need to find her.'

37

Rosalie Marshall had been missing for fifteen years and eight months, and no one had picked up so much as a trace of her whereabouts in all that time, until now. Before we got back to the office after our long drive the next day, we had our first lead on where she might currently be.

Colin Vale greeted us with a beatific smile. 'You asked, and we delivered. We've found that vehicle that went missing from Windholt House – the van.'

'Already?' I said, stunned.

'Well, automatic numberplate recognition software found it, to be honest. The plate pinged for a traffic car in Brentford.'

'I can't believe she drove it all the way to London.' *When* she had done that was the next question, I thought.

Derwent clenched his fist, triumphant. 'Finally. What did we ever do before ANPR?'

'My first nick, I worked with a guy who was like human ANPR. Never forgot a number we got in briefings. He was infallible. Those are the skills that you lose once you bring in computers, even though computers are supposedly more reliable, like cabbies not needing The Knowledge any more because they have satnav. It used to be all up here.' Colin tapped his temple.

I knew from experience that Colin could go on more or less indefinitely if he was given the chance to compare humans and computers. 'So what's our best course of action?'

'We're taking it slowly. There's a unit stationed nearby at the moment, with eyes on, hopefully out of sight. I've just heard from them and there haven't been any developments so far.'

'They must be delighted,' I said. 'That's the kind of shift that makes you question your life choices.'

'Some people like a nice quiet job, Maeve.' Derwent's eyes were gleaming. It was a hunt, now, not just a mystery, and he had the scent of his quarry.

'Basically,' Colin said earnestly, 'we've got two main options. We can take the vehicle in for forensic analysis and see what we can find out from that, or we can get a surveillance team to watch it in case she comes back to it and we can pick her up.'

'We've got to go for option two,' I said. 'She could be anywhere nearby, or she could be nowhere near. The only fixed point we have for her is the Ford.'

'Yes, but before you make that decision, you should see it.' Colin clicked a file on his desktop and I leaned over to look at the picture that appeared: a battered red Ford Transit caked in dried mud. The windows were filthy and one was rolled down a couple of inches. Some dead leaves had caught behind the wheels.

'Oh. That looks abandoned,' I said, crestfallen.

'I don't think it's moved for weeks.' Colin zoomed in on the image, examining it. 'What I think is that she parked it there when she got to London and she didn't move it again.'

'That makes it easier. We should get it picked up. Where is it exactly?' Derwent had crossed the room and was looking at the big, detailed map of London that occupied most of one wall of the office.

'It's parked in a dead end called Goat Wharf, by the river.'

I went to look over Derwent's shoulder and pointed. 'There. Not far from Richmond, as the crow flies, which makes sense if she was heading for home.'

'What's around here, Colin?' he asked. 'Not much, from memory, but I haven't been there for a few years.'

'That area's been redeveloped a lot. I had a look on Google. Flats, a hotel. We checked with the hotel – no current guests matching Rosalie's age, with children or without, although she could have stayed there in January or February. I didn't think there was any point in going back too far at the moment, but

244

it's worth a look if we can't trace her through the van. It would be very nice to get some up-to-date CCTV images.'

'Anything,' I said. 'Anything at all. A description would be a start.'

'We've asked the local response teams to give us a list of possible places she could be – squats, that kind of thing – and they're putting the word out to anyone who's usually helpful. The local charities, clinics . . .'

I was still staring at the map.

'What is it?' Derwent asked quietly, the question for me only.

'Just wondering why she parked there, if she had the two kids with her. It's not near anything much except the river. Why there?'

'She had the river at the bottom of the garden when she was a kid.'

'Yes.' I could imagine the pull of the water on her, after years in the spare beauty of the mountains, threadlike streams cutting down the steep inclines. At that point in its journey the Thames was calm and tree-lined, sedate and lovely. 'Maybe it reminded her of the house in Richmond. Or maybe she felt she'd reached the end of the road.'

Derwent grimaced at the thought, but it wouldn't be the first hunt for a killer that ended with a body.

'What do you want to do?' he asked.

'Go there.' The words were unpremeditated.

'Tomorrow?'

I turned to look at him. 'What's wrong with now?'

By mutual consent, we ditched Georgia. It wasn't about her being irritating, or about wanting to be alone together. She had come back complaining of a headache. I'd found her in the kitchen knocking back paracetamol, her face pale. She agreed that she needed to go home, and so Derwent and I left the office with her, then continued to the car park without Una Burt or anyone else noticing that we were going anywhere on our own. It felt ridiculous to sneak away as if we had something to hide.

245

It was work, that was all, but I had a feeling that tingled at the back of my neck, telling me that this was our chance to find Rosalie.

'You think we'll do a better job of finding her than the locals,' Derwent said, carefully neutral in his tone. He was driving – had insisted on it – and I had given in because I had won the main battle about going to Brentford straight away.

'I think the local cops have a lot of other things to worry about and they don't know Rosalie.'

'And we do?'

'I've thought about her constantly for weeks.'

'Me too.' He glanced at me. 'But we know her as a nine-year-old. She's twenty-five now. She's probably changed a fair bit.'

I glowered. 'I had factored that in, believe it or not.'

He snapped his attention back to the road, his eyes wide, his shoulders up around his ears, pretending to be terrified.

'Twat,' I said softly.

'There she is. That's my Maeve.' Another fleeting look across the car, this one filled with affection. I couldn't help the small smile that curved the corners of my mouth upwards. Warmth spread through me: happiness, I thought hazily, and tried to hold on to the feeling even as I thought about Rosalie, who might have killed several people, who might have been a victim or a killer, or both.

Derwent peered through the windscreen with disapproval all over his face. 'The thing is, they can knock down every industrial building from here to Kew Bridge and build over the land and call these luxury riverside apartments. It's still a shithole, and if you go five minutes away from the river you can't hide it.'

'Brentford isn't bad,' I said. 'There are nice areas and a football team and the river is beautiful. It's just not posh.'

'It's not about being posh. It's about knowing I can walk down the street and find a reason to arrest someone within five minutes.'

'There's no one around,' I pointed out, which was true. Hardly anyone seemed to be out in the afternoon sunshine.

'Don't speak too soon.'

A stocky figure was walking towards us, clipboard in hand. Kev Cox smiled as we got out of the car.

'Come to supervise?'

'No, just having a look,' I said. 'We didn't know you'd be here already.'

'All right, Kev.' Derwent nodded at the van, which had a flatbed truck parked beside it, preparing to whisk it away. 'What do you think?'

'It'll take a while to process it once I get it back to the garage. Loads to look at. No one's wiped it down, I can tell you that much. Prints and all sorts. DNA, obviously.' He beamed happily. 'Now, whether that'll help you in any way is another story.'

I walked to the van, feeling jarred by the reality of it as it sat there. It had come from Windholt House. It was registered to a dead man. It had no business being in London, parked in a street that ended in the river. I moved past it until I could see the water, and beyond it the red brick of Kew Palace above the greening branches of the gardens.

If I was Rosalie, where would I go?

If I stepped out of the van, not knowing where I was or what I should do . . .

I turned, letting the place sink into my mind, trying to see it with the eyes of someone unused to an urban environment. Even if she had been in Keswick, Brentford would be a culture shock. The traffic alone . . . I couldn't imagine her walking towards the high street, alone or with the children. The hotel. Maybe.

Back to the river.

Why here?

I looked right, then left, and I saw it.

'Josh?'

He was squatting by the front bumper of the van, talking to Kev about some damage to the left side, but he looked up. 'What?'

'There's an island.'

'So?'

'With a bridge. Pedestrian and bike only. And there's a gate.' I had my phone out, zooming in on the map. 'Lot's Ait, it's called.'

He straightened up, weary now. 'And you have a feeling about it.'

'I don't *have a feeling*. It's a private island,' I read from a helpful Wikipedia entry. 'There's nothing on it now except a boatworks. Otherwise it's uninhabited, to all intents and purposes. The two islands in the river here were planted with alders and willows to hide the gasworks on this side of the river from Kew Gardens.'

He came to stand beside me, looking downstream at the island. His hands were in his pockets, his hunter's instinct on hold. 'Interesting from a historical point of view, I grant you, but how is this relevant?'

'That's smoke,' I said, pointing at a faint blue smudge rising from the other end of the small thicketed island. 'It's not coming from the boatworks – they're near the bridge. Someone is living there on the island, out of sight, and I think we should find out who it is.'

38

Half an hour later, we were standing in the middle of a small clearing on Lot's Ait, accompanied by two large uniformed officers, and I was revising my opinion: not one person, but several. Seven of them stood or squatted in front of us. Some looked surly, others detached, and one or two looked frightened, but none of them gave the impression that they were prepared to be helpful. Travellers with matted dreadlocks and piercings and homemade clothes: four men and three women. They were the sort of people who floated from festival to festival all summer, performing or selling art or braiding hair, and melted away for the winter, finding somewhere to hibernate while they waited for the long days to come again. Someone else had mentioned travellers, I remembered, and waited for it to come back to me: Louisa Stern, huddled in Derwent's jacket, in her delicately perfect house.

Here, their shelter consisted of haphazard structures that circled the clearing: a breeze-block shed that looked damp, a square structure made of corrugated metal, and a couple of wood and plastic shacks. Clothes hung from lines strung around the trees, drying, and a small fire ringed with stones was at the centre of the clearing. Someone had kicked earth over it at the sound of our approach, but it had been far too late to hide once we were on the island.

'Do you really live here?' Derwent's distaste was obvious.

'It's a community of artists and creatives.' A bearded man with hair to his waist, his chest broad, his hands enormous. He looked like a leader even though I suspected the true power lay elsewhere, with one of the women. It was that sort of group.

'We don't need your approval. We live here together in peace. We're harming no one.'

'The people at the boatworks can't be happy about you being here.'

'We don't bother them and they don't bother us. They're decent people.' His voice was a rumble. 'We haven't done anything wrong.'

'You should go somewhere else,' one of the response officers said coldly. 'You shouldn't be here.'

'We're not causing any harm.'

'Why are you here?' A red-haired woman, her septum pierced with a large silver ring that hung down to the bow of her mouth. She had wide cheekbones, slanting brown eyes and the strong hands of a woodworker. 'What brought you to the island?'

'We're looking for someone,' I said. 'We were hoping you could help us find her.'

'We don't help cops.' That was from a man at the back. His hair was a fuzz of silver and his eyes were hostile. I eyed the blurry tattoos on his hands and placed him as someone who had been in prison, probably often.

'You would be helping someone who needs it, badly. We're very worried about her. She's a young woman who may have been travelling with two young children.'

No one moved. I felt as if they were holding their breath.

'She left her van on the riverbank.' I looked around at the clearing, the trees, the gleam of water beyond thick undergrowth. 'It's beautiful here, and quiet, and you're kind people. You would look after someone who needed help. You would take them in, if they needed shelter.'

'Fuck off.' The words burst out of the silver-haired man and two of the others jumped: a painfully thin man with blue eyes and curling hair who was clinging to a guitar, and a young woman with long dark plaits who was hugging her knees to her chest.

'She's been missing for a long time. Sixteen years. Since she was a child.' I looked around again, making eye contact with all of them in turn. 'We know she suffered. We know life was hard for her. We know that she was running away from something or someone that she feared greatly.'

A movement, instantly arrested, and I couldn't tell who had made it; I had only seen it out of the corner of my eye. It felt as if what I'd said surprised them, or didn't match with what they had heard.

'We want her to be safe. That's the first and the most important thing.'

'Go away.' The bearded man spat a gobbet of phlegm on the ground. 'You're just fishing. You don't know anything about her.'

'And you do?' I said softly. He realised his mistake and clenched his teeth.

'We don't have to talk to you.'

'Yeah, yeah.' Derwent had been silent at my shoulder while I spoke, but that just meant his rage had been building. 'We get it, all coppers are bastards, fuck the police, whatever. You're freemen of the land and the law doesn't apply to you, blah blah blah. You're worried that talking to us would be a breach of trust. Each of you thinks the others in this group will turn on you if you speak up. That's selfish, not noble.' He jabbed a finger at the bearded man. 'And as it happens, you're right. We don't know much about her. Her name was Rosalie, when she was kidnapped from her home in the middle of the night. She was nine years old and she never came back. We don't know exactly where she's been or what's happened to her, but I can tell you this: she probably hasn't known a single day without fear since she disappeared. We need to find her and the kids she was with, and it's not about making an arrest or locking anyone up. She has family who love her and they've spent sixteen years hoping and praying she's not dead. They want to see her. Her brothers miss her.'

Silence. The woman with dark hair had her eyes locked on the ground. Her face was bright red, as if she was suppressing very strong emotions. I looked around the group, hope fading that we would break any of them. I flipped open my notebook and ripped out a page that I'd written earlier.

'This is my name and number. And the number below it – that's Ivo's, her older brother. I have Magnus's number too, if Rosalie wants it. All she has to do is phone me and I'll give it to her. And any of you can call 101 anonymously if you want to pass on any information. Just say it's about Rosalie Marshall. We're from the Special Murder Investigation Team in Westminster. They'll get a message to us.'

I put the paper on the ground and weighted it with a small stone instead of trying to hand it to any of them. Better not to challenge them if I didn't have to.

'Helping Rosalie is the right thing to do, even if you don't trust us.' I stood up again. 'If you see her, please tell her she has people who care about her and want her to be safe.'

'Are you fucking off yet?' The silver-haired man had folded his arms and the muscles in his forearms looked like rope.

Derwent followed me out of the clearing, the two response officers' boots loud behind him, branches hissing across their high-vis jackets. There wasn't a sound from the little group of islanders we'd left behind.

'Total waste of time,' one of the officers said, and the other one gave a hum of agreement.

I waited until I had crossed to the riverbank before I turned to Derwent. He was grinning.

'Nice to see your eyes shining again,' he said.

'Well, you look happy too.' It was as if a cord that had been pulled too tight had now relaxed, somewhere deep within him. I hadn't realised how worried he had been.

'I don't get it,' one of the response officers said. 'They didn't help you.'

'They still might. At least the fire was out so they didn't have a way to burn the paper with my number on it.'

'Doesn't mean any of them will use it.'

'They might not need to,' Derwent said. 'They'll tell her. That's if she wasn't there somewhere, listening.'

The uniforms were both looking baffled. 'What makes you say that?'

'You didn't see the washing on the line? Two little jumpers, side by side. Hand-knitted. Not new.'

'So?'

'The kids are alive,' I said simply.

'And they were on the island, if they aren't right now.' Derwent kept his back to it, as if he was no longer interested, as if every thought he had wasn't about the island and the people on it. 'All we have to do is be patient.'

39

Patience was not one of Derwent's defining attributes but if he was setting a trap he would wait more or less forever. We were sitting in our unmarked car which he had parked unobtrusively behind a van. We had a perfect view of the end of the pedestrian path from the island to the mainland, and snacks, and no one to interrupt us. As we talked to pass the time, avoiding any difficult subjects by tacit agreement, I found myself laughing more than I had in months. Covertly I watched the way the creases lengthened around his eyes when he grinned, and the way he tapped his hands on the wheel when he felt the need to fidget. The bright day faded to blue twilight, and I could have sat there for hours without minding it.

Georgia's voice floated into my head.

you need someone to stop you from making some bad choices

I wasn't doing anything, I argued with her silently. I wasn't choosing anything. It wasn't a big deal.

But I knew I shouldn't feel disappointed when a slim figure in a hoodie slipped through the gate and off the path, melting into the dusk.

'I'll go.' Derwent eased the car door open. 'You stay here.'

He was gone before I could say anything in response. I watched him jog away, insubstantial as a shadow, which was an achievement for someone of his height and build.

My attention was on him, so I almost missed the movement in front of me: a couple stepping through the gate, one in a hood, one wrapped in a shawl. One went left, the other right, at speed.

'Shit.' I hissed it, popping the latch on the car door as quietly as I could. Even as I jumped out, another person jogged off the

254

path, moving with lanky grace. He had a hat pulled down over his hair but I knew it was the curly-haired boy. Nothing could hide his distinctive build. He went straight down the centre of the road and I flipped a coin in my head: I could stay and watch every single person leave the island without knowing which of them was important or I could send a message to Rosalie. The curly-haired man's blue eyes had promised me a soft heart. I went after him at a run, the slap of my trainers loud on the ground. He picked up his pace, aware of me immediately, and I chased him down to the high street and across it thanks to a lucky gap in the traffic, gaining on him because I wanted to catch him more than he wanted to get away. When my breathing was beginning to labour, when I was starting to think Derwent might be right about my fitness levels, he jinked sideways into a dark alley. I went after him, and ran full tilt into his narrow body with an impact that winded us both.

'You – you were following me,' he said when he was capable of speech.

'Are you . . . going to find . . . Rosalie?' I asked, gulping for air.

'That was the idea.'

I drew him into the streetlight so I could see him, holding on to his arm tightly in case he was thinking about running again. He was looking nervous, licking his lips, his lean face tight with tension.

'Where is she?'

'I can't tell you.'

'It's important. She might be in danger.'

'I can't.' He looked over my shoulder, yearning to get away. 'It's not up to me.'

'You can't make up your own mind?'

'I can, obviously.' He seemed to be on the verge of tears, fidgeting with unease, and I leaned on him hard, pushing him to talk, telling him that no one would know, that it was the right thing to do, that he would want someone to help him if he was

255

in a similar situation. He wilted under the barrage, but he didn't give me anything for all that.

We went back and forth, getting nowhere, and my prisoner looked more and more agitated, until a car engine hummed, going in the opposite direction from where we stood. I twisted to see and he caught hold of my arms with surprising strength, his fingers digging in as he dragged me back to face him.

'No. Keep looking at me. You don't need to see.'

'Is that – is that her?' I closed my eyes for an instant, the realisation kicking in. 'Did she run while we were following you?'

'I couldn't say.'

My shoulders slumped. 'You were a distraction.'

He grinned, transformed from the frightened rabbit to a confident, slightly languid young man who had never been going to break, no matter what I tried. 'Don't feel too bad.'

'You're a good actor.'

'Thanks. That's actually my real job.'

I had gambled and I had lost, not for the first time. I leaned against the wall beside me, exhaustion slamming into me like a truck. Footsteps were Derwent, jogging towards us, his face full of concern. I managed a half-hearted wave.

'They tricked us.'

'Yeah. I worked that out.' He glowered at the lanky actor. 'Did you stay to gloat?'

'Not exactly.' The actor was looking at me, at the despair that was hollowing out my chest. 'You really care, don't you?'

'I really do.'

'I told her that.' He sniffed. 'It's hard for her.'

'Are the kids OK?' That was Derwent, anxiety putting edges on his words.

'Fine. The kids are fine.'

'And Rosalie? Wait, what do you call her?'

'Why do you want to know?'

'Because if I find her I want to know what to call her,' I explained patiently.

'Ellie.' He said it on an exhale, quietly, as if he wasn't sure he wanted to give us any information we didn't have already. 'She's been through a lot.'

'That we know already.' Derwent was standing with his feet braced wide apart, his arms folded, glowering at my informant. I wished he would tone the alpha male posturing down a smidgen; it wasn't likely to work on the actor. But then maybe I was wrong about that . . .

He glanced away, over his shoulder, and then back to us. 'I shouldn't tell you this.'

'I won't tell anyone,' I said softly. 'If it helps her, it's the right thing to do.'

'Ellie . . . wasn't OK.' A mutter that I almost didn't hear.

Derwent laughed, without humour. 'No, I imagine she wasn't.'

'Why do you say that?'

'She left a dead man in her house.'

I hurried to soften it. 'We don't know who killed him or what he did but I – I think he probably deserved it. And whatever she did – it'll be all right. She's been through a nightmare since she was kidnapped. That's a defence straight away.'

'No. I don't mean that she was upset or worried. Not about that.' He swallowed. 'She's not OK *physically*. She's sick. Really sick. She needs help. We should have persuaded her to talk to you, but she wouldn't. Promise me you'll help her.'

'That's all we've been trying to do,' I said, tiredness skinning my voice of professional calm, my frustration absolutely clear.

'Can I go?'

'Run.' Derwent's voice was grim, and the actor obeyed, speeding away towards the island.

'They conned us,' I said.

'Yeah. It's what I expected.'

'Did you?'

Derwent looked at me, surprised. 'Didn't you?'

'I thought we'd find her.' I blinked back the tears that I didn't want to shed, and his face softened.

'What do you want to do now?'

'Go home.'

'At least it's the same direction for once.' He put his arm around my shoulders and pulled me in for a sideways hug that was as consoling as it was brief.

The journey across London was quick. As we got closer to the flat, I felt my anxiety rise. I didn't want to be on my own. I wanted him to stay with me, to distract me from my thoughts as they spiralled down to a dark place. My arms ached where the actor had dug his fingers into them. We weren't popular with people like that. They thought the worst of us and we generally thought the worst of them. There was no trust, and I didn't know how to build it.

And I was tired. All I wanted to do was sleep, and I feared my thoughts getting between me and rest. Derwent was yawning too, his eyelids drooping with fatigue. We could do anything if we had hope, but despair ran the batteries right down.

As the car turned into our street, my phone began to ring.

Derwent groaned. 'Don't answer it.'

I stopped with it halfway out of my pocket. 'Seriously.'

'No. You'd better get it.'

My heart jumped as I saw the number. 'Hello? Ivo?'

Derwent stopped the car then and there, the hazards blinking as he occupied the centre of the street.

'Slow down. No – look, hold on. Tell me slowly. What?' I listened, my eyes widening. 'She *what*?'

Derwent pulled a face at me, impatient, and I shook my head, still listening to Ivo's disjointed sentences.

'OK. We won't be long. Just hang on.' I ended the call.

'She went to him,' he guessed.

'Yeah. I'll tell you about it on the way to Clapham.'

'We have to go there?' He kept the disappointment out of his voice reasonably well but he was tired and so was I.

I nodded. 'Right now.'

40

They were sitting at the dining table in the big, glamorous basement room, squashed together on one chair. Four unblinking eyes watched us walk down the stairs, like a pair of small owls trying to make sense of their new surroundings. Lisa Marshall, Ivo's wife, was sitting opposite them. She was a slight Black woman whose hair was held back with a silk scarf, and she fiddled with the end of it as she watched them. Her expression was half shock, half wide-eyed awe, which I understood completely thanks to the briefing we'd received from her husband before we came downstairs.

'Lisa – she didn't wait as soon as Rosalie asked us to have the children. She said yes straight away.'

'She didn't want time to think about taking on the two kids and what that would involve?' Derwent sounded sceptical and Ivo eyed him, wary.

'No. She didn't need to think about it.' He hesitated, then went on in a rush. 'We can't have children, if you must know. Tried, gave up. This is – this is a gift.'

A gift. A gift from his long-missing sister, who had phoned him and asked if she could see him, and had stood on the doorstep, refusing to come in, as she pushed her children inside.

'She didn't want to stay and I couldn't make her.' Ivo lifted his hands, helpless. 'Seeing her again . . . I was crying. We were all crying. She made me promise not to ask questions when she phoned, before she came.' Ivo's voice was low, even though he had shut the study door behind us. 'I know you probably think it's crazy that we didn't find out everything about who took her and where she went but she said she couldn't tell us anything, or wouldn't, and I wasn't going to push her, in the circumstances.

When she was here, I asked if she'd been happy and she nodded, but I don't know. I mean, what *is* happy? She was happy about the children. With the children. I mean, she clearly adores them. Wil and Posy.' He said the names tentatively, still learning them. 'Wil with one L. It's short for Wilbur, from *Charlotte's Web*, and Posy is from another book.'

'*Ballet Shoes*,' I supplied, and he nodded with a quick smile. Derwent took a second to raise his eyebrows at me, and I knew he was filing it away for later when he could ask more about my childhood ballerina dreams.

'Wil is three. Posy is two. Rosalie – she wanted us to have them. To adopt them, formally. But we know that might not be possible. Social services – I mean, it's complicated, isn't it?'

'Depends on the family situation,' Derwent said as if he knew all about it. 'They want to keep families together as much as possible, so anyone with a family connection has a better chance than someone who isn't related. They won't want to take them into care unless there's a risk involved to their safety. I don't know if adoption will be possible in the future, but for now you can relax. We'll need to inform social services, but I'll make sure they understand the circumstances.'

Ivo swallowed, clearly relieved. 'She said their father was dead.'

'Did she tell you his name?'

'Piers, she said. She didn't tell me his surname. She said she wanted the children to be Marshalls.'

'Did she tell you how he died?' Derwent asked the question diffidently, but Ivo picked up on it.

'No. Is there – is there something I should know?'

'Assuming it's the same man, which is a pretty safe bet because you don't get many Piers to the pound these days, he was murdered.'

Ivo's face drained of colour. 'Who killed him?'

Silence. Neither Derwent nor I had the heart to tell him, but he got to the answer anyway.

'Poor, poor Rosalie. No wonder she was so frightened.' He cried then, hacking sobs that shook his body. When he got himself under control again, he managed a watery smile. 'I never cried when she disappeared. I never cried about my parents, before or after they died. I locked it all away. And now I can't seem to stop crying.'

'Grief is like that,' I said. 'It comes out eventually.'

'Mr Marshall, why did Rosalie want you to have the children? Why didn't she keep them?' Derwent asked. 'Was she worried about being arrested?'

'Um. No. She didn't say that.' His eyes filled again. 'She's sick. Really sick. She said she can't look after them and she doesn't trust anyone else. She wanted them to be . . . with her family.'

'What do you mean by really sick?' I asked.

'I don't know but she looked very frail. Unwell.' His face was working as he tried to hold back his emotions, unsuccessfully. 'She looked – honestly, she looked as if she was dying.'

And now we were standing at the bottom of the stairs, face to face with Rosalie's children. They had their father's fair hair and their mother's dark eyes and they were utterly, stunningly beautiful, but also filthy from head to toe. Posy was chewing a corner of toast. Wil sat with his arm around her, not moving. His face was thin and his hair tangled around his shoulders.

'Oh *God*.' I said it under my breath, without meaning to, and Derwent heard it.

'What?'

'I saw them,' I whispered, as Ivo went forward to stand beside his wife and the two sets of eyes fixed on his face instead of mine. 'The first day, in the park, when I was messing around instead of going straight in to view the bodies. They were feeding the ducks. I *saw* them. And she was there.'

'Are you sure?' The words were barely a breath, certainly inaudible to the other people in the room.

I nodded, and he took hold of my arm just above the elbow, with a comforting kind of pressure. 'You couldn't have known it was important. The park was full of mothers and kids. They blended in.'

'I know, but—'

'But nothing. Don't say anything about it here. It's interesting that she was there a few hours after they died, but it's not evidence of anything. Put a pin in it for now. We have other priorities.'

I followed him to the table where he introduced himself and me to Lisa, and grinned at the children.

'All right. Which one of you is Wil?'

A solemn little lift of his chin was the answer.

'That means you must be Posy.' She slid slowly under the table and Derwent checked. 'Wait a second. She's gone. She's disappeared into thin air. Where did she go?'

A giggle floated out from under the table and the rest of us laughed in surprise. Wil looked panicked though, as if this was the prelude to trouble of some kind.

'It's all right,' Ivo said, taking the words out of my mouth. 'Don't worry, Wil.'

'Have you had any food, Wil? Do you want anything, buddy?' Derwent sounded cheerful, normal, reassuring.

He shook his head.

'Has he said anything?' Derwent asked Lisa quietly.

'No.' Lisa looked up at Derwent, her face unguarded. 'What should I do?'

'Give him time. Big day.' He moved away and indicated that Ivo should follow him. I went too, amused that he was taking charge of this professional couple as if they were a pair of thick probationers, and that they were letting him.

'You should take them to a doctor. Get them checked over before anything else happens. If there is a question about adoption you need to have a proper record of how they are now.'

'How? It's late in case you didn't notice.' He was taut with tension.

'Got any friends who are doctors?'

Ivo blinked. 'Friends of friends. One of them is a paediatric consultant, actually.'

'There you go. Call in a favour. Call in every favour. Get it done, whatever it takes. If someone offers to help, grab it. This isn't for you, remember. It's for them.'

'We need to buy things. We can do some online shopping, but they need stuff now. They don't have much.' He looked at his watch, distracted. 'She left us a list. Clothes and things. Shampoo and toothpaste. I thought we'd go to the supermarket . . .'

'Give me the list,' I said. 'We'll get everything for you.'

'No, I couldn't ask you to . . .' Ivo shut his eyes for a second, and I knew Derwent's words were coming back to him. 'I mean, thank you. That would be amazing.'

He scrabbled in his pocket, coming up with a credit card and a scrap of paper. I took it from him and unfolded it, looking for a resemblance to the straggling childish handwriting of the story first because I couldn't quite switch out of investigative mode, and then reading the words.

Wil is my brave wolf. He likes green and blue, dinosaurs, anything salty, and rhymes.
He finds it hard to get to sleep. He has nightmares and sometimes wets the bed but please don't shout at him because he doesn't mean to.
He needs more warm clothes and T-shirts and underwear and some books and shoes. He likes reading and stories.
He needs a lot of love.
Posy is a sweet little rabbit. She loves food especially sweet things. She sleeps on her tummy. She's brave.
She likes putting things in order.
She likes it when I sing to her.
I love them both so much. I always will.

The last words were a straggle, the letters unformed. I thought it had taken enormous effort for her to write so much, the pencil smudged in places where she had rubbed something out. Water stained the paper: not too farfetched to think the marks were fallen tears. I handed it to Derwent, wordless, and he read it too. He shook his head as he got to the end.

'God . . .'

'She said goodbye to them.' Ivo was trembling. 'She said goodbye for the last time and then she left. I don't know how she could do that, but she did it.'

41

'You don't mind doing this, do you?' Derwent asked as we walked into the supermarket.

'Of course I don't mind. It was my suggestion.'

'You wanted to go home.'

I glared at him. 'This is important.'

'I think it is too.' He flattened out the list. 'Can you get clothes for them? Wil looks small for his age. They both do. They need everything – socks, underwear, pyjamas, the works.'

'No problem. Shoes?'

'Not tonight. They'll need to get their feet measured.' He stopped for a moment, and his mouth tightened.

'What's wrong?'

He was still reading the list. 'Nothing. Just . . . Thomas loves getting his feet measured.'

I swallowed. 'Josh, I—'

'Let's get on with it. Meet back here in ten, OK?'

I went off obediently, thinking about Thomas, and Derwent, and why he might be so familiar with the adoption rules and regulations. Thomas still had a father, even if Melissa was scared to death of Mark Pell. Maybe she had wanted to cut him out completely. Maybe Derwent had been looking into it for his own reasons. Adoption would give him rights that he didn't currently have.

Stop thinking about it, I ordered myself, and concentrated on choosing tiny socks and vests and little T-shirts.

He came back with a basket piled high with nappies, Calpol and cough mixture, toothpaste and toothbrushes, hooded towels and a detangling hairbrush. 'I bet they've never had their hair brushed properly. That'll be fun.'

'Did you get conditioner?'

'Nope.'

'You'd know you have a boy,' I said, thinking of my nieces and their waist-length hair that had required careful handling.

'I don't.' He dropped the last thing into the trolley: nit shampoo, I saw with an inward shudder. 'He's not mine.'

Stupid of me. Unforgivable.

He stretched, relaxed. 'Unless you mean Luke, of course.'

'You can't tell me Luke doesn't know his way around the hair-care aisle.'

'He spends hours on his hair. And skincare. He has a routine, for God's sake.'

'Speaking of which, I know you nicked some of my moisturiser when you were staying in the flat.'

He looked wounded. 'Where's your evidence? Listen, copper, I know you're just trying it on. I want my solicitor and I'm not saying another word until she gets here.'

I grinned. 'What have I forgotten?'

'Let's have a look.' He flipped through the clothes in the bottom of the trolley. 'Any reason you went for the most boring options?'

'Lisa and Ivo seem classy. I thought they probably didn't want anything too lurid.'

'Lurid is what kids like.' He set off down the aisle and came back a minute later with some pairs of camouflage and neon tracksuit bottoms and a hoodie with wolf ears for Wil. He'd picked out a rabbit onesie for Posy that was impossibly cute.

'What about books and toys?'

'The section is closed.' I pointed to the barrier that someone had thrown across the aisle.

'Bollocks.' Derwent stepped over it, taking his own sweet time about choosing some picture books, boxes of Lego and Duplo, and a lift-the-flap book about dinosaurs that 'actually has proper facts in it, look'.

'Do you want a copy for yourself?' I asked eventually, and he snapped it shut with a glower for me.

'What else?'

'I can't think of anything.' I checked the time. 'We should get going.'

'Yeah.' He flicked the credit card in my direction and I caught it. 'I want to get something else. You go ahead.'

There was never any point in asking follow-up questions. I did as I was told, and he caught up with me at the car, a shopping bag at his side.

'What's in there?'

'Just a couple of things I thought they might need.'

'With your own money?' I had had the credit card.

'What of it?' He threw the bag in the back and got into the driver's seat. Intrigued, I left it for the time being. I would find out what was in the bag eventually.

On the way back I asked, 'Why do you think she was there, at Battersea Park?'

'Not killing her parents, whatever else she was doing. She'd never have had the kids with her if she was planning to off them, and I can't see her leaving them with the island lot.' He glanced across at me. 'She's off my list of suspects for that, whatever about murdering Piers.'

'I agree. So who killed them, and why?'

'Someone who didn't want her to go back to them. Someone with something to hide.'

'The person who took her in the first place?'

'I assume so.'

I thought of Tor Grant, who was still out there somewhere, and I wondered if he was hunting Rosalie the way we were hunting him.

'She was so close to coming home. Do you think it would have made a difference to Helena to see her?'

'Maybe it would have been worse for both of them to come face to face with reality instead of whatever they'd dreamed of. Rosalie is sick, it seems, and Helena was far from her old self. It would have been difficult.'

'If the killer's goal was to keep Rosalie from seeing her family again, Ivo and Magnus are in danger.'

Derwent nodded. 'We should warn them. Especially Ivo. Rosalie would do anything for her kids. They'd be perfect bait in a trap.'

But Ivo, when we got back, was stubborn. 'I'm not taking them to a hotel. They've had enough upheaval for one day. We have a burglar alarm and I don't think either me or Lisa will sleep much tonight.'

'What did the doctor say?' I asked.

'He gave them a quick once-over. He said they were basically healthy and there was no reason why Wil wasn't talking but he'd need some time to gain confidence. He said they were too thin and they needed to see a dentist. Their fingernails and toenails need cutting. I suppose we have to do that.'

'After a bath.' Derwent handed over one of the bags of shopping. 'Everything you'll need is in there.'

'I don't know – maybe Lisa . . .' He looked at me. 'You could help her.'

Derwent stepped closer to Ivo, getting his attention. 'Listen, the best advice I have for you is to get on with it. You'll get more confident as you go on. Don't leave it all up to your wife or you'll never feel like their dad.'

'Their dad,' Ivo repeated, the thousand-yard stare back. 'Yes.'

Derwent's face softened. 'It's a huge responsibility, but you can cope. And make them laugh, if you can.'

In the end, I did help, running the bath to the right temperature and coaxing Wil into the bathroom to see it. He was rigid with horror at the prospect of being put into the water but he let Lisa peel off his clothes. He backed away when Lisa reached out to lift him into the tub.

'Let's give it a minute,' I said to her, and to Wil, 'Come and see the ducks swimming. We can have a race with them.'

Curiosity drew him over to the side of the bath, and as we pushed rubber ducks up and down the bath on the currents we made with our hands, gradually he forgot to be scared. Behind me Lisa was taking Posy's clothes off and singing a nonsense song she was making up on the spot. Lisa, I thought, was going to be all right. Ivo came in and stood by the door, not quite running away but not getting involved either. I stood up.

'Ivo, do you want to help Wil into the water? I think he's ready to get in.'

He came forward and picked up the little boy, who clung to him. 'It's all right, Wil. Nothing bad is going to happen. Look, your sister is in already.'

Posy was crouching in the water, her eyes wide but with joy rather than fear. Brown dirt spiralled away from her feet and hands: the bath was going to be filthy when they got out.

Ivo lowered Wil into the bath and he gave a short cry as his feet touched the water, but he stood still once he was in, bolt upright.

'Do you want to sit down?' Lisa asked him gently and he shook his head. 'No? That's fine. You just stand there.'

'Here's a washcloth.' Derwent passed it to her, and as he moved back he edged me out of the room so smoothly that none of them noticed. Lisa started singing again and Posy laughed as she pushed a rubber duck under the water to see it pop up again. Ivo held on to Wil's hand, talking to him quietly. The new family, finding their way.

'Let them handle it now,' Derwent said in my ear.

'Are we leaving?'

'I want to wait until they're finished. I have something to say to Ivo.'

I spent the next half hour wandering around the flat admiring the light switches and artwork and taps while Derwent dozed on the cloud-like sofa. When the four of them came back from the bathroom, the children with damp hair and pink faces, Ivo stopped short at the sight of us.

'I thought you'd left.'

'Just going.' Derwent stood up. 'If Rosalie comes back, Ivo, let us know. We really need to find her.'

'I'm not going to help you lock her up,' Ivo said quietly, but his eyes were steady: he meant it.

269

'I want to help her.' Derwent sounded sincere. 'I want to keep her safe.'

A long pause and then Ivo nodded. Lisa had sat down in the big chair. Posy was curled up on her lap, her head lolling as she fought sleep. I noticed that Lisa wasn't looking at us and her face was impassive, giving nothing away. Ivo might have bonded with Derwent, but Lisa wasn't convinced, and she would tell us nothing.

'One last thing.' Derwent picked up the shopping bag and took out a toy rabbit. He handed it to Posy, who gave a little squeak of pleasure.

'A bunny.' Lisa tightened her grip on the little girl, who had pushed the rabbit under her chin. 'Thank you.'

'That's all right.' He turned, looking for Wil. The little boy was standing behind Ivo, peering out from behind his legs, wary. Derwent crouched. 'Come here, buddy. Come and have a look at this.'

He walked forward slowly, his eyes fixed on the bag. Derwent slid it towards him.

'This is for you.'

Wil reached into the bag and pulled out a soft dinosaur with a long neck and tail. He held it with two hands.

'Do you know what it's supposed to be?'

'Diplodocus.'

The room was still. It was the first time Wil had spoken. His voice was soft but every syllable was distinct.

'What do you know about them?'

'It was the longest dinosaur.'

Derwent nodded. 'With a tiny brain. So not the brightest. You'll need to look after him.'

The little boy nodded, then hid his face in the toy. He ran blindly, straight into Derwent's arms.

42

The car was parked around the corner from Ivo Marshall's flat and Derwent set off towards it as if he was in a race.

'Slow down.' I jogged after him. 'Are you all right?'

'Yeah.' He threw the word over his shoulder.

'Sure?' I was trying to see his face so I could judge for myself. No reply. His head was bent as he fumbled for the car key and opened the driver's door. Instead of getting in he slammed the door closed again, walking away with the long stride that proclaimed, as clearly as if he'd shouted it, *don't follow me*.

I followed him, obviously. He made it fifty metres or so before he fetched up at a blank brick wall by the side of a house and stopped, bracing one shoulder against it. Something that might have been a sob shook him. I stopped a couple of steps away from him, wide-eyed.

'Josh?'

'Just leave it,' he mumbled.

'Come here, you idiot.' I stepped in front of him and put my hand on his arm, planning to hug him, but he moved back, out of reach, straightening up. *Take the hint, Maeve.* His eyes glittered with unshed tears in the streetlight but his expression was forbidding.

'It's nothing. Go back to the car.'

'It's not nothing. You're upset. Anyone would be. Those little kids . . . and the way Wil responded to you. I thought – well, it reminded me of Thomas and how he was when you met him first.'

'It's not that.' He shook his head. 'I mean, it is, but that's not the whole story.'

'What's the whole story?' I leaned against the wall too, my hands in the pockets of my coat so he knew I wasn't going to make any unwise moves. I would never attempt to touch him again, I had decided, knowing that the way he'd stepped back would haunt me in the small hours for the rest of my life. 'What's going on? I've never seen you like this.'

A movement made us both look around: just a cat crossing from one pavement to the other, slinking with its belly low to the ground. It was the only sign of life apart from the two of us.

He lifted one shoulder helplessly. 'This case. Not being at home. Those kids. The uncertainty. It's getting to me.'

'Is that all?'

'Isn't that enough?'

I frowned. 'For most people. What aren't you telling me?'

'Melissa.' He said it reluctantly, drawing out the syllables.

'What about her?'

'She wants.' He stopped.

'A baby?'

He took a half-step backwards, jolted. 'No. Why would you say that?'

'I – I don't know.' I was caught out, embarrassed. 'So it's not that?'

'She wants to get married.'

'Makes sense. I should have guessed.'

He was lightning-fast. 'Why?'

I blushed. 'Because of what you said when Bill Howlett asked you if you were married.'

'Which was what, exactly?'

'You said, "not yet".' I squirmed, wondering how he had turned the conversation around so I was the one giving myself away. 'You didn't say a straightforward no, so I thought maybe it was on your mind.'

'It's bothering Melissa, not me.'

'What's bothering you?'

'I can't talk to you about it.'

272

I was shocked by his tone – flat resignation edged with something I couldn't place – and I knew it showed. His face softened.

'Look, it's about what I don't have.' He kicked the wall with the side of his shoe, looking down at the ground. 'Seeing Wil and Posy, making them laugh, buying things for them, talking to them about dinosaurs and rabbits – I want that. I want it all. The waking up in the middle of the night and the bathtimes and the why-is-the-sky-blue questions and the sensible car and the school run. I want it more than I can tell you. I missed it with Luke, and Thomas isn't mine. He feels like mine, but he's not.'

It explained his reaction to what I'd said about Melissa wanting a baby, at least.

'What does Melissa think?'

'I haven't asked her. And I'm not going to.' He glanced up at me for a second, then went back to scowling as if the pavement had personally offended him. 'It would be a lifetime commitment. Worse than marriage, which doesn't have to be permanent. It would tie me to her forever.'

'Josh, you sound so unhappy.' It had gone badly the last time I talked to him about this, but I couldn't stay silent. 'You can't stay with her. It's over. I know she said she wouldn't let you see Thomas if you broke up—'

'That's the deal.' He managed a small and twisted version of his usual smile. 'She means it.'

'Even more reason to break up,' I said firmly. 'She can't blackmail you into staying.'

He sighed. 'She's not a bad person, Maeve. She's just trying to be happy.'

'At your expense.'

'I've made my share of mistakes, and now I'm paying the price. That's how it goes.' He raised his eyebrows. 'Have I told you enough to satisfy your curiosity?'

'I'm not asking you about it because I'm curious,' I said, hurt. 'I'm asking because I care about you.'

'Of course you do.' He let the sardonic mask slip for a second, exhaustion in every line of his face. 'I know that really.'

'Then stop forcing me to interrogate you to find out what's going on in your life. I have to drag information out of you. You'd never let me get away with it. You always make me tell you everything.'

I was trying to make him laugh, but he just looked at me with that quiet, stoical misery I'd noticed before.

'I wish I understood why you don't talk to me,' I said lamely.

'I don't want to want anything from you, Maeve.' I was still trying to work that one out when Derwent shook his head, 'But God, I just *need*—'

There weren't the words for what he needed, I discovered, not in the split second between the two of us standing a foot apart and him moving, his hand catching my jaw to turn my face up to him, his mouth finding mine with unerring, practised intent.

My first reaction was pure shock that this was happening at all. Somehow I had convinced myself, despite everything, that he would never give in to the physical attraction that hummed between us like electricity, and if he did, it wouldn't be like this: honest, unguarded, full of longing that was more complicated than desire. All of that passed through my mind in a split second, like a lightning flash, and then I gave in to the rush of heat that made me burn at his touch.

He'd started it but it was my choice to kiss him back, my choice to press against him and say his name in a small, hurried voice that I barely recognised as my own, my choice to let it go on and on and on . . . He tilted my head back to kiss my neck, the hollow under my ear, my mouth again, slower now, achingly sweet. I was learning his face in close-up glimpses (that curved lower lip, the precise angle of jaw and neck, the pleasing sweep of his lashes) and all I wanted to do was stay there for a hundred years to study him some more. Standing on an anonymous street corner, at the end of a long, difficult day, my whole life turned upside down and for the first time it felt as if it was the right way up.

And yet, there was an uneasy undercurrent to it, a hint of discord. I couldn't help thinking of Melissa and her suspicions, and guilt made me turn my head away from him.

'Sorry. Sorry, I shouldn't have—'

'You don't have to say that,' I said quickly. 'I understand.'

'Do you?' He leaned back, frowning a little. His eyes were dazed.

'These things happen. They've happened before. A moment of madness.'

He went still. 'Is that what you want it to be?'

'No – I – I don't know.' I hesitated. 'You said . . . you need me.'

His arms went around me and he pulled me close. 'All the time. As if you didn't know.'

'I – I didn't.'

The corner of his mouth curled. At least he could still be amused. 'You have a brain the size of a galaxy, you pick up on every tiny detail of everything you see and hear, but you can't work out what's right in front of you, can you?'

'Apparently not.' I was struggling to put my thoughts into some kind of coherent order. 'Is this why you wouldn't stay in the flat with me?'

'Might be. And it might be why I've been avoiding you.'

I perked up. 'You're admitting it.'

He grinned and my heart flipped over. 'Tricked into making a confession. You always get there in the end, don't you?'

'Often.' The warmth of satisfaction faded slowly. 'Josh . . .'

I felt his sigh as if it had been mine. 'I know. Don't say it.'

It's not the right time. We both knew it.

I put my hand on his chest, which wasn't enough but better than nothing. 'We need to talk about it, don't we? But not here.'

'It's just complicated.'

'I know. I think we should head for home.'

And after we had driven back across London, mostly in silence, we said a perfectly civil goodnight to one another on our doorsteps, without touching. He went into his flat and I went into mine, and I stood in the dark hallway, alone at last, able to close my eyes and imagine I could still feel his hands on me, his breath on my skin, his heart thudding against my chest, his need for me and mine for him.

It was only much later, as I lay in bed, sleepless, replaying those moments for myself over and over again, that I realised what had been unsettling me. Not guilt about Melissa at all: something much worse.

He had kissed me as if it was the only kiss there would ever be, as if this was the last kiss instead of the first.

He had been kissing me as if it was goodbye.

43

The next morning I pushed open the office door to a room full of interested faces, and every single one of them looked away from me when I glanced around. I frowned, trying to work out what was going on. They were acting as if I was in trouble about something. Liv was looking for something in her bag, a tried and tested technique for avoiding conversations. I switched my attention to Georgia who was pathetically easy to question, as a rule. She was typing, her eyes fixed on the screen, a patch of colour high on each cheekbone that had nothing to do with her usual expensive make-up.

'What's going on?' I kept my voice casual but low. The office was usually humming with noise: phone calls, conversations, rattling drawers and squeaking chairs. Now it was deathly quiet.

Georgia cleared her throat. 'What? I'm just working.'

'I see that,' I said evenly. 'Georgia. Talk to me.'

'Look, I understand, all right. No judgement. These things happen.'

'What things?' It came out as a hiss.

'I don't want to get involved.' She pushed her chair back and hurried away from her desk, biting her lip.

'Maeve.' I knew Una Burt's voice, and I knew the tone: cold disapproval. 'Could you come into my office, please?'

'Of course.' I followed her, aware of eyes burning holes in my jacket as my colleagues watched me going to – what? My doom? Ridiculous to be so paranoid, but—

The thoughts evaporated as Una moved to one side and I saw someone was already in her office, slouching in one of the two chairs in front of her desk. Derwent didn't even glance at me. He was scowling, which wasn't all that unusual when Una Burt was on his case, but it made my mouth go dry.

He regretted that anything had happened between us, because now, if Melissa asked, he'd have to tell her the truth.

He resented me for not having realised how he felt.

He was sorry he'd kissed me because it hadn't lived up to his expectations – but no . . . A shiver of pleasure raced over my skin as I sat down next to him. Just being near him was enough to throw me off.

'I need to talk to you both because of this. Colin saw it this morning when he was checking for any new information about the case and drew it to my attention.' She was turning her monitor around but she paused. 'Josh was in early, and he has already seen it.'

I couldn't help looking at him for guidance. The scowl had deepened, if anything.

Back to the monitor. Una scrolled slowly through a webpage, a forum of some kind.

'This is a fan site for all kinds of true crime. Documentaries, books. Podcasts,' she added, with heavy emphasis. 'And these were posted this morning. I don't know if you can see . . .'

'I can see,' I said faintly. Photographs, hundreds of them, taken split seconds apart but making it look as if Derwent and I had been glued to one another for hours, not a few minutes. 'You can stop scrolling through the images if you like. I get the idea.'

She let another few slide up the screen though, and stopped on one that was particularly bad, from my point of view, because Derwent had turned his back to the camera and the focus was on me. I stared for a moment, taking in the full rabbit-in-headlights expression on my face, starry-eyed and about to get run over, emotionally speaking. I decided I simply wouldn't see the picture, and looked at Una instead. Beside me, Derwent cleared his throat and picked a piece of fluff off his trousers.

278

'Was there something you wanted to say about it, boss?'

'A couple of things, yes.' She stared him down, daring him to argue.

'Was there a post with the images? What did it say?' I asked.

'It was brief.' She had printed it out, which meant that she didn't have to scroll up to read it, and my picture wasn't going anywhere. Well, some you win, I thought, and steadfastly continued not to look at the monitor while Una read, in a flat voice:

'"The top police officers investigating the murder of Helena and Bruce Marshall, parents of missing Rosalie Marshall, getting on very well indeed. Funny, I wouldn't have thought murder and kidnapping was that much of a turn on, but what do I know?"'

'Is that it? Have we worked out who wrote it?'

'Our best guess is someone who is involved with the podcast,' Burt said heavily. 'He's posted about it before and he seems to be very familiar with the facts of the case, the personalities of the suspects and so on.'

'Tor Grant.'

'That's what we think. We're trying to trace his whereabouts through the posts on this site. We've requested the IP address from the owner of the site and he's being very cooperative.'

I was halfway out of my chair, panicked. 'If it's Grant, we need to warn Ivo Marshall. Those pictures were taken right around the corner from his flat.'

'I rang them,' Derwent said. 'I told him. They're going to go somewhere else for a few days.'

'Was he upset?'

'He wasn't pleased.'

'Grant must have tracked us down there somehow. Maybe he was following us. Maybe Rosalie.'

'Or he was just in the right place at the right time,' Derwent said. 'Don't take it to heart.'

'I didn't know anyone was there. The street was deserted.'

'You still shouldn't have assumed you could behave that way in public. On duty,' Una Burt added, her face mottled with disapproval. 'I take it that's not a regular occurrence.'

'Of course it isn't,' I said hotly.

'It was nothing,' Derwent drawled with maximum arrogance, contempt for the entire conversation clearly written on his face. 'And we had finished work so we weren't technically on duty. The end of a long day. You know how it is. You need something to make you feel alive again.' He paused for a moment and smiled, not pleasantly. 'Maybe you don't know.'

Most unusually, Una rose to the bait. 'I know better than to *grope* a junior colleague.'

'He wasn't groping me,' I protested. 'The pictures are misleading. It was just a kiss.'

'Really, not even a very memorable one.' Derwent glanced at me, unsmiling. 'I wouldn't have bothered if I'd known we were going to end up here. It was an error of judgement on my part but it won't be repeated.'

'I warned you.' Her face was hard as flint.

'I remember.'

She pointed at him. 'You. Go. Maeve, stay for a minute, please.'

He got up and walked out of the room, leaving me sitting there unacknowledged, as if I didn't exist. He shook his head as he closed the door behind him. *What a waste of time that was.*

I turned back to face Una, who had adjusted her monitor so I couldn't see the picture any more: a small mercy. The anger had faded out of her face, replaced by something worse: pity.

'I'm not going to tell you that was a mistake. You know it already.'

I nodded.

'I could see what was coming.'

'I didn't,' I said simply.

'Josh is . . .' She pressed her lips together, holding back whatever she wanted to say. 'Anyway, I don't think you were to blame.'

'Is he in trouble?'

'You shouldn't worry about him. He doesn't worry about you.'

I nodded. He had certainly seemed not to care at all during the previous few minutes. If that was what he wanted Una to believe, I would go along with it.

I hoped that was all it was.

'You are very talented and very important to this team. I told you before I would choose you over him if I had to.'

'Are you getting rid of him?' *Please no.*

'I warned him to stay away from you and he didn't. He's always been difficult to manage but this was a red line for me. And if you think that's me being unreasonable, it was Charles Godley who told him to keep his distance from you originally.'

Superintendent Charles Godley, who had been our boss – a man I had trusted absolutely and unswervingly.

I leaned back, shocked. 'When was this?'

'I don't know. Does it matter? Josh knew the rules and he broke them for fun.'

'Not fun,' I said. 'He was having a difficult time.'

'And I'm sure he told you all about it.'

'Eventually. I had to ask.'

'Yes, well, he's very good at manipulating people into doing what he wants them to do.'

He was. I knew that.

'Was there anything else?'

'No.' She flipped open a file. 'Once this Marshall case is over we can make new arrangements. But you don't have to worry. You won't find yourself in this situation again, because you won't be working with Josh Derwent.'

I walked out of Una's office in a daze and made my way to my desk. Words in Derwent's voice echoed in my head, from a long time ago: *You don't cry at work. Don't be that girl who cries at work. You've worked too hard to be that girl.*

So I didn't cry. I sat and went through my inbox, replying to emails with robotic competence, and I ignored my colleagues, including any curious or sympathetic glances they might have been intent on offering me. I only looked up once, when Chris Pettifer leaned over my shoulder and said, 'It'll all blow over, love. Worse things happen.'

I nodded, trying to smile while my throat tightened. Somehow his kindness made me feel worse. I went back to work, concentrating so furiously that I almost missed the moment when the meeting-room door opened and Derwent came out, his face ashen. He waited for Liv and Georgia to go past him, both of them with their eyes fixed on the floor as they walked past me. I had just enough time to wonder what had happened when he stuck his finger and thumb into his mouth and whistled, a sound that cut through the room and brought instant silence.

'All right, everyone. To save you speculating about what happened, it was all my idea, it hadn't happened before, and it won't happen again. Maeve was just there. Nothing to do with her. If you have any other questions about it, ask them now.' He waited a beat. 'No? Then the subject is closed.'

He turned on his heel and walked out. He hadn't looked at me once.

To say it was awkward to be left sitting in the office after that was an understatement. Over the roar in my ears I heard stirring, and murmurs, and then, by some miracle, the ordinary sounds of the office as a phone rang and the photocopier hummed into life.

Maybe confronting it head on had been the right way to go, but I'd have appreciated some warning.

Don't think about it.

I pushed Josh Derwent out of my mind, sat up straight and focused instead on wondering why Tor Grant had spied on us, and how he had known where to find us, and where he might be at that precise moment, and what Rosalie had planned to do once her children were safe. And all of the possible answers I came up with worried me.

44

'Got him.' Colin Vale came trotting across the office heading for Una Burt's office, waving a sheet of paper.

I went to join him. While Chris Pettifer, Vidya and Liv had been doing everything they could to find Rosalie, I had been trying to shake some information loose about Tor Grant and finding only dead ends: the friends that I traced said they hadn't seen him in years. His main source of income was cash from his loving mother which gave him financial freedom and no need to work, so he had no ties to a job. I found a handful of old addresses where he'd left abruptly and never returned. His life was chaotic and unhelpful, and it was frustrating me. I was determined to track him down. He owed me an apology, for one thing. 'You've found Tor Grant?'

Colin was too cagey to be definite about something he couldn't prove. 'When I say we've got him, I mean we've traced the IP address of the computer that posted the pictures on the forum.'

'Does that give us a geographical location?' Una asked.

'It does indeed. A business. Rafe and Gunther.' He handed the page over with a flourish. 'And it's not far from here, funnily enough.'

'What sort of business is that?' Una frowned at the page.

'An auction house,' I said, dry-mouthed.

'How did you know that?' Colin gave me a quizzical look. 'I had to look it up. They're a niche business.'

I turned to Una Burt. 'I know who posted the pictures, and it wasn't Tor Grant after all.'

* * *

'Magnus Marshall. What a surprise.' I closed the door of the interview room. 'Thanks so much for joining us.'

'I didn't feel as if I had much of a choice.'

I could appreciate that. Liv and Chris Pettifer had picked him up. They found him in his office with his feet on his desk, headphones on, watching a film in his lunch break. Safe to say his day had taken a turn at that point, even if I didn't know exactly what they had said to him. Currently, Liv was sitting at the other side of the table from him, watching him like a cat at a mousehole, silent and focused. It was unsettling to face that kind of scrutiny and she knew it.

He dug into the table with the edge of his thumbnail, sullen. His hair flopped over his forehead. He looked like nothing more than a truculent schoolboy.

'Oh, you had a choice. You always have a choice about what you do.'

That dragged his eyes up for a moment. Whatever he saw in my face couldn't have been encouraging. He went back to the table.

'Nothing to say?'

A shrug. 'Am I in trouble?'

'With me? Yes. Legally? Hard to say. This interview isn't being recorded. It's just a conversation. I don't think I can arrest you for a *massive* invasion of privacy, no matter how angry I am about it.'

'You don't want to be caught out, don't feel up your colleague on the street where anyone can see you. Weren't you supposed to be on duty?' A flash of pleasure. 'Are *you* in trouble?'

'Not in the least,' I said smoothly. 'But let's talk about that. Why would you want to get me in trouble?'

'I suppose I was just bored, Sergeant Kerrigan, and I thought it would be good content to share with the mouth-breathers on the internet. It was very popular, incidentally. Lots of comments about the two of you and what might happen next. Some of the posters have extraordinary imaginations.' He grinned slyly. 'And some of them just watch a lot of porn.'

'That's why you did it? For internet clout? Because you were bored?' I was trembling. I clamped my hands around the folder I was carrying, holding it in front of me like armour.

'Why not? It's as good a reason as any.' He slid down another inch in his chair. 'My job is painfully dull.'

'OK. So your story is that you were just looking for a distraction.' I dropped the folder on the desk. 'A hundred and thirty-seven times over the last year?'

'What?'

'We've compiled a full record of the posts on that website that came from your IP address, which is the computer on your work desk, if you were wondering. Comments, new threads, details of Rosalie's disappearance that other users debated endlessly. You drummed up interest in the case, in Rosalie, and in the podcast.' I sat down opposite him, folding my arms. 'You were working with Tor Grant on the podcast. You and he have been in touch for some considerable time.'

He rolled his tongue in his cheek, considering it. 'Yeah. So what?'

'So how does that fit in with you vomiting your guts up outside the café the other day, because you were so worried about misleading the original investigators?'

'It was a shock, all right?'

'Yet here you are, still promoting the podcast. Still on his side,' I said softly. 'It's almost as if you wanted us to think he was a suspect for some reason, when you knew he was nothing of the kind.'

He looked uneasy for a moment. 'That wasn't what I wanted – look, I just wanted to do something with the pictures and I knew they would get a huge reaction on the boards. The members of that forum are all sex-starved basement-dwellers. They love speculating about Sadie, our nanny, and whether my dad was knocking her off. I knew they'd wank themselves stupid over the pictures of you and the other cop.'

'It was just a kiss,' I said, my voice catching, which made Liv switch her attention to me for a split second before she returned to Magnus.

'Well, it looked like a lot more.' He grinned at me lazily. 'You should thank me. You looked very fuckable. Everyone agreed.'

'It was a shitty thing to do, and you know it.'

The grin widened. 'Well, I'm a shitty person.'

'No, you're not. You're faking it to hide your real feelings. When we spoke to the original SIO – William Howlett, remember him? – he said you were a nice boy.'

His eyes widened before he reverted to nonchalance. 'Well, he got a lot of things wrong, didn't he?'

'Not that. He said you were a little wild, but you were devastated when Rosalie disappeared. More than Ivo – or at least you showed it more than he did.'

'Ivo has always been cold.' He sniffed. 'He's a cunt.'

Liv smiled. 'If you think that's going to shock us, you're wrong.'

'Oh, I'm sure you've both heard that word before, lots of times.'

'Once or twice,' I said levelly. 'From people I was locking up for a long time.'

'Well, as we discussed, I'm not technically in trouble here.' He pushed his chair back. 'And since I'm not under arrest, I think I'm going to leave.'

'You were hurt, weren't you? Rosalie went to Ivo, not you. She didn't even wait to see you.'

My words nailed him to his seat. 'No.'

'You raced over to Ivo's when he told you she had been in touch. You didn't get there in time.' I tilted my head. 'Did you pick up when he called you, or did you let it go to voicemail?'

'He sent me a text.'

'And you missed it. You missed your chance to see your long-lost sister.'

'Look, fuck you—'

'You got to Clapham. You found his flat. It was probably the first time you'd ever been there. And you were too late. You didn't even speak to Ivo, did you? You didn't knock on the door. I've been talking to him, so don't lie.'

286

'I got there and I knew she was gone. I saw you coming out. You'd never have left her there. She would have been with you.'

'You lost your temper,' I said. 'You lashed out.'

His face was flushed. 'Yeah, I was pleased that you started snogging your boss or whatever he is. I wanted you to feel as bad as I did. I'll admit it. I wanted to fuck things up for you.'

'Like a toddler having a tantrum.'

'Again, fuck you.' He swallowed. 'I just wanted to see her, that's all. And you're right, I was hurt that she went to Ivo, not me.'

I had taken a certain amount of pleasure in torturing Magnus to make him talk, but in all good conscience I couldn't let him think Rosalie had chosen Ivo over him. 'That's because I gave her Ivo's telephone number.'

'Not mine?'

'I was hoping she'd make contact with me and ask for yours.'

'Why the fuck would she do that? If you had just given her my details, she might have called me.' He swallowed. 'I know you don't think much of me, but I don't think you can understand what it was like for me when Rosalie disappeared. I missed her so much. She was my little sister and I loved her. That's why I've been helping with the podcast and posting on the boards. I'd have done anything at all to find out what happened to her.'

I believed him, for what it was worth. This was the real Magnus, the kind boy who had hidden behind an uncaring mask because feeling had brought him nothing but pain.

'Even if she'd had your number she would probably have opted for Ivo and his wife anyway. She was looking for somewhere to leave the children.'

'The . . . children?'

I stared. 'You didn't know?'

'Ivo's been calling me. I didn't want to talk to him.' He leaned forward, his face twisted as if he was in pain. 'Children?'

'Two of them. A boy and a girl. They're three and two.'

'And she left them with Ivo?'

I nodded.

'Why would she do that?'

'We don't know,' Liv said. 'We're trying to find her.'

He gave a little cracked laugh. 'So what else is new? Where did she get children?'

'It's a long story.' I was nowhere near forgiving him for the invasion of my privacy, but my anger had faded. 'I think you should go and see your brother and let him tell you what he knows. Meet your niece and nephew.'

'I – why are you still being nice to me?'

'Because I want something in return. Tell me when you started helping Tor Grant. Did he contact you? Was the podcast his idea or yours?'

'His. He got in touch.' Magnus swallowed. 'I hated Grant, you know. We didn't get on, then or now. I just thought it might be the best way to find out what happened to Rosalie. But I never thought we would find her. I thought she was dead.'

'You weren't the only one,' I said, thinking of Howlett and his theory about the river. If he hadn't believed Rosalie was dead, he might have handled the investigation differently. 'What did he want from you?'

'The inside story. He wanted to know what happened when she disappeared, and how my parents behaved. He wanted all the little details.' Magnus looked sick. 'I knew he was too scared to approach Ivo, and Ivo would have told him to get fucked anyway. I didn't feel any loyalty to my parents. I've only ever wanted to get to the truth about Rosalie. I wanted to know where she was and who took her. Then when you and I talked the other day, I realised I might have been helping him hide what he did. I felt like shit. That's why I was sick.'

'Have you talked to him since then?'

He shook his head. 'Not a word. He's not using his phone or answering emails.'

'If he makes contact with you, don't tell him about Rosalie being alive and definitely don't tell him about Wil and Posy. Promise me, Magnus.'

'Wil and Posy?' He smiled and it was such a contrast to his usual cynical sneer that it made him look like a different person. 'God, those names are so Rosalie. She can't have changed much.'

'You'll have to ask Ivo.'

The cloud settled back over Magnus. 'I bet he didn't even care that she'd turned up.'

'He cried yesterday. He couldn't stop.'

'*Ivo?*'

'You might find he's changed a bit more than you expected too. People do that.'

Magnus rolled his eyes. 'Point taken, Sergeant. I'll call him.'

'Speaking of calling, if Tor Grant contacts you, tell me. Don't agree to meet him. He could be dangerous.'

'Tor? I can't believe that. He's pathetic.'

'A cornered animal will fight,' Liv said. 'He's on the run.'

Magnus's cocky air faded. 'What if it was him all along? The things I told him . . .'

'It's high time you learned how to keep your mouth shut, Magnus.' I picked up my folder. 'I suggest you start practising now.'

45

That evening, when there was a knock on my front door, I seriously thought about not answering it. With great reluctance I came down the stairs and opened the door.

'I won't keep you for long.' Derwent was standing well back, several feet of cool evening air between us. 'I just wanted a word.'

'You could have spoken to me in the office,' I pointed out. 'Instead of ignoring me all day and leaving without me.'

He shrugged. 'No privacy.'

'I don't think we need privacy for an apology,' I said evenly, and his face darkened.

'For what, exactly?'

'When you said what happened last night was an error of judgement. When you made Una think I was an idiot and you were a shit.'

He looked pained. 'She thinks I'm a shit anyway. She always has. And isn't it better that she thinks you're an idiot than the kind of woman who would be happy to sleep with a colleague even if he was cheating on his partner?'

'That's not how it was.'

'That's exactly how it was.' He was watching me, his gaze steady. 'Don't dress it up as anything more romantic.'

'That's not what I meant at all.' I swallowed, trying to put into words why I was so angry with him. 'And we didn't sleep together. It was only a kiss.'

'Exactly. Not worth getting upset about.'

'Whatever it was, I didn't expect you to – to dismiss it as a mistake, or announce to the entire office that I was just the nearest convenient female.'

'Maeve . . .' He made to move towards me, but checked himself. When he spoke again he was brisk. 'Look, I wanted to make Una believe it wasn't important so she didn't overreact. She was furious with me. I spent the day talking her round. And as far as the team went, I felt I should take responsibility for what happened. I wanted them to leave you alone. Better to head off the gossip than let it get out of hand. You and I both know it wasn't how I made it seem, and that's what matters, isn't it?'

I folded my arms as an answer and he took a deep breath. 'Having said that, I meant it when I told everyone it wouldn't happen again. I'm here to make sure you understand that.'

'Why do you feel the need to tell me that? Where is this coming from? Una? Or was it whatever Liv and Georgia said to you in the meeting room? Did they tell you to put me off? Or is that just an excuse because you crossed a line and now you regret it?' My anger was a hot, heavy stone in my chest.

His mouth thinned, and he stepped into the hall, sweeping the door shut behind him as I backed away. He took hold of my shoulders and spun me around so I was staring into the mirror that hung on the wall, my eyes wide and dazed. For a moment neither of us moved. His expression was tight with determination, the planes of his face hard where mine were curved. What light there was came from upstairs and it was soft and dusty, like a Vermeer portrait. Slowly, he tucked my hair behind my left ear and murmured into it so quietly I felt what he was saying more than heard it.

'It's a fantasy, Maeve. A dream. Make-believe. That's all it was last night and that's all it is now. The reality wouldn't be like that. It wouldn't be anything other than grim. It would ruin you with guilt and jealousy, and I won't do that to you.'

I flinched and he went on, relentless.

'I don't want to be afraid of getting found out. I don't want to have to tell lies and I really don't want you to have to lie too.' His voice was lower and slower as his hands moved down to cover mine. His fingers slid over my knuckles and tightened,

291

locking my hands within his. 'I don't want to know you're wondering when I last slept with Melissa while I'm inside you. I don't want you to think about what she likes in bed when I hold you down and make you come.'

I caught my breath.

'I don't want your friends to tell you I'm lying about how unhappy I am, or how much I need you. I don't want to leave you in bed on your own while I wash away every trace of you before I go back to her—'

It was mesmerising, watching him in the mirror as he dismantled the dreams I had almost allowed myself to have. I wriggled free from the hold he had on me, breaking the spell. 'Then don't. Don't do any of that.'

'I was just making sure you understood.'

'I got it. Thanks.' With an effort, I pulled myself together. 'Where are you going?'

He stopped, halfway to the door. 'I was leaving.'

'You may think the conversation is over but I haven't had a chance to speak. You owe me that much.'

'All right,' Derwent said, a world of reluctance in his tone. He left as much space between us as he could when he moved past me to sit on the stairs. He braced his elbows on his knees and stared at the floor instead of risking eye contact, and that was enough to remind me how angry I was. The least he could do was to pay attention to what I had to say.

'I don't know why you think I'm not capable of reaching the same conclusion as you. I don't want that kind of life any more than you do.'

'What *do* you want, Maeve?'

That question again. At least this time I had an answer. 'I've already said I want you to break up with Melissa. Not for my sake. For yours.'

'You know I can't.'

'I know you won't.' I folded my arms. 'And I know you should. You're unhappy.'

'If you cared about me you'd keep your distance instead of trying to break up our relationship,' Derwent said tightly.

I felt my temper slip away from me again. '*You're* the one who's made all the running. Why do you want me to stay away from you? Because you don't have any self-control and you wouldn't be able to resist me? That sounds like your problem, not mine.'

'Maeve,' he snapped, a one-word reproof.

'You were the one who kissed me. You're the one who made it clear you have feelings for me and acted on them. None of that was my fault. You need to learn some self-restraint instead of telling me I did something wrong by standing too close to you.'

He glowered. 'I have no difficulties with self-restraint. It would be nice if you gave me some credit for not sleeping with you since we've been working together, even on the ten or twelve occasions when it would have been the easiest thing in the world to let it happen.'

'Ten or twelve occasions?' My face was hot. 'First of all, no. Twice, maybe, if I'm being generous. And secondly, if we're handing out medals, what about every single day we've worked together, when I could have had you any time, anywhere.'

'I am very good at not having sex with you.'

'Absolute rubbish,' I snapped. 'It's just that I never tried.'

A muscle tightened in Derwent's jaw. 'Really, no. Don't flatter yourself.'

I walked over to stand in front of him, staring him down. 'We are in the middle of an argument that started with you telling me how vital it is that we don't sleep together, and I could still make you want to, and that's what you're afraid of.'

'You don't know what you're talking about.'

Furious, I pushed him back, pinning him against the stairs by the shoulders so I could kneel with one knee on either side of his thighs. That took him by surprise, I could tell, but he didn't resist, letting it happen. I settled into his lap slowly and deliberately and in a cold state of rage. He tipped his head back to look at me, the tendons of his neck in lovely relief. I thought about kissing the notch at the base of his throat and felt dizzy. *Focus.*

'What was it you said to me last year? Oh yes.' I leaned forward and whispered, 'It would be the best thing that ever happened to you.'

His hands came up and tightened on my hips, but instead of lifting me off him as I had expected, he pulled me a couple of inches closer to him, tilting my body by a fraction, and suddenly there was no gap between us at all and it wasn't about winning the argument any more. I found myself staring into his eyes which were ink-dark with desire; I assumed mine were the same. My heart was thudding and I seemed to have forgotten how to breathe. He let go of me, but only to reach up and pull my face down to his. There was nothing tender about the way he kissed me this time: it was utterly ruthless and demanding and intoxicating. I kissed him back because of course I did; I was lost, completely.

I had known him for years and I would have said I knew what to expect from him, after all the times we had shared a moment of mutual attraction, whether it was a look or a touch or the time he had made me melt with desire in a stranger's kitchen. This was different. I realised the iron control he'd shown before, the restraint that he was abandoning. His hands moved again, sure and deliberate, and I gasped against his mouth, a small sound that sent a tremor through him. I knew he wanted me as much as I wanted him – maybe more – and that it would be easy to let it go on.

But one thought emerged from the haze of desire that fogged my brain. It was both concise and unarguable. He had said this couldn't happen, and he'd been right.

So I had to get up.

Prehistoric animals scrambled out of tar pits with less panic and more elegance than I managed as I went into reverse, struggling to my feet and stepping out of reach. He let me go

294

but stayed as I'd left him for a few seconds, sprawling on the steps, his elbows braced at shoulder-height, his legs spread wide. He gave me a heavy-lidded look, lingering in the moment like a lion in a sunbeam. Then, reluctantly, he sat up.

'All right. You've made your point.'

I'd won but triumph was on hold: I had very nearly lost my grip on the situation, even if he didn't realise it.

'I'm glad you agree. So we've established that you would, in a heartbeat, despite the consequences. I don't want you to cheat on Melissa. I don't want to be the other woman. You came here to put me off, because you can't stop thinking about it and you can't choose between us and you don't trust yourself.' I pushed my hair back off my face, striving for dignity. My knees were trembling. 'And you could have said all of that. You could have talked to me like an equal instead of trying to manipulate me.'

'I'm trying to do the right thing,' he said quietly. 'For you, too.'

'I know. Your trouble is that you go about things the hard way. You seem to think whatever happens is up to you to fix on your own. Life has taught you that no one is coming to help you and it's all up to you.'

He nodded grudgingly.

'There are two of us in this stupid situation,' I said. 'We both know it would be wrong to act on our feelings while you're still with Melissa, so we won't do it.'

'You make it sound easy.'

'Not easy, but possible.'

'And if I broke up with her?'

'Then it might be different.'

A glint. 'Might be?'

I hesitated. 'I don't want to be the reason you can't see Thomas any more. I don't want you to resent me.'

'It wouldn't be your fault.' I had time to be grateful for that before he added, 'Then again, it's not his fault either and it would be tough on him. I can't do that to him. I should have known you'd understand.'

'Yes, you should.' I swallowed, hard; a stupid, romantic part of me had been hoping he would tell me it wouldn't matter, and it was vital he didn't realise that. 'Honestly, you go on about my trust issues but you don't trust *anyone*.'

'I've learned not to,' he said with a wry smile. 'As you just found out, I can't even trust myself.'

'I wish I'd put money on it. I could have won my tenner back.'

'You'd have deserved it.' He stood up and gave me a look that could have started a forest fire. 'Quite a revelation, Kerrigan.'

'Goodnight, Josh.' I went to the door and held it open and he walked out without another word.

46

I opted for a tight bun, small gold earrings, minimal make-up and a severe black trouser suit the following day, to signal that I was in professional mode and whoever had been sitting in Josh Derwent's lap the previous evening was not going to be making an appearance again, in the office or out of it. I might as well not have bothered. By the time I walked in I could have been wearing a clown costume and he wouldn't have noticed. He was talking to Una, Pettifer, Vidya and Liv in front of a big map of the UK, and all of them looked worried. Una saw me before anyone else did and beckoned me over.

'What's going on?'

'Ivo's bringing Lisa in.' Derwent said it over his shoulder, his attention on the map. 'These three spent all day yesterday trying to trace Rosalie and coming up empty-handed.'

'She didn't go back to the island?'

'No.' Vidya sounded certain. 'I went and spoke to them. I spent quite a bit of time there. I think I got them to trust me.'

'Or they took great pleasure in misleading you,' I said.

'Just because you're still angry they tricked you,' Derwent said absently. 'They probably liked Vidya more than you.'

'You were the one who was rude to them,' I snapped, and Pettifer patted the air with his big paws.

'Whoa, whoa, whoa. Calm down. Stop squabbling about who did what. We know Vidya did a lovely job on talking to them yesterday because they told us what they could about Rosalie.'

'They were worried about her,' Vidya explained. She was earnest by nature, small and serious. 'I was pushing an open door really.'

As she said it I remembered what it was like to be a new member of the team and young and good at your job and aware that the very fact you were all of those things might make people not like you, and I was ashamed of myself. 'I'm just cynical, Vidya, and Josh is right, I am still angry they tricked me. You were there yesterday and I wasn't – you'd know better than me whether they were being honest. What did they tell you?'

'She knew they were living on the island because she'd met one of them – Jessica – in the Lake District last year. Jessica called to the house – she was walking from Scotland to Blackpool, apparently, and she went looking for some food and shelter for the night. Initially Rosalie turned her away but then she came after her. The two women got on well and Jessica told her where she was planning to go after Blackpool and described the island. That little community of travellers has been using the island for a few years so Jessica told her to head there if she ever needed help.'

'She was already planning to leave,' I said.

Vidya nodded. 'But then when she got to the island, she was sick. She was struggling with shortness of breath and exhaustion. She slept a lot. They thought she was in pain but she wouldn't talk about it.'

'Doesn't sound good,' Una commented. 'I wonder what's wrong with her.'

'Well, whatever it is, she thinks it's serious or she wouldn't have given her children away.' I still found it hard to believe she had been able to do it.

'They said she was an amazing mother,' Vidya commented. 'They showed me all the children's things that Rosalie left with them when she took the kids to Ivo – boxes of books and clothes and toys. They didn't know if they should keep them or not.'

'Why would she leave them behind?' I asked.

'Too much to think about when she was taking the children to her brother, maybe,' Derwent said. 'Packing all of that up would have taken a lot of energy.'

'But she took them from the house,' I said, recalling the bare, comfortless rooms.

'She might have been focused on getting the kids settled before she goes to prison for murdering her bloke,' Pettifer said. 'Prison's hard on the mothers. They know no one can really take their place as far as the kids are concerned. It's a nightmare for the staff. They're a suicide risk – the ones with long sentences especially – and visits are horrible. It feels like the kids are the ones being punished too, not just the mums. It all takes a toll.'

'She must know how this is going to end,' Una Burt said. 'Why doesn't she just hand herself in?'

Derwent turned his head to look at her, his expression just the right side of scornful. 'Because she's free for the first time in her whole life. Why would she want to be locked up when she can go anywhere and do anything?'

'She'd stand out,' Liv said. 'We should be able to find her easily.'

'And yet, no luck.' Derwent frowned at the map again. 'Did she tell the islanders where she wanted to go, Vid?'

The casual intimacy of the nickname. They had been working together a lot, I reminded myself, and it was nothing to do with me anyway. Melissa could be jealous of Vidya, with her glossy black hair and her thousand-watt smile that was a rare treat.

Vidya was going through her notes. 'She talked about the seaside, and Stonehenge, and Cornwall. She really wanted to see Tintagel.'

'All right. That's a start.'

'And we haven't picked up any trace of her on public transport?' Una checked.

'Nothing,' Pettifer said. 'I started in Clapham because that's the last location we have for her and we have some idea of when she might have been there. I've checked buses and the tube stations.'

'Clapham Junction is walkable from Ivo's flat,' I said. 'You can go just about anywhere by train from there.'

'If she did, we haven't spotted her,' he said simply.

'Vidya, did you find out who drove her from the island to Clapham?' I asked.

'It was Cameron, the older guy with grey hair.'

'The prison tattoos,' I said. 'I know the one. Where's his car now?'

'Parked by the river. He's the only one of them who has a vehicle – it's a VW camper van.'

'Of course it is,' Derwent muttered under his breath.

'He wouldn't talk to me,' Vidya went on, 'but Jessica – the one with the plaits – said he came back without her. She thought he'd probably dropped Rosalie and the kids off and then come straight back. Jessica was the one who went to the house in Richmond with Rosalie, by the way. Of all of them she was closest to her.'

'But she won't tell us what Rosalie's plans were, and Cameron definitely won't.' I sat on the edge of the nearest desk. 'Rosalie can't walk to Cornwall. She must be somewhere.'

'Hitchhiking, but that's difficult if you look alternative. Truckers don't love new age hippies.' Derwent turned around at last and I tried to assess his appearance without staring at him: normal, I concluded, which was something, even if I wasn't sure what. 'So let's assume she has transport or she's relying on public services. Have we circulated a description to BTP?'

'Yesterday,' Pettifer said laconically. 'Nothing.'

'So far,' Una Burt corrected. 'Nothing so far.'

'If we can't find her here' – Pettifer leaned forward and circled the end of his pen over the very small area of the map that covered south-west London – 'I think we'll struggle to find her here.' His pen swung in a huge circle that covered most of England and Wales.

'Yes, thank you, Chris. I don't think we have a choice.'

'Why are Lisa and Ivo coming in?' I asked Derwent.

'He just said they have some information we might need.' He turned to Una. 'They want to talk to me and Maeve. I think he trusts us.'

'Fine. That's fine,' Una said, but her eyes flicked from him to me and back again, as if it wasn't.

I met Ivo and Lisa in the lobby, smiling in welcome as they came in through the revolving door.

'How are you?'

'Yeah, OK,' Ivo said. Lisa said nothing. Her hair was scraped back off her face and she wore tracksuit bottoms under a long pearl-grey cashmere coat. A fine scarf wound around her neck and she ducked her chin into it, hiding her mouth. She looked as if she was there against her will. Ivo's hand was holding hers tightly.

'How are Wil and Posy?'

Ivo's face softened. 'Amazing. They're with Lisa's parents. They were so excited to help out for a couple of hours.'

'I'm sure they were.'

'We should be with the children,' Lisa said. Her eyes were red. 'We shouldn't be here.'

'This is important.' Ivo looked at me. 'Can we get this over with quickly?'

I took them straight up to the meeting room, where Derwent was already waiting. He read the situation from the expression on my face. In a matter of seconds they were sitting down at the table, having refused his offer of tea or coffee or water. No messing: he went straight to the point.

'Ivo, you said you had some information for us that we might need.'

'I may have been slightly misleading.' He looked at his wife, his face tense. 'Lisa?'

She didn't respond, staring at her hands which were folded on her lap.

'She won't tell me anything,' Ivo said to us, 'but I found out today that her car keys are gone and her car is missing. I went downstairs, when Rosalie was at the flat, to get her some water and painkillers. It took a couple of minutes. That must have been when they talked.'

'Lisa's car is missing?' Derwent looked at her. 'Did you give it to Rosalie?'

She sank an inch further into her scarf. This wasn't working.

'Did you promise her you wouldn't tell us anything?' I asked gently, and Lisa bit her lip. 'I understand you want to be loyal to her. She's given you the one thing you wanted. You owe her everything. That comes before any other consideration.'

Lisa looked at me, her eyes wide.

'But Rosalie needs help,' I said. 'Everyone says she was sick. Really sick. I think she's scared to go to a hospital in case she gets arrested, but my priority is to find her and make sure she's all right. It always has been. I want what's best for her. We can talk about whatever she did or didn't do after she's better, once she's safe.'

'I promise we'll look after her if you help us,' Derwent said, with that direct compassion of his that was so persuasive.

'All right.' Her voice was husky. She turned to Ivo. 'I'm so sorry, darling. I didn't know what to do.'

'It's fine, I understand.' He put his arm around her and held on to her. 'This is difficult.'

'I don't want her to be ill and on her own. I want her to be all right.' She gave a long, quavering sigh. 'It's a vintage Mini.'

'Write the registration.' Derwent slid a piece of paper across the table and she wrote it down, which was psychologically important rather than essential for our purposes. We could have found out the car reg in about a minute but Lisa writing it down herself was a first step in sharing whatever she knew with us.

'Did she ask you for it?' I asked. 'Try to remember exactly how the conversation went.'

'She asked if I had a car she could borrow and I said yes. I checked she could drive it and she said she learned on a manual. She asked if it had a full tank of petrol and if I had a map and I said I usually used satnav on my phone but she didn't have a phone and she didn't know how satnav worked so I gave her an old road atlas that we had in the study. She asked for money and I gave her all the cash I had.'

'Did she say where she was planning to go?'

Lisa blinked, tears welling up in her eyes. 'She said she was going home.'

'What did she mean by that?' Derwent's voice had an edge and I knew what he was thinking. What did home mean to someone who had been taken from hers?

'She didn't say.'

'Did Rosalie ever talk about her life before she was adopted?' I asked Ivo, thinking about what William Howlett had told us.

'No. I know she didn't want to see anyone from her foster family after we took her away and I was surprised. Looking back on it, I don't think they were kind to her. But she did ask about her actual relatives from time to time and my mother – well.' He tried to smile. 'She wasn't always a nice woman.'

'What did she say?' I asked.

'She always said, "Forget about them. No one wanted you, Rosalie. Only me."'

'Christ,' Derwent said, caught off guard, and Ivo nodded.

'It was never the dream family, whatever my parents pretended after Rosalie disappeared.'

We kept them for another few minutes, trying to shake loose any other scraps of information but this time Lisa's silence was because she'd told us everything she knew. Ivo ran his hands through his hair.

'Can you find her now that you know about the car?'

'It'll help.' Derwent paused. 'No tracker, I take it?'

Lisa shook her head.

'Too bad. But not the end of the world.'

'You've done the right thing,' I said.

'I'm going to feel guilty, whatever happens,' Lisa replied simply, and I knew it was true.

After I'd taken Ivo and Lisa down to the lobby and said goodbye, I went back up to the office and found Derwent loitering outside the lift.

'What do you think?' I asked.

'I wish I could have a word with Helena Marshall.'

'I know. It's starting to feel as if Rosalie was rescued, not kidnapped.'

'Poor kid.' He was frowning.

'What's wrong?'

'I've made a mess of this case. All the way through. I've been . . . distracted. It feels as if there's a lot we don't know yet. We've been too slow, over and over again.'

'That's not your fault.'

He looked at me, his eyes bright. 'Una Burt says it is.'

'Since when did you listen to her about anything?'

He nodded, and started to move away. Halfway down the hall he turned to walk backwards for a couple of paces. 'Hey, Maeve?'

'Yes?'

'Nice suit.' He reached the door to the office, shouldered it open and was gone.

47

The question of what might constitute 'home' for Rosalie occupied Una Burt for all of three minutes before she decided how to deploy her resources having briefed the media and the Met's response teams. 'I'd like to think she meant Richmond, mainly because it's convenient for us, which I'd assume means that won't be where we find her but you never know. Who wants to go to Richmond and wait to see if Rosalie makes an appearance?'

'I don't mind going,' Chris Pettifer said.

'Isn't it on your way home?' Derwent asked and Chris whipped a finger up to his lips to shush him. Una ignored them both.

'Georgia, you go with Chris. Don't just sit outside the house. Drive around. That Mini is going to be distinctive – you don't see many of them on the road any more.'

'And it's bright red,' Derwent said.

Georgia sighed. 'I'd love a car like that, wouldn't you?'

'I had one. My first car. I rebuilt her from scrap.' Pettifer folded his arms above his belly. 'You wouldn't think I'd fit into one, would you?'

'We were all thinking it,' Derwent said. 'You were never a small man, I imagine.'

'No, I always had these shoulders.'

'Yeah, that's what people always say about you. Chris with the big shoulders.'

'I think that's enough banter given that we're looking for a killer,' Una snapped. Derwent looked down at his notes, his face impassive, but I knew he was irritated by the reproof in general, and specifically by the description of Rosalie. I was too. She was a victim as far as I was concerned, not a murderer, until she was safe and we could find out what had happened in a room where a man died.

'Obviously we also have to cover the house near Keswick.' Una looked around at us, considering her options. 'I did ask the locals if they could handle this, but they declined. They're keeping an eye out for Rosalie and for the car but they're struggling to cover their current commitments and are understandably reluctant to drive miles into the middle of nowhere on what might be a wild goose chase. So Maeve, you can do it.'

I nodded, trying to muster a smile. Typical Una, a flick of discipline dressed up as duty. All the way back to Keswick, to hang around the cheerless farmhouse waiting for something to happen. 'On my own?'

'I'll go with you,' Derwent said, and Una stiffened.

'You certainly will not. You're needed here to – to coordinate the investigation.'

He smiled, but there was nothing friendly in his face; it was more a baring of the tips of his teeth than an actual smile. 'Yes, I thought you'd say that.'

'I'll go with Maeve.' It was Liv who volunteered, which surprised me, and it nonplussed Derwent and Una to the extent that they forgot about squabbling.

'What about Cornwall?' Vidya asked.

'It's a big place and she could be anywhere between here and there.' Una shook her head. 'There's no point in sending you all the way there to wander around without knowing what you're looking for. If we can narrow it down to some specific locations, then yes.'

'I could make a list of the places Rosalie lived before the Marshalls adopted her,' Vidya suggested.

'One of the private detectives tracked down a foster home. There's a folder somewhere in the boxes that's about Rosalie's early years,' Liv said. 'I didn't think it was important, given that she was so young when she was adopted.'

I looked at her quickly, and then looked away, hoping no one had noticed my frustration. Maybe it didn't matter – but I caught Derwent's eye, and knew he was thinking along the same lines as me.

'Great.' Vidya didn't sound happy though, and I thought she would have preferred to go up to the Lake District and see the crime scene, while I would very much have liked to stay in London – which was exactly why, I assured myself, it was a good thing that I was going.

'We'll head off this afternoon. I need to go home first and get some clothes,' I said.

'You don't have time,' Una said. When she saw my face, she added, 'We need to move fast, Maeve. It may be sixteen years since the girl disappeared but that's no reason to think this isn't urgent. Don't you have a change of clothes at work?'

I nodded. I had a navy-blue suit hanging up in my locker; I had been at some bad crime scenes in my time and I knew better than to rely on being able to go home in what I wore at the start of the day.

'Me too,' Liv admitted. 'But no pyjamas for overnight. And no toothbrush.'

'You can buy something on the way,' Una said, unmoved.

'I can't say I'm looking forward to sleeping in my gym kit tonight,' I said, dropping my bag into the boot of the car.

'At least you have gym kit.' Liv grinned. 'On the other hand, I'll be sleeping on my own, undisturbed. I don't actually need to wear anything in bed.'

'As long as there isn't a fire alarm, you should be fine.'

'What are the chances?' She put her bag beside mine and shut the boot. 'Do you have a toothbrush?'

'No. Shower gel and shampoo, yes, but I don't brush my teeth at the gym. We can buy stuff at the services.'

Liv slid her sunglasses on. 'I'll drive. Do you think we're going to find her? She's a day ahead of us.'

'I honestly don't know. She's not well and she's probably staying off the main roads so maybe she's taking her time, wherever she's going.'

ANPR had come up short so far; the Mini hadn't gone through the congestion charge zone in central London and it hadn't been seen on the M25 or any of the major routes out of London. Colin was working his magic but I actually agreed with Una this time; the sooner we went, the better our chances of locating her.

I waited until we were on the outskirts of London to ask the question that had been bothering me since Liv had volunteered to come with me.

'How come you're able to leave London? What about Sonny?'

'I had a conversation with Joanne. I created a spreadsheet to show her how much time I was spending on Sonny admin and home stuff compared to her.'

'Not a spreadsheet. Ouch. Straight in with the big guns.'

'Don't laugh! I know what she's like. Facts and figures mean a lot to her. She didn't even argue – I think I was pushing an open door, really. She knew she was leaving a lot up to me.'

'And?'

'She said she wants to be more involved. Get this, she said she feels left out. She isn't confident with Sonny because I'm so quick to know what he wants and he goes to me whenever he needs help with something.'

I looked across at her. 'She wasn't suggesting it was your fault for being too good at being his mother, was she?'

'No, genuinely not. She said it was her own fault for working so much and not being around. The more I did, the less she felt I needed her. Meanwhile I felt completely overwhelmed but she had no idea. I think it'll be good for them both to spend more time together, and I get a trip with my pal.'

'Just you and me and the open road,' I replied automatically. I had snagged on one word. 'You said overwhelmed? Is that what it's like? I thought you loved being a mum.'

'I do. I really do. But you lose something of yourself. You stop being just you and start being someone else's life-support system. Sonny needs me and what I need has to come second. That's a huge change. But it's a privilege too. And, you know, I'd die for him in a heartbeat, but the further I get from Sonny the more I feel like me. I'd forgotten what it was like to be free.' She sighed. 'It's complicated.'

'I don't know how I'd cope.'

'Well, it's not in your stars at the moment so you don't need to worry.' A pause. 'Or is it?'

'No. Definitely not.'

'Not something you've been discussing with anyone?'

I shook my head. Derwent's yearning to have a baby wasn't something I wanted or needed to talk about. And it was nothing to do with me, anyway.

My phone rang and I looked at the screen where his number was flashing, as if I'd summoned him. I bit my lip before I answered it.

'Hi.'

'It's work,' he said immediately, which I appreciated.

'I'll put you on speakerphone.'

His voice filled the car, loud with triumph. 'You'll never guess what's happened.'

'You've found Tor Grant?'

'Not personally.' He sounded disappointed. 'How did you know? Did someone tell you?'

'Lucky guess,' I said. 'Where was he?'

'It's no fun if I just tell you.' I could hear by his voice that he was grinning. 'Want to make it double or nothing?'

'Just get on with it,' Liv said. 'I know you two never get tired of playing games but I want to know.'

'Cornwall,' he said. 'Just outside Falmouth. He's staying in a holiday cottage because it's cheap at this time of year, but he doesn't look like your typical holidaymaker. He stuck out a mile.'

I thought about it. 'She mentioned Cornwall to the island folk, didn't she? Do you think she was going to meet him?'

'That's a possibility. But get this, Vidya found out Rosalie lived there for a while when she was little, with her aunt and uncle, after her parents died but before she went to the foster home.'

'Near Tintagel or Falmouth?'

'St Ives.'

'Oh. Well, maybe he couldn't get a holiday cottage in St Ives.'

'Or it's a coincidence,' Liv offered.

'We're going down to interview Grant anyway,' Derwent said. 'Is there anything you think I should ask him?'

'Why is he such a creep?'

'That's on my list already.'

'Are you going with Vidya?' I had to ask, even though I was aware of Liv turning the big sunglasses in my direction.

'Yep. We've managed to get out of the office, in spite of the boss's best efforts.'

'Well, have fun,' I said lamely. 'And don't be too nice to Grant.'

'You don't need to worry about that.' He ended the call and I held on to the phone for a fraction too long before I put it back in my pocket.

'You told him to back off, didn't you? You and Georgia.'

'We staged an intervention.' Liv pulled a face. 'I know. Nothing to do with us.'

'No, you were right.'

Her eyebrows shot up. 'What? I wasn't expecting that.'

I told her about the previous evening – the edited highlights rather than the full details that made me feel weak with desire when I thought about them, as well as faintly mortified.

'And I told him I didn't want to be the other woman. Actually, he told me I didn't want to be the other woman.'

'And then what?'

'Then nothing.' I was glad she was driving and couldn't see my face. 'He's with Melissa and he won't leave her. Well, he won't leave Thomas.'

She drove on for another mile. Then, 'Is that why you were asking me about being a parent?'

'Sort of.'

'OK.' She hesitated. 'Look, Maeve, have you thought about this in terms of what you want?'

'People keep asking me that. What I think is that I should try to find someone else.'

'Yes. Good.'

'But I don't want anyone else,' I said in a small voice. 'And don't tell him I said that. I'm pretending I don't care.'

'More games. You should try being honest with him.'

'I – he's never honest with me.'

'Break the cycle?' she suggested.

'What good would that do? I can't have him and that's that.'

'Look, I know he's attractive, even though he's not my type. You don't get more heterosexual male than Josh Derwent. But there are other men like him. There are also other men who *aren't* like him and they might be a better choice.'

'In what way?' I could hear the ice in my voice and if Liv couldn't she wasn't listening.

'Nicer. Kinder.'

'I've never met anyone kinder than him,' I said curtly, and she pushed her sunglasses up to the top of her head to look at me, wide-eyed.

'Seriously? OK. Well, here's one thing he definitely *isn't*. Available.'

'I know that.'

'Yes, but honestly, Maeve, isn't that part of the appeal? He's unattainable. You don't have to risk anything. You can kid yourself you're in love with him but really he's the safe option. He's your excuse not to get your heart broken again.'

As we drove on up through England on the straight, tedious motorway, all I could think was that it was probably the first time Josh Derwent had ever been described as the safe option, and if having feelings for him was supposed to save me from hurt, it wasn't working too well.

48

Windholt House didn't look any better without the hum of police activity around it, especially at the end of a long and tiring drive. The dry spring weather meant that the track up to the house was firmer and we were able to make it all the way through the many gates to park in the yard, where the muck was still soft and unspeakable. Something about the house looked different, as if it knew it was abandoned rather than neglected now. The windows weren't actually broken but it gave me the impression it was only a matter of time before decline set in.

'Bleak house,' Liv said.

'They should have called it that. Windholt sounds too nice.'

'It sounds cold. And it is.' She pulled her jacket around herself, flipping the collar up. 'Can we go inside?'

'Yeah, but it's not going to be any warmer,' I warned her.

'Out of the wind, though.' She stopped on the doorstep. 'Mind you, look at the view. Beautiful.'

'There's a lot of it,' I agreed abstractedly.

'What?'

'Just trying to work out if anyone has been here recently.' The marks from our car ran straight across the mud, over any number of prints and tracks, but then again, the local police had been in and out. I'd never seen the yard in a pristine state.

'No sign of a red Mini.' Liv's teeth were chattering. 'Can we go in?'

'Of course.' I had picked up the key from the police station in Keswick, and had a chat with Superintendent Eli Parker, who was more than happy for me and Liv to be at Windholt House.

'More than likely we'll come across her before you do in this bright red Mini. It'll stand out around here.'

'If she comes here. If she's still driving the car.'

'A lot of ifs.' He hesitated. 'Are you staying up at the house?'

'I booked the same hotel as before. We should probably stay there for surveillance, but . . .'

Superintendent Parker shuddered. 'I wouldn't like to think of you staying there overnight.'

'Me neither,' I said emphatically, and Liv rolled her eyes.

'It can't be that bad.'

Now she caught her breath as I pushed the door open and ushered her in. The cold sank its teeth into us immediately. 'That's brutal.'

'These flagstones keep the place nice and chilly.' I pointed down the passageway. 'The kitchen. Let's go and see if anyone has been living here. That's where I'd camp out.'

The range was dark and cold in the kitchen, though, and there were no fresh crumbs or splashes of water in the sink, the tell-tale hints of occupancy. I held a hand against the chilled kettle and shrugged. 'Nothing.'

'No one here but the mice.' Liv wrinkled her nose at the tiny brown pellets that freckled every flat surface.

'I'm pretty sure there are rats too. They did some damage to the body upstairs.'

'Oh *yuck*. Why did I volunteer to leave the office?' She looked around. 'It must be cosy in here when the range is working.'

On a second visit the room wasn't as bleak as I'd believed: handmade cushions on the chairs around the big table, plant pots on the windowsill, and a procession of homemade clay animals on a high shelf. Maybe it wasn't so impossible to imagine Rosalie living there with the children.

'Come on. Upstairs is more interesting.'

'Warmer?'

'Not as such.'

We toured the house, Liv taking it all in for the first time. I was still trying to spot anything that might have changed since my first visit.

You have a brain the size of a galaxy, you pick up on every tiny detail of everything you see and hear, but you can't work out what's right in front of you, can you?

He was heading to Cornwall, with Vidya, for work. At home he had a girlfriend. Not mine. Never mine.

The dining room, with its stiff dark furniture and cold linen. The sitting room, where something small and fast hurled itself under a fat leather sofa and I caught my breath. The hall, dark and unwelcoming. Upstairs, to the room with the tiny handprints, where Liv's eyes filled with tears. A bathroom that was pure vintage, with tiles and sanitaryware that had to be a hundred years old or more. The cluttered bedroom at the end of the hall, where there was still a smell of death.

'So no one's been here.'

'I can't blame her for not coming back.' I stepped around the area of the floor where the body had been, the rug absent for forensic analysis so the old floorboards were bare. 'It's not what I would think of as home. If I got away, I wouldn't rush to return.'

'The kitchen could have been cosy, if the fire was lit. In here too, without the smell. They used to light a fire, look. There are ashes in the grate.' She rubbed her arms, shivering. 'What do you want to do?'

'We should wait.'

'Ugh. In here?'

'I suppose.' I was looking out of the window, trying to imagine being Rosalie. How on earth had she ended up here? Had she been happy? The blood on the wall and the dead body on the floor suggested a very definite no. 'I was going to have a proper look around the house. The local cops searched it but you never know, I might find something they overlooked.'

'If it's all right with you, I'll go down and sit in the car. I've got some phone calls to make and it's more comfortable than anywhere in here.'

'No problem.' In some ways, I'd prefer to be alone. I had the nagging feeling I'd missed something. 'I'll see you outside in a while.'

After Liv had gone, I wandered through the upstairs rooms again. They were sparsely furnished and it didn't take long to look at everything, and stare out at the imposing, oppressive view, and imagine the grinding misery of short dark winter days. I took out my torch, though, and looked at the carpet, seeing indentations where furniture had stood. Someone had moved everything into the main bedroom and the rooms downstairs, I thought, making a note to check what was in the outhouses. The children's room had been stripped, dust marks showing where furniture had stood against the walls. Vidya had said there were toys and books on the island, left behind when Rosalie took the children to Ivo's house. I tried to imagine the room full of colour and life. Was that how it had been? And if so, why was it so bleak now?

I spent most of my time in the bedroom where Piers Wilmington had died. I wasn't sure what I was looking for but I couldn't stop myself from looking, sliding open drawers and checking behind pictures. The only movement was my own reflection in the starry glass of the broken mirror. I paused to look at myself, at the shadows under my eyes and the unhappy downturn of my mouth. The last time I had looked at myself with that close attention, I had been standing in the hall of the flat with Josh behind me, and he had warned me to stay away from him, for his sake.

Una had said our old superintendent Charles Godley was the one who'd forbidden Josh to make a move on me, at some unknown point in the past. He had believed I needed protecting, presumably, and Godley knew Josh better than anyone. But the thought of my boss at the time – a boss I had worshipped – thinking he needed to intervene before anything had happened . . . my skin prickled with embarrassment. I would rather die than ask Josh about it, I decided, and looked past my reflection to the background, and the fine spray of blood that marked the wall. Rosalie's blood. It was as close as I'd got to her so far.

I went over for a closer look at the blood and spent quite a long time there, shining the torch on it, considering what it told me about what had happened, and frowning to myself.

Before I went downstairs again I used the bathroom, wincing at the ice-cold water that gushed from the tap labelled 'hot'. A towel hung behind the door, stiff and rough. As I dried my hands I looked down at my feet and saw a small yellow duck, a bath toy that had been stuck behind the door, unnoticed. I picked it up and set it on the edge of the bath, ever more unsettled by the feeling that we had been primed to see one thing when reality was quite another.

On the ground floor there was more furniture but less of a sense that the rooms had ever been inhabited; it was like a museum, as Georgia had said. I wandered into the dining room and opened drawers in the mahogany sideboard, finding a treasure trove of string, matchbooks and old, crumbling corks. I looked at the pictures, and the dust in the corners of the room, and I was just about to leave when I idly opened the huge Bible. One ribbon marked the family history of the Wilmingtons in spidery ink and impeccable calligraphy, a few different types of handwriting recording the births, marriages and deaths down through three centuries. The last entries were in black ink in awkward, small letters, and they had smudged.

Wilbur Magnus Wilmington

Posy Ivy Wilmington

Magnus and Ivo, commemorated in her children's names. I took a photograph of it. Magnus would want to know, I thought, that he had been her first thought, not Ivo.

And then my eye travelled up to the previous entry, where the same hand had written of the (common-law) marriage of Piers Wilmington and Eleanor Wilmington. The bride had written her maiden name in pencil, pale but legible.

I read the name, and stood rooted to the spot, and read it again, and realised that we had been entirely wrong from the start, about pretty much everything, and the facts of the entire case slipped into logical order like a run of dominos falling, one after another.

I had to talk to Derwent. Urgently.

A glance at my phone confirmed my worst fears: no reception. Not even a bar of it. I held the phone up uselessly, and tried to remember if I'd used it at Windholt House the last time I was there, or if anyone else had been able to use theirs. The local police had radios, I recalled.

'Shit.'

I hurried to the back door, and out across the yard, my eyes on my phone screen to see if by some miracle it managed to connect to the network, and it was only when I was right beside the car that I glanced into it to see Liv slumped sideways in her seat, her face waxy, her eyes closed.

'Liv!' I scrabbled at the door handle, clumsy in panic, horrified. No reaction from her. No signs of life. Something had happened – someone had done something to her. She had only come with me because she loved me and I'd told her she needed to get out of the office more often, to show commitment to the job that absolutely was not worth her life. 'Liv – oh God, please be all right. Please wake up. Please—'

And then something was in front of my face, clamped to my mouth, my nose, a wet cloth of some kind that I couldn't escape because the hand that held it was too strong, and it was pushing my head back at an awkward angle, hurting me, and I couldn't get free or get any purchase on his arm, and my lungs were aching and I had to breathe . . .

And that was all I knew.

49

The police station in Falmouth was modern and uncompromisingly blocky. It was still a sight for sore eyes after the drive from London, which had taken almost seven hours and all of Vidya's patience. It wasn't the first time she'd worked with Josh Derwent, but it was the first time she'd seen him behaving this way: snapping with energy, intolerant of delays or distractions, impatient with her attempts at conversation. He'd insisted on loud music all the way and the briefest of stops. This was the Derwent they'd warned her about.

A good copper but an awkward sod . . .

Don't get on the wrong side of him . . .

He only really likes working with Maeve . . .

'And you know why that is,' Pete Belcott had added with a smirk.

'Because she knows how to handle him,' Georgia said earnestly, and Pete crowed.

'Bet she does.'

And Vidya had assumed it was all talk. He had been polite to her on their previous cases, professional, a little distant as if his mind was on other things. What she was realising now was that he had been that way, not because he liked her or thought she was good at her job, but because he fundamentally didn't care about whatever they were doing. Now that she saw him driven, focused, taut like a strung bow, she realised she'd been fooling herself.

Vidya wished that she'd spent more time watching Maeve deal with Josh. There had to be a better way than sitting in silence, hoping he forgot she was there. Vidya wanted to spend more time watching Maeve in general. If she had a role model on the team it was definitely Maeve. One day, she promised herself, she would be as confident and astute as the sergeant. Until then . . .

'At last.' He slung the car into a space behind the nick and leapt out of it. 'Come on.'

'Why are we in a hurry?' Vidya was slower, stiff after the long drive. 'He's not going anywhere.'

'I can't wait to see his face when we walk in, that's all. He thought he'd skipped away in time.' Derwent looked across the roof of their car, his eyes bright. 'I don't like people who lie to me, and I don't like him.'

The feeling was entirely mutual, Vidya thought, sitting opposite Tor Grant half an hour later. His hair was lank and sweat glossed his face. He stared at Derwent with a kind of sick fascination.

'How did you track me down?'

'Easily.' Derwent leaned back, his arms folded. 'Why were you so keen to head for the hills? You knew we wanted to know where you were.'

Grant sniffed, rubbing his nose with the back of a hand. 'I don't like being arrested. Questioned.'

'Well, you're out of luck, aren't you?'

'I don't know what you want with me. I have an alibi for the night the Marshalls were murdered. I'm just an interested bystander. You're wasting your time on me.'

'Rosalie Marshall.'

Grant wriggled. 'I don't know what happened to her. That's why I'm making the podcast. To find out.'

'Is that so?' Derwent's voice was soft and Vidya felt a chill run down her spine. She was discovering the inspector was actually less intimidating when he was shouting than when he was quiet.

'I didn't have anything to do with her disappearance. You have to believe me.' Grant ran a tongue over his lips, fidgeting.

'Why did you leave early for university? Why did you change your plans?'

'I was fed up with Magnus. I had saved enough money. My mother was driving me insane.' He touched his forehead, examining his fingertips as they came away wet with perspiration. 'You'd have run too. And it was long before the girl disappeared.'

'Conveniently.'

'No.' He slammed his hand down on the table, panicked now. 'Whatever you're implying, you're wrong.'

'What made you leave then?'

'I wanted to.'

'Why?' Derwent was implacable. 'What made you decide it was the right time?'

'I – I don't know.'

'Did it have anything to do with being caught masturbating in Magnus's bedroom?' Derwent leaned back in his chair. 'Just a suggestion.'

The air hissed out of Tor Grant. 'Fuck. He told you.'

'Yes, he did.'

'Don't read too much into it.' Grant shifted his weight, still fidgeting, still sweating. 'I was embarrassed.'

'Why were you touching yourself in a child's bedroom?'

'I wasn't – well, I suppose I was, but – look, I don't know. I just wanted to. I did it a lot back then. It was . . . comforting.' His eyes darted to Vidya's face. 'Does she have to be in here?'

'Yes.' Derwent leaned forward. 'You'd been in there on your own with Rosalie, hadn't you?'

'That – that wasn't relevant.' He was almost sobbing. 'I wasn't *attracted* to her. If anything, she scared me. I tried to talk to her and it – it went wrong. She laughed at me. She was bright, you know, and – and tough.'

'She was nine years old.' Derwent said it through clenched teeth.

'Yes, well, she wasn't like any nine-year-old I'd ever met. Understandably, when you know about her background.'

Derwent was still for a second. 'What about her background?'

'Her parents.' Grant sniffed. 'Rosalie's dad went insane and murdered her mother. He stabbed her fifty times. It was a bloodbath.'

'So what?'

'Rosalie was in the room when it happened.' Grant looked from Vidya to Derwent, triumphant. 'You didn't know *that*, did you? No one knew. She was only three years old. She saw the whole thing.'

Vidya knew that Derwent didn't like being caught unawares, especially by Tor Grant, but he managed not to show it.

'How did you find this out?'

'I found her mum's sister and husband. The podcast, you see. Their son saw some reference to it on Reddit or Facebook or something and got in touch, and then I got them to trust me. They didn't like the police who investigated Rosalie's disappearance, so they wouldn't tell them much – your colleagues fucked that one up.'

Vidya thought it was exactly the kind of detail the original investigation should have found out, and from the look on his face, so did Derwent. He made a meaningless note on the pad in front of him and without looking up asked, 'What are you doing in Cornwall? Looking for Rosalie?'

'No. I wanted to do another interview with the aunt and uncle. They live in Falmouth now but they were in St Ives before. I wanted to ask about the time they spent looking after her before she was fostered. They didn't want to keep her. Guess why?' Grant didn't wait. 'She was a little weirdo. A freak. They were glad to see her go. And the foster family were the same. Helena never understood what she was taking into her home, but the girl was damaged goods.'

A hush settled on the interview room and Vidya resisted the urge to fidget: the tension was almost visible.

Derwent stirred. 'Let's go back to the start again, shall we? One more time.'

He conducted the rest of the interview with cool professionalism, turning Grant inside out. What was absolutely apparent was that Grant was exactly what he had said, an overzealous podcaster on the trail of a big story. As time passed Grant warmed up enough to start getting cocky, and at the end, after the recorder was switched off, he winked.

'I'd like to interview you for the podcast, Inspector. I think that would be really fascinating. You have a perfect voice for it.'

Derwent's expression was stony. 'I'm busy.'

'I can do any time that suits you. Name the day. I'm at your disposal.'

He didn't even look up. 'It'll never suit me.'

Vidya waited until Grant went back to the cells. The room felt twice as big once he'd left it.

'What did you think?'

'Total prick.'

'I meant what he said about Rosalie.'

Derwent shrugged. 'Check the details for me. You might as well chase up the aunt and her husband. Find out whatever you can, in case it's useful. There's nothing in the files, which could confirm what he said about the Marshalls not knowing Rosalie's background. But I don't necessarily believe him about any of this. And alibis can be broken.'

His phone rang and he sighed before he answered it. 'Una. This should be annoying. Hello? Yes. Just finished.'

There was a pause before he spoke again, and in that few seconds, his face changed. Vidya shivered in spite of herself. Something was very badly wrong.

'I'm on my way,' Derwent said into the phone. 'If she's missing, I'll find her.'

50

The ache in my right knee was the first thing I noticed. I groaned, and tried to move my leg to ease the tension in the joint, but it was impossible; something was pinning my legs. I was stuck, sitting upright, unable to move my hands, unable to lean forward because of a line of pressure that ran across my throat. I was blind, confused.

There had been an accident, I thought.

I was trapped.

I was—

'Awake?' The voice was familiar and yet it had sounded different the last time I'd heard it: it had been more tentative. Now it was clipped and totally lacking in warmth.

'What,' I said, brilliantly, and then stopped. The question wouldn't form properly in my mind. It was as if my brain was smothered in a thick blanket of fog. The reason I couldn't see anything, I worked out, was because my eyes were covered with something soft. I was sitting on something that felt like a dining-room chair, hard and unyielding. There was a vile taste in my mouth. As far as I could tell, I was indoors, but this wasn't Windholt House; my hands were warm.

'"What happened? Where am I?" I think those are the traditional things people want to know at this point.'

I heard a movement near me and jerked my head back as something touched my lips.

'It's water. You'll need it. You'll be thirsty.'

Never drink the water, I thought, and drank it anyway, because as soon as he said it I was aware of a raging thirst that I couldn't begin to satisfy. While I drank I tried to force my thoughts into some kind of order, knowing that I needed to be alert, that this was the kind of situation that could slide out of control easily if I panicked him, or myself.

He took the water away. 'Do you know where you are?'

I shook my head.

'Do you know who I am?'

'Yes.'

'You do.' He sounded surprised. 'How?'

I didn't answer that one. I certainly wasn't going to tell him that I had only worked it out two minutes before he'd grabbed me, and that I hadn't had time to tell anyone else.

'They'll be looking for you,' I said instead.

'They've always been looking for me and they haven't found me yet.' His breath, close to my face. 'I found *you*. You're in my custody, not the other way round. And considering where I found you, I don't think you had the least idea where to start looking for me.'

They would start at Windholt House, when they didn't hear from me. They would start with the last known point and work from there. Wherever I was, it couldn't be far from Windholt House; I couldn't have been unconscious for long. So all I had to do was stay alive until they came and found me. They would start at Windholt House and find the car.

The memory jolted me: Liv, slumped and unconscious.

'What did you do to Liv?'

'Who is Liv? Oh – the other woman? She was looking at her phone when I went over to talk to her. I had a story prepared about being a lost hiker in need of help, but I didn't need it. The car was unlocked. I tried the door, it opened, and then I knocked her out.'

'You hit her?'

'No, she had the same treatment as you. A little chloroform.'

That explained the filthy headache, I thought, and the lack of response from Liv when I'd knocked on the window. My brain was working more efficiently now. Given that I had woken up with the mental capabilities of a potato that wasn't a huge leap forward, but it was better than nothing.

'Where did you get chloroform?'

'I made it.' A giggle; he was pleased with himself. 'There are videos on YouTube, did you know that? A simple chemical reaction between acetone and bleach. Amazing what you can do with household products.'

Chloroform. Another piece of the puzzle. I squashed down my worry about what homemade chloroform might have done to us and tried to focus.

'Is that what you did to subdue the Marshalls? Knocked them out so they couldn't fight back?'

'I don't think they would have been able to fight back, but it suited me to be able to take my time. I wanted to get it right.'

'You didn't do a very good job.'

Silence for a beat. 'What did I get wrong?'

'Where do I start?' I allowed myself to be waspish to see how he reacted. 'The position of the bodies. The bedclothes were too neat. The window was open in the bedroom and they never opened their bedroom window at night. You forgot to shut it.'

'Ah. I should have remembered. I wanted to let the air clear. Maybe the fumes had affected me more than I knew.'

'It must have been difficult, even if they were unconscious. Killing them. Holding a pillow over her face. Shooting him.'

He sounded as if he was gritting his teeth. 'I don't want to talk about it.'

'Did they see you when you went to kill them? Speak to you? Did they know you were there to harm them?'

'Shut up. Shut *up*.'

I backed off. I didn't want to panic him. 'How did you know how much chloroform to give us?'

'I didn't. I guessed.'

'But you could have hurt Liv.' My anxiety had been fading because if Liv felt the way I did she was probably miserable but she would be all right, and if he had left her in the car she was better off than I was, currently. Now it went right back up to the red zone. 'You could have killed her if you gave her too much. Did you check she was all right? Did you make sure she was breathing before you left?'

'No. I didn't.' He leaned in. 'Because I didn't give a fuck about her and I don't give a fuck about you either. You were in my way.'

'You were hoping she'd come back to the house,' I guessed. 'Rosalie. You don't know where she is, do you? You've been desperate to find her, all this time. And you were afraid we'd scare her off.'

'Well, you weren't likely to help. Why were you there?' He hesitated and came out with the question he really wanted to ask. 'Do you know where she is?'

'Is that why I'm here?'

'It's not because I wanted the pleasure of your conversation. I have other things to do.'

'Like what?' I wanted to keep him talking. I had worked out that my arms were restrained, and that moving them tightened the rope that ran around my throat. With small, careful movements I was trying to work out how much play there was in the ligatures. 'Why don't you take my blindfold off?'

'I don't want you to see me.' He leaned closer. 'I don't think you do know who I am. I think you're bluffing.'

'Really, Dennis, you have to get over the idea that you're some sort of criminal mastermind,' I snapped. 'No one ever seems to have thought of you as a suspect in Rosalie's disappearance, but that was just luck. Let's be honest, no one seems to have thought much about you at all. You barely came up in the original investigation. Bruce never mentioned you.'

'It wasn't luck.' He pulled the hat off my head so he could stare into my face, angry now. Dennis Hood, still neat, his beard perfectly trimmed, but his eyes were red-rimmed. Dennis Hood, who had tracked the Marshalls from their old house and had inserted himself into the family again, knowing that Rosalie would come to find them. Dennis, who had decided Bruce had to die, and Helena too, to make it look like suicide. Dennis had pretended to be devastated. Dennis had limped around London bravely, bewildered, playing the part of a kind old man.

He sat back into the small armchair that faced me, looking whip-thin and fit and a world away from the frail, lame man I'd met before. 'It wasn't luck,' he said again, and I'd wounded his pride. 'It was planning and organisation. We had already left London, as far as anyone knew.'

'Which is why Bruce wanted to check the dates,' I realised. 'He was trying to remember where you'd been.'

'What?'

'He left a note.'

'A note?'

'He knew that there was something wrong with your story. You must have given yourself away.'

He lifted his upper lip in a snarl. 'We were talking about Nell – they called her Rosalie – and the things she took with her. She didn't have much. A book. A toy dog. The bloody gun. I could have murdered her when I found it in her bag. She said she thought it might be useful. He was listing everything and I suppose I was impatient. I said, yes, and the back door key, trying to hurry him up but they hadn't told anyone except the police that it was missing. The police had made them keep it quiet.'

BDK? How?

Back door key? How did he know?

'Why did you kill them? To stop Rosalie from being able to see them?'

'No. I was only there to try to talk to her. I was hoping I'd find her first. Then I put my foot in it with the key, and I saw Bruce react, even though he tried to hide it. I pretended to leave and said a big goodbye to them both, banged the front door and went back to hide behind the boxes. I stayed there while the carer put them to bed. I waited until they were asleep before I went in.' He beat his hand on his thigh, irritated. 'I was kind. I put them out of their misery. They didn't feel anything after the chloroform. I'm the one who suffered because I had to see it all.'

327

'You never left after the murders, did you? You made it look as if the killer escaped by using the balcony, but that was just to mislead us. We were looking for someone able-bodied, not an old man.'

A smile. 'I stayed. I let myself out while the carer was cleaning the bathroom, and went to the park. It didn't matter if anyone saw me then because it was long after they had died. I waited for her to call me. It worked perfectly.'

I had been focused on him completely. Now I looked around, taking in the details of his small cottage. It was a comfortable home, if simple, with plain furniture and good amateur art on the walls and a few low shelves crammed with books. It felt like somewhere he had lived for many years. The curtains were drawn and I couldn't begin to guess what time it was, or how long I had been unconscious.

'You're good at hiding, aren't you, Dennis? Did you hide in the house the night you took Rosalie?'

The breath hissed out of him. 'How did you know?'

'When something works, you keep doing it. You hid at the Marshalls' flat. You hid in Windholt House, just now.'

'Just now,' he repeated, and smiled as if he knew something I didn't. 'You were very deeply unconscious, weren't you? Easy to manage. But heavy to carry, I won't lie. If you have a few bruises, that's my fault.'

I swallowed, knowing that he was enjoying my discomfort and the power he had over me. 'Why did you kidnap Rosalie, Dennis?'

A spasm crossed his face. 'You talk about her being kidnapped but she came willingly. Willingly. She wanted to leave. She was unhappy.'

'She missed her brothers.'

'She was a loving child. She gave love freely. Piers took advantage of that when he came across her in the mountains. He persuaded her she loved him. She didn't know any better.'

'You took advantage of that loving nature too. What did you do to her? Did you hurt her? Abuse her?'

He looked scandalised. 'No. Nothing like that. She was ours. Our child. My wife was the one who decided to take her, not me. I didn't want to do it, but I had to. I couldn't leave it up to her. She would have been caught.'

'Whereas you knew exactly what to do and how to get away with it.'

He shrugged. 'I got away with it, as you say, for sixteen years. That's longer than most.'

'Why are you looking for her now?'

'You first.'

'Untie me and I'll tell you.'

'Tell me or I'll tie you up even tighter.' His eyes were implacable and I reminded myself that this was a man who had killed two vulnerable people with ruthless efficiency to protect himself, when he could have left Helena alive. He was thorough to a fault. I told him what we knew about Rosalie, and where she had been, and what she had done with the children.

'She gave them to Ivo?' He sounded shattered.

'He'll look after them. He and his wife are good people.' I tried to rotate my wrists. There was no give in the ropes at all. 'We're worried about Rosalie. About her health. And they suspect she killed Piers.'

He swallowed. 'Are you going to arrest her?'

'There's an investigation,' I said. 'I'm not running it. I'm not involved with it, so I don't know for sure, but it's a possibility.'

'They need to leave her alone.' Hood took a deep breath. 'I killed him.'

'Why?'

'He knew who she was – because she told him. Practically the first person she'd met after we came here, and she *told* him. Piers said he'd tell the police if I ever got in his way. He'd send them after us. I had to protect my wife. And then she died, and I was afraid. I knew there would be consequences if I was found out.' He spread out his hands, and I noticed a tremor in his fingers. 'I only ever tried to do what was best. Piers wasn't a bad man. He wasn't very bright, that's all. He loved her, absolutely, but he wouldn't let her go. She wasn't well. I wanted her to see a doctor, but Piers refused.'

'She never saw a doctor after you took her,' I spat. 'So don't pretend you were worried about her.'

He looked at me as if I was insane. 'She had my wife.'

'Your wife . . .'

'Lydia. Dr Lydia Fuller. My wife. She used her maiden name because she was already qualified when we met.'

I closed my eyes, beyond frustrated. How many times had my eye slid over the name in the files? How many times had witnesses mentioned Dr Fuller? That was on me; I had assumed that Dr Fuller was a man. I had never made the connection with Dennis Hood. Rosalie had been a regular patient, which explained how the doctor had got to know her so well. Above reproach, utterly respectable. No wonder the Hoods had never been suspects.

'Rosalie was worried about the children,' Hood said, almost to himself. 'I was going to take them but then – I didn't get the chance.'

'So you killed Piers.'

'I did it for her. I didn't know she would run away. I thought she'd be happy.'

I didn't feel sorry for him; I didn't need to because he was sorry enough for himself. It was Rosalie who haunted me – Rosalie who had suffered alone, Rosalie who had gone from one prison to another, Rosalie whose choices had narrowed down to what it took to survive.

He made a vague gesture towards the kitchen table, where there was a small notepad. 'I've written a note. I've said that I was the one who killed him.'

'You don't need a note. You can go to the police and confess, just like you confessed to me.'

'I can't go to prison, that's the thing. I'd never get out. I can't do that.'

'Dennis,' I began, and his eyes came back to me.

'I'm sorry.'

330

'Why are you sorry?' I tried to loosen the ropes again. The one that ran across my throat dug deeper into my skin. 'Look, untie me and we can talk. I'm sure there's a way to help you.'

'I don't need any help.' He stood up and walked away, moving like a sleepwalker, and it occurred to me, with a chill that went right through me, that Dennis Hood had absolutely nothing left to live for.

51

'Don't you want to see her again? Rosalie?' My voice cracked. 'Don't you want to say goodbye to her?'

He looked at me vacantly. 'What's the use of waiting? She could have given me the children to look after instead of Ivo Marshall. She chose not to. And she's not here now.'

'She wanted them to have the life that she didn't have.'

'We gave her a wonderful life. Lydia and I gave her everything. And she adored Lydia. If my wife was still alive, maybe things would have been different.'

'You miss Lydia.'

'All the time.'

'There are people who will miss me if anything happens to me, Dennis.' Josh's face flashed into my mind, serious in the streetlight after we had kissed, tender and sad. 'People who love me.'

He went to the kitchen, ignoring me. I turned my hand within the rope tie, trying to loosen it, and only succeeded in burning my skin. Every time I moved, the rope around my neck tightened, which threw black spots across my vision and made panic spiral through my mind.

One last try. 'Lydia wouldn't want you to hurt anyone else.'

'She would want me to protect Rosalie. Nothing else matters.' He read through the note one last time. 'Everything I've done was an act of love. Even this.'

A wave of anger swept over me and I let it out. I had nothing left to lose. 'Let's be serious here. If she had turned up here, sick, in need of help, you wouldn't have taken her to a doctor, would you? You had the chance to do that and you didn't, because you were afraid you'd be found out. You put yourself first and

332

you left her to suffer. So all this talk about protecting Rosalie is bollocks. We both know if it was up to you, you'd have left her to die alone.'

'Everyone dies alone,' Dennis Hood said heavily, and walked out of the room.

Nothing I could do. Nowhere I could go. I struggled against the ropes and made no progress. I listened to him walking around the rooms of the small cottage, the legs of a chair squealing as he dragged it across the floor. At some point he opened a door and a cool breeze washed into the room, clear iron-hard air that smelt like the early morning. It was a small thing but I wished I knew what time it was, and how long I had been there, and what Dennis Hood was planning to do next. I was lost in every sense of the word.

What he did at last was to climb onto a chair in the small hallway of the cottage. He took the rope he'd hung from the stairs, I found out later, looped a noose around his neck, and kicked the chair away. The clatter of it made me jump, and the noise of him choking, his legs kicking as he died, was something I knew I would never forget. He died hard, and I couldn't do anything to stop him.

I would have saved him, if I could. In spite of everything, I would have tried.

When Dennis Hood was silent and still, and the only sound was the slow creak of the rope, I sat up. I needed to get out of the chair and get help.

It didn't occur to me then that I might not be able to free myself. It was many long, agonising minutes later that I realised I had underestimated Dennis Hood's talent with knots. I could see and feel that the rope looped around my body in a complicated sequence of ties, circling my upper arms as well as my throat, tying my forearms and wrists to the chair and holding my shoulders back. The actual knots were too far away for me to be able to reach them with my fingers and the rope was too tight to allow me to work my arms free. The more violently I struggled, the more the rope sawed against my throat.

Something else he had seen on the internet, I guessed, with a vague recollection of elaborate Japanese bondage, and it was very much not the kind of thing that the tied-up person could undo on their own. My hands were numb already.

I needed a new plan. I thought about tipping the chair over and trying to break it, but a couple of experimental hops confirmed my worst fears: it was solid and I didn't think I could count on the force of a fall to break it. Also, there was every chance I would fracture both of my arms, given that they were in a stress position behind me. And if the attempt to break it didn't work, I would be stuck on the floor, in even less comfort than I was already.

That left only one solution. Wait to be rescued.

I shut my eyes for a while and imagined the efforts of my colleagues. Liv would have sounded the alarm, if she was able to. But if she had died—

I couldn't think about that. She hadn't died. She had recovered and gone for help. Even now, she was standing in the police station in Keswick, helping to coordinate the search. Maybe she had seen him, or his car. Maybe she was on her way to me at that very moment.

I thought I had probably dropped my phone when Dennis Hood attacked me, but if it was in my pocket, or if Dennis Hood had taken my phone – assuming it was connected to the network now – they could pinpoint my location.

Or they might find something that directed them towards Hood; I had, after all.

They might have found Rosalie.

They might . . .

It wasn't a good moment when I faced up to the fact that these were little better than fairy tales – stories with a happy ending, a comforting nonsense.

It's a fantasy, Maeve. A dream. Make-believe.

I felt tears squeeze out from under my lashes. Josh.

Don't think about him either.

I don't know how long I sat in that chair. Long enough to ache in every bone of my body, long enough for every muscle to burn. Long enough to cry. Not long enough to pull the rope tight around my neck for the sake of hurrying the inevitable, but long enough to register that it was a possibility. I still hoped: stupid, unreasonable hope, the dogged determination that meant I never gave up.

But I went through twenty different kinds of hell holding on to my hope.

And time passed.

When I heard footsteps coming from the back of the house, I thought I was hallucinating. I lifted my head and found myself staring at a figure in the doorway: a stranger.

It was a woman, painfully thin, with long, tangled dark hair, a long skirt and a big hand-knitted grey jumper swamping her frame. Her skin was yellowed and her face was gaunt but her eyes were wide and dark, unchanged, and I had spent weeks looking at photographs of them.

'Rosalie?' The word was a ghost, soundless. I tried to clear my throat.

'What – what happened?' She faltered forward a couple of steps. 'Who are you?'

She was here, in front of me, and all I could think was that I had to get free.

'Cut the rope,' I said, in a rush.

She stood still instead, her eyes wide.

Oh God, I had to be patient.

'I'm a police officer. Please. Help me.' I tried to gather my thoughts. 'My name is Maeve. I was looking for you.'

Instant, total panic. She scrambled backwards, her eyes wide, and I cursed myself.

'Rosalie, it's all right. I'm not here to arrest you.' I tried to smile. 'Not that I could, from here.'

'No.' She was taking in how I was tied, my total helplessness. 'Who did this to you?'

'Dennis.'

She started and looked around. 'Where is he?'

'I think he's in the hall.'

Her mouth straightened to a line and she turned towards the door.

'Wait. Don't go out there.' I said it with as much authority as I could manage. She looked back at me, dubious.

'Why not?'

'You don't want to see him like that.'

'Like what?' Her eyes widened. 'He's dead?'

I nodded.

'Why?'

'He confessed to killing Bruce and Helena . . . to taking you . . . and to shooting Piers.'

'Did he?' She seemed stunned.

'His confession is on the kitchen table.'

She stumbled over to it, staring down at the written pages that Dennis Hood had left behind.

'I never thought he'd admit it.'

'He was worried that you'd get the blame.'

'If he hadn't confessed,' Rosalie said slowly, 'would I have been in trouble?'

'I don't know.' My lips were dry and I tried to moisten them. 'Could I have some water?'

'I should let you go.' She said it in an unfocused way, her thoughts elsewhere.

'Please.'

'I – sorry.' Her hand went to her head. 'I'm not feeling well. I get . . . distracted.'

'It's all right. I know.' I managed not to scream at her. 'If you cut the rope, I can get myself something to drink.'

'I'm just tired.' She slid into one of the chairs at the table, with her back to me, and leaned her head on her arm.

'Rosalie. Please.' I felt a tear slide out of the corner of my eye. So close and so far. 'I can get us both help if you let me go.'

There was no sound but the ticking of a clock somewhere, and Rosalie's breathing, and my heart thumping. She wasn't well. She might collapse, unconscious.

She might die too, and then it would be a matter of time until I followed suit.

I needed her to get up.

'Rosalie? It's the last thing I'll ask you to do, but please, please, let me go.' I begged. I coaxed. I let her sit for a few minutes to gather her strength. I talked about her children – about Wil and his love for dinosaurs, about Posy's laugh. I talked about Ivo and Magnus.

I got nothing back.

A long, long time later, she shifted on her chair and looked around at me. Clear-eyed. She hadn't been asleep, or unconscious.

'Why are you here?' she asked.

'He took me from Windholt House. I was looking for you there. Waiting to see if you'd come back. He wanted to find out where you were. He wanted to know what we knew.'

'You shouldn't have let that happen.' There was pure steel in her face, and I understood how the small child had survived, had lived, had given everything to her children and not minded the sacrifice. I had felt sorry for her, all of this time, but now I felt I understood her.

'It was a mistake,' I agreed.

'Are you good at your job?'

'As a rule. Maybe not today.' I tried to smile, but I couldn't. 'There are people who'll miss me, just like you. People who'll wonder where I am. There's someone who loves me, I think—'

'You think? Don't you know?'

'Yes,' I said. 'I do know. But he hasn't said it yet.'

She got to her feet, slowly, as if everything in her body ached, and came towards me, holding on to the furniture for support. Up close she looked even worse, the skin stretched tight over the bones of her face, her eye-sockets hollow.

'You need something to cut the rope,' I said gently.

'I have a knife.' Off-hand. Laconic.

Why did she have a knife? I twisted my head, trying to watch her hands as she moved behind me. The hair stood up on my arms, the nape of my neck.

Say nothing. Maeve, say nothing . . .

'Did you come here to kill him?'

The silence was heavy. I listened to my heart pounding, to the short breaths that Rosalie was taking, and I shut my eyes. Oh, Josh.

Her voice sounded as if she was a long way off. 'He wanted Wil and Posy. I couldn't let him have them. I couldn't take the risk. He was a coward, and I thought I'd done enough to keep him away from them, but I was wrong. I thought he'd be too scared to come after us.'

The skin on my neck tensed, waiting for the cold kiss of metal. How long would it take to bleed out if she got the right angle and hit an artery? Not long. Slower if it was a more superficial injury, but I would still slide into shock.

'Where did he learn to tie knots like these?' She said it almost to herself.

I felt the knife catch against the skin of my wrist and I bit my lip to stop from crying out.

'Sorry – it's tight.' She set to work on the rope, dragging the blade against it, pulling it lower so it seared the skin of my throat. I could have wept with frustration as she sawed at it, her breathing laboured. She was pitifully weak.

She was all I had.

'Why didn't you go to the police, when you ran away from Windholt House?'

She went still for a moment. 'I was brought up to avoid the police. I was afraid.'

'We would have helped you.'

'You didn't save my mother – my real mother. No one helped her.'

I bit my lip. It was true. 'Do you remember what happened to her?'

338

'I remember a little.' She sounded fierce, her breath hot against my skin, and I wondered again at my inability to play it safe, my need to know the truth that drove me beyond what was sensible or rational. 'She was pretty. She sang to me. She used to shut me in my room when Da was angry – but there wasn't time, that day. The sun was shining, I remember that, and the blood was very bright, and I remember she stopped moving and I thought she was asleep – and afterwards, he cried.'

A rustle behind me was her picking up the knife again, and I tensed, but it was the rope she cut, not me.

'Getting . . . there . . .' Her breathing was harsh and she was shaking with effort.

I pushed against the ropes, and a second strand went, and a third. It took a long, long time, even after that, for Rosalie to saw through the remaining rope – so long that I thought it would be better to call for help and let someone else do it. But when I suggested it, my throat raw and burning inside and out, she shook her head.

'There's no phone here.'

'Internet?'

'He uses the library.' She looked around. 'This place isn't even on the electricity grid. There are solar panels and a generator. It's genuinely the middle of nowhere.'

Bad news. I reached somewhere deep inside myself for the resolve to wait, and she had enough determination to persevere, and at long last the rope gave way. I slid forward, not meaning to, and collapsed on the floor. Every muscle in my body was protesting. I couldn't move even if I'd wanted to. I was vaguely aware of Rosalie slumping to the ground beside me, her head tipped back, struggling for air.

Rosalie. The fact of her being there was incredible. The woman I had searched for, the child who had been hidden, who had been lost. A stranger now to the people who had loved her most.

I'd thought I might save her, but she'd rescued me instead.

339

She was staring into space, her body slack, her mind somewhere else. The effort of cutting the rope had been too much for her, I realised, and stretched out my hand to hers.

'Thank you.'

'We'll have to drive out.' I was looking at an ordnance survey map of the area, which Rosalie had found, and the tiny rectangle far from any proper road that was the cottage. She had shown me Windholt House too, and I saw Hood had moved me further than I'd realised. There was nothing to connect the two properties, nothing to tell rescuers where we were. I was glad I hadn't known that when I was tied up in the chair.

I had recovered enough to be able to hobble around the cottage, avoiding the hall where a quick glance confirmed Dennis Hood swayed at the end of his rope. My body ached and my knee was screaming a warning with every step that it was damaged and I was making it worse. Rosalie had slept for a while, flat out on the sofa.

'We can't drive.'

'I can manage,' I said, with more bravado than I felt.

'No, it's the car.'

I turned to look at her. 'What about the car?'

What about the car indeed. I leaned against the wall of the cottage, staring at the Toyota Land Cruiser that Dennis Hood had driven straight into a ditch. It was nose down, wedged, unrecoverable except with a tow truck.

'Why did he do that?'

She shrugged. 'Maybe it was an accident?'

Or it was his way of ensuring he had no choice but to take his own life. A coward needed to have no alternative to do something final, something selfless. He had trapped himself, and in doing so he had trapped us like spiders under a glass.

'What about your car?' I asked. 'The Mini?'

'It ran out of petrol. I left it a few miles from here. I had to walk across the hills to get here.' No wonder she was so exhausted. It was a blow, all the same – even if the police found the car it wouldn't tell them where we were. She sat down on the doorstep of the cottage, huddled in her clothes, worn out. 'I can't do it again. I can tell you where to go if you want to try to walk.'

'I don't want to leave you.' I sat beside her with some difficulty. 'Also, I'm not sure I'm capable of walking anywhere with my knee like this.'

'It's surprising what you can do when you have to.'

'Well, we know you can do anything.' I was running through the possibilities, feeling increasingly dismayed and trying not to show it. No phone, no internet, no transport, both of us weak to the point of failure. The mountains surrounded us. Overhead the sky was clear, blue, empty of anything except a couple of birds that wheeled and swung on invisible currents. There wasn't a breath of wind. Nothing moved.

No one was coming.

No one knew where we were.

And currently, we were as invisible as if we'd been hiding.

I thought about hiding, and what gave people away, and an island in the Thames came to mind.

'Stay here.' I went back into the cottage to find one of Dennis Hood's tea towels, and a box of matches, and a bottle of whisky, and (averting my eyes from his livid face) the keys to the Toyota which were in his pocket.

'What are you doing?' Rosalie asked when I came back, the tea towel now saturated with whisky.

'Smoke signals.' I limped over to the Land Cruiser, and by great good luck I could just about reach the petrol cap to unlock it. I shoved the tea towel into the tank, leaving a tongue of it sticking out. It probably wasn't long enough to get close to the petrol that was left in the tank, and I was crossing my fingers that there was enough petrol left in it anyway for my purposes, but first and foremost I just needed vapour.

'Go inside. Stay away from the windows.' I waited until Rosalie had disappeared into the kitchen and lit the end of the tea towel. A flame ran up it, and I made for the cottage at my top speed, which was not going to break any records. I was just shutting the door when the cloth charred through to the petrol tank and ignited with a sound like the end of the world. I heard Rosalie scream and I hurried through to where she was huddled behind the sofa.

'Are you hurt? No?'

'I wasn't expecting it.' She uncurled herself, staring out of the window.

I looked out too, at the column of dark smoke that was billowing out of the burning Land Cruiser, stretching up into the sky already, swirling higher and higher, marking our position for anyone who cared to see it.

'They'll come now,' I said. 'They'll know we're here, and they'll come.'

52

'Here you go.' Georgia came in carrying a mug of tea, the most beautiful sight I'd ever seen.

I took it from her with a sigh of happiness. 'Thank you.'

'Are you sure you shouldn't be in hospital? You look . . .'

'I know how I look.' I was sitting in the police station, in the small room they had set aside for us, wearing tracksuit bottoms and a hoodie that I'd borrowed from one of the local police officers who was about my height but much bigger. I knew the clothes swamped me. I had taken off my poor abused black trouser suit, now sadly mud-stained, bloody, torn and filthy, and dropped it into a bin in the bathroom of the police station. The hoodie didn't hide the red marks across my neck and wrists, the tiny blood bruises that bloomed wherever the ropes had dug into my skin, or my pallor, or the dark circles under my eyes. Nothing could make me look like anything except someone who had barely escaped with her life. 'It's fine.'

'They checked her over.' Liv, who was standing with her back to the window, watching me worriedly. 'They said it was just bruising and dehydration and a sprained knee.'

'No lasting damage – nothing that time won't fix. So I'm very grateful for the tea,' I said, and meant it. 'It really is what I need.'

'They told you to rest too,' Liv pointed out. 'And it's late. You should get back to the hotel and get some sleep.'

'I can't yet.' I was still fidgeting with leftover adrenalin and the thought of closing my eyes did not appeal. When I did that I was going to have to confront what had almost happened to me, and I wasn't ready. I wanted any distraction I could find instead.

'Do you still have a headache?'

I nodded. 'The chloroform is taking a while to wear off. You?'

'Same.' She shuddered. 'It was horrible.'

'He wasn't much of a chemist.'

Georgia dragged out a chair from the table and sat down. 'What's the news about Rosalie?'

'Nothing good,' I said. 'Ivo and Magnus are coming from London to be with her.'

'Magnus?' Liv's voice was sharp. I shrugged.

'She brings out the best in him. He truly loves her, you know. She was his little sister and he was devastated to lose her. Now at least he has a chance to see her again.'

'Is she dying?' Georgia was still trying to understand what was going on and I got that, but I wished she hadn't put it so baldly.

'From what I've heard, the doctors can't help her. All they can do is make her comfortable. They don't think she'll last until this time tomorrow, but they can't be sure.'

'Is it cancer?'

'Yeah. If they'd seen her when she first felt unwell they might have been able to help. As it is . . .'

'It's so sad,' Georgia said, and I nodded.

'She's in and out of consciousness now, because she's on so much morphine. She was in agony but she never complained.'

It had taken an hour or so for there to be a response to the smoke, and it came in the form of a drone that circled the cottage. Then it had been another hour before the first engine noise, the first vehicle in the distance, the lights bouncing and dipping as it lurched up the track towards us through the gathering dusk.

'I wish you'd been there when we realised Dennis Hood was the one we were looking for,' Georgia said dreamily. 'That was big.'

'How did you know?'

'The last photograph you took. Liv found your phone in

the mud beside the car and we checked it to see if there was anything helpful on it – I mean, we were desperate. We were trying everything and anything. Rosalie's name was just visible in the top right corner. Eleanor Hood. The travellers had told us they called her Ellie, so we guessed that was Eleanor.'

'I didn't think anyone else would spot it. I'd only just worked it out when Hood caught me.'

'We almost missed it,' Liv said.

'Who noticed it?'

The two of them exchanged glances before Georgia answered. 'Josh.'

'He usually leaves that kind of fine detail to me.' I was trying to sound casual but the very mention of his name was electric. 'Actually, where is he? I thought he'd want to give me a hard time about all of this. I thought he'd be furious with me for not noticing Dennis Hood creeping up on me.'

'I'm not sure where he is,' Liv said slowly.

'What does that mean?'

Another look passed between them, full of meaning.

'One of you tell me what's going on,' I said quietly but with enough menace to get some answers.

'He was in Cornwall when I raised the alarm. As soon as he heard, he wanted to come up here and look for you.' Liv looked across at Georgia, who was chewing her thumbnail. 'There was a conference call. We were all on it. Una told him we could manage without him, and if he was finished with Grant he should go back to London.'

I pulled a face. 'I bet that went down well.'

'Yeah. He wasn't happy.'

'She told him to be a professional for once,' Georgia said, round-eyed. 'And then he really lost his temper.'

'What did he say?'

Liv shrugged, wordless, and Georgia shook her head. 'I don't think we can do it justice.'

'The highlights?'

'It's for him to say, really.'

Liv glanced over her shoulder for maybe the thirtieth time, and visibly relaxed. 'Sorry, I just have to . . .'

'Don't run away!' I was too late; she was gone, slipping out into the hallway leaving me with a very apprehensive Georgia. I decided to be kind.

'So everyone was worried about me.'

'You were missing for twenty-four hours but it felt like forever. I came up from London with Chris yesterday so we could help Liv and the locals. Once we had Dennis Hood's name, things moved a bit faster. Josh and Vidya went from Cornwall to Bristol and found the address he'd given us was unoccupied. The neighbours had an address for him on the Isle of Wight, so Josh and Vidya went all the way there, and found it was the same story – a derelict shop. Hood was really good at covering his tracks.'

So Josh had criss-crossed the country looking for me, on a wild goose chase that must have driven him insane. And then once he knew I was safe, he had what? Backed down when Una Burt told him to? Gone back to London, because there was no reason to come and find me?

I nodded brightly, not letting any disappointment show.

'We got on to the Royal Mail,' Georgia went on, 'and they gave us the re-direct information, which went to a PO box in Keswick. Basically, we knew he was living in this area but we weren't any closer to actually finding you. We showed his picture around town and a couple of people recognised him but no one knew where he lived. We would have worked it out eventually, though.'

Maybe, and maybe not. I wouldn't have lasted, I thought, if Rosalie hadn't come to confront Dennis Hood. I owed her my life, as she was losing hers. It felt important, somehow. It felt as if I should do something better with mine.

The door opened and I looked up, expecting to see Liv, and she was there, but Josh was standing in front of her. Neither of us spoke or moved for a second; we just stared at each other. Then my tea went flying, and, careless of my knee, I ran to him.

53

Derwent hadn't been there for five minutes before I was furious with him.

'I'm not going back to the hotel.'

'You are, you know.'

'Tell me what happened with Tor Grant.'

'Not a lot.' He was looking around. 'Where are your things?'

'What things?'

'Your actual clothes.' He paused to eye my borrowed outfit. 'Don't tell me you were walking around in public like that.'

I closed my eyes for a moment of pure irritation. 'Forget it. What does "not a lot" mean in the context of Tor Grant's interview?'

'I'll tell you tomorrow.'

'Josh.'

'Maeve.' He gave me his most inscrutable blue stare; if I wanted to know more, I was going to have to cooperate.

Liv and Georgia had withdrawn to one side of the room, watching us as if they were at a tennis match. Liv's expression was conflicted; Georgia's was pure glee.

'It's just nice to see someone boss Maeve around,' she said.

'That's my job.' He jerked his head towards the door. 'Come on. Let's get out of here.'

I went, because there was no point in arguing with him when he was in that kind of mood. Liv followed us out into the hall.

'Can I come with you?'

I waited for Derwent to say no, but he shrugged. 'Of course.'

His car was thrown in a space outside the station and I stopped to admire the way he'd blocked the spaces on either side by parking at an angle.

'In a rush?'

He grinned at me. 'Maybe.'

'You wouldn't have wanted to miss the chance to tell me what to do.'

'That's it. That's why I spent the last twenty-four hours breaking the speed limit on every single journey.' He held the passenger door open. 'Come on. Hop in.'

I hopped, and he shut the door. I had to be looking even worse than I felt, I thought, if I was getting the door opened for me, and a quick look in the mirror confirmed it. Maybe that was why he didn't mind Liv climbing into the back seat.

I waited until he had started the engine. 'On the way to the hotel you could tell me about Tor Grant.'

'Give up.'

'Never.'

'Tomorrow.' He batted away every other question I asked him during the short drive.

'I'll take her to her room,' Liv said after we'd parked, and Derwent went to check in, not noticeably bothered about Liv taking charge of me.

The hotel room was the same one I'd had the last time I stayed there and I stared at the watercolour on the wall opposite the bed, wondering who had chosen it, wondering what I had made of it on my previous stay. Somehow I couldn't remember.

'Should I draw the curtains?' Liv had her hand on them.

'No, leave them. Thanks.'

'Do you want to get changed?'

I sat on the edge of the bed and looked down at my clothes. 'I only had gym kit to sleep in, remember? I might as well wear this.'

'You should try to lie down.' She sat beside me, looking at me with concern. 'Just see if you can sleep.'

'I will.'

'Do you want me to stay?'

'No. That's OK.'

She hesitated. 'Maeve – you and Josh.'

I said nothing, waiting.

'I didn't realise how you felt. The things he said about you on that call – I mean, he didn't care that we were all listening. And then seeing your face when he got here tonight. I thought it was casual and it's not. I was wrong.'

'So?'

'So be careful, that's all. I don't want you to get hurt.'

'Is that why you escorted us to the hotel?' I smiled. 'Having actual feelings for one another doesn't mean he's any more available.'

'I suppose not.' She got up. 'Are you sure you don't want me to stay?'

I shook my head. 'You need a good night's sleep to get rid of your headache too.'

She bent and hugged me. 'I'm so glad you're OK.'

After she'd gone, I curled up on top of the covers. I was aware of being tired but I couldn't bring myself to try to sleep. The horrors were all too close to the surface. And something else was nagging at me like a stone in my shoe.

I needed to talk to Derwent.

My phone hadn't made it back to me; I thought there was a good chance I'd never see it again. I used the phone by the bed to call down to reception and got them to put me through to Derwent's room. I listened as the phone rang and rang and rang.

He wasn't there.

He'd gone . . . somewhere. A lurch of sadness and uncertainty swamped me.

I put the phone down and had time to feel bereft before there was a soft tap at the door. I hurried to open it. He was in shirtsleeves, his hair ruffled, his eyes narrow with tiredness, but he smiled at me.

'I was just calling you.'

His eyebrows drew together. 'Everything OK?'

'I have a question.'

The frown cleared. 'So what's new?'

'I can't sleep until I know the answer.'

'All right. One question.' He came in and shut the door behind him. I sat back down on the edge of the bed.

'Do you think Rosalie killed Piers after all?'

Not what he had expected. 'Why do you ask?'

'She had a knife when she came to the cottage. She was going to kill Dennis to keep him away from her kids, after what he'd done to the Marshalls. She had to make sure he wouldn't harm Wil and Posy. I don't think she was expecting him to take the initiative by killing Helena and Bruce and when he did, that changed everything.'

'That explains how she behaved towards Dennis, not Piers.'

'She was prepared to kill for her children. And she was surprised at Dennis's confession – not what was in it, but that he'd written it. She knew it was a lie and she knew she was the top suspect.'

'What else?' He was watching me closely.

'The blood on the wall in the bedroom. It was a fine spray. That's not how it looks, when someone beats you up and splashes your blood on the wall.' I tried to smile. 'I should know, after all. That's how it looks when you spit blood at something. She staged it. She made the house look miserable before she left it, but the children had books and toys and clothes that she left behind on the island, and it would have been warm enough in the kitchen and their bedrooms with the fires lit, so I don't think the house was as bleak as it seemed when we saw it. It was an insurance policy, in case she needed a defence for murder – if Piers had been abusive, she had a reason to kill him. She was going to get Dennis Hood locked up for killing him, I think, or at least threatened him with that, but if it didn't work for some reason, she had a back-up plan.'

He slid his hands into his pockets and leaned back against the wall. 'I don't know is the short answer. But Tor Grant said she watched her father murdering her mother, and said her aunt and uncle were scared of her – that's how she ended up in foster care. He also said she was cleverer than him, even aged nine. She was capable of terrifying him. I can't imagine that sixteen years have changed her that much. It's entirely possible she had detailed plans for every eventuality.'

'When she came, she didn't untie me straight away. She thought about leaving me there.' I took a long, quavering breath. 'She let me live but she waited until the very last second to decide about that. I don't think she'd have hesitated if she'd thought she'd be better off with me dead.'

He shook his head slightly, as if he didn't want that thought in it. 'Does it matter if she killed Piers?'

'To me, yes. I want the truth. Don't you?'

'No.' He looked down at me, sombre now. 'Even if she only did one good thing, she saved your life. That cancels out everything else for me.'

'When I believed she was going to kill me,' I said slowly, knowing there was no way back from it, 'I thought about you.'

Be careful, Liv had said. Apparently I was incapable of that today.

He looked surprised, and then compassionate. 'It was bad.'

I nodded.

'But you don't want to talk about it.'

'No.' I was shivering. I wanted more than anything to ask him to hold me, but I couldn't. He wasn't mine. I had no right to tell him I needed him.

He sat on the edge of the bed so he could yank off his shoes. Then he settled himself against the pillows and held out an arm. 'Come here.'

I crawled across to him and put my head on his shoulder. He drew me in close, so I was curled up against him.

'You were never lost, you know.' His voice was quiet, a low murmur. 'I wouldn't have let that happen. Wherever you were, I would have found you.'

I woke before he did in the morning, instantly aware of where I was and who was lying behind me. I stayed still for a moment before I began to extract myself from the bed. Every time I had stirred towards wakefulness during the night, he had gathered me against him and soothed me back to sleep, his instinct to comfort, to reassure, even when he was barely awake himself. We had been wrapped around each other, but too tired for anything except sleep. Now he was sprawling across the bed, still fully dressed, his face unguarded. I watched him – the rise and fall of his chest, the tilt of his chin, his hands open and relaxed. I never saw him like this, and I committed every detail to memory: the angle of his eyebrows, the line of his jaw, his mouth when it wasn't tight with anger or curling into a sardonic smile. Then I went to the bathroom and locked the door and set about making myself presentable.

He was loitering outside the bathroom when I opened the door, looking troubled. When he saw me, his expression changed instantly to the usual detachment. He raised his eyebrows at the suit I was wearing (navy, not my favourite but clean).

'Off to work?'

'I want to go to the hospital to see Rosalie.' I looked down at myself. 'This suit is all I have with me, unless you want me to wear the hoodie again.'

'Anything but that.' He yawned. 'I don't suppose you have a spare toothbrush.'

'The one I bought on the way here came in a packet of two.'

'Convenient.' He flashed a grin at me and went into the bathroom, humming under his breath.

I came to two conclusions. He managed to hide the strain he was under pretty well, except for every now and then when I caught him off guard, so what I saw was only a fraction of what he was feeling.

And I couldn't let things drift on as they were. Something had to change.

54

She was in bed, in a room full of soft white light: a clean room, with clean cotton sheets under her and over her. Her fingers found the sheet and folded it, over and over again, pinching the fabric. It reminded her of a skirt she had worn as a child, a skirt with a pattern on it, and she couldn't remember the pattern exactly. Apples or circles. Who to ask? No one seemed to know.

They were all dead, she remembered. All the people she could ask. All dead and gone.

Was it when she was Rosalie Marshall that she had worn the dress? The sheet pleated between her fingers and thumb. There was a graze on her knee, in her memory of it, and she had looked down from high in a tree, past her skirt and her knees, to where someone was standing looking up at her.

'Hello, Sally. Funny to see you here.'

Yes, it was Magnus who had looked up at her, and laughed, and called her Sally.

He was here now, in the bright room. She looked at him and saw him as an adult, a man, handsome now but still very definitely her brother. He took her hand, freeing it from the sheet.

'Magnus.' She wanted to say *I never thought I'd see you again* but the words were too clumsy and difficult. *I missed you most of all.*

'It's all right, Sal.' He sniffed, and his eyes were wet. 'I'm here now. We both are.'

The other side of the bed was too far away for her to look – turning her head was exhausting – but she felt someone take her other hand.

'It's me, Ivo. We love you, Rosalie. And so do Wil and Posy.'

'My babies,' Rosalie managed.

'They're well. They're doing really well. They're wonderful.' His voice broke on the last word. She was still looking at Magnus, whose face was wet.

The children. They were the only thing that had ever belonged to her, and she had let them go. She let them fall away from her like petals from a beautiful flower, a rose. They were safe now.

They were the future. And this was what was past.

'There you are.' Her father, slipping into her bedroom in the villa. The shutters were drawn against the evening sun but it crept in around the edges of the wooden slats, golden and hot, as if the earth was burning outside the dim, bare room. 'I've got something for you.'

'What is it?' Rosalie sat bolt upright, pleased. She hadn't wanted to go to bed yet. The days of the holiday were slipping by too quickly and bed was a waste of time.

'Something to help you sleep. Like – like Sleeping Beauty.' Bruce smiled, pleased to have come up with a reference his small daughter would understand. She regarded him gravely.

'Sleeping Beauty pricked her finger on an enchanted spinning wheel. There was blood. I don't want to prick my finger.'

'No, no. Nothing like that.' He held out his hand, showing her a pill on his palm. 'Just swallow this with some water – you have some water, don't you? Ah, yes, here it is.'

He poured out a glass from the carafe by the bed, which Rosalie knew was as flat and hot as bath water, but she didn't argue with him. Obediently, she took the pill and managed to choke it down. It felt as if it was stuck in her throat and her eyes watered, but Bruce nodded approvingly.

'That should be the end of the waking up. We want you to get a good night's sleep, don't we? So your mother gets a good night's sleep and doesn't get cross with you. Or me.' He reached out and tweaked her nose, and Rosalie smiled back.

'Did you check I get the whole pill?' Rosalie had learned to check this after Bruce tried to give her a massive overdose of

Calpol, having misread the bottle, but at least this was only one pill, even if it was a big one.

He pulled the packet out of his pocket and frowned at it. The prescription was in Helena's name and the pharmacist's label covered most of the box, but even so, Rosalie could read NOT TO BE GIVEN TO CHILDREN UNDER SIXTEEN in bold letters across the top of the instructions.

There was a short pause as he took it in, and doubt in his eyes when he looked back at her. 'I'm sure it's fine. They always put warnings on these things. Ridiculous.' He leaned forward and kissed the top of her head. 'Now get to sleep. I'll come in and check on you.'

Rosalie put out a hand and grabbed her father's wrist. It felt clammy in the heat and his watch dug into her.

'Am I going to die?'

'No. You're going to sleep well. No nightmares.' He shoved the box back into his pocket. 'But – er – don't say anything to your mother, will you? Or Sadie? Let's keep this as – as a secret between us. And I'll come in and check on you during the night.'

A wave of dizziness passed over Rosalie, and she closed her eyes.

'OK?' Bruce's voice seemed to be coming from a long way off. 'Rosalie?'

Their secret.

She was groggy the next morning, and she was glad Bruce never tried to give her a pill again, but she kept the secret. She never told anyone.

'I'm bored,' Rosalie said, and slid off the chair, pushing her hair off her face with the back of a hand that was none too clean.

'No, don't go. Stay here for a while.' JV got to the door before her, just in time to slam it shut and hold it there. He was very tall when he was standing over her. Enormous. 'Stay here, little one. There's – there's something else I want to show you.'

'What?' She had already decided that Magnus's tutor was hopelessly tedious – getting excited about rectangles, as if he was a toddler playing with shapes – but she was prepared to see if he had anything more exciting to share with her.

'In my bag.' He reached for it, suddenly awkward. It was a very ugly blue rucksack with brown leather edging. 'You remind me of this anime character. Have you ever heard of Sailor Moon?'

The book was a small, battered hardback. A girl in a short sailor dress filled the cover, her eyes huge, her hair dark blue and curling around her face. She wore white gloves and her fingers were long and spidery.

'Pretty Guardian Sailor Moon,' Rosalie read from the cover. 'Who is she?'

'The character's name is Usagi Tsukino. She's really cool. There's a whole series of books about her. This is the second one, actually.'

'Can I have it?' Rosalie had flipped it open and was staring in wonder at the artwork, which was like nothing she had ever seen.

'No. It's one of my favourite books.' His voice cracked: a giveaway that he was uneasy.

'It's for children, though.' She looked at him severely. 'Are you a child?'

'No, but—'

'You should read books for grown-ups. Give it to me.'

'M-manga is hard to find. They have to import it from Japan.'

'I want it,' Rosalie said, holding the book with both hands. 'I want it.'

'I was just showing it to you,' JV said, desperate now. 'I'm sorry. I can't let you have it.'

There weren't many people who were scared of Rosalie, but she knew what to look for when it came to fear, and she saw it in JV's face. Fortunately, she knew how to exploit it too. She remembered one of the girls in the foster home, and her foolproof way of getting what she wanted. 'If you don't give it to me, I'll tell Mummy you tried to take off my knickers.'

'*What?*'

'And she'll believe me.' Rosalie blinked, her eyes wide, innocent. 'She said you were a weirdo.'

'Keep the book.' JV scrambled away from her, holding his rucksack in front of him like a shield, as if he could use it to ward her off. 'Just leave me alone. There's something wrong with you. Something sick. You're not right.'

Rosalie felt her triumph dissolve.

If even JV noticed that, she wasn't doing a very good job of hiding it.

The sun was slanting across the lawn at the front of the house, through the trees. Rosalie was playing a game about being a high priestess in a temple, like in her myths book, because Ivo was out with his friends and Magnus was playing on his Xbox and told her to fuck off, and her parents were drinking gin on the terrace at the back of the house, languid and uninterested in what Rosalie was doing. There was an illustration of a beautiful woman in white tending a sacred fire and Rosalie had studied it carefully, deciding that her mother's dressing gown and the birdbath might stand in for the robes and plinth in the image. She had some crumpled paper and a box of matches, palmed from her father's desk the last time he'd let her into his study. He put a lot of effort into pretending to read her work – it would have been easier, Rosalie felt, if he actually read it – and that gave her an opportunity to liberate anything useful. His study was full of interesting things. A compass. A fountain pen that spurted black ink all over her fingers when she tried to write with it. Bullets, in a desk drawer at the back, loose, and the gun in a box on a low shelf, hidden after Magnus had knocked it down from the top of the bookcase. As if she wouldn't find it. She had visited it a few times, early in the morning when everyone else was asleep. It was heavy and old but she liked to point it at things: her father's chair, a portrait of a woman in a pink hat, her own face in the bathroom mirror.

It was only going to be a small fire in the birdbath (which was dry; no one ever seemed to fill it up). She looked around carefully, though. Her mother didn't like fires and she didn't like Rosalie borrowing her clothes, but she was distracted. Part of the fun – most of the fun – was getting away with things, Rosalie found. She pushed back the sleeves of the dressing gown, which were far too long for her and fell over her hands. She needed them out of the way for when she struck the match—

'Hey. Hey!'

She looked around and saw a man standing at the gate. His dark hair flopped over his forehead.

The man who took her story.

'What are you doing, Rosalie?'

'Nothing.' She crossed the lawn, trailing the dressing gown behind her. It was embarrassing to talk about things you made up. Grown-ups never seemed to understand, or they were horrified, or both. 'What do you want?'

'I wanted to see if you were OK. Was everything all right, after I left?'

Rosalie considered it. Yes, because she had certainly not missed him, but also no, because her mother had been angrier than ever before. She settled on a shrug.

He looked past her, wary. 'I couldn't stop thinking about whether you were in trouble because of me. I'm sorry.'

'It's OK.'

'I loved your story.' He smiled. 'You're a very talented writer. You should keep going. Keep inventing things. Imagining, like you're doing now.'

A noise came from the house and Rosalie gave a tiny gasp of fear, not pretending. The man backed away, then ran for his car with an impressive turn of speed. The car roared as it accelerated away and a cloud of exhaust hung in the air afterwards.

'Who was that?' Her mother was crossing the lawn, furious. 'No one.'

'Was it the journalist who was here before?' She grabbed Rosalie's arm and squeezed, and it was always worse when she had been drinking. 'Don't lie to me.'

'I don't know what you mean.'

'What are you wearing? What were you doing? Are those *matches*?' Without waiting for an answer, her mother's face tightened. 'Come on. You're going in a cold bath.'

She dragged the little girl across the lawn as Rosalie screamed and tried to free herself, her legs tangled in the dressing gown, her arm burning in her mother's implacable grasp.

'What happened here?' Dr Fuller's face was kind, as always – warm and concerned and understanding. Rosalie looked forward to seeing her bedroom door open when she knew the doctor was coming, and even though her body was aching she still felt a little lift of happiness.

'Fell downstairs.' It was a whisper.

'Fell? Or did someone push you?'

Rosalie giggled weakly. Jumped was the actual answer. Jumped because it was now or never.

'Where does it hurt?' The doctor's hands were strong and certain as they ran over Rosalie's limbs, checking, pressing.

'My neck. And my ankle.' She pointed at her stomach. 'And here.'

'Oh dear. Everywhere, really.' The doctor took out a stethoscope. 'Let's have a listen. Can you lift your top up?'

The pyjama top was too small and Rosalie struggled with it.

'Maybe take it off?'

That was a better idea. She pulled it off and sat there in her vest, waiting for the cold kiss of the stethoscope on her back.

Dr Fuller was frozen, halfway through reaching out to her. 'What are those bruises?'

The marks dappled the skin of her arm, blue to green, oval in shape, overlapping in places.

'Who did that, Rosalie?'

'Mummy,' she whispered, with a sudden lurch of fear that she might be hovering in the hall, listening – that there might be terrible consequences for saying it. 'But she didn't mean to. She was angry with me.'

The doctor's eyes were wet. 'Oh, Rosalie . . .'

'You can't go.' Rosalie held on to the doctor's hand. 'You can't leave now.'

'The house is sold – I was only here to say goodbye and then Helena said you'd hurt yourself—'

'Take me with you.' She dug her fingers in. 'They don't have to know. I want to go wherever you're going.'

'They wouldn't let me – I can't. It's madness.' Dr Fuller hesitated. 'I would if I could. I really would. I don't have a little girl and I wish I did. I've always said, I'd like one just like you.'

'I wish you were my mother,' Rosalie blurted. She leaned forward and wrapped her arms around the woman's neck. 'I love you, not her.'

By the time she went downstairs, madness or not, Lydia Fuller had made up her mind.

Rosalie hadn't meant to go to sleep but she did, wearing all her clothes, under her covers. She opened her eyes to see him bending over her in the darkness, a black shape against the night, and she almost screamed before she remembered.

'Are you ready? Don't make a sound.' His breath was bad and it came to her in a flash that Dr Fuller's husband was nervous, that he was scared they were doing the wrong thing, and that there was still time for him to leave her there if he lost his nerve.

'Thank you,' she whispered into the darkness. 'Thank you for helping me.'

'What's that?' Her bag had swung against his leg as she picked it up, and it was heavy. 'I thought you weren't taking anything with you?'

'Just a book and my dog, Gilbert.' And the gun, which Rosalie had decided might be useful to have, but she knew better than to mention it.

'Gilbert?' He sighed in relief. 'A toy.'

'Yes, obviously.' Rosalie wasn't allowed to have a dog, which was one of the things that made her feel leaving was a good idea. Mr Hood was a bit slow on the uptake but you couldn't have everything.

She was sure – as she followed Mr Hood down the stairs and into the kitchen, and watched him slide the bolt out of its socket, and when she turned the key in the back door, and opened it on the night – that she was doing the right thing. Mr Hood left the door open because he was afraid it would make a noise when he shut it, and they slipped down the garden to the river, to the small boat that he would row downstream, to where Dr Fuller was waiting for them by the car, and Rosalie found she was still holding the back door key but it didn't matter. She looked back as the house disappeared around a bend in the river, and felt safe for the first time.

She was sure no one would miss her at all.

A skitter of paws and a flash of black: a sheepdog, nosing at her hair. She was lying at the base of a big slab of rock, high on the mountain. The satchel was nearby, spilling its contents: the food and money she had scraped together, and her favourite books. It wasn't that she didn't need more than that to run away; it was that she had nothing else to take.

She didn't want to stay in the mountains without Dr Fuller, that was the thing. Her real mother. She had gone into hospital, grey and gasping, and there had been an operation, and she hadn't made it. That's what Dennis said, through his tears. She hadn't made it.

Rosalie was going to make it. There was a world out there and Dennis was never going to be ready to let her experience it. He was scared of losing her, scared of being found out, scared to death.

But she wanted to live. She wanted to get away from the cottage where she'd grown up. She wanted to experience the world that she only saw in books – to travel, to work, to fall in love. She was an adult now, and she wanted to be independent. Lydia Fuller had wanted that for her, but Dennis . . .

Dennis had scared her, when she talked about leaving.

Dennis had more or less told her that he'd kill her before he'd let her go.

Rosalie had learned to take that kind of threat seriously.

The plan, such as it was, involved getting away from the cottage, hiking through the mountains, finding a town and making her way back, somehow, to the house by the river, and the Marshalls. Their long-lost daughter, returning in time to benefit from the wealth that she had often considered in the tiny cottage, where Dennis and Lydia had tried to give her a good education but life had been . . . dull. Limited.

The Marshalls would feel guilty that they hadn't looked after her properly, and guilt meant money.

What she hadn't planned on was a fall, and a sprained ankle that was too painful to attempt to walk on it. She was far from the cottage and nowhere near civilisation, and the sun was slipping down behind the mountains already. She knew what that meant. Could she survive a night in the open? Maybe. Two? No.

The dog was all paws and lolling tongue and bright eyes. He barked, and barked again, and she shut her eyes at the sound of footsteps. When she opened them, a man was standing in front of her, staring down at her, his mouth hanging open in surprise, and after a moment he introduced himself as Piers.

Rosalie blinked up at this square-jawed farmer, wide-eyed and sunburned, and she knew immediately he was her way out. He carried her all the way back to the cottage, where Dennis was beside himself, and she looked at Piers as if he was Prince Charming and Mr Rochester and Mr Darcy and Heathcliff rolled into one, and saw him fall head over heels in love, there and then.

Piers. Not the brightest of men but surely among the best, sweet-natured and kind. He came back, every day, and she told him who she was, and explained to him what that meant for Dennis Hood, and Piers went and towered over Dennis and threatened him the way they'd rehearsed it.

And she'd got away.

Well, she'd got *somewhere*. It was only ever supposed to be temporary, that was the thing. She had been eighteen, and ready to be romanced, and Piers was more than willing to oblige. And then – what? It wasn't the children; they had come later. It was more that she had found her limitations, like an injured animal that can never return to the wild. She had spread her wings and then discovered her flight feathers were gone. She told herself that she wasn't ready, that there was no rush, and she let the days slide by . . . and even when the children were born, she thought there was time.

Then she started to feel unwell, and it was too late.

And she discovered one more use for Piers, who didn't want her to leave him, who wasn't capable of looking after the children, whatever he thought, so it was up to her to give them to someone she could trust. She knew what it was like to shuffle from one home to another, never belonging. That wasn't what she wanted. They deserved a home, and opportunities, and love.

When she looked into herself, Rosalie found darkness. She'd come to understand that other people weren't like that. Other people hadn't watched their mother die. Other people didn't know what it took to survive. Other people wouldn't have cleared away every trace of life and comfort from their house to set a scene for the police in case they caught up with her: pretending he was an abusive husband, that she had managed a lucky escape. Other people wouldn't have decided, lying within his arms, that he was better off dead so he couldn't get in her way.

Sometimes she thought about what would have happened if the dog hadn't found her on the mountain. A slow death, like the one Piers had endured while she waited for Dennis to literally get the message and come to the house, so he'd understand she wasn't going to let him interfere with her plans either – so he'd know she was capable of anything. Death with the sky above her, and the earth below her.

She thought of all the things she would never experience again.

The wind on her face.

Rain.

The stars.

Piers had died with a stained plaster ceiling above him, and dusty floorboards below him, and blood seeping into spaces within him where it was never meant to go.

If they had known what was going to happen, he might have lain down beside her on the mountain all those years ago, and stayed there until they were both dead.

The bed lifted and swung under her and it was the sea, she was floating in the endless blue of it all. She had been in the sea, on holidays with Mummy and Daddy and Ivo and Magnus. She had waded in the water, amazed by the glitter and sting of it, the energy, the way it pushed and pulled like her breath, like a heartbeat.

'Water,' Rosalie said, and Ivo leaned forward to put a straw to her lips, but that wasn't what she meant. It was kind though. Loving. The room was full of love, Rosalie thought, from the two men on either side of her bed to the nurse that was hovering nearby, checking the machines, and in the corner, although her sight was dim and clouded at the edges now, there was the police officer and a man who was watching her, the only person in the room who wasn't looking at Rosalie.

There's someone who loves me, I think—
You think? Don't you know?
Yes. I do know. But he hasn't said it yet.

'Love,' Rosalie said.

'We love you, Sally.'

'Yes, we love you.'

Magnus looked up, urgently. 'Come this side, Ivo.'

A shuffle and a scrape of chairs on the floor.

She had been loved, she thought. She had loved.

She remembered Dr Fuller coming, to check her latest injury, making her laugh. She remembered the way she had looked at her, smiling in that special way that made her feel warm inside.

And Piers had loved her fiercely, and had been so shocked when she shot him.

But that had been loving too, in a way, because she couldn't leave him on his own in that lonely house. He would have been lost without her.

Now she was coming back to find him, and everything would be all right.

'It's all right,' Ivo said, and she opened her eyes and smiled at him and Magnus, their faces side by side, so different, so alike. Their hands were on hers, all of them knotted together.

'You can go now,' Magnus whispered. 'You've done enough. You can go.'

All that anyone wanted, Rosalie thought, was to be loved. She had known nothing but love, if you understood people, and why they did what they did. She had been lucky.

She closed her eyes and slipped out of the world so quietly that even though they were watching her, it was a few seconds before they realised she was gone.

55

I took some holiday before I went back to work. It wasn't entirely my idea – Una Burt insisted that I'd been through too much to go back immediately. I suspected she wanted to keep me and Derwent apart. No one had told me exactly what he'd said on the conference call, but I had some idea – enough, anyway, to know that he'd made a few things clear to everyone else, if not me. I went away to a small coastal village in Norfolk, miles from anywhere, the landscape flat as paper. I had had enough of mountains for the time being. I switched my phone off the day I arrived. I told my parents how they could find me, if they needed to, but no one else knew where I was.

The sun shone every day and I walked on the beach and plunged into the cold sea for as long as I could stand it, thinking about life and what mattered most. My knee gradually stopped aching. My hair tangled and the bruises faded. Only the marks on my soul remained.

I thought about requesting a transfer to Norfolk Constabulary. I thought about not being a police officer any more.

I thought about the conversation I'd had with Derwent before I left, in the small hotel room where he'd held me all night. I had packed; I was saying goodbye.

Be honest, Liv had said, and I'd tried, as he stood with his arms folded, listening.

'In the cottage, I realised that I want you to be happy. I can't bear that you're tearing yourself apart. I need you to know—'

'Maeve—'

'I need you to know,' I repeated with more emphasis, 'that I understand you have to choose Thomas. I could never resent you for it. Sometimes things don't work out. We both know you and I would be special together, but we just have to make the best of what we have. Friendship. That's important too.'

He considered it for a moment. 'This is what you concluded while you were waiting to die? I suppose you were a bit oxygen deprived. I shouldn't be surprised.'

'Don't make a joke out of it. I'm serious.' I took a deep breath. 'I'll find someone else. I know they won't be you, but I'll make sure it's someone good for me. You won't have to worry about me any more.'

He flinched. 'Why are you saying this?'

'I think you need permission to stop trying to make it work out. This way it's not your decision. You'll get over me. You'll be happy again.' I picked up my bag. 'And it's the right thing to do.'

He had let me go without an argument, without a word of reproach, because he knew I was right.

When I'd been there for a week, I went for an early walk on the beach, the gulls wheeling and screaming overhead, the sand deserted. The tide was going out and the wind had dropped to a gentle breeze. The sun was warm on my skin and I felt soothed, at last. I turned back after a mile and saw someone coming down through the dunes, a long way away, moving with purpose. I knew him immediately, and all the peace I'd been cultivating blew away.

As he came nearer, I looked at him, trying to be objective. He was thin, but not excessively so; whatever had been driving him for weeks had relaxed its grip, it seemed. He looked like his old self.

When Derwent was close enough, I called, 'How did you find me?'

'Your parents.'

'You asked them where I was?' I wasn't sure how I felt about that.

He looked amused as he closed the distance between us. 'Your mum rang me.'

'She did *what*?'

'She was worried about you going off on your own. She wanted me to make sure you were OK.'

'I'm fine. I'm coming back to London in a couple of days.'

'I did tell her that.'

'And you couldn't convince her?' I frowned. 'She usually listens to you.'

'Well, I didn't try too hard. I wanted to talk to you before you got back.' Before I could guess at what he meant, he went on, 'I need to tell you I've moved out of the flat downstairs. Jonny is coming back from his trip tomorrow.'

I nodded, as if it was all right. Of course, he had only had the place for a month.

'I've gone back to Melissa.'

I felt the shock run through me, and knew he'd seen it before I could stop myself from reacting. It was kind of him to tell me now so I had time to recover, I thought, dully, but I wished he hadn't felt he had to tell me face to face.

'I talked to Luke,' Derwent went on. 'I asked him about what it was like, growing up without me in his life, and how he felt about it now. He said he was glad to have got to know me and it had come at the right time. He said Thomas would know I only wanted what was best for him. I can be there for him when he's older. Listening to me and his mum fighting isn't good for Thomas, and if that's the only reason I'm staying with her, I'm not helping anyone.' He paused. 'So it's over with Melissa. I'm only there because I need time for her to get used to the idea. I owe her that.'

'Josh—'

'Just to be clear, I'm not choosing you instead of Thomas,' Derwent said. 'Melissa and I would be finished even if you didn't exist, because our relationship has turned into something I hate. She's angry with me and I probably deserve it. We should have broken up ages ago – I've let it drag on for too long already.' He paused. 'It's going to be a rough couple of months, and I want clear blue water between me and Melissa before anything else happens.'

'Anything else?' I raised my eyebrows. 'What does that mean?'

'You'll have to wait to find out.' He dug his hands into his pockets, uncharacteristically awkward. 'But I can't guarantee you a happy ever after, Maeve. It's not that easy . . . and I'm pretty sure I'm not good enough for you.'

The truth, in a rush, when he had always maintained a veneer of self-confidence in front of me. This was uncharted territory for us in all kinds of ways.

I grinned at him. 'Come off it, Josh. You've seen my exes. The bar is very, very low here.'

His smile warmed his eyes and it was like the sun coming out. 'I really want to kiss you but I'm not coming any closer than this. You know I can't control myself.'

'I remember.'

He sighed. 'I promised myself I'd never tell you how I feel about you.'

'And you never have.' Not in so many words, anyway. A breeze tugged at my hair. 'But I'll find out the truth.'

'You always do.'

I studied his face, needing to tell him how I felt. 'You know, I'm willing to bet this will all work out in the end.'

'What do you want to bet?'

'A tenner?'

The corner of his mouth lifted. 'Haven't you learned anything? You always lose.'

'Yes,' I said, 'but one of these days, my luck is going to change.'

Epilogue

Catastrophe comes when you least expect it, and I should have known that, but I had no sense that anything at all was wrong when my phone rang. I was in the middle of a crowded platform, hoping against hope that the next District Line train would be empty and going my way. It was rush hour, the last three trains had been cancelled, and I was a long way from home. The only positive was that the station – West Kensington – was above ground, so I had both phone reception and fresh air while I waited in the swelling, jostling crowd. I had just been reminding myself that things could be worse when my phone hummed in my pocket. Out of habit I glanced at the screen before I answered it. When I saw it was my father, a tiny knot of worry drew itself tight inside my stomach. He never called me.

'Hello? Daddy?' The childish name for him came out of nowhere.

'Maeve.' His voice burst out of the phone, loud and panicked. 'Maeve?'

'Yes, it's me.' A train slid to a halt at the platform opposite, brakes squealing. I jammed my knuckle into my free ear and pressed the phone hard against the other one. 'Sorry, it's really loud here. Are you all right?'

'Maeve, I—' he broke off to hush someone who was making noise in the background.

'Daddy? Is everything all right?' I was cold all of a sudden. 'Is it Mummy?'

'No. No.'

'Is that Thomas?' They had been looking after him that afternoon, I knew. 'Is he *crying*?'

'It's Thomas.'

'What's wrong with him? Is he OK?'

'He's fine. You're fine, Thomas. Stop your whining, there's a good boy.' My father, infinitely patient, sounded almost irritable, and that made me more worried than anything else that had happened so far. I could hear a siren in the distance at his end of the call, and it was getting louder.

'Daddy, what's going on?'

'Maeve, my darling, I'm sorry . . .'

'What is it?'

The tone of his voice, his reluctance to get to the point. I knew what he was going to say, and I needed him to say it, but when he spoke I sank to my knees in the middle of the platform, careless of everything that was happening around me. Two words only, but they brought my world crashing down around my ears.

'It's Josh.'

Acknowledgements

Huge thanks, as ever, to the team at HarperCollins who saw this novel through from an outline to a finished book – Julia Wisdom (the wonderful publisher to whom this book is dedicated), Kathryn Cheshire, Lizz Burrell, Fliss Denham (who has made publicity such a joy), Maddy Marshall, and everyone else who has offered their support and encouragement, from the most junior members of staff to the most senior.

I'm very lucky to have Ariella Feiner as my agent: she is unfailingly kind, thoughtful, astute and reassuring. I'm also so grateful to Amber Garvey, Jennifer Thomas and the entire team at United Agents; they look after me and my work so well.

I'm so glad to have so many friends in the writing world and outside it, especially Catherine Ryan Howard, Catherine Kirwan, Andrea Carter, Vanessa O'Loughlin/Sam Blake, Andrea Mara and all the Irish murderesses, Sarah Hilary, Erin Kelly, Ruth Ware and of course Colin Scott who knows just about everything there is to know about crime; Alison, Claire and Sarah (the best fat babies); Harriet Evans, Anna Carey and Sarra Manning; Cressida McLaughlin who is one of the kindest first readers I know, and last but not least Sinéad Crowley and Liz Nugent, who get the first and last word on all subjects.

Philippa and Kerry, thank you for the trips, wisdom and moral support. Edward and Patrick, thank you for providing a reason for continuing with writing by growing out of your shoes roughly every three weeks. James, thank you for being you and for that one line in chapter 14. Thank you to Felix for adding a regular dose of violence and disdain to my day, and to Rory for the companionship even if it is bordering on obsessive.

And finally, readers, my thanks to you for trusting me with the characters you've come to care about. I'm so grateful for your messages and for your support. Maeve and Josh will be back very soon – with a full explanation for that ending.

Keep reading for a sneak peek at
The Secret Room, the next brilliant book
from Jane Casey following
Maeve Kerrigan and Josh Derwent.

Prologue

She walks into the hotel like she owns it. She moves fast, breaking into a little run a couple of times, her heels clicking on the marble floor. It means she gets to the reception desk just ahead of a large group of tourists from South Korea – eighteen of them milling around a guide, handing over passports and documentation before they all check in. No matter how efficient the receptionists are – and they're trained to be very efficient indeed – the tourists will take a long time to organise themselves and fill in their registration cards and find out which rooms they have been allocated and collect their keys. It's worth hurrying – worth being a little rude, in fact, and pushing in ahead of the guide, who was really at the desk first. She sidesteps him with a brilliant smile that cuts off his murmur of polite protest as sharply as if it was a knife. The reception staff greet her with manufactured warmth, wide smiles and blank eyes that hide their real thoughts. They are professionals.

She doesn't have to say anything to set one of them tapping at the computer in front of her. The other turns to leaf through the box of welcome folders behind the desk. There is one folder with her name on it – or the name she uses for them. There is no need to go through the welcome spiel, they acknowledge, with a conspiratorial nod that stops just short of a wink. She is there every week and she has never stayed long enough to book a table in the Michelin-starred dining room on the top floor or the hotel's more casual restaurant next to the lobby, where a breakfast buffet is available in the morning between 7 a.m. and 10 a.m. She will not be there for breakfast, although the room is booked for the night.

She will not visit the highly equipped gym or the swimming pool in the basement, not even to make use of the steam room or the award-winning spa facilities, which currently have a special offer for a half-price massage if you book any facial treatment. The receptionists do not bother to mention this. The woman has the soft, glossy hair, immaculate nails and flawless complexion of someone who knows her way around a spa, but she is not in the hotel to pamper herself. That has all happened already, in preparation for her brief, weekly stay with them.

There is no need for help with luggage, either. As usual she only has a tote bag slung over one shoulder, this one jangling a gold C and D from the strap, a little reminder that it was made by Christian Dior. Her handbag is Hermès, in soft calf leather that is the delicate pink of the inside of a shell. Her shoes are buff suede Aquazurra slingbacks with towering heels and a bow on the back of the ankle, and the coat is the palest fawn cashmere, full-length, the sort of clothing that has never – even in nightmares – encountered the grime of an underground train. It is a coat for a world where cars come with drivers, where a taxi is a last resort, where public transport simply doesn't exist. There's a hint of white under the coat, a froth of lace at the neck and a delicately pleated skirt, but really there's no way to know what she's wearing might look like without the coat. It is a dress that cost more than the girls on reception make in a week, but soon it will be flung on the floor of room 412, the coat thrown over the chair in the corner, forgotten along with her memory of this brief interaction.

What happens at the reception desk is a ritual so familiar to her that she barely looks up from her phone now that they are preparing her key card and slotting it into the paper folder and murmuring the only information that interests her – *no, Ms Nevin, the other key has not been collected yet* – and she knows where the lift is, and how to get to the room that is booked every single week, that has been booked every Wednesday for the last eleven months, whether they could use it then or not.

She turns away from the desk with a small, private smile on her face that doesn't waver as the tourists edge out of her way. She walks straight across the lobby to the lift, and turns as the doors slide shut, looking out through the gap with ladylike composure.

Once she is on her own and unobserved – oblivious, like most people, to the cameras mounted in the corners of the lift – she drops the act for a moment. She leans in to get closer to the mirror, inspecting her eyes, running a fingertip under her lower lashes to smudge away some mascara, tilting her head left and right with a critical frown. Something catches her attention – some mark, some imperfection – and she gets close to the glass again, worrying at her cheek with a long nail, until she is satisfied it's gone. Then a step back and she considers herself, turning sideways, putting one leg forward and leaning back like a model. She sweeps the coat back and props a fist on her hip, posing more outrageously now, tipping her chin up so the bright overhead spotlight catches her cheekbones. Unexpectedly, charmingly, she pulls a face at herself as the lift slows to a halt. She abandons the mirror and turns to face the door.

The cameras pick her up as soon as she leaves the lift, her stride longer now, her impatience apparent from the way she is chewing her lower lip, and the quick, almost irritable movement that pulls her bag onto her shoulder when it slides down. She looks nervous, or possibly excited. Room 412 is at the end of the corridor, which is shaped like a T. The door is on the right side, facing room 411, set back so that the cameras can't see it, and this probably doesn't seem important to her, if she's aware of it at all.

She pauses at the end of the corridor, framed against the blank wall, and she fumbles the card wallet as she pulls out the key. With one quick flick of her wrist (at 2.13 p.m. exactly, according to the timestamp on the CCTV image, confirmed by the hotel's own data from the electronic lock) she opens the door and then disappears from view. The camera captures only a flare of light from the room before the end of the corridor fades to dimness again as the door is closed.

The next time the camera in the corridor sees her, she will be lying on a metal trolley, zipped inside a body bag, as the undertakers wheel her quietly and discreetly past the closed doors of rooms that are now empty. No one will stay on the fourth floor until the police are finished, and no one will stay in room 412 until it has been comprehensively, thoroughly cleaned of every trace of what took place there.

First, it will be necessary to find out what actually happened behind that closed door. Much time will be spent watching the footage over and over again, especially for the period after the door closed. Much effort will be expended on identifying and assessing everyone who comes and goes on the fourth floor, even those who don't seem to pass anywhere near room 412.

But everyone who watches from the beginning – from the first moment that she steps into view, striding past the doorman as if he doesn't exist – will have to fight the strange, pointless urge to warn her, to call her back from the lift, to usher her out of the hotel and onto the street, to slip her back into her life again, as if there might still be a chance that someone could stop her from hurrying towards her death.

PART ONE

Curtain Up

No two people see the same one thing alike.

Harry Houdini
The Right Way to Do Wrong:
An Exposé of Successful Criminals
(1906)

1

The job was never the same, and it was always the same. I walked into the hotel room – more of a suite, in fact, at the exclusive Governor Hotel – and it felt familiar, immediately. Death had arrived just ahead of me, and it greeted me like an old friend, which was fortunate because the welcome from the staff downstairs had been distinctly chilly. Here was the familiar nightmarish sense of everything normal having shuddered to a stop, the ordinary and everyday turned strange. I had had that feeling in small, grubby houses and immaculate mansions, barely habitable flats and filthy alleys, in car parks and woodland, and now here, in an elegant five-star hotel that occupied a sliver of expensive, exclusive Mayfair.

Ahead of me, there was a small dressing room, the cupboard doors open to show empty hangers. To the left, a bathroom, the door slightly ajar, and from inside the rustling movement of crime scene technicians. Light seared the air for an instant: a camera flash. Heat and steam seeped out through the gap in the doorway. I left it for the moment and went on into the bedroom.

If you ignored the crime techs, the clothes strewn on the floor and the scattered bits of disposable equipment the paramedics had left behind, it was a beautiful space. A huge bay window curved around two armchairs so you could sit and stare out at the heart of privileged, wealthy London, or look back at the enormous bed that your money had temporarily bought you. A tray stood on the table between the chairs. It held a single champagne glass beside a bowl of out-of-season strawberries that scented the air with an unlikely breath of summer. The heavy curtains were still looped back with gold ropes and the lights of the building opposite gleamed in the November afternoon gloom.

The furniture was a combination of modern luxury and carefully chosen antiques. The sort of hotels I stayed in ran to a sheet of mirror glass on the inside of a cupboard door, or next to the door, inevitably in the darkest corner of the room. Here there was a full-length mahogany-framed mirror on a stand, so it could be adjusted for the best and most flattering reflection of the person using it. There was a tall glass-fronted bookcase opposite the bed filled with a curated selection of reading material and decorative pieces: a small model of St Paul's Cathedral, a bust of Charles Dickens, a porcelain shepherdess bending over her sheep. It felt unique and specific instead of exactly the same as every other room in the hotel, and that was part of what you were paying for too – the sense that someone had taken time and care in furnishing the space. It was a room you could fall in love with, a room where you could fall in love, if you had someone to fall in love with . . . I gave a small, unhappy sigh.

'Maeve.'

I jumped and turned to see my colleague Liv Bowen, elegant in steel-grey, her dark hair plaited and pinned into a neat knot.

'When did you get here?'

'About ten minutes ago.'

'Have you been in there?' I nodded to the bathroom.

'Only briefly. Too many people in there at the moment. The pathologist is waiting to have his turn.' She glanced around to make sure no one was close enough to hear her. 'Are you OK?'

'Fine. Don't I look it?'

'You look good.'

I knew. I was wearing a midnight blue trouser suit and a long coat the same colour. My skin was clear and glowing, my hair was clipped back and behaving itself, my head was high. Winning all round.

Until you looked into my eyes, which was where people who knew me well tended to start worrying.

'I hate sudden, suspicious deaths in hotels,' I said, which was true but not what she had been asking about. 'The more luxurious the hotel, the worse it is. Getting the management to cooperate is always a pain in the arse because all they want is for you to pack up and leave so you stop getting in the way of their precious guests.'

'This is an interesting one, though.'

'Is it? I don't really know what the case is. I got a call from Una telling me to come here.' Una was Superintendent Una Burt, a woman of great efficiency and no personal charm. She was never prey to self-doubt, which I admired, but on the other hand total conviction was only useful if you were always right, and Una was not infallible. 'All she said was a dead body and suspicious circumstances and the hotel had asked us to be discreet, which I was. Much good it did me. The concierge actually winced when I told him who I was and why I was here.'

'Well, you can see his point. A dead body on the fourth floor doesn't really fit with the hotel's image.'

'And that's my main priority, obviously. Tell me more about the dead body.'

'The victim is Ilaria Cavendish, who was a regular guest here,' Liv said. 'She booked the room under a different name – Anne Pusey. The first police officers who responded found her real ID in her bag. According to the reception staff, she met the same man here every week. They would stay for a couple of hours and then leave, even though the room was booked for the night.'

'It's just a wild thought, but maybe they were having an affair.'

'Do you think?' She grinned. 'Anyway, today she came up here on her own. She ordered champagne from room

385

service, which was delivered to her room at 2.32 p.m. At ten to three, the man she was meeting – Sam Blundell – turned up. Nine minutes later he was on the phone to reception, telling them to call an ambulance. He'd found her in the bath and he couldn't get her out.'

I frowned. 'Why not?'

'The bath was full of scalding water. She was submerged. Still is. He said the water was still running when he came in. He turned the tap off, then tried to lift her out but all he managed to do was burn his hands.'

'Why did it take him nine minutes to get around to calling for help?'

'Good question. We haven't been able to talk to him yet. He's gone off to hospital to have his injuries looked at.'

'One champagne flute,' I said, looking around. 'Where's the bottle and the other glass?'

'In the bathroom. The champagne was in an ice bucket.'

'So she was having a bath and a drink and what – passed out and died? That's an accident, not murder.'

'She has a significant head injury.'

'She could have slipped getting into the bath and knocked herself out.'

'We'll have to see what the pathologist thinks, but it doesn't look like that kind of head injury.'

'And she was on her own here apart from the lover?'

'Apparently so.'

'We can confirm that with CCTV. Unless the manager is reviewing it right now. If it looks problematic for the hotel, he'll discover that oops, that camera wasn't working and the maintenance team were supposed to have fixed it last Friday. Sorry, he can't think how it happened.'

Liv laughed. 'That's cynical, even for you.'

'Wait and see. But really the mystery here seems to be how she died, not who killed her.' I shrugged, frustrated. 'At least it looks straightforward. Una could have told me all this on the phone.'

'What else did she tell you about this case?'

'Nothing. Why?'

Liv looked around, ultra-casual. 'She didn't mention who was in charge?'

I felt my stomach drop. 'He's not.'

'He absolutely is. The senior investigating officer on this extremely fascinating case is none other than Detective Inspector Josh Derwent.' She leaned closer to whisper, 'He's only just got here. He was held up.'

A sudden jolt of anxiety ran through me. 'Everything OK?'

'It must be, or he wouldn't be here.'

'Good point.' I swallowed, trying to loosen the knot that had suddenly tightened my throat. 'Una could have warned me.'

'I thought she was keeping the two of you apart.'

'She isn't, actually. He's the one who wants to avoid working with me.'

Liv looked surprised. 'Are you sure about that?'

'He told me so himself.' No room for ambiguity in it, either; it had been a straightforward statement that I couldn't interpret in any other way. 'I presume he had to take me this time because there's no one else, apart from you. Everyone else is tied up with the Russian gangsters in Chelsea.'

'Well, at least we're not on that one,' Liv said, trying to sound positive. 'It's a total shitshow.'

'Give me three tortured and disembowelled gangsters in a five-million-pound flat any day if it means I can avoid . . . certain people.' I looked around, half hoping to see his dark and glowering presence, half afraid he would be standing behind me. Derwent had a gift for appearing at the wrong moment. If anyone needed to arrive in a warning cloud of sulphur, it was him.

'Look, it'll be fine.' Liv put her hand on my arm and squeezed it for a second. 'I know it's hard but you're both professionals.'

'Both professionals? That's generous. He might be a professional but he doesn't often act like it.'

If anything, Liv's sympathetic expression intensified. 'Look, it's been a few months since you last worked with him, but you'll fall back into the usual routine soon.'

The usual routine was the problem, I thought. The usual routine was why he had been avoiding me.

A white-suited figure emerged from the bathroom. He pulled his mask down so it hung below his chin, revealing the face of Kev Cox, my favourite crime scene manager. He was eternally cheerful even though he spent most of his days examining the worst things that people did to one another, in the closest possible detail.

'Maeve! I didn't think you'd be working on this one.'

'Why not?'

He looked evasive, which sat oddly on his open, honest face. 'Well. I don't know.'

I took pity on him. 'I do. Is he here?'

'He had to take a phone call from the hospital.' Kev looked around, checking the coast was clear. 'Have you heard anything about Thomas?'

'No,' I said. There was a knot of tension in my stomach. 'Nothing. And we'd better not talk about it here.'

'It's hard to ask him about it. I don't want to upset him.'

I nodded. I knew. 'What have we got?'

'She's still in the bath.' He brightened. 'You won't like it.'

'Why?'

'Skin slippage.' Kev's eyes narrowed with amusement at my reaction, which was unfeigned nausea. 'We'll be pumping out the bathwater before we lift her out. We'll sieve it for fibres and anything else that might be useful.'

'Liv, see if you can track down the CCTV. I'd better go into the bathroom and have a look,' I said with minimal enthusiasm.

'Suit up first,' Kev ordered. 'And don't touch anything if you can help it.'

I had started to walk away but now I stopped so abruptly that Liv walked into me. 'Kev, how long have we worked together? Do you really think you still need to tell us not to touch anything at a crime scene?'

'Better safe than sorry. I'm a scientist, Maeve. I don't take anything for granted.'

'I'll let it go, but only because I like you.' I was smiling as I got changed, and even as I slipped through the bathroom door, but that didn't last for long when I saw what was waiting for me.